ESCAPING MR. ROCHESTER

ESCAPING MR. ROCHESTER

L.L. McKINNEY

HARPER TEEN

An Imprint of HarperCollinsPublishers

HarperTeen is an imprint of HarperCollins Publishers.

Escaping Mr. Rochester

Copyright © 2024 by HarperCollins Publishers

All rights reserved. Printed in the United States of America.

No part of this book may be used or reproduced in any manner whatsoever without written permission except in the case of brief quotations embodied in critical articles and reviews. For information, address HarperCollins Children's Books, a division of HarperCollins Publishers, 195 Broadway, New York, NY 10007.

www.epicreads.com

Library of Congress Control Number: 2023936864

ISBN 978-0-06-298626-9

Typography by Corina Lupp

23 24 25 26 27 LBC 5 4 3 2 1

First Edition

*To the Black girls determined to live how they want
and love who they want, you are the blueprint.*

PART 1

I am no bird;
and no net ensnares me.

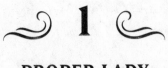

PROPER LADY

JANE . . .

This is better than the alternative. I've told myself so time and again. I repeat the assertion while I wait near the road for a coach that will carry me into the unknown. Not for the first time do I face such a fate, but it will be the first time I have *chosen* to do so.

The truth of this does nothing to assuage my fear.

So I shove my thoughts aside and focus on the moment itself. Despite the cloudless sky and bright sunshine, the late morning is so cold my breath mists. I shiver, partly from the chill plucking at me with icy fingers, and partly from nerves. Perhaps mostly from nerves, if I am fully honest with myself.

My fingers dig into the fabric of my coat as I clutch my arms for warmth. Paper crinkles in my left hand, caught between my palm and my sleeve—the letter that came last week. The wax seal has crumbled away due to my fidgeting, leaving a bloody kiss on the envelope.

Dear Miss Eyre,

I hope my correspondence finds you well. I am pleased with your decision to accept my offer of employment as governess in Thornfield Hall. As such, I will send for you at the earliest

possible convenience. A coach will arrive at Lowood the morning
of Saturday of next week. That is the sixteenth. I trust this
will provide plenty of time for you to make the necessary
preparations. Room and board will be provided as part of your
wages. Please bring anything else you feel you will need.

Regards,

E

I've read the letter often enough to commit its words to memory. And to know this coach is late.

The single traveling chest containing all my belongings rests near my feet—tightly packed and, truthfully, more prepared for this journey than I am. There's a twisting in my gut that's been there since I woke before dawn. A breakfast of cold porridge and leftover broth did not settle my unease, and taking such an early meal means my stomach is now empty. There's nothing to weigh down the nervous hummingbird fluttering viciously. My fear is alive inside me.

It takes every ounce of willpower not to glance over my shoulder, past the high gates of Lowood School, to the dingy windows where faces no doubt crowd the panes to watch me.

She's still out there, they likely whisper, mocking me for standing in the cold for so long.

Foolish.

She's surely lying.

The letter is fake.

No one is coming.

The imagined taunts ring like bells in my ears, and my grip on my arms and thus the letter tightens. I could go back inside, if no one came. Back to the bleak and lonely halls that are as much my home as the muddy path stretched before me. Back to the sideways glances and snide remarks about my family or hair or dress. Back to being told what to do and when to do it. To so few choices and even fewer possibilities.

"No." The word crawls free from somewhere deep down, spoken by a part of me that knows this is the only way. The same part of me that knows, without Helen, I'd never survive Lowood.

Thoughts of her fill my mind and my heart, and I feel her absence as keenly as I might a blade in my side. She made this place bearable, with her sharp mind, soft words, and unyielding being. My Helen, whose smile I can still see as clear as if she were standing before me. My Helen, who would want this for me.

My Helen . . .

A horse whinnies and my eyes fly open. The sight of the approaching coach sends a thrill through me. As the horses pull up, the scent of oil, leather, sweat, and something sour washes over the area. The fluttering that had taken residence in my middle dissolves, as do the unpleasant feelings surrounding it.

"Miss Eyre?" a hoarse voice crackles from the driver's box. A squat blanched man gazes at me with one bright blue eye, the other milky. He sniffs, his large nose heated red from the autumn chill. Or, given the pungent stink of ale wafting off him, the previous night spent halfway down some bottle. That would explain why he's late, at least.

I nod. "Yes."

He stares at me with a look that says he doesn't quite believe me, then gazes past me and to the school.

Pushing aside the beginnings of a familiar burn in my chest, I lift my chin and clear my throat. "Busy morning?"

The man blinks, his eyes finding me again. "What's that?"

"I was curious if the roads were busy this morning to upset your schedule so."

Those eyes of his narrow. "All's fine, ma'am."

"I'm glad to hear it." I go to climb into the coach when a harsh cough stops me.

"Hand up your trunk first."

"What?"

"Your trunk. Hand it up." His gloved fingers fidget with the reins before setting them aside.

"Oh." Clambering down to the road, I take hold of my trunk to pull the thing forward. The lower edge sticks in the mud a couple of times, despite a relatively light load.

"Come on now, we don't have all day," the man grumps.

Heat fills my face as anger spills through me. But I smile and straighten from where I've been dragging my belongings across the ground. "I apologize. Forgive my tardiness, as I've forgiven yours."

His lips become tight, and my smile widens. I bob a half curtsy, just enough for the gesture to be recognized but left unmistakably and intentionally incomplete, then return to my task. Slipping slightly in the muck, I manage to wrestle the trunk into my arms and up high enough for the driver to take hold. He yanks it free with such force that he nearly takes me with it, and I have to wonder why he could not do it himself. First late and now this? Lazy sod.

The insult dances on my tongue, but I snap my lips shut. *No.* I swore I'd be better about that, especially now that I am to be a right and proper governess. No matter how much he deserves it.

Right and proper. I scoff faintly as I settle onto the bench. I barely manage to situate myself before the coach jerks forward and we're on our way. Thankfully, the cab is unoccupied, as it appears Mr. Rochester sent his personal coach. Whatever the circumstance, I'm grateful for the time alone to gather myself and allay my rising irritation.

This driver is not the first to show such unkindness in my nineteen years, and he will not be the last. People find ways to justify their mistreatment of others. The wrong lineage, the wrong upbringing, the wrong affluential status. An enumeration of charges for the crime of being born different. I learned long ago that I had committed such a crime. I also learned that fighting with every cruel person in the world will leave me time for little else, and I refuse to let them have all of me.

Besides, I doubt my future employer would appreciate such openly critical commentary of his other staff. Mr. Brocklehurst certainly didn't, and he made sure I was aware of this at least twice a day. He also made clear his displeasure that I often forgot to refer to him as Headmaster or Sir. Neglected was more like; it pleased me to see him so agitated.

Well, I will no longer have to be concerned with what pleased or displeased that man, or anyone save my new employer. For the first time, my fate is now my own. My life is my own.

And I will do everything in my power to keep it that way.

2

STOLEN SUNLIGHT

BERTHA . . .

I snatch at one of the boards covering the single window at the far end of the room. The wood groans, as if in pain, while the nails strain against my efforts. I've been working at it since last night and my hands and arms ache. My fingers tingle, but I tighten my grip.

One more tug ought to—

Crack!

I nearly topple over when the board finally comes free, along with a chunk of the window frame. That was not part of my plan.

"*Damn*," I hiss under my breath, and steal a look over my shoulder at the bedroom door, shut and locked tight from the outside.

For a moment, I don't dare to move. I barely dare to breathe. My senses strain to hear any signs of life, especially the familiar sound of Grace's feet shuffling hurriedly toward me. But silence presses in from all directions.

After counting to sixty I allow myself to relax, but only barely. I shift the now-dangling board in my grasp and inspect the damage. The bit of wood that broke away from the sill remains intact. If I can balance this board on the one beneath it, I can press the hunk back into place. The deception won't hold up under scrutiny, but to anyone present for the scant amount of time it takes to deliver my meals, the damage should go unnoticed.

Carefully, I swing the board along the remaining nail like a hinge and lower it to hang. For the first time in days, sunlight pours past me. It cuts a swath through the darkness, scattering the sleepy morning shadows and revealing more of the space. This room that has been my cage for the better part of a year, ever since that monster trapped me here.

The furnishings, what few remain, are agreeable for a prison. The bed is large, the linens changed regularly by Grace, my chambermaid and warden. A small table at the bedside holds a single lantern with barely enough oil to feed the flame through a full night. There's the battered wardrobe that contains what remains of my clothes, and a table where I eat with a single chair.

Most everything else has been removed, after an incident this past summer when I broke a chair leg free and used it as a club. I managed to reach the kitchens that time. It was the farthest I've ever gotten. I also broke Sophie's arm when she tried to stop me. Her screams alerted the others. Then I was dragged back in here and most of the furniture was removed—all but what I needed to live "somewhat contentedly." If one can be content with being held captive.

"You are my wife," Edward had said, in that way of his that's capable of making a person feel like they were less than nothing despite all the compliments he paid. Like the very breath they lived by was a gift he personally bestowed and could just as easily take away. "You will be afforded the necessary comforts."

Comforts he chipped away as time went on. Like my mirror, wood for the hearth, a bowl for washing, and my thick, seasonal linens after I used them to fashion a rope. Last week he managed to take the sun itself when he had my window boarded after I climbed through it and attempted to use said rope to reach the ground.

But now I have reclaimed the light.

Dust glitters in the warm September rays. At least, I'm fairly certain it's September. It's difficult to mark the passing of time, but the way the green of the trees has begun to bleed into the rich burn of orange and red marks the change of the season.

A sharp band of sunlight reaches my table and illuminates the surface. I hurry to my chair and take up my pencil. What remains of it. Adèle snuck it to me under the door a fortnight or more ago, along with several leaves of torn paper. The black at the tip is nearly depleted, and the thing as a whole is barely the size of a thimble. Pocked and gnarled from my makeshift sharpening with dining knives when I can, there is perhaps enough lead for a few pages.

I write furiously.

September, maybe

It's as I thought; Sophie is gone. I suspect this is in part because Edward is disappointed with her performance as governess. Then there were her injuries. I'm not sorry for what I did. She was in my way, and more importantly, she was working to keep me trapped here. I had suspected as much when she delivered my dinner one evening. Then there is the fact that Edward doesn't bring anyone into his full employ unless he feels he can eventually control them.

I should have known better, should have trusted my instincts. Adèle never liked her either. That child is smarter than anyone gives her credit for, and an excellent judge of character. She is, perhaps, the only true friend I have in this hell. I will miss her when I leave this place, and leave it I shall.

The hole is nearly finished. I only have to wait for an opportunity to present itself. Once free, I will sell what few possessions I have left to pay for passage back home, back to my family. I will ne—

The familiar tap of approaching feet fills the silence and I freeze. It could be Grace, come to bring my breakfast. I strain to listen for the rattle of dishes against a tray. There's nothing but her clomping shuffle, and it stops shy of reaching my door. Hinges squeak and rattle. Grace has returned to her room, likely coming in from her morning prayers. She talks to God more than she does any living soul in this house. I wonder if He answers. If He tells her that, despite her devotion, what she does is wrong.

There are a couple of thumps from the room before the door squeaks closed again, and her footsteps retreat back down the corridor. Grace must have put away her Bible and rosary and is likely on her way to the kitchens to fetch the morning meal.

I spare a moment for my own prayer that the shawl she wears will catch fire. Then her hair. Then her skin. I long for that almost as much as I long for escape.

Anger simmering within me, I put pencil back to paper.

—ver have to look Edward Rochester in the face again. I will let all memory of him, of this house, fade. Then I will have peace. Then I will have true freedom. For that, I know I would burn this wretched place to the ground.

These are the writings of one Bertha Mason. On this day, I am being held against my will by my husband, Edward Rochester. Any statement to the contrary by him or anyone in his employ is a lie.

I'm startled by the sound of Grace's shuffling gait coming down the hall, followed by another. She shouldn't return for another quarter of an hour, and yet I hear the dishes on the tray as she approaches. The rattling is soon drowned out by the pounding of my heart.

Gathering the pages with similar entries scrawled across them, I wrap them in a napkin I kept from one of my evening meals. The words may smudge, but I have no time to be gentler. These writings will be all that is left of me someday, and if they are found, I want the truth of what has happened here to be known.

I take the bundle, along with the last inch of pencil, and hurry to my bedside. Dropping to my knees, I crawl halfway under and pry up a loose bit of wood to reveal a small hole. There are a few other things present: a small brush, a bit of lace, and a beautiful sketch of the gardens. I tuck the napkin amongst my treasures, then slide the plank into place.

The first lock on the outside of my door rattles. There's a *click* as it gives.

I nearly trip over my skirts in my haste to reach the window. Wood scrapes against wood as I swing the board up, balance it, and finally press the chunk of frame into place. My hands shake so hard the plank slips, swinging away.

I bite back a curse and try again.

The second lock jangles as Grace fumbles with the key. Sometimes it sticks.

I wrestle with the board. Thankfully, when I withdraw my hands, it stays in place. I turn as the second lock gives and the door swings open.

Grace steps into the room. "Good morning, madam." Her long, reedy fingers tremble slightly where they grip the tray. Her skin is pale, ashen almost. Dark spots circle her bony wrists. Her black hair, streaked with shocks of white, is pulled into a severe bun at the back of her head. She wears a thin smile.

My gaze lingers on the open door behind her. There's a buzzing in my limbs, my body preparing to run. *Wanting* to run. But there is little point to it.

Just outside the door, leaning against the corridor wall, stands Edward's stable hand. Devin, I've heard Grace call him. A younger, not-quite-roughened sort, a deceptively kind smile reclines across his disarmingly handsome face. He or the old manservant Marsters accompany Grace whenever she comes to my room. It has been this way since I attempted to overpower her the first week of my capture. That was nearly a year ago.

"Eggs and a bit of bacon this morning, with fresh milk." Grace sighs, almost wistfully. She finishes pouring my tea, then nods at her good works. "Such blessings. Go on, then. I'll be back for your dishes in half an hour." Her smile widens, pulling at the flesh of her face, tightening it in odd places. "Enjoy."

As she turns to depart, a small war rages inside me. I wish to spend as little time as possible with her in my presence, and I want even less to speak to her. But I have questions.

"How is Adèle?" I ask. I keep my voice even, more curious than concerned.

Grace pauses and eyes me with an expression that holds a healthy dose of both interest and caution. "How do you mean?" Her eyes dart about the room, then back to me, as if I can somehow stand before her and simultaneously pounce from the shadows.

I clasp my hands behind my back. This makes me seem both less imposing and unlikely to attempt anything. I want information, and she won't give it to me if she feels I'm up to no good. "How is she since losing her governess?" I hold genuine concern for the girl. She was present during my confrontation with Sophie, saw us grapple with one another. I surely injured more than the woman's arm, but the break was the worst. I was comparatively unharmed.

I fought when Devin and Marsters came to drag me away, but through the flurry of my desperation I saw Adèle standing at the far end of the hall, half-hidden around the corner, her face pale with terror. No one else seemed to notice her. I'm glad. Though she has not been to visit me since.

Grace sniffs a laugh. "You mean since you cost her her governess."

I merely shrug. As I said, I'm not sorry.

"Your concern is touching," Grace continues. "You would have made a fine mother for the girl. Alas, the master has found another to look after Adèle. Should be arriving today, in fact."

Those words set my mind spinning. Another governess, after only a month? Surely, Edward could not have convinced someone to join his farce so swiftly. Sophie had arrived *with* Adèle some time back and was loyal long before. This new governess might not be, which means at best she might be a potential ally, or at least a distraction. With all eyes on her, judging her trustworthiness, her pliability, there will be less attention on me for a time. This could present a unique opportunity.

"You needn't worry," Grace says, likely interpreting whatever expression I wear as apprehension. "The tot will be well looked after." She departs and locks the door behind herself.

As her and Devin's combined steps wander off, the beginnings of a plan take form in my mind. I look to the meal. The smell of bacon and eggs calls to my stomach, but thoughts of someone new in the house, someone I could potentially reach out to for aid before Edward sinks his claws into her, replace all hunger with a sharp and anxious nausea.

Despite this, I force myself to eat. Not doing so would raise suspicions, and if I finish quickly, I can use the fork to carve away at the steadily widening hole in the back of my closet. It's nearly large enough for me to crawl through to the adjoining one belonging to the unoccupied room next to mine. That door will not be barred from the outside. If all goes according to plan, by this time tomorrow I will be a free woman. My life will be my own again.

And I will do everything in my power to keep it that way.

3

SHADOWS OF THORNFIELD

JANE . . .

I reread the letter for the fifth time since Lord Punctual and I—that's what I've decided to call the driver, since introductions were never made—set off from the gates of Lowood. The passing hours have done little to calm the excitement welling within me. Excitement that has built steadily over the previous days.

With little else to occupy my thoughts, I close my eyes and try to picture Thornfield Hall in all its glory. I imagine a magnificent house bright with chandeliers and warm with firelight. It sits amidst great lawns and gardens still lush with the remnants of summer now burning with amber leaves and autumn flowers. Blue skies are reflected in pristine ponds, glasslike and serene. I see myself in this place, teaching lessons in lavish drawing rooms or at stately desks in a grand library. There has to be a library. I beg silently for one.

"We've arrived," Lord Punctual booms as the coach begins to slow.

I blink out of my reverie and tuck the letter away, then press against the side of the cab, wanting to see everything. The wide smile that had broken across my face fades as my mouth drops open. A carpet of green dotted with plump red and pink bulbs lies before me. Clusters of trees, their branches aflame with the turning of the leaves, paint the land with patches of shade. There is no water feature that I can see, but the walls of a hedge maze peek around the western edge of the house. The hall itself rests like a stone giant stretched on its side, reclining comfortably. There are three—no, four floors.

"It's breathtaking," I say to no one, unable to contain the truth of it.

The coach jerks to a stop at the innermost point of a circular drive. Before Lord Punctual can make his way down from the box, I push open the carriage door and climb out.

The grand entrance looms before me. Large wooden doors set in great stone, old and strong. Boxed windows peer down from various points along the walls. I wonder if one of them belongs to my room.

My room.

The thought hammers into me with a sudden giddiness.

"In a hurry, missy?" Lord Punctual calls from somewhere behind me. He grunts and mutters, panting around broken breaths. Struggling to retrieve my trunk, no doubt.

I turn to find my assumption was correct. "I believe Mr. Rochester expected me much earlier. I don't want to give him the impression I am ungrateful for this opportunity."

"Well." Lord Punctual puffs as he yanks at the trunk, which is caught against the baggage railing. As short as he is, he can't gain the leverage to lift it over. "Mr. Rochester—*blast it*—is out for the day."

"Out?" I ask before I can help myself.

"Aye. An important man with, erg, important business to attend. Damn it all!" He yanks on the trunk in a sudden fit. The handles creak in protest. "Ya fill this thing with rocks?"

With a huff, I approach the back of the coach. Bracing one foot against the step, I grip the edge of the window and push myself upward. Half hanging from the door, I'm able to stretch my taller frame and get my hand beneath one side of the trunk to lift.

It's enough for Lord Punctual to give one good tug before my luggage finally comes free. Then he and it tumble to the ground. The trunk is old, but thankfully the latches are sturdy—they hold. Lord Punctual is not so fortunate. He goes rolling a few additional feet, cursing the entire time.

By the time he rights himself, I've managed to haul my trunk to the front steps. He glares as he climbs back into the driver's box, but I pointedly ignore him. With a snap of the reins, he's on his way, off to whatever other errand he's likely late for as well. Or to find the nearest pub. All the same, he's no longer a bother, and I'm glad for it. I'm not even sour he didn't help me to the door.

Pushing Lord Punctual from my thoughts, I'm stricken by the fact that no one has emerged from the house to greet me. Mr. Rochester might be away at the moment, but surely there must be staff. Maids and manservants to tend to this place.

Straightening my skirts and smoothing the slight catches and wrinkles in the fabric, I reach for one of the brass knockers. They are massive, shaped as twin cherubs dangling scrolls to be lifted and dropped against the door.

Bang. Bang.

The sound runs hollow through the rest of the house, loud enough that I can hear the echoes. I wait and listen.

No one. Nothing.

I lift one of the scrolls again.

Bang. Bang.

Still nothing. Strange.

"Hello?" I call, though not too loudly. Discourteous as it may be to leave me standing on the doorstep, I don't wish to seem pushy or put out. Not on the very first day. "Is anyone there?"

Something jostles the curtain in the large window to my right. There's a flash of a small, light brown face curtained by dark hair. And then it's gone.

"I'm here at the request of Mr. Rochester," I say to the door now that I realize someone is listening. I'm fairly certain that someone is a child, most likely the very one I'm here to tutor. "But I'm afraid I've arrived while he is out."

No response.

I clear my throat. "Is there someone I could speak to? The housekeeper or a butler, perhaps."

Silence.

I curl my fingers into fists at my sides. "Please. The day wanes, and I fear I may catch a chill."

More silence.

Oh, enough of this. I raise my fist to knock directly when the *clickity clack* of a lock sounds on the other side. Finally, one of the massive doors swings open, and a narrow woman fills the small space between them.

She's older than me, though not by much. Her pale face is pointed, her cheeks flushed, her lips pink. Most certainly not the face that peeked out at me before. Bright red strands of hair are pulled into a high knot atop her head. She is lovely, and there's a sudden flurry in my stomach.

My previous irritation fades immediately. "H-hello."

"Can I help you?" A Scottish burr clips the woman's words. She pats her hands against a stained apron, sending small ivory clouds swirling into the air.

"Yes! Yes, I'm Jane Eyre." I fumble for the rumpled letter now tucked in my pocket, my fingers clumsy with nerves. "I'm here at the request of Mr. Rochester." I thrust the paper toward her.

She takes it in her powdery fingers, smearing white against the envelope as she opens it.

"To be a governess for his daughter," I continue.

The woman doesn't look up at me but instead focuses on the letter for much longer than it would take to read so few lines. There's a sudden urge to play with my curls or the pins in my hair, but I do my best not to fidget, the silence growing around us once more.

Finally, she looks at me, to the letter, to me once more, and then her eyes drop to the trunk. "That yourn?" she asks, pointing.

"Yes."

"Bring it inside." The woman steps back, drawing the door open fully.

Worried she might change her mind, I hurry to haul the chest forward. She closes the door, plunging the both of us into dingy light.

"Mr. Rochester isn't in right now," the woman says over the catch of the locks sliding into place. "But I can show you to your room. We'll have to be quick; I've pots bubbling for supper." She doesn't wait for a response and instead steps past me and down a hallway that branches off the vestibule.

I take a moment to orient myself. The struggle with my trunk has left me winded and a little dizzy. I let my eyes drift over the ornamentation of Thornfield's foyer and immediately find myself . . . underwhelmed.

The splendor of the grounds is not carried through to the interior in the least. Shadows wreath the atrium's high ceiling, clinging to the corners and upper walls like living creatures. They curl along the top of the grand staircase that snakes along the far wall and circle an unlit chandelier, then bleed out into the adjacent halls. Thick, velvet curtains hang heavy as battlements against any intrusion from the sun. Without the fullness of day allowed inside, darkness doesn't just live here, it thrives.

"Are ye here to sightsee?" the woman asks. Her tone pierces my thoughts.

I whirl to face her.

She stands where she's stopped several feet down one of the corridors. Dust hangs in her wake, glittering faintly in the scant shafts of light that manage to pierce the gloom. One of her brows arches sharply. She seems unbothered by the fact that this place appears to be slowly withering around her.

"N-no. No, sorry." Taking hold of my trunk, I drag it along, nearly bending in half to do so. The going is slow and clumsy. She has to stop every so often to allow me to catch up.

The hall we take is just as murky as the entryway. There are no candles, no fires. Paintings and tapestries decorate the walls on either side, many of them covered in sheets. Some are beautiful. Were beautiful. And I can't help but notice a couple of spots where the floral paper is faded in the shape of a missing frame. The entire place is shuttered against the outside, giving it a hollow feeling despite the presence of what looks to have once been very fine trappings.

The woman has gotten ahead of me again, her pace brisk and mine encumbered. "I don't believe I caught your name," I say, hoping she'll slow or even stop.

She continues walking, back straight, steps swift. "I dinnae throw it."

My irritation returns but I push it down. "Do you work for Mr. Rochester as well?"

"In a manner. I prepare meals for the house."

A cook. That explains the stained apron.

She continues, "From time to time I help with some of the housekeeping or keep an eye on the wee one. But I'm not her caretaker." She finally stops and spins to face me, sending another cloud of dust spewing forth. "Not like you'll be. Here we are." With that, she reaches to twist the knob on a nearby door, pushing it inward.

The door creaks in protest and stops partway. I have to give it another shove to make room.

"Thank you," I manage a bit breathlessly. *For nothing.*

"You are welcome." Her tongue tumbles over her *r*'s elegantly. "I've got to finish supper. It should be ready at the top of the hour. Do ye need anything else?"

I straighten and sweep a few strands of my dark hair from my face. My hand comes away slick with sweat, and I pray I'm not drenched enough to smell. It's been a few days since I had a good scrub, I'm embarrassed to admit.

"I think I can take it from here, Miss . . ."

She looks me over. "You can call me Emm."

"Emm." I try the name with a nod. "A pleasure."

"Aye." She turns to go.

"There is one thing," I call before she manages her first step.

Emm heaves a sigh into the dusty air. "Yes?" Annoyance is hung on the end of that word, elongating it by at least two extra syllables.

"Adèle. I'd like to meet her." I feel I likely did, at least somewhat, via the window earlier. "Where is she?"

Emm shrugs. "Yer guess is as good as mine. Always adventuring about, that one. Can't sit still to save her life. No doubt she's around here somewhere. If you go looking, watch your feet. The flooring can be a bit dodgy, and a fall in these halls would be a bad time, especially with no one here but us to hear you scream." Emm chuckles at her little joke as she starts forward, but then she draws up short again. "On second thought, better if you let her come to you. Mr. Rochester doesn't like it when folk go wandering about."

It's not hard to see why. With the deceptively lovely lawns presented to the world, Thornfield Hall's interior tells a different story. How odd to let what must have been so impressive a place as this waste away, especially when the man of the house has such means.

"Oh, I'm sure I'll be all right." I suppress an undignified sound as I shove the trunk the rest of the way into my room. There is little light here, too, so I haven't gotten a good look. It's likely as drab as the rest of Thornfield. "He did hire me as a governess for his daughter, after all."

Emm snorts, looks me up and down, and starts off again. Her voice carries on the thick air. "Don't say I dinnae warn ye."

4

TEARDROPS AND PEARLS

BERTHA . . .

I pace the space between my bed and the door, occasionally throwing glances at the latter. Each step riles the twisting in my center, but I cannot stop myself. Nor can I unwind the tension tightening my body.

Grace is late with supper.

Memories of previously delayed meals play through my mind.

Once, when she did not arrive with breakfast in a timely manner, it was because Edward had wanted to bring it himself. He set the food aside, then sat between me and the table for more than an hour, speaking of happenings with the estate and rumors spreading through society, as if I were truly his wife. The whole while, he helped himself to the meal for one. I stood in stunned but furious silence, trembling so hard my vision blurred. When he was finished and the plates were bare, he stood and crossed the room to press in close. I flinched when he leaned in to kiss my forehead.

Then he departed, leaving the empty dishes for Grace to collect later. That was one of the milder encounters. It was the rare occasion he left without some sort of threat, veiled or direct, or a promise of future torment if I didn't behave as a wife should.

I push away the memory, and the feeling of wanting to crawl out of my skin that came with it. While I know the delay cannot be due to him—he is away—I am still stricken with distress that he could come through that door at any second.

The sound of steps drifts down the hall. I freeze, listening.

For a moment I can't tell who it is, but as they grow closer, I recognize the scratchy drag of Grace's feet against the wood, and a wave of relief crashes through me. She moves a bit slower than usual, and it sounds as if she's alone.

I move to the other side of the bed as the locks come undone. The door swings open, and Grace comes hobbling through. She closes it behind herself and moves to set the tray on the table.

"Dinner, madam," she pips, far too cheerfully.

I ease into my chair. "Quite the delay."

Grace busies herself with setting out the small plate and cutlery. "Just seeing to a few additional responsibilities. Nothing you need worry about."

When she lifts the silver dome, the smell of roasted meat and earthy broth hits my nose. I try not to seem eager while my stomach nearly ties itself in knots. I've not eaten since this morning.

"Adèle's new governess must have arrived." I keep a neutral tone, so as not to sound too invested in this news.

"She has, though I've not had the pleasure of making her acquaintance just yet. I thought it best to give her time to settle in." Grace positions the cutlery before setting the plate in front of me. She always makes a show of *properly preparing* my dinner.

"There you are." Grace takes the dome and withdraws. "I'll be back to collect the tray within the hour."

"Thank you." I squeeze my hands between my thighs and wait for her to leave the room.

Before the last lock clicks into place, I grab the knife and stand, gripping it hard enough my fingers ache. I wait and listen. Grace's shuffle carries her to and down the stairs. When I'm certain she's truly gone, I hurry for the closet.

The muted light from the boarded-up window doesn't reach this far. I must feel my way through dust and darkness, then along the farthest wall. My fingers brush over wood, smooth and polished at first until the surface dips inward and turns suddenly rough and jagged.

I grip the knife and drive it into the wood. Again, and again, and again, I chip away at the gradually thinning planks.

Every few moments I stop, hold my breath, and try to listen past the beating of my heart for signs of anyone coming to investigate.

For now, I am safe from interruption.

After several minutes of quietly digging, I pause to feel along the serrations I've created. Every few inches or so I apply pressure, testing the give of the wood. My breath catches when one spot dips outward. Then another. The third time I push, what remains of the plank gives with a soft snap.

A rush of excitement moves through me, and I press my entire palm against the area. It bends but doesn't break. Yet. I'm so close. With another few hours of work, I will be through.

It takes everything in me to resist trying to pry or kick the planks free. The noise will surely bring Grace or others running.

No, no, I have to be patient. I've waited so long, what is another day? And if I work through the night, I'll break through by morning. Edward will not be home until the following evening, and my plan is to be long gone by then.

"Pace yourself, Little Bird," I whisper into the gloom. Maman used to say this whenever I grew frustrated or overeager in some aspect of my life. My studies or music lessons or, frankly, anything. There's a pang at the center of my chest when I think of her. I miss her. I miss her face, her voice, even the sharpness in her tone when she scolded me.

Without thinking, my fingers fall to my chest and the one treasure I cannot bear to part with. A string of pearls ornaments my neck. It was a gift from Maman on my wedding day. Passed down from her mother, and her mother before, so on and so forth. It is a simple thing, beautiful, delicate, and all that remains of my life before Thornfield.

If I close my eyes, I can remember the last time I laid eyes on my mother. It was a crisp and clear morning. She stood with my father amidst a sea of well-wishers gathered at the New Orleans port, there to see off any number of ships. Her thick hair was pinned into magnificent rolls carefully tucked beneath a blue hat. The pale but beautiful color sticks out in my memory. It was her favorite. She waved her hands frantically, matching gloves catching the sunlight, her smile wide and her eyes bright with tears.

I fight the sting of my own at the memory. I feel her absence keenly, and my father's. I fear I may never see either of them again.

"Madam?" Grace's voice causes every muscle in my body to stiffen to the point of pain. My breath catches in my throat. I should have heard her coming long before she reached my door. Instead, I lost myself so deeply in the past that not even the rattle of the locks drew me out of it.

"What are you doing down there?" Grace asks. Her tone remains more curious than suspicious. For now. She's still standing in the doorway. I think. And it's hard to think while fighting off the beginnings of panic.

My mind scrambles for an answer as the sound of dragging steps brings her closer. If I am caught, if the damage to the wall is discovered, I will be thwarted. And when Edward returns . . .

I need a distraction.

"Oh, Grace," I say, forcing emotion into my voice. I clutch at my necklace, my fingers working along the pearls anxiously. "I was . . ."

Then I'm struck by the suddenness of a thought. It is an idea. An awful idea. One that pains me immediately. But rather than shove the hurt aside, I cling to the sharpness of the feeling, allow it to fill me. This will make what comes next, loath as I am to do it, more believable.

I sniff and whimper audibly.

This causes Grace to pause. "Whatever is the matter?"

There's a grunt from outside the bedroom door. Devin or Marsters no doubt listening for signs of trouble.

My hand shakes as I tighten my grip on the necklace and yank. "I thought I'd lost them!" I shout over the sound of a few pearls peppering the floor, bouncing and rolling off. The rest are still on the string clutched in my hand. I let some slip silent into the folds of my skirts while hurriedly plucking up the others.

Grace trundles forward. "What are you on about?"

When she draws close, but not too much, I turn and hold out the damaged bit of jewelry.

"I—I don't know how, but I've broken it." My voice flakes away under the weight of my genuine sorrow. I look up and into the old woman's eyes. "Some of the pearls rolled under the door. I was trying to fetch them." I make sure not to let forth too much emotion. Just enough for it to seem like I'm fighting and failing to keep my composure. Which isn't all that far from the truth.

Grace looks from me to the darkened closet. With the window boarded up, I pray she cannot peer too deeply into the shadows to see the mess I've made of the wall.

Her fingers slide over a glass of what I can only assume is wine that she's brought to go with my dinner. I hadn't noticed it was missing.

After an eternity of seconds, Grace huffs. "You poor dear." She moves to set the glass on the table.

I deflate a little, on purpose, as part of my act. The tears continue to flow. I swipe at them with my free hand. Relief and anger battle one another in my chest. I have tempered her suspicion, but at a cost.

"You shouldn't search around in the dark like that." Grace moves toward my chest of drawers and the lantern there. "Let me get a light."

"No need." I push to my feet and close the closet door. "I've got them all, I'm certain." I carefully place the necklace and loose beads upon the tray, along with the knife, making sure to conceal the action with my body.

Grace hobbles to join me near the table. Her fingers press my shoulder in a gesture that is likely meant to be comforting. It takes everything in me not to flinch away from the touch.

"Perhaps I can inquire after repairs." She fixes me with a look one might give a child who's been misbehaving. "The master may not be amenable after your last tantrum."

I feel a muscle in my jaw jump. To hide the shift in my expression, I turn away as if chided. "Please? It is dear to me." Revealing the truth of this is dangerous. Almost as much as releasing the necklace into Grace's and thus Edward's possession. But I must be convincing.

She huffs as if put-upon by the request, then begins to collect the remnants of the jewelry. "Very well." Her words are pleased. She's enjoying this, the fact that I am now beholden to her in this way. "It'll have to wait until he returns, of course."

When he returns, I will have left this place—and thus my pearls— behind. The reality of this burns through me, hot and furious. I *am* furious. But I force out a shaky "Thank you." My eyes linger on the necklace clutched in her thin hand. The knowledge that I won't be able to take it with me, even in pieces, is like a blade in my heart.

"Lovely," Grace says, considering. "Now, you get back to your dinner before it goes cold." With that, she makes her way to and through the door.

By the time the sound of her departure fades, I am all but shaking with rage. A jagged, ugly feeling claws at my insides, hollowing out my chest. My vision blurs with it. More tears. But I will not let them fall.

One more thing has been taken from me.

5

DINNER, DESSERT, AND DESPAIR

JANE . . .

Heeding Emm's warning against wandering Thornfield's halls for the moment, I spend my time before dinner unpacking. Thankfully, my room is not in the same dilapidated condition as the rest of the house. The ceiling is high, and a row of large windows dips outward to cradle a bench just large enough to sit and read. It is more space to myself than I've ever had. The furnishings are clean. The linens on the bed fresh. A fire dances in the hearth, filling the room with warmth and light. Clearly, my arrival was expected. Perhaps even eagerly.

Despite being little more than four walls and a few large windows, the space feels less oppressive than the rest of Thornfield. I can breathe in here, stretch myself and my being. There's no sense of something hidden in the corners waiting to pounce. The firelight reaches every inch of the room, banishing the shadows. Still, I imagine them waiting outside my door, ever vigilant, biding their time.

It does not take long to put my belongings away. I do not have very many, but they are mine. The last item is a journal. My journal. I know the perfect place for it. Upon entry, I immediately spied a small desk tucked away against one wall. A quick perusal of the drawers revealed no pens or ink, but I'm certain I can request these.

My task complete, I have nothing to distract me from the fact that I have not eaten since before dawn. After such a lengthy ride, mitigating the scuffle between Lord Punctual and my luggage, then fully unpacking, I'm fit to starving. Well, if I'm not to meet Adèle just yet, perhaps I can be of help to Emm in preparing supper. I take one last look around my room, then depart.

There's likely another few hours until sunset, but the waning daylight has already stripped all familiarity from the corridor. I move in the direction we came before. At least, I think it was this way. Everything is dust and sheets and slowly lengthening shadows. It's easy to imagine something resembling fingers reaching to try to snag my skirts with claws or talons. The house is slowly being devoured by the encroaching night.

I quicken my steps.

Around the next corner I stop just in time to avoid slamming into a body as it leaps from the darkness, and my heart in turn leaps into my throat. I scream.

"Heavens!" cries an elderly woman, who presses her hand against her chest as something bounces against the carpet. Several somethings. They scatter along the floor.

"I'm sorry," I manage, reaching to steady her. "I didn't see you. Here, let me he—"

"Pay attention to where you're going!" The woman huffs and turns her attention to the carpet. Her spotted and lined face creases with a frown. "Oh, that's just lovely, isn't it?"

"I apologized." There's an edge to my voice I don't take care to dull.

She doesn't reply, just mutters to herself as she shifts onto her knees to begin plucking at the rug. "Racing through here like some brat. The impertinence."

Forcing a practiced smile into place, I simply nod. "As I said, I didn't see you." I move to step around her, then pause, my thoughts peeling themselves from beneath my anger.

This woman, mean-spirited as I can already tell she is, is likely another of Mr. Rochester's employees. She's been here longer than I have, meaning she most likely has a trusted and less precarious position than mine. Being on her bad side so soon would be less than ideal. I take a deep breath and push my feelings somewhere deep down.

"Here," I offer before dropping down beside her. "Let me help."

"No need," the woman grunts, but I'm already gathering up the small baubles that have spread around us. I place a few in my palm and lift them for inspection.

Pearls, I realize with sudden surprise. Actual pearls. They glisten softly in the low light, almost seeming to glow.

"Don't go getting any ideas." She thrusts her hand out, wagging her fingers demandingly. "Hand them over."

"Only one of us has their mind on thievery," I say evenly. I pour what I've gathered into her waiting palm.

She looks me over. Her eyes hold the familiar weight of judgment. I feel it settle into my bones, but I shift my shoulders, shaking it off. I deserve to be here.

"Lovely pearls," I say, gesturing at her now clenched fingers. "Are they yours?"

"Yes." The old woman glances around, likely making sure she's collected all of them. She shifts as if to rise but looks to be having a bit of trouble getting her feet under her.

I rise to mine and reach for her. "That's all of them, I think."

She eyes me but doesn't resist. Together, we get her upright. She rocks with the motion of standing.

"I'm Jane." I nod in greeting. "Jane Eyre."

"Eyre? You're to be Adèle's new governess, then?"

"Yes. I arrived not too long ago. I've just gotten settled and was attempting to find my way to the kitchen."

There's a pause as a look of consideration passes over her face. It's brief, then she sniffs again. "I can show you to the kitchen, but I suggest you stay out of Emmaline's way." She shuffles past and gestures for me to follow.

We fall into a less than amicable silence, even though I have countless questions—what it's like to work for Mr. Rochester, who else I can expect to potentially crash into while roaming these dark halls—but I say nothing. I don't imagine she is the talkative type, and I want nothing from her. I know her kind.

The aroma of roasted meat and vegetables reaches us before we arrive at the kitchen, along with the sharp scent of burning wood. There's also a sweetness in the air, and the crisp smell of something baking.

Stopping just inside the door, I take in the wide space with walls lined with cupboards on one side and pots and pans hung along the other. Emm stands at the stove, fussing over a pan filled with something steaming, surely the source of the delicious scents that have all but called us here. At a nearby table, I spot a little face greatly resembling the one that peeked out at me when I stood at the door earlier.

Still round with youth and slightly rosy, it belongs to who I must assume is Adèle. Such a pretty thing, looking every bit the age of ten, her brunette hair braided back and ribboned, though it rises here and there in the peaks of coils wishing to be rebellious. Freckles dust her light brown cheeks and wide nose, and she looks up at me with large, dark eyes before hurriedly returning them to her plate.

I bite down on my eager greeting. The way the girl shrinks herself, timidity all but radiating off her, is enough to pull at my sympathies almost painfully. I've known shy children. I was such a child myself. I'll have to be careful, go slowly, let her open to me so I don't go stomping over boundaries I may not recognize immediately.

"Took ye long enough," Emm snaps. She gestures to a nearby station. "Help yourself, but don't get too excited. A few other bellies need filling."

"Thank—" I turn to say to Grace, but she's vanished. There's no sign of her in the hall either. ". . . you."

"Yer welcome." Emm straightens from sliding the pan into the large brick oven. "What I do?"

"Not you; Grace." I glance around, but it's as if the sour woman simply vanished into thin air. "She showed me how to get here, but now she's . . . gone."

"Aye, quick as death, that one, when she wants to be." Emm wipes her hands on the apron around her waist. "I figure it's because she's out footing 'im."

"Neat trick."

There's a faint sniffle of laughter from the table, then a shift in attempt to conceal it. I pretend not to notice, fighting the smile that wants to pull at my face as Adèle ducks her head once more.

"You should see the ones she does at parties." Emm smiles and winks.

The tight feeling in my stomach from before eases a bit, though the confusion that replaces it is equally uncomfortable. This Emm, quick with a joke and a smile, seems so completely different from the cold and irascible woman who answered the door. What could be responsible for such a transformation?

I step farther into the kitchen. It's warm here, and full of life, unlike the rest of Thornfield. I imagine it's the same in Emm's room, as with mine, and likely Adèle's as well. Pockets of vitality dotted throughout Thornfield like islands spread across cold, unforgiving seas.

As I take up the ladle to stir what looks like stew, I'm hit with the briefest pang of regret. A memory bubbles up unbidden, of an afternoon spent on kitchen duty, poking fun at common enemies with another fetching face. I recall a smile. Sweet laughter. And a kiss behind the pantry door. It's a pretty memory of a moment stolen long before I knew the value of it.

Shaking myself free of my own mind, I ladle helpings of stew into a bowl. I hope it tastes half as good as it smells.

Emm offers me a spoon, which I take with thanks, then she sets to filling her own bowl. "I want to apologize."

"For?"

"For my less-than-pleasant manner when I greeted you earlier. I was in the middle of cooking and no one else bothered to answer the bloody door, so I admit I was a bit short. Uncalled for."

Relief plays through me, and I fairly feel faint with it. I'd begun to fear I wouldn't find a friendly soul within these walls. "Oh, I understand. No apologies necessary, really."

"Maybe not, but I give them anyway." She motions toward the table with a hunk of bread.

"I appreciate the gesture." I take the offered loaf to slice and butter enough for the both of us and Adèle, who I've noticed stealing glances in my direction. "You can make it up to me by telling me just who else I can expect to run into here at Thornfield."

Emm titters softly. "Well, I assume you've met Marsters, otherwise you wouldn't be here. You've met Grace and my lovely self. All that's left is Devin, the stable hand, though I doubt you'll run into him lest you venture outdoors at some point. He tends to prefer the open sky to a roof."

"The sky can be nice on certain nights."

"Indeed, it can. Of course, there's Mr. Rochester, but he's not here."

"Ah," I cut in. "When will he be returning? If I might ask."

Emm twists her lips together in thought. "Tomorrow, though I'm not certain of the time. By supper, is what I was told."

I nod, wondering at the oddness of not being present when a new member of one's staff and thus household arrives. And then to be gone another day? I've not met him, and yet I'm a mite curious at the oddities of one Edward Rochester.

"That leaves young Adèle there," Emm says.

The girl lifts a small hand in a slight wave.

So, my assumptions were correct.

I smile, clearing my throat gently. "Hello, Adèle. I'm Jane. Mind if I sit with you?"

The girl shakes her head, and I pull back a chair. Emm draws out the one across from me and plops into it, setting her bowl down.

"Jane here is to be yer new governess, lass." Emm stirs her stew, then takes a bite.

Adèle's brows lift as she looks to me. "You are?" There's a slight roundness to her words, the vestiges of an accent hidden behind her teeth. I can't place it just yet.

"Indeed I am. And I'm very happy to make your acquaintance."

Adèle doesn't speak. Instead, she looks to her bowl, tracing the edge of it with her spoon. She worries at her lower lip while sinking into herself just slightly.

"Jane here came all the way from Lancashire," Emm says, distracting me from my thoughts. "She was at Lowood School, if I'm not mistaken."

I blink at Emm, somewhat surprised she knows so much about me. Then again, it makes sense that Mr. Rochester would inform the others in his employ as to who I am and where I have been . . . educated. And yet, the realization that such details about my person are already spread unnerves me, even if only slightly.

"Have you been anywhere else?" Adèle asks, her voice soft, small, the words almost fragile, like fine glass. Contrarily, they help solidify my previous speculations as to the origins of her accent. It's French. How peculiar.

I shake myself from my musings. "I've been many places. And you'll learn of many more, if you like. We'll learn together."

"And go there someday?" Her face brightens just the faintest bit, but it's enough to bring a smile to mine.

"If we are so fortunate. The future is full of possibility."

She manages a small smile as well. "Monsieur doesn't take me many places." The way she says it, like it's an unfortunate fate she's accepted, breaks my heart. Though I'm distracted by her words.

Monsieur?

"Mr. Rochester's a busy man," Emm cuts in between spoonfuls of stew. "Besides, all his travels involve dealing with boring business stuff, yeah? I'm sure things will be far more entertaining with Jane."

"I *promise* they will be." I wink, and Adèle huffs another of her soft laughs.

"There we are. Now, eat up." Emm taps the table beside Adèle's still mostly full bowl.

To my delight, Emm's cooking is indeed incredible. All three of us have second helpings, and there's even mention of cake. That's what was in the pan before and is now left cooling, tantalizingly so, on the nearby station.

While we wait, I want to ask why Adèle referred to Mr. Rochester as *monsieur* instead of *father*, which would certainly be far more forward than any newly made acquaintance has any right to be. My curiosity has often been the cause of trouble in the past. Instead, I ask Emm just how she came to be in Mr. Rochester's employ.

"Oh, I'm only partially employed." Emm busies herself with putting things away and preparing for tomorrow's meals as I see to the dishes. "I split my time between here and town, as a favor to Mr. Rochester more than anything."

I quirk an eyebrow inquisitively. "Favor?"

"Aye." Emm nods. "Rather, I'm repaying a favor with a favor. He helped my family with a precarious situation a while back—no, I'm not going into detail—and I agreed to utilize my skill in the culinary arts to help him keep his wee one fed these past few months."

"Was there no cook? No other servants or staff?" I ask.

"Well, Grace took care of that before. Sturdy as they come, that one. She'll likely still be working while you and I are cold in the ground. All the same, the master thought an extra pair of hands and eyes would be best."

My nose wrinkles at the mention of Grace. I don't bother adjusting my expression as I towel our plates dry. "Then you're fairly new here as well."

"Relatively." Emm looks at me. I sense there's more to that statement, but she doesn't say anything else.

Adèle fiddles with the ribbons on the sleeves of her dress while she listens.

"Then, as far as staff"—I set the final clean bowl in the pile I've made to be put away—"there's you, me, Grace, Devin, and Lord Punctual?" I count the names on my fingers.

Emm makes a face.

I wave a hand. "Marsters, sorry. He was late this morning."

Emm sniffs a laugh. "Right you are. Mr. Rochester isn't your usual socialite. He's not prone to lavish displays like a full staff or the like. Says he prefers working with a small group. That way, we're more like a family. His words, not mine."

"And does it genuinely feel that way? Like a family." Because that is most certainly not the impression I've gotten so far, present company excluded. I hope my tone doesn't betray my slight dismay, or my eagerness. In the week leading up to my arrival, I'd imagined working closely with Adèle in her studies, my skills seeing to it that I become a confidante as much as a tutor. Winning over my charge and then her father would ensure a great many things, one being a sense of security of my place in the world.

"It can. At times." Emm rolls her shoulders in a shrug. "But, as I'm sure you know, even family has its complications."

34

I don't miss the brief glance Adèle casts my way before focusing on her dress again.

"Quite," I murmur. "Then you enjoy your time here at Thornfield?"

"I wouldn't be here if I didn't, favor or no." Emm taps the top of the cake lightly, testing the temperature again. It seems to have cooled to her liking, and she reaches for the small bowl of white frosting nearby. "Mr. Rochester is the simple type and seems to favor a simple life."

This time *I* sniff. "He wouldn't if he actually knew what it was," I murmur.

Both Adèle and Emm look at me.

Heat fills my face and I studiously, though uselessly, shift the now clean dishes about on the counter. "And what of Mrs. Rochester?"

Whatever warmth and camaraderie had filled the room prior flees in the face of my question. Silence doesn't just descend, it sweeps in like a hurricane wind and slams into each of us, weighing upon Emm and Adèle almost physically. While Emm's shoulders slump, Adèle's hitch upward. Both of them pretend to be engrossed in what they are doing and say nothing.

I drown in the quiet.

Glancing between them, an apology dances on the tip of my tongue.

"She's gone," Emm says, the line of her shoulders tense. "Passed on."

Adèle has sunk so far into her seat she's practically melted into it, and I'm struck with the carelessness of my inquiry. I should have realized on my own. The clues were there. Surely, he would have mentioned his wife in his letter if she were still with us. And meeting the lady of the house certainly would have been a priority, if there was one.

Blast it, Jane. "I—I . . ." *I'm sorry*, I want to say, but the words shrivel on my tongue.

"It's best if you don't mention her around Mr. Rochester. For his sake and yours." There's a clatter as Emm sets out a small stack of plates. "Cake's ready."

It takes the delicious sweetness of Emm's dessert and a completely different topic of conversation before some of the heaviness that had befallen the mood lifts. The three of us discuss the different types of desserts we've had. From biscuits to pies to sweet creams, Adèle has tasted many more than I, but it's still a paltry amount by Emm's standards.

At some point during the discussion, Grace enters with a tray of empty dishes. It appears she took her meal alone, which is just fine by me. I don't imagine her inclusion would've made for a pleasant time.

She washes, dries, and puts the dishes away herself before disappearing again, but not before bidding good evening to Adèle and Emm. She only sniffs in my direction.

Two can play at this game. I pointedly ignore her, focusing instead on scooping up the last bit of leftover frosting on my saucer.

"Don't take Grace's sour mood personally," Emm says once the old woman has gone.

"Would it be rude if I admit it's hard not to?" While Grace's seemingly unreasonable dislike of me is nothing new in this world, it's not something I'm inclined to put up with.

"Not at all. It's just, she was close to Adèle's previous governess."

Adèle shifts again as she works on her second piece of cake.

"Misfortune is no excuse to take out one's woes on passersby." A lesson Grace, and many others, could stand to learn.

"I'm not providing excuses, merely explanations. A bit of insight."

"What happened to the previous governess?" I'm in no mood to discuss Grace any longer.

Emm eyes me a moment, and I fear she may press the issue, but I can see her acceptance of the shift in topic in the way she relaxes her shoulders, and I'm grateful.

"Poor thing broke her arm," Emm explains. "Fell down the stairs. I told you this place could be dangerous."

The clock hung above the door chimes six, the ring of the bell echoing faintly. Outside, the setting sun fills the sky with fire that will soon be doused by starlight. The mere thought of the night is enough to draw a yawn from me, and I stifle it with apology.

"You must be tired after traveling most of the day." Emm makes to rise, and I do the same.

She's right; I am. The truth of this settles over me like a blanket of sudden exhaustion, and my early rising will no doubt catch up to me soon. "I should probably help Adèle get prepared for bed as well. Thank you for dinner and dessert, Emm. It was delicious."

As Emm gathers up the dishes, I offer my hand to Adèle, who blinks at it in surprise.

I explain, "It seems I require a knowledgeable guide to navigate your . . . lovely home. Would you be so kind as to show me the way to your room?"

Adèle hesitates, glancing at Emm, then at me again, before taking my hand. Hers feels so small tucked away between my fingers.

"Good night, ladies," Emm calls as we slip from the kitchen.

The shadows of the hall stretch before us, ever lengthening with the dying of the day. Adèle's fingers slip from mine, but she remains at my side as we walk, our steps muffled against the carpet.

"Thank you for the escort," I say, my voice seeming much louder in the quiet than it is. "I fear I may have gotten lost on my own."

There's a faint quirk at the corner of Adèle's mouth. "It's not so bad, at least not on the first floor."

My own smile returns. "I'd wager you know every inch of this place after growing up here."

The quirk vanishes. "I didn't. Grow up here."

I blink rapidly, my brain stuttering over the newly presented information. "Oh?" is all I manage at first. "Where did you grow up?"

"Paris."

That explains the accent. I'd been pondering it during dinner. Though this revelation brings on even more questions. Taking in the way Adèle has begun to shrink herself again, I push my inquiries to the back of my mind to be asked and answered later.

Instead, I inquire after her opinion on toffee apples. They're the perfect treat in autumn, and I'm certain we can prepare some at a later date. Adèle seemed more than delighted by the idea. We become so caught up in our mutual love of sugary things that it doesn't take us long to reach a door that opens onto what is obviously a child's room, though twice as big as mine. The windows on the far wall are similarly bayed and allow in enough fading sunshine for me to find and light a few lanterns.

From the look of the furniture, toys, and other trappings, Mr. Rochester may want a simple life, but he's clearly spared no expense when it comes to his little girl. There's a fine line between showering someone in affection and attempting to buy it. I wonder just which is going on here.

"That's quite a collection," I say as my attention is drawn to a cabinet of shelves packed to the brim with all manner of books, some far too complex for many adults, let alone a child. Perhaps my ward is quite the accomplished thinker. "What do you say to a story before bed?"

Adèle nods as she plucks a lavishly dressed doll from the floor, then sets it inside a house that's nearly as tall as she is. At ten, she's far too old for such things, or at least that's what my aunt would say. But I understand how a companion, even one stitched together from cloth and cotton, is better than being entirely alone.

"Do you have a favorite?"

"No." She makes her way over to the wardrobe.

"I don't believe that," I say playfully before I move to help her with her dress. "Everyone has a favorite story."

She stills as my fingers work at the ribbons and laces, undoing them.

"Je peux le faire," she says suddenly, pulling away. "I can do it."

I stare, taken aback a moment before nodding and making my way once more to the shelf. Perusing the titles scrawled in silver and gold lettering, a familiar name pops out. Smiling, I pluck the book free.

"How about 'Cinderella'? It's one of my favorites." I turn to find she's made swift work of pulling off her dress, which she's left in a heap on the floor, and drawing on a nightgown.

She bends to gather up the garment and I step over to her again. "Why don't we trade." I hold out the book. "You take that and go get settled. I'll put this away." I give the dress a little shake where I take hold of it.

After a moment, she lets go almost reluctantly and moves to crawl into the massive bed. I hang the dress and put her shoes and stockings away.

By the time I'm finished, she's tucked herself beneath the blankets, though she's left the book on the side table. The fabrics nearly swallow her whole, and if it weren't for the shock of her dark hair against the linens, I may have missed her entirely.

"All right," I breathe as I settle on the edge of the bed and take the tome in hand to begin flipping pages.

"You're an orphan?" Adèle asks, her voice as soft as the sheets surrounding her.

I blink, not certain I heard correctly at first. "I beg your pardon?"

"Emm said you're from Lowood." She peers at me from where she's sunk into a massive pillow. It's almost comical the way everything in the room seems to dwarf its sole occupant.

But my thoughts are wandering, and I wrestle them back into place. "Ah." I close the book, marking the spot with my finger. "Yes. I'm an orphan. Does that bother you?"

She shakes her head, and a feeling I'd barely begun to notice, like a serpent winding around my lungs, eases.

"When did you lose your parents?" Her voice quiets with each word, until the last one is nearly a whisper.

"I was young. Too young to remember the full circumstances surrounding their passing, but I'm haunted by what could have been." My even tone is a result of years of practice, betrayed only by the shaking in my fingers, which clench around the book. "Even though I only knew them when I was still small, I still find myself missing them sometimes."

"You . . . you miss them?"

I smile softly, sadly. "Every day."

Adèle shifts beneath the blankets. She has more questions; I can see them play across her expression as she purses her lips and crinkles her brow. I wait patiently.

"Do you think they would love you, if they were here now?" There's a hitch of hesitation, as if she is afraid of the asking rather than any possible answer.

Still, the inquiry catches me off guard. My mouth opens and closes as my mind turns over the memories of time spent with family in my earlier years. I've often thought about how things would be different, *what* would be different, if typhus hadn't claimed my parents. If they had been there to raise me with love and kindness. What would have become of that Jane, I'd wonder. Would I recognize her? Would she recognize *me*?

It's a daydream so familiar I could wrap myself up in it like a favored blanket. Instead, I blink away the fantasy. "I do. I believe it with my whole heart."

The smile that breaks over Adèle's face is like a balm against the faint ache in my chest, and I return it.

"I miss my mother too," she admits with a sigh.

"I know." I set a hand over a lump in the covers that looks to be one of her arms. "But at least you still have your father."

She glances away at that.

"And, though I never met her, I'm certain Mrs. Rochester wouldn't want you to suff—"

"No." The denial takes me by surprise, especially as I am unsure what it is she's denying, and so vehemently at that.

"What?"

"Mrs. Rochester wasn't my mother," she mutters, her brow drawing into a frown. Then she turns onto her side, facing away from me. "Maybe we can read a book tomorrow. I'm tired."

The force behind her words is gone, but the weight of them has trapped me. I'm stuck sitting on the edge of the bed, my hand hovering in the air where Adèle has pulled away. Her little shoulders are stiff, tight. My throat is as well. It's difficult to breathe, let alone speak.

Not her mother? Then how . . . who . . . *That's none of your **business**, Jane.*

And yet, my wonderings do not cease. They scatter about the room, and my gaze follows, trying to catch them. I take in the furnishings and clothes, the toys, the books, all things expected to be found in a little girl's room. I also take in the fine layer of dust over most of them. Nothing here bears the well-worn signs of use and care. Of a mother's careful hand and touch. Of love.

I swallow thickly and push myself to my feet. This is best left for another time.

"Very well. I'll see you bright and early in the morning."

Adèle says nothing.

"Good night," I urge, pushing a little bit of a song into my words.

Still nothing.

Sighing, I set the book on the bedside table and turn down the flame in the lantern before slipping out the door and closing it behind me.

6

SACRIFICES

BERTHA . . .

My dinner, delicious though it may be, is stone cold as I shove it into my mouth. I barely chew before I swallow, my throat stretching painfully, but I need to get as much of this down as I can to avoid suspicion.

Foolish, I chide myself as Grace's steps reach the door. *Foolish!* I should have been paying attention to the time. I should have stopped to eat long before now. But the progress I'd made on the hole had distracted me.

Taking the bowl in both hands, I lift it to my lips and drink from it straight. Some of the broth dribbles down my chin to my chest, no doubt staining the front of my dress.

The locks click as they're undone.

I set the bowl down and snatch the napkin free, wiping at my breast as the door swings open. I switch to dabbing the corners of my mouth, then calmly set the napkin aside.

"All finished, madam?" Grace steps over to the table to inspect the dishes.

"Mm." I concentrate on keeping my hastily swallowed meal down as something in my stomach tumbles and tries to climb back up my throat. "I wanted to let you know, you don't have to trouble yourself with looking after my necklace." Perhaps I can talk her into returning the pearls before I have to leave them behind.

"It's no trouble at all! In fact, I've your precious pearls tucked away to await mending." Dishes clack and clatter as they're gathered. "Though I fear my trip may not be for a few more days yet. I don't like to be away when there's a new body in the house."

Well, that certainly is an about-face. I wonder what changed her mind. "You mean the new governess."

"Indeed." She chews on the word in a manner that's . . . It snags my attention the way the disdain catches against her teeth. It's not too drastic a change, but it's enough to let me know she doesn't approve of the girl.

Interesting.

"What do you make of her?" My tone isn't overly friendly, and I'm careful to sound more mildly interested than truly.

Grace pauses in her fussing with the tray to look me over. She's quiet for a moment, then huffs a breath. "We only met briefly, but I fear the master may be in for disappointment."

"Oh?"

Her head bobs in assurance. "She's clumsy. Rude. Willful, I can tell."

"Does she get on with Adèle, at least? That's what's important." I know the smart thing to do would be to mind my own business, but there's a flutter of guilt every time I think of the innocent girl. She is as trapped here as I am, bound to Edward as well. While I would take her with me if I could, I have little enough to fend for myself outside these walls. I couldn't bring a child into that on my own. I want to know she'll be all right.

Grace goes back to gathering the tray. "Who's to say. They had dinner together, seemed amicable enough. But only time will tell with this sort of thing." The dishes clatter as she lifts them.

And now comes the next part of my plan. "Ah, Grace?"

The old woman turns from where she's nearly reached the door. "Yes?"

"I'd like a bit of tea while I read tonight. With honey." I fold my hands in my lap and swallow thickly as a bit of air rises at the back of my throat. "Please," I add, more to disguise my slight burp than as any true attempt at pleasantries.

Grace sniffs faintly. "I'm not certain the master would—"

"Edward isn't here," I snap, then clear my throat. "And if he were, I doubt he'd be pleased to learn I'm no longer afforded something so simple as tea. He does want me as . . . comfortable as possible, after all. And I would be ever so grateful."

Grace's face has gone slightly white. Well, whit*er*, and she nods with a slight dip of her body. "Tea. At once, madam."

"With honey." I soften my voice and do my best to sound grateful. "Thank you."

Grace nods again before backing out of the room. She closes the door behind herself and her steps hurry along the hall.

I begin to wonder if I heard what I think I did when she swiftly realizes her mistake, hurries back to the door, and the locks click into place.

My disappointment is short-lived when I glance at the closet door. Just behind it is the crumbling wall and my progress to freedom. The small opening in the wood is now large enough for me to fit one arm and my head through. If I work quietly through the night, using the spoon Grace is sure to bring with my tea, I should be able to fit my entire body through by morning.

Smiling, I reach to tangle my fingers in my necklace, only to catch at nothing. It's gone. The reminder is like a battering ram against the fragile tendril of hope that's sprouted within me, but I steel myself. The sacrifice will be worth it.

I almost want to be here to see the look on Edward's face when he returns to find me gone.

7

GAMES

JANE . . .

Adèle is still withdrawn when I greet her the next morning, and it continues to grieve me. It is to be expected, after I tore open such a wound with my words, unwitting and clumsy as they were. I've hurt her, and I've spent most of a sleepless night and all morning pondering how to make amends.

Despite my attempts at striking up conversation, she remains silent as I see to getting her dressed and prepared for the day. It's not until I announce my intention to fetch breakfast that she finally speaks.

"I'll go with you," she says as she grabs her doll from the small house.

Surprised, I position myself to wait by the door. "Of course." I won't deny her.

Children can be forgiving things, letting you know you've not lost them entirely with small gestures such as this. I'm grateful and determined not to waste the boon granted.

As we walk, I let my gaze wander along with my mind. The halls of Thornfield are a touch more resilient in the fullness of the bright morning. A few of the windows are open to let in fresh air, and a number of the shadows have retreated, but most are far from banished.

It is like walking through a portrait painted by one of the Renaissance masters, the bold contrasts of light and dark masking our surroundings with a surreal and somewhat frightening edge. Only instead of the allure born of chiaroscuro, there is an inelegance here that is hard, almost cruel. I would marvel more, perhaps, were I not distracted with how to broach the current subject.

"I wish to apologize," I finally manage to say.

Adèle looks up at me. "What for?"

"What I said last night. It was careless, and I apologize. I understand that it can be painful to speak of those we've lost."

Adèle lowers her eyes.

I take a breath and continue. "You don't have to talk about it if you don't want to. Not now, not ever. But if there comes a time you *wish* to—"

"I don't *wish* to talk about Maman," Adèle says, her words rushed and thick with emotion. Fear or anger, I cannot tell.

"I know," I say quickly and squeeze the little hand tucked in mine. "I know. I'm not asking you to. I am simply offering, should you ever change your mind. I want you to know, I'm here to listen. About that or anything, really."

Silence descends. From this angle, Adèle's face is estranged from me. I can find no sign of pain or anger or even disregard upon it. For a moment I feel a claustrophobic press of panic, and I fear I've undone what little I've managed to gain with her.

Without a word, she stops. I don't realize immediately and take a couple of steps before pausing as well. She pulls her hand from mine before becoming engrossed in retying a ribbon in her doll's hair.

"I want to go back to my room," come the small, soft words. "Can I?"

My heart aches and my throat clenches. I nod, unable to form words for a moment. "Of course."

In a blink she is running back the way we came. We haven't made it too far, and I watch her reach her door and slip inside. It bangs closed behind her, and I am alone with my guilt.

Well done, Jane. Your second day and your charge already hates you.

Well, *hate* may be a strong word, but it's easy to see that I am in for a difficult time when it comes to winning her over.

Sighing softly, I wonder if maybe I should ask any of the others in Mr. Rochester's employ exactly what became of Adèle's mother, who it seems wasn't married to her father. Not uncommon, to be sure, but a puzzle of sorts that I'll have to put together to mind my tongue around the girl. Or perhaps I should set the puzzle aside entirely. What does the girl's lineage matter to me? Who was Adèle's mother, and how she knew Adèle's father, are both irrelevant to the reason I am here. And besides, such a matter is far too delicate to be the subject of gossip, and that is certainly how it would come across to anyone else, despite my want simply to comfort the girl.

No. Adèle will tell me, or no one will.

With that decided, I make my way toward the kitchen. The smell of Emm's cooking is enough to lead me to her.

I enter to find her busy, of course, setting out helpings. Grace is there as well, putting things together on a tray. Even Marsters is present, though he's set on a stool in the corner, snoring softly, likely drunk, considering the smell of alcohol is strong enough to reach me all the way over here.

The only other change this morning is the door that opens onto the grounds, situated on what I think is the east side of the house, given the almost blinding sunlight that pours through the frame.

Birdsong and the low hum of someone singing filter in. The stable hand, perhaps?

"Come for the wee one's breakfast?" Emm calls.

"Late." Grace shakes her head. "Was she awake when you found her, or did you wake her yourself?"

The memory of Adèle already sitting up when I entered her room flashes before me. "I think my entering must have woken her."

Grace gathers her tray and moves past me toward the door. "*Tsk.* Children should rise early, and breakfast should be waiting for them or they'll get a stitch for the rest of the day." Then she's gone, but not before throwing an ugly look in my direction.

I watch her disappear down the corridor before turning to Emm. "Did I insult her in some way?"

Emm barks a faint laugh. "I told you not to take it personal. She's like that with everyone who's new."

The part of me that's learned to hear what isn't said and read what isn't there tells me it's more than that, but I let it go.

Emm ladles something thick, steamy, and white into a bowl before offering it to me. "Grace has served this house and its masters longer than most of us have been alive. I suppose she's feeling territorial with your being here."

"Was she like this with the last governess?" I ask as I set about gathering things onto my own tray to bring to Adèle. "Before coming to like her, as you claim. Which seems an impossibility. . . ."

There's a pause as Emm frowns in consideration. "You know, I'm not sure. They were both here before me, though I do know she was a right peach at my arrival. It's never a good idea to upset the cook. There's nothing you can do but give it time. She's old and stubborn, but she'll come around."

I'm honestly not sure I want her to. "Thank you." Taking the tray in hand, I make my way across the house toward Adèle's room. I only get turned around once, but it delays me long enough that my arms are aching by the time I arrive.

I set the tray on a small table just to the side before knocking. "Breakfast smells delicious," I call as I open the door, then elbow my way through.

And it does smell delicious, particularly the savory scent of the fried ham and the sweetness of the sugar atop the bowl of porridge.

But my preemptive appreciation of Emm's cooking is short-lived.

Adèle is gone.

She's not in the window, at the desk, on the bed, or anywhere else I can see from the doorway.

"Adèle?" I call, moving farther into the room. There's no answer. I hurry to set the tray on the neatly made bed before dropping to my knees to peer under it. She's not there.

I search the wardrobe and behind the dressing screen, calling her name the entire time.

The beat of my heart quickens as I look behind the thick gatherings of curtains lining the windows. Still nothing.

"Adèle!" I hurry from the room and down the hall, throwing open what doors aren't locked and peering inside. My search turns up no sign of her.

Two additional halls and six empty rooms later, my worry is mounting. Where on earth could she be? I pause and take a beat to gather myself. There is no need to assume the worst. Thornfield is massive; there are plenty of places for one so small to hide. Perhaps she is somewhere out on the grounds. There is the garden maze, but with the morning chill still thick in the air, I doubt it provides too tempting a prospect.

"Maybe . . . maybe she went to get breakfast herself," I muse aloud. "Knowing I was going to get it for her." I don't think I was gone *that* long. Perhaps when I got turned around, she decided to seek me out. Or seek her meal out.

Assured I'll find her in the kitchen, and ignoring the fact that if she *had* gone to the kitchen, we would have likely passed by each other earlier—I race across the house.

I stumble into the kitchen, earning a confused look from Emm.

"Adèle?"

Across the room, Marsters wakes with a jolt, grumbling and glancing around as my shout jostles him from sleep. A pale man, looking to be around the same age as Emm and I, glances up from where he's sweeping along the edges of a now empty porridge bowl with a bit of bread. He pauses mid-chew, so his cheeks are puffed with food. It would be amusing, if I weren't fighting my rising frustration.

"Steady on, lass, what's wrong?" Emm approaches me, wiping her hands on her apron.

"A-Adèle." I stammer out her name, my tongue tripping over the syllables, despite there being so few. "She's gone! I can't find her!"

Emm's startled expression shifts to confusion briefly before she bursts out laughing. The sound is bright and loud, and I'm annoyed and slightly entranced all at once. Is it possible to laugh with an accent?

"Calm yourself. You'll find she does this quite often."

"Does what?" I ask, not entirely sure what is going on.

"Goes running off somewhere to be alone or play or whatever it is little girls from wealthy families do in their youth." Emm goes back to tending a pot she'd stepped away from.

My panic eases slightly but still continues to buzz in my chest like an agitated bee. "But . . . but breakfast," I say, thinking about the tray of food I've left sitting on her bed, which will no doubt be cold by the time I return.

"She'll turn up when she's hungry enough," Emm says. "Speaking of hungry." She fires a look over her shoulder at the man at the table. "Will three helpings be enough, then?"

Interrupted for the second time in as many minutes, the man looks less amusingly ruffled by it this time. He takes his dishes and stands, walking them over to the sink. "Three will be fine," he calls, his voice carrying a note of laughter.

"It had better," Emm says, though there's no real threat in her words. "Since you're done stuffing yer gob, come introduce yourself before you head out."

The man seems to hesitate a moment before approaching. An easy smile takes his face.

"How d'you do?" he says to me, dipping his chin in a nod. "Name's Devin Cabbston. I tend Mr. Rochester's stables."

I offered a mirrored smile, one of practiced pleasantries rather than genuine delight. "Jane Eyre. A pleasure." It's not his fault that my mind is elsewhere, specifically on how I've now managed to alienate and lose track of my pupil all in a matter of hours.

"Jane is Adèle's new governess," Emm says without looking at either of us.

Devin's smile widens, and I notice there's a roundness to his face, the last vestiges of boyhood that haven't melted away entirely. It lends him a hint of charm.

"Well," he begins, "she tends to spend a fair amount of time outside when the weather permits. If I see her, I'll send her your way."

"Thank you," I say.

"Ladies." Devin nods again before turning to head for the door. He stops in front of Marsters, who'd quickly gone off to sleep again, to kick lightly at his boots. "Day's calling, old man." The words are teasing.

Marsters grunts, then mutters again before finally hauling himself upright. He doesn't spare either Emm or me a glance before following Devin through the door. The younger man waves, then reaches to close it behind them.

"Try not to get yourself too wound up," Emm says, and faces me. "Adèle has been through a lot. Took her the better part of a month before she'd even look me in the eye, let alone speak to me, and you got whole sentences on your first day!"

At Emm's words, I recall our less-than-pleasant exchange last night. The way Adèle shuttered herself away. Then again, in the hallway this morning, her retreat to her room. All to get away from me. Yes, I'm doing splendidly.

"She's fine, I'm sure," Emm says, pulling me from my thoughts.

"Yes," I agree, my previous trepidation now shifting into concern. "But she's still my responsibility. I'll search the house for her, then the grounds. If she comes this way, let her know I left breakfast in her room?"

"Of course," Emm says. "Remember, Mr. Rochester doesn't want folk to go wandering. The two upper floors are expressly forbidden."

That comes as a surprise. How peculiar. "Did he say why?" Of course, it's only after I pose the question that I wonder if it's any of my business.

Emm shrugs without looking up. "I don't question a man about the rules of his house, long as they don't interfere with doing my job."

Fair enough.

I leave her to her work and make my way through the house again, calling for Adèle as I go, offering assurances that I'm not upset or angry, I just want to know she's all right. With no set destination in mind, I walk. And walk. And walk. Calling into the silence. And silence is what answers me.

I try a few other doors as I pass them. Two are locked, but the third swings open.

"Adèle?" I try again, lifting my voice as high as I dare.

This room is large, but dark and sparse. What little furniture there is, is covered by dirty sheets. There's barely any light thanks to the windows along the far wall being shuttered against the day, the thick curtains drawn. The sun tries in vain to squeeze what it can through the thin seams between what was once luxurious velvet draped from the ceiling. At least, it looks like velvet. Rank, dusty velvet.

I start to close the door when the faintest echo of a voice catches my ear.

"Adèle?" I step fully into the room to get a better look. Perhaps she's hiding beneath one of the sheets or behind one of the chairs.

That's when I notice a staircase tucked away in the shadows. One of the gold ribbons I'd tied to the end of Adèle's braid rests against the bottom step, just out of sight of the door.

I pluck the ribbon from the floor and peer up the staircase, into more shadows and dust. Whether the girl is still up there is uncertain, but I now know she came this way, and not too long ago. I start to follow, the wood creaking beneath my feet, but then I pause.

Emm's warning echoes in my mind. *Mr. Rochester doesn't want folk to go wandering.*

Adèle has to know the upper floors are off-limits; this is her home, after all. And yet the upper floors are clearly where she's gone. I'm not surprised. Telling young children what they ought not do all but guarantees they do it. The question now becomes whether I also break the rules in order to go after her. The fact remains that the girl is my charge, my responsibility. Surely Mr. Rochester would prefer I prioritize his daughter's safety over any dislike of people "wandering."

Steeling myself, I keep climbing. The stairs carry me to the second floor, where more dingy, shady halls chopped up by struggling sunlight and locked doors await. The dust is thicker here, likely from being undisturbed for longer. For a moment I get the idea that perhaps I can follow Adèle's trail in it, like tracking someone across snow, but alas, it's not *that* thick.

As I continue, a sort of foreboding settles over me. There's something about this floor that feels deeper, more withdrawn, than the ones before. If a house could be withdrawn, that is. I wonder if it's a trick of the light, or lack thereof, that makes the shadows seem lengthier, lending them a somewhat maleficent edge. Here, they are allowed to run free. They seem to churn and writhe and stretch along the walls, painting the illusion of the ceiling rising to impossible heights. They crawl across the floor, stealing sight of it altogether in some places.

I'm reminded of stories of sylphs and fae, tall tales of sprightly beings whose beauty was unmatched by all but their cruelty. It would be fitting to imagine such creatures lurking in the trappings of this esteemed estate, waiting for unwitting passersby to step on what they believe to be a shady bit of carpet, only to fall through a hidden hole to a painful or deadly drop.

Pushing the images conjured by my agitation aside, I continue calling for Adèle, and I continue receiving nothing in answer. My previous concern is beginning to wax, due in no small part to the twisting in my stomach. Adèle's breakfast isn't the only one going cold. I'm of a mind to abandon my search altogether and just wait her out in her room or the kitchen when I hear the thud of steps overhead. They're swift and light, the steps of a child.

The relief I feel is tempered with annoyance. "Adèle?" I call, aiming my voice upward. "Is this a game? Are we playing?"

I find a second staircase, much smaller than the first, tucked away in a corner. I take it quickly, waving away the dust that springs forth, disturbed by my steps.

My eyes search the shadows, and my ears strain to hear any other signs of my charge. "Adèle, this is rather fun, but breakfast is going to get cold."

More silence. But then . . .

Laughter sounds somewhere to my left.

Or is it coming from somewhere in front of me?

I pause, listening.

Then I realize with a sudden jolt that it's not laughter I hear, but instead a high, faint crying.

"Adèle!" I break into a run, gathering my skirts as I go. The darkness of Thornfield rushes forward to swallow me. I don't care. "Adèle! I'm coming!"

8

CONSPIRATOR

BERTHA . . .

With one final jab from my knife, the last plank loosens. I press my hand against the roughened wood and push. There's a sharp *snap*, and it comes free altogether.

I release a rush of breath, joy beating to life inside me, then grip at the splintered edges and work them open and away to widen the hole. My arms tremble from exhaustion, my fingers throb, and my vision doubles from lack of sleep and leaving breakfast uneaten, but I've done it.

Crack. Pop!

More and more wood comes free. I sling chunks of it aside, big and small, and crawl forward until I'm able to work my way through. My nose stings when I disturb a layer of dust, sending it scrambling into the air around me. I hold my breath and fight against the sneeze that builds.

The folds of my dress catch along the jagged edges and I yank at the fabric. It tears, but I don't care. I'm near dizzy with delight as I push onto my knees and feel around in the dark. The opposing closet is small and empty. My fingers find the knob and I have to force myself to stop.

Slow down. I take careful breaths, listening for signs of Grace. She just dropped off my breakfast, so she shouldn't be back for an hour yet.

My preference would be to sneak out at night, when the house is asleep and the world is dark, but two things work against me in that. I want to go before Edward returns. He seems to be aware of everything that happens within these walls, and the fewer eyes looking for me, the better. Also, with winter approaching, the nighttime chill would likely slow me, if not stop me entirely. Perhaps I can wave down a passing horse or coach once I reach the main road. But none of that will matter if I let my eagerness get the better of me and rush forward without thought.

Slowly, I open the closet.

Darkness and gloom greet me, everything wreathed in shadow and the curtains drawn tight against the far window. My eyes have already adjusted from working in the closet, and I'm able to make out the shapes of covered furniture here and there.

Gaining my feet, I quickly cross to the far door. I curl my fingers around the knob and try to will my racing heart to calm.

The hall is empty from what I can tell, though I wait a minute or so more before finally easing through. The knife in my hand feels heavy with my intent to use it if I must. My last bid for freedom resulted in a broken arm, and still I was captured. Getting away from this place may cost someone more. May cost me more. . . .

I move as quickly as I dare. If I remember correctly, I should make a left, and that will bring me to a back staircase. At the end of the hall, I check both directions before continuing. My heart thrashes in my chest. It's beating so loud I fear it may give me away, but I can't stop.

"Adèle!" a voice calls.

I near trip over my feet as I slam to a stop. I press my back to the wall and hold my breath.

"Adèle!"

The voice is unfamiliar. The governess, I realize. What is she doing up here?

Edward allows no one new into the upper halls, not until he's certain he can convince them of my supposed insanity, or he can buy their loyalty. But Edward has been gone since before her arrival, so it could very well

9

OFF-LIMITS

JANE . . .

I would much rather be chasing Adèle through the high walls of the hedge maze, letting the sun warm my face and the smell of the crisp autumn air tickle my senses. Instead, I'm shuffling around in the gloom with dust coating my throat and the walls shunting me back and forth.

However, a skylight offers a brief reprieve from the dark and I turn my face to the heavens. The day is clear and likely gorgeous. The morning sky is bright blue with just a hint of cloud. I draw a breath in slowly, then let it out. I can't let my ire get the better of me.

Adèle isn't doing this to vex me personally. None of the times I hid as a child were an attempt to upset anyone, but because I myself was upset or scared. I need to remember that, and to focus on how I can ease her discomfort and prove I'm here to help her in any way I can. I want her to trust me, but I must earn it.

"Adèle!" There's less force behind my voice this time. "If you wish, we can come back up here after breakfast, but you at least need to eat something first." I squint as I make my way along the corridor once more, waiting for my eyes to adjust after standing in the light. My fingers slide along the wall for guidance.

The smell of dirt, of mud, and something distinctly rotten and moldy wafts up with each step. Perhaps someone attempted to wash these rugs, and there was so much dust the result was less than desirous. Then they put them right back partially wet for others to slog across.

And it is a slog, the thick carpeting feeling more like sludge beneath my shoes. I go a bit slower, afraid of either catching an unseen rise in the fabric or maybe even sinking into it, never to be seen again. The shadows are thinner here, longer, thanks to the angles of windows and skylights, but no less menacing. They stretch up the walls to seemingly towering heights and loom overhead, with spindly fingers reaching to pinch and pull at passersby. I feel the grooves in the wall, the catches in the wood where it has split from age, hung open like wounds.

If the lower floors of Thornfield are the haunted domain of malevolent spirits and shades biding their time during the days and crawling free at night, then the upper halls are certainly dark, decaying forests that swallow lost children and unwitting maidens. I'm torn between the desire to find the stairs to descend back into relative safety and the need to find Adèle.

This is her home, part of me says. *She knows how to get around. She's not afraid, you heard Emm, this is practically Adèle's playground.*

Even so, a less frightened part of me counters, *it wouldn't do to abandon the girl. You are responsible for her.*

But what if she's already downstairs?

What if she's not? What if she's fallen and is hurt, or somehow unconscious? What if the house has indeed swallowed her up? Taken her to bait you into the darkness, wanting to get you alone, biding its time until . . .

A hand falls upon my shoulder and squeezes. A surprised shout rises within me, and I clap a hand over my mouth to conceal it as I spin in the middle of the hall.

A man stands before me. I have to look up into his white face, which is cast just slightly in shadow with the sun at his back. Even so, I can make out the lines of his features with little difficulty. Deep, dark eyes gaze at me from beneath a shock of brown hair. Sharp cheekbones my aunt would've called distinguished and a strong jawline mark him as rather handsome.

He arches a brow and tilts his head curiously. There's an inquisitiveness in his gaze, though his lips are pursed slightly. He can't be more than a handful of years my senior.

"And just what are you doing up here?" he asks, the timbre of his voice smooth and even.

"I—I . . ." I clear my throat, embarrassment hot in my cheeks, and try again. "I'm searching for Adèle. She's my charge. I thought I heard someone and—"

"Ah." He sounds amused, and yet simultaneously miffed. "I see. You must be Miss Eyre."

I nod, facing him fully and looking over him quickly. "That I am. Jane Eyre."

The man straightens just so before offering his hand. "A pleasure, Miss Eyre," he says as I place my fingers in his. He bows and gives them a squeeze. "I am Edward Rochester."

My previous embarrassment is now full bloomed into shame. I stammer over an apology, which only seems to amuse him more, given the smile that quirks his lips. I pull my hand from his and drop back into a slight dip.

"I am so sorry, I—I don't—I went to get Adèle for breakfast, and she was gone, I—"

Movement over his shoulder catches my attention, and I wonder if Adèle has finally come out of hiding. I shift to try to see past him, but Mr. Rochester sets a hand at my elbow lightly, guiding me around and leading me on down the hall. "I'm afraid it is I who must apologize." He sets a swift pace, and I have to concentrate on keeping up. "Adèle is prone to these little adventures through the house, even though she knows certain areas are off-limits."

It could be a trick of the light, what little there is, but the look he gives me is cutting. At least until we pass by the dim glow of a window and I notice he's still smiling faintly.

My face heats for a completely different reason. "I did not mean to go against your wishes, but I heard her up here and I—"

"I know," he cuts in. "She can be a handful."

"That's not—"

"Please." Mr. Rochester gestures with his free hand, the other still lightly holding my arm. "Let me finish. Adèle is a sensitive child. Even at this age. And she has a habit of testing her limits when said sensitivity is provoked. I fear her mother's relatively recent passing may have something to do with that. And I have not been the best at . . . seeing to what she needs to cope with such a loss. So, once more I must apologize. You have done nothing wrong."

I blink in surprise, stunned silent. I don't know what I expected in response to my flagrantly flouting the rules of the house, especially when discovered by the *owner* of said house, but it certainly wasn't an acquittal of my actions. My mouth works uselessly a few times before I finally find my voice. "I understand. It's hard to lose those we love."

His brow furrows. "Spoken from experience?"

"It was a long time ago."

"If there is one thing that unites all of humanity it is that each of us will one day be wounded in such a way. We have our scars in common." He clears his throat. "On a less melancholic topic, I must also beg your forgiveness for not being here when you arrived yesterday. Normally, I prefer to greet new employees personally and show them around Thornfield, make introductions, warn them of issues with the house."

"And what areas are off-limits as a result," I say, smiling faintly as my feet work to keep up with his.

He doesn't seem to notice, though his smile returns as well. "Yes, it's quite embarrassing. There was a leak this past summer that went unnoticed. As a result, several floorboards here and there have rotted from the inside and are weak. Why, the young woman in your position previously had an unfortunate time when her foot went clean through the floor." A dark expression crosses his face. "I would like to avoid such things until repairs are completed."

Well, that explains why the carpet smells like a marsh. A leak, and not neglect. I shouldn't be so judgmental at times.

"Many have been made," he continues. "And there are many more to be done. In the meantime, I hope the state of things, shameful as they are, isn't too terribly off-putting."

"Oh, no, of course not." I knew there had to be a reason for Thornfield to be in such a state, though my proposed reasonings had been less favorable, I hate to admit. Even if only to myself. "The grounds are beautiful, and the house itself remains very impressive. Grand, even. I'm certain those repairs will restore its previous majesty."

"Indeed," he says, looking at me briefly. "I hope you're still around to see Thornfield in all its glory."

"Do you foresee a reason I should not be?"

A chuckle leaves him, and the sound is not unpleasant. "I suppose not. Alas, I don't have my crystal ball on hand. But repairs are extensive and may take time. Who knows what could happen between now and then? Sophie is no longer with us."

"Sophie?" I ask as we practically run along another hall that eventually brings us to the top of the grand staircase just inside the front entryway. To think we were so near this familiar juncture; it felt as if I had wandered up there for an eternity.

"Adèle's previous governess. She left to be married. Perhaps the same fate will befall you." I'm not sure if he's taken note of my plight in being nearly a head shorter and trying to keep up, but he slows his pace.

I clear my throat, taking a moment to recover from both our jaunt and his somewhat forward but not entirely untoward statement. "The future is a mystery, I daresay, even with a missing crystal ball. And I meant it when I said I'd like to see Thornfield in her grandeur."

"Hopefully, that comes to pass." He finally stops and smooths a hand over the front of his jacket before offering the other to me. "Now then, Adèle is in the dining hall having a bit of breakfast. We should join her, don't you think, Miss Eyre?" His smile is broad enough that it crinkles his eyes.

My insides are still somewhat wrecked from the shame of having been caught and then admitting my failure in keeping track of Adèle. And while our conversation has done much to quell that particular beast, there's something about Mr. Rochester's countenance—the way it seems less sharp, more open and understanding—that eases my remaining anxieties. He truly doesn't seem upset or bothered by my mistakes, so perhaps it's best if I put them behind me.

"Of course, Mr. Rochester." I place my hand in his and smile in return, though it's not the practiced, spurious expression I offered Devin earlier. No, this is more genuine.

"Please," he says as he leads the way down the stairs. "Call me Edward."

10

HOME SWEET HOME

BERTHA . . .

My heart thrashes, same as my arms and legs as I am dragged along the hall. I try to scream but the fingers clamped tightly across my mouth squeeze hard enough that my jaw aches and agony detonates behind my eyes. The hand those fingers belong to smells of alcohol, sweat, and something foul.

"Quit your fidgeting," a low, rough voice grumbles near my ear. Marsters tightens his hold around me and pulls, yanking me off my feet. With one meaty arm around my torso, trapping my arms to my sides, and the other keeping me from shouting, he half pulls, half hauls me along the corridor, back toward my room.

"Such a troublesome woman." Grace shakes her head as she shuffles along after us. "Thank you for your assistance, Marsters. Oh!" She sets a hand over her chest as I kick out at her, but it's no use.

"Oi!" Marsters grunts and gives me a shake so hard my teeth rattle. "You want a wallop? Do ya?"

"Easy now," Grace cautions. "The master doesn't want her harmed."

"He's too good to this tr—"

"Ah!" Grace barks, silencing him.

It's all the distraction I need to draw my knee up as far as I can before driving the heel of my shoe onto the top of his foot.

He howls and his grip slackens. I twist to pull away, breaking free and making it down the hall a handful of steps before something slams into me from behind.

The impact sweeps me clean off my feet and I hit the floor hard enough that the air is forced from my lungs. My head throbs. My entire body thrums with pain.

Grace says something in that high-pitched tone of hers she uses when upset, but I can't make out the words over the sound of my own struggling breaths.

"I know, I know!" Marsters growls before hands grip my arms hard enough to hurt, then yank me upward.

I can't quite get my feet under me, but that doesn't matter. I'm dragged along like so much dirty laundry.

A door opens—my door, I realize with a sudden swell of dread—and I'm flung into the room.

I catch myself against the floor. Fresh pain rattles my already aching body.

"Clever, digging your way out like that," Marsters says, his voice low and full of menace. "Smarter than you ought to be."

He slams the door, leaving me alone in the gloom.

"No need to be rude," Grace chides over the sound of the locks clicking, her voice muffled by the door.

Marsters spits out a response, but he's already started down the hall and is well outside of my hearing.

Grace goes after him, and I am left alone, lying on the floor and hurting.

So close. I was so close!

If I hadn't stopped, if I had just . . .

How could I be so foolish?

Anger roils through me, hot and heavy. My vision blurs with the sting of tears as I curl into myself, muffling my screams with my skirt. I pound at the floor until my fingers are numb to it. Instead of pain, my swollen hands tingle with cold.

So close, and now they know about the hole in my closet.

My fury is near to boiling.

I hate Edward. I . . . *hate* him.

Not the usual hot, ugly feeling reserved for someone who's done you some egregious wrong, but a blistering, primal thing one might find in the wilds. A ravenous monster that hollows you out with teeth and claws until there is nothing left *but* the hate.

"Damn you," I whisper to no one, because no one can hear me. "Damn you," I say louder.

The silence answers me. So I fill it.

"Damn you!" I scream.

I stomp over to the tray of uneaten breakfast, catch my hands against the edge of the table, and heave. Dishes, cutlery, everything clatters to the ground. The table falls over with a heavy thud. Kicking aside the mess, I snatch up one of the plates and fling it at the window.

"Damn you!"

Bread and butter go flying before the plate slams into the boards. Pieces of china shoot in every direction. The loose plank falls free. I throw the half-empty bowl of porridge next, still screaming.

"Damn you! Damn you!"

Another bowl, the cup, the cutlery, then the tray all sail across the room, scattering their contents.

There is nothing left, but I'm still . . . I can't see straight. The world tilts and fractures. My heart thrashes in my chest, my head swells. I can't stop.

I snatch at the items on my dresser, throwing them as well. A cross, an empty vial of perfume, bits of jewelry. Next are the pillows, the sheets, all of it. I rip them free. Feathers burst into the air.

I'm still screaming, my breath coming in gasps, though now something warm and wet runs along my face. Tears, I realize. They blur my vision as I fling the chair, then grip the side of the dresser and pull. It slams into the floor with a sound like thunder.

By that time my throat burns and my voice is spent. My fingers clench so tight all color flees them. My knuckles ache. The whole of me quakes and heaves. Looking at the wreckage, it appears as if some great tempest has savaged my chamber. I stand there panting and shaking, shaking so hard my teeth rattle. So hard I feel I may crumble.

There is nothing else. It is all destroyed. Just like my life.

My rage abates and leaves me at the mercy of the sorrow waiting at the fringes. It sweeps up to consume me, just as ravenous as the fury but far less forgiving. I've always fought to keep the sadness at arm's length, to embrace the rage because rage sustains.

Sorrow subdues.

My screams turn to sobs, and I can stop them no more than I could stop my earlier cries.

"Damn you . . ." It's a whimper now. I have no air nor strength left for screaming. I am hollow.

My legs tremble before giving out, and I drop to the floor. I lie in the eye of the storm, my hands pressed to my face as all of me comes undone.

By the time I manage to lift myself, my senses swimming and my head thick from crying, the room has darkened significantly. I don't know how long I've been down here. The room is still a mess, with food and linens scattered. I know they have to have heard me, but have likely kept their distance.

It doesn't matter if they come; all the fight has left me, and I'm weak in its absence. Despair wedges itself between my lungs, hard and heavy. I haven't felt such hopelessness since I arrived at Thornfield, and what was to be my new home became my prison.

It was a clear night, a beautiful night, the stillness and quiet occasionally interrupted by the song of crickets and toads. A symphony that reminded me of home in New Orleans. The stars twinkled brightly alongside the face of a full moon. The weather was warm, and a pleasant breeze shifted through the darkness. I was sick for home, despite the beauty of the English countryside, and my new husband's worsening mood wasn't helping.

I was still angry with him from our argument earlier in the week and, as a result, had elected to remain silent during the final leg of our journey. He'd received a telegram that left him in a sour mood. I'd suggested a walk in the gardens of the inn where we had stopped so he could make correspondence. He'd declined. I'd come around to his side, hoping to persuade him to at least come to dinner, but he recoiled as if harmed. Then he howled accusations of my attempting to pry into his affairs.

I was not trying to see the bit of paper as he insisted; I'd merely hoped to offer my new husband comfort. He warned me, with such vehemence in his eyes, that I should mind my place. After that, if he spoke to me at all, he was gruff and curt. It was such a drastic change from who he had been as we sailed across the ocean.

I'd hoped returning to Thornfield would ease his temper, and I was indeed excited to see the grand estate he'd described to me, detailing its splendor more than once.

"The grounds are something to behold, lush and green in the spring, flowers in bloom on all sides," Edward would say. "It reminds me of the grand paintings one might see in museums, the birthplace of color."

The way he'd spoken of Thornfield was as if he were describing some faraway kingdom, the kind ascribed to tales of fantasy.

"Thornfield boasts some of the loveliest gardens in the county. There's nothing quite like beholding the entirety of it on a clear, bright day."

Unfortunately, we would be arriving in the dead of night, so I would have to wait until the next morning to see the grounds. Still, as the coach carried us down the long road at the edge of the estate, I let my imagination run wild. I built a replica from passing shadows and filled it with all manner of flowers and trees. I lost myself running through the fields of this dream world.

When the coach finally came to a stop, it jolted me from my fantasy and back into the cold, dark reality where my once warm husband now sat apart from me, more interested in reading papers by lantern light.

"Finally." Edward shoved the missives into a case and snapped it shut. He didn't wait for the door to be opened but instead pushed it aside himself and climbed out without so much as a glance in my direction.

I remained seated for a few moments so as to put some distance between us. His foul mood was rather contagious at that point, and my own temperament was beginning to suffer. *Anger is better than tears, Little Bird*, Maman would say. *Anger is focused. Tears make things unclear.* And I was indeed angry for having been all but ignored for days.

The coach rocked as Marsters climbed down. The smell of alcohol filled the air as he wandered past the window nearest me, no doubt headed for the back of the coach to fetch down our things. My nose wrinkled. He must have been drinking this entire trip. I'm not one to judge what another does with their coin and time, though I did wonder how he was able to find his way while being three sheets to the wind, in the dark no less.

There was a thud and a grunt, then the familiar bang of a large door. Finally, silence descended. That's when I surmised enough time had passed, and Edward by now had to be inside and tending to things upon our arrival. I hoped that the business of returning after so long a venture would keep him occupied while I made my way to bed. Tomorrow, I planned to see which version of him greeted me.

I climbed down out of the carriage. My legs ached from sitting so long and I was thankful for the chance to stretch them. Thornfield rose before me out of the shadows of the night, a monster of stonework. Even in the dark I could tell it was a formidable structure, unlike anything I had ever laid eyes on back home. Light flickered in many of the windows, the house coming alive at the return of her master and lady.

I smiled, thinking I *could* make a home here, weather whatever storm had taken Edward, and wait until he returned to himself and to me. I took a few steps and turned my gaze toward the brightness of the moon.

That's when everything went dark.

Something made of cloth fell over my head. The hem pressed into my throat, choking me. I tried to grab for it, but hands seized my arms in painfully tight grasps. I was lifted and dragged forward.

I kicked and screamed, shouting for Edward, Marsters, anyone who could hear, begging for help.

My feet stumbled along as I tried and failed to dig my heels in. I was hauled up the stairs and through Thornfield's front doors.

Burglars, my panicked mind said. Brigands had invaded my new home and taken me captive.

"Edward!" I screamed again.

Still, there was no answer.

The hands adjusted their hold as they pulled me up a massive set of stairs. I fought as best I could, throwing my weight forward and back, stomping at where I thought feet would be. One of my shoes managed to connect and I heard a grunt.

Pain erupted from along the side of my face as my head wrenched around with the sudden force of a blow.

I'd been slapped, I realized as I blinked through the resulting daze.

"Don't!" another voice snarled.

I didn't know their number, but it was enough that they overpowered me completely and dragged me through the house until, finally, the fabric was yanked from my head. I blinked the world into focus, catching sight of a simple bedroom just before I was pushed inside.

I caught myself against the bed as the door slammed shut behind me. Locks clicked into place. Even so, I pulled at the knob, twisting and shaking it with all my might. I pounded at the wood with both fists, yelling to be released, demanding to know what they had done to my husband! The hinges rattled furiously with my efforts, but they were in vain.

Soon steps wandered away from the door and I was left alone in the dark.

And alone I remained, for two entire days, with no food, no water, and not one word from another soul, no matter how loud I shouted. For two days, I feared the worst for Edward, and for myself and any number of grisly fates I could meet.

Questions tumbled over themselves in my mind: *Who had done this? What did they want? What would they do to me now?*

Until finally, the sound of voices preceded steps along the hall, coming toward me. Despite my pounding head and aching muscles, weak from hunger, I grabbed a nearby chair and readied myself to fight.

I had decided, whatever my fate, I would not go quietly.

I was no longer afraid. I was *angry*.

The locks clicked as they were released.

The door opened.

And to my utter shock, Edward filled the frame. He didn't look haggard or harassed. In fact, he looked prim and pressed, the very same as when I'd last seen him in the carriage.

Part of me wanted to go to him, to throw myself into his arms and sink under the weight of the relief that washed through me. But the rest of me remained in place, frozen in my surprise.

Edward adjusted a cuff link and sighed. Just over his shoulder, I spied Marsters, glowering at me, his face red with drink.

"Bertha," Edward finally said, his voice far calmer than it had any right to be. "I'm afraid there are a few things we need to discuss."

PART 2

You must neither expect nor exact anything celestial of me, for you will not get it.

11

FOOLED

BERTHA ...

I don't turn away from the window when I hear the locks clicking. The door swings open and Grace's distinct gait enters the room, along with the clatter of the tray.

"Here we go," she coos. "Oh dear, it looks like a board has come loose."

I say nothing, simply continue to gaze through the slats covering my window and out across the grounds. From here, I have a perfect view of the hedge maze. It's lovely, everything I ever imagined when I heard tales of it in the beginning. Now? The vision has soured.

"No matter, I'll have Marsters come set it right. You hear that, Marsters?"

There's a grunt from the hallway, the old drunk keeping watch.

The tray clacks against the table, but there's something off about the sound. Something . . . hollow.

I finally turn to find lunch waiting for me on wooden plates. A wooden bowl and wooden spoon and fork are there as well. Blinking in surprise, I look to Grace. "What is this?"

Grace scrutinizes the setting. "Bit of bread, some meat and cheese, and—"

"No," I say, stalking over and lifting one of the utensils. It's rough and small in my hand, confirming my assumptions. "Is . . . is this a toy set?"

"Oh, yes, I'm afraid so." Grace sighs, as if the truth somehow pains her. "You've broken every dish I've brought you for nearly a week now. The master doesn't think you can be trusted with proper settings. I regret this is all that's left. I borrowed it from Adèle's room. Eat up!"

I stare at the place setting as Grace shuffles away, the door closing behind her.

A toy set. So, what, now I am not only a prisoner but I'm to be treated as a child?

Throwing down the fork—it bounces against the table—I return to the window. The sight that greets me sends my blood cold and stirs a fury in my chest.

Edward is down there, strolling along with the new governess. I only got a brief look at her those days past, but I can tell it's her, especially when she turns her face toward the sun. That face is branded into my mind. Every curve, every rise, the fullness of her nose and mouth. She is a gorgeous creature. And Edward, bastard that he is, walks with her at his side.

They stroll leisurely, arm in arm, as Adèle moves about them, chasing butterflies or riding the wind. If I perhaps were some random onlooker not privy to the machinations of this hell, I might think the three a quaint, handsome family.

Perhaps it might have been *my* family. I can't deny having dreamt of it in the past. When it was I on Edward's arm as we'd promenade through one of New Orleans's glorious parks. He smiled then as he does now. His handsome face, though I detest it, lights up in a way that further ignites my anger and stirs a sadness I can't place.

I maybe loved him, once. Or thought I did. The way he would speak gently to me, or how we'd laugh together, as they laugh now.

But that part of me is long dead. Killed by his betrayal. I have reconciled myself with this death and the knowledge it has provided me. Thus, with the truth now awash in the blood of my broken heart, I see Edward for what he is and I remember what he pretended to be.

I can recall the day I first laid eyes on him. It was perhaps two years ago, some time in the spring. The last chills of winter were fading, and the green of the world was shaking away the final vestiges of frost. New Orleans during that time is dazzling.

The day was soon done, and the newborn evening brought with it a smattering of stars against the still faintly blue sky. My grandmama used to say that the sun likes to be here when the stars come out to play, so he takes his time sinking into the horizon.

My parents and I were exiting the Théâtre d'Orléans. We'd just seen a charming little show, a local troupe attempting to modernize Shakespeare, and the two of them were in heated debate about what my father perceived as a very obvious but wholly unnecessary plot hole in the second act. My mother chided him for ruining the "magic" of the theater.

Meanwhile, I was preoccupied with a completely different type of magic. He was tall, handsome, with sharp features and an even sharper wit given the way everyone around him laughed. His voice carried, even above the rumble of the exiting patrons, but he wasn't loud or belligerent in the way some men can be. Instead his tone was even, thoughtful, as he spoke.

The entire atrium seemed full of him, and yet I was only able to steal scant glances between people as they passed. Then he laughed, and with that laughter came the brightest smile. I felt one wanting to take my lips in response.

I stared at him, barely hearing my parents argue. My father said something about calling for the coach, then slipped out the door. There was a pause in Edward's conversation, and he glanced up and directly into my eyes. Time slowed in that moment, and for a stretch of eternity there was nothing and no one else. Just us. I was convinced he felt it, too. I told myself that I had *seen* him notice, due to how his expression softened and his boisterous demeanor seemed subdued. The suddenness of the change is what convinced me.

"Bertha?" my mother called, curiosity coating her tone. "Did you hear me? Goodness, child, whatever are you looking at?" She shifted beside me, no doubt peering across the room.

"Mm?" I quickly turned to face her, shaking my head. "Nothing. I thought I saw someone I knew, that's all."

"Who, dear?" Mother looked to me, then across the room again.

I followed her gaze, a twinge of fear that my wandering thoughts and the subject of them might be discovered, but he was gone. The space where he once stood was empty, and it felt like all the air had fled the room with him.

I couldn't help my disappointment, though it was quickly followed by embarrassment and self-deprecation. Imagine, being so caught up by a pretty face and little more.

"No one," I finally answered my mother. "Or, at least, I was wrong. I thought perhaps I'd seen Maisey Unclest."

"She's still away with her family in France, remember?"

"Which is why I was so surprised when I thought I saw her." I fidgeted with my gloves for something to do with my hands. "Look, there's the coach, and Papa."

My mother angled her body toward the door and adjusted her hat. "So it is. Let's go, and don't forget to open your parasol. Can't have you fainting in this sun."

I made what I hoped was a polite noise as we moved for the exit. The doorman drew it open; we stepped through. Before we emerged from the shadows, I opened my parasol and propped it against my shoulder with a practiced grace.

As we climbed into the coach, I stole one last glance over the crowd, but the stranger had vanished. If I had been born with just a bit more luck, I would never have seen him again. I would have lived my life in peace, perhaps found a husband who cared, or spent my days with my family. But, as my poorest of fortune would have it, I would cross paths with Edward Rochester two months hence, at a celebration hosted by a dear family friend.

Amidst the early evening glow and the shade of blooming magnolia trees, I fell into his trap.

12

SPIRITS, SWEETS, AND SECRETS

JANE . . .

Things have been . . . strange here at Thornfield, as of late. Upon my arrival weeks ago, there was already an uneasy air about the house. When Mr. Rochester returned, things only worsened. I can't rightly explain it, but it's as if the gloom permeating the house has thickened. A sort of muddiness, heavy and palpable, fills the halls. And while everyone seems in cheery enough spirits, there are times when I'm struck with a sense of melancholy from seemingly nowhere and for no reason.

"The willies," my beloved Helen once said when I described similar misgivings about Lowood one night some years ago. "That's what my momma called a feeling you get from a house, because houses can have spirits, too, if they're old and have seen enough."

Helen always did have the most delightful stories about fantastical places or mythic creatures, faraway kingdoms or magic spells. Her favorite stories involved ghosts and hauntings, tales of the unknown and the occult. Such a strange girl. I miss her so.

I wonder what she'd make of the most mysterious matter I've started calling the Nighttime Howlings of Thornfield. A few times I've been unable to sleep, and so sought the kitchen for a bit of tea to help calm my thoughts. More than once I've been walking along by candlelight in the dark when I heard what I'm certain is crying. It's faint, and seems to come from somewhere above, though never the same place twice all thanks to how massive the house is. The first time I heard it, I thought I'd imagined the entire thing. Especially after checking on Adèle and finding her sound asleep then and every time after.

I also wonder what Helen would make of Mr. Rochester. With the exception of our first introduction in the upstairs hall and a tour of the grounds, he's mostly kept to himself and his study since returning. The reason being that he has to catch up on and attend to the affairs of the estate. Now and again, he's made mention of how he would like the chance for us to get to know one another better, but the opportunity has yet to present itself. Because of this, I still know very little of my employer.

The few instances we've spent any amount of time in the same room have often been during meals he shared with Adèle and me. Any conversation made pertained to the girl's progress with her studies, all while she herself stared at her food, her head bowed, her eyes down.

Despite the fact that Adèle is rather reserved in her father's presence, I always do my best to assure him she's doing quite well. That, in spite of our less-than-ideal start, she is opening up more and more. She now takes to her studies like a fish to water.

Each time he seems pleased, and yet I can't help this slight turning in my stomach that says Mr. Rochester is somehow cross with me.

"The master gets like that after trips," Emm assured me when I confided in her one morning that I thought I had offended him somehow. "Give it another day or two and he'll emerge bonny enough for the both of you."

I have attempted to take Emm's advice to heart, but cannot shake the feeling that I've made some sort of misstep. Still, I won't let it distract me from my duty to Adèle, especially given how her mood seems to have soured with her father's return. Poor thing is likely upset he's so caught up in his work. I want to ease her anxiety, and my own, which brings us to my current plan. We are elbow-deep in it at the moment.

"You want to squish it between your fingers," I say as a smile plays across my lips. I roll a bit of dough about on the wooden table at the center of the kitchen, the surface dusted with flour. "Make sure everything mixes together."

Adèle stands beside me, her hair pinned back, her sleeves pushed up, as she kneads the dough as well. Her arms are powdered white, along with the too-large apron draped across her front. There's a bit of flour on her cheeks as well, which round to their fullness when she smiles up at me.

"You want to be thorough when making biscuits." I knead and press beside her. "They can tell when you're not."

Near the stove, Emm prepares for the evening meal. She scoffs somewhere at the back of her throat. "I don't appreciate your turning my kitchen into a nursery for a wee bit of story time."

I glance up at her but keep kneading. "And what makes you think I'm telling tall tales?"

"Biscuits can tell when you're not thorough?" Emm looks at us over her shoulder, her gaze disapproving, though not sharply so. "Ridiculous. And so is the notion of a young lady learning to bake, might I add. She will have servants for that."

"Yes, she might. And your opinion is noted, thricely now." I smirk and Emm shakes her head, though there's amusement clear on her face. "Besides, baking is an art form. You have to practice to be good at it, and the best in the world take it very seriously."

"An art form, you say?" There's a curious note to Emm's voice.

"Oh yes. You must be purposeful." I speak to Adèle now. "Exact. You must know what you're doing at each step, just like with each stroke of a brush or pen. You must be confident. All apt qualities to instill in a young lady, wouldn't you agree, Emm?"

She makes a noncommittal sound that isn't a rebuttal, and Adèle and I share a secret smile behind her back.

"Plus," I continue, "sweets brightened my day as a child, when I got to have them, and are the perfect treat for a job well done. They'll be the best incentive, wouldn't you say?"

"Of course!" Adèle says excitedly as we continue to press the dough.

"Excellent." I withdraw my hands and swipe them against my apron. "Keep that up. I need to check on the oven."

Adèle nods eagerly and I step away from the table, moving to join Emm where she's stirring something that will likely become a base of some sort.

I set about preparing the oven, stealing one more glance at Adèle before sidling closer to Emm. "Have you heard strange noises these past nights?"

Emm looks at me, her face pinched in confusion. "Strange noises?" she asks.

I flap a hand quickly, looking to Adèle once more, then back to Emm. "Yes." I lower my voice conspiratorially. "Like someone crying."

A look crosses Emm's face. "Crying? In the dead of night?"

A sudden heat fills my face and my tongue trips over my embarrassment. "I—I, yes. It sounds . . . it sounds like someone is crying. And I know *that* sounds strange."

"To say the least." Now Emm glances at Adèle, then back to me as well.

"But I know what I heard, and I just thought . . . I don't know what I thought. That maybe I could help whoever it is."

Emm arches a brow before grinning faintly. "Maybe it's a banshee, come to warn us of the mister's lingering doldrums." Her smile widens and I narrow my eyes. She hiccups lightly, trying to hide it behind her hand. "Oh, you're serious. I thought you were playing at a bit of fun."

"I didn't— Well, no, I am. Serious, that is." My hands still and I stare at my fingers. "There are nights when I have trouble sleeping. I find lavender tea helps. Sometimes, on my way to or back from the kitchen, I hear

83

it. It's faint, but I'm fairly certain someone is crying. A woman, maybe a child."

There's a moment when I think Emm might actually believe me. Then she huffs in that way of hers I've learned means she thinks I've said or done something simple. "Likely the wind. This place is drafty, you've seen the state of it."

"Never heard any wind that sounds like sobs, and I've been in many a drafty house." I can't keep the slight sting of my irritation from my words.

"This place is also old. Maybe it *was* a ghost." Emm says it with such certainty that for a moment I believe that *she* believes this. She continues stirring, not really looking at me, though I can see the corner of her mouth twitch just slightly.

"A ghost," I say, skeptical.

"Oh, aye." She nods. "There once was a chimney sweep. Fell off the roof. Now he roams the halls, leaving trails of soot everywhere and black dust on the drapes. You can hear the spirits of past maids weeping at the state of it all."

"Now you're poking fun at me."

"Then there's the time the cook before me lit his mustache on fire." Emm strokes at the space beneath her nose. "He was fine, but they say that at night, during a full moon, the smell of singed hair accompanies a wee voice begging for mercy from the hot flames!" Her smile breaks wide over her face. "Maybe that's what you heard?"

I can't help the first giggle that escapes. "A dead mustache?"

"Long enough it tripped him when he walked, now haunting these here halls!"

Trying to bite down on the swell of amusement results in an embarrassing snort, which just makes the two of us splutter with laughter.

"I'm being serious!" I chide, swatting at her with a flour-covered hand.

"What's so funny?" Adèle asks, her curious gaze moving between us.

I can't help jolting slightly in surprise. I had meant to keep the conversation quiet, so as not to scare the girl, but watching Emm wipe away tears of laughter, she's right. I am being a bit ridiculous.

"Jane thought she heard a specter in the dark." Emm curls her fingers around her own throat before waving them through the air with a dramatic "OoooOoooOoooo!"

Adèle's eyes widen. "A ghost?!"

I heave a sigh before shaking my head. "No, no. I . . . I thought I heard someone crying last night."

Adèle doesn't look at all comforted by the explanation provided, quickly lowering her eyes to where she's been piecing out balls of dough. I feel a tug of sympathy and guilt. I should've waited to say something to Emm when Adèle wasn't around.

"Emm's right. It was likely the wind." I take the tray Emm has set out for us and start placing the balls upon it. "Nothing at all to be afraid of."

Despite my words, all enthusiasm has faded from Adèle's eyes. Completely my fault. I hope the biscuits will be enough to coax her back into bright spirits.

I take up the tray. "Help me put these in?"

Adèle nods and follows me around the table to the oven. "All right, we slip them in like this, and now we wait!"

"How will you know they're done?" Adèle asks.

"You can smell it!" I smile as I close the oven door. "Just wait, you'll see. Now we clean up the mess. Rule number one of a great baker: always keep things tidy."

"Ah ah ah!" Emm holds up a finger. "That's rule number *two*. Rule number one is to mind your nose."

"Mind my nose?" Adèle asks.

At that, Emm reaches to swipe her lifted finger against Adèle's apron and then along the girl's nose, leaving a trail of white. Adèle goes a little cross-eyed before smiling brightly and laughing as she rubs at the flour.

I'm glad to see her smile more and more, and that all worry of potential specters has left her face. My embarrassment from before is dulled but still present. If any of the girls back at the school had heard such claims, I'd be ridiculed for certain.

Seeing ghosts and ghoulies again?

Jane and her overactive imagination.

That's what reading so many books will do to your mind, fill it with things that aren't there.

I know well the difference between fantasy and my actual perceptions. And while I can admit that, perhaps, my somber assessments of the state of the hall might have influenced me to call what I heard crying, I will attest to my dying breath that I did indeed hear *something*.

Still, I put the worry out of my mind as Adèle and I set about cleaning up after ourselves.

Soon the kitchen is filled with the smell of cooked sugar, vanilla, and cinnamon. It mingles with the rich, heady scent of Emm's food. Adèle bounces eagerly where she stands to the side as I peer into the oven, the heat of the fire warm on my face.

"Do you smell that?" I ask.

"They're done!" Adèle cries.

"Let's check." Taking a towel, I quickly pull the tray free and set it aside. Adèle presses forward, but I wave her off gently. "Careful, they're hot."

Emm hands over the spatula and I test a few of the biscuits. "They're perfect!"

Within moments they're racked and cooling, though I chance the heat to split one up the middle, offering half to Adèle. "Still a bit warm, but should be all right."

86

She bites into it and her face balloons with joy, though the expression falls in the next instant.

I begin to ask what's wrong when a voice sounds behind me.

"So that's what this delicious smell is."

I turn to find Mr. Rochester stepping down into the kitchen, a faint smile pulling at his handsome features.

"Good afternoon, sir." I nod in greeting.

Emm does as well. Though she is still tending to preparations for dinner, I do notice one cheek partially stuffed as she chews, likely on a biscuit.

"Quite the distraction." Mr. Rochester stops near the table.

Adèle edges behind me a bit, pressing against my back.

"Distraction, sir?" I ask.

"Yes. It's not easy to be about one's business with the smell of sweets singing their siren song. Please, don't apologize."

I close my mouth, the words shriveling up on my tongue.

He breathes deep before gesturing to the rack of cooling biscuits. "May I?"

"Of course." I grab a saucer in order to prepare one, though he waves off the gesture and plucks one free with his fingers, biting into it.

There's a moment when I'm not sure what he makes of them, before he sighs heavily and closes his eyes. "It seems, Miss Eyre, that you are a woman of many secret talents." He finishes the biscuit in another bite and reaches for a second.

Warmth fills my face at the compliment, and I nod again. "Thank you, sir."

"Feel free to make these as often as you like. I'll see to it that you always have the necessary ingredients." He takes a bite of the second biscuit and gestures to Emm. "Dinner smells delicious as well. I'll leave you to it, then."

And like that, he's gone. For a moment, it's as if he's taken all the air in the room with him, leaving the three of us stranded and unable to move. But then I heave a sigh and the spell is broken. Emm tends her pot. Adèle hurries around to the other side of the table to snatch up her doll, which I hadn't realized she'd left behind. I study her, the tight line of her shoulders, the way her small mouth seems to nearly vanish as she purses her lips, their corners turned down. I've gotten so used to her being more open and jovial that the periodic return of the painfully shy girl I met my first day at Thornfield is always drastic enough to catch me by surprise. Why, if I didn't know better, I'd think she was afraid of her father.

But I don't know better, I realize. In fact, I know very little about these people, this family. While I've been here nearly a month, this pales in comparison to how long everyone else has known one another. While nothing seems out of sorts on the surface, my experience in life—and with people who are well versed in disguising their transgressions against others—has left me equipped with the knowledge that not everything is always as it appears.

"I . . . best put these away until after supper." I plate the biscuits and move to set them beneath a tin top meant for cakes. "All right. We'll take the rest of your lessons in the garden, Adèle, how does that sound?"

She nods, though doesn't say anything, and I am at a loss as to how to draw her once more out of her shell. And determined to find out why the mere sight of her father sent her scrambling back into it.

⋰ 13 ⋱

ONCE SMITTEN, TWICE SHY

BERTHA . . .

The clack and click of wood against wood fills the air as Grace collects the dishes from lunch. I sit on the bed, my back straight, staring at the window.

The old woman meanders toward the door.

"I'm out of lamp oil," I call without turning to face her.

She pauses, no doubt looking from me to the lamp on the table near the bed.

I can hear Devin just beyond, humming a jaunty tune as if all is right and perfect with the world. Maybe it is in his.

"So soon?" Grace asks.

"I have to burn it during the day now, with the sun all but blocked out." I gesture at the window. "Or am I to suffer in silence *and* darkness?"

She clicks her tongue. "You're lucky the master didn't board up the very door, you know."

"He may as well have," I murmur, though she doesn't respond. I don't know if she didn't hear me or is ignoring me. I don't care.

"I will ask." That's all she says before she slips out.

The door is locked and bolted behind her. Their footsteps thump as they retreat, and I listen for the stillness of their complete departure.

When I'm certain they are gone, I drop to my knees beside the bed and reach into the secret space amidst the floorboards. My journal waits for me, along with the almost nonexistent pencil. Tonight, instead of writing, I read what I have already penned.

September, maybe October

After the evening at the theater, I didn't see Edward again for nearly two months. It was at a birthday party for Charlotte DuBary, another young socialite from an old family in New Orleans. My mother and I were invited to the soirée. I never did enjoy such things, and my afternoon was a frightful bore until I spotted the face of one Edward Rochester across the way. . . .

As I write, the memory rises fresh and raw. I didn't know who Edward was then, but I recognized him instantly as the man I'd glimpsed in the foyer after watching a dozen or so budding thespians stumble through a passable rendition of *King Lear*.

A strange and yet familiar buzzing moved through my middle as I watched the stranger. "Once smitten, twice shy," my grandmother used to say. It meant that if you saw your love twice in a row and turned away each time, a third encounter meant you were bound to be together. I didn't believe in such things, but at that moment . . . I wanted to.

He stood with a group of gentlemen on the far side of the lawn, chatting and laughing and handsome as the sun was bright. I stole glances when I could between my own conversations. I had hoped to be inconspicuous, but when Edward next turned, our eyes met, same as before. Or perhaps I imagined they did. Either way, I snapped forward and nearly sent my teacup spilling into my lap.

"Oh!" I managed to catch it and save myself the added embarrassment of a mess, though the other ladies on the veranda paused in their discussion to look at me.

"Are you all right, Bertie?" Charlotte asked, her brown eyes wide with concern. She was a lovely girl, with full, soft lips that were perfect for stealing kisses, and rich, dark skin that sparkled like smoky quartz. In that moment, draped in folds of fabric and lace colored eggshell white and powder blue, she reminded me of those paintings of ancient goddesses stretched amongst the clouds, being fed grapes and fanned by plump little cherubs.

I nodded rapidly in response to her question. "I'm fine." Though the flush in my face might've said otherwise. Thankfully, it could've been explained away by my fluster at the near accident. "Just lost my grip on the saucer is all."

Charlotte gave me an understanding though teasing smile and reached to squeeze my hand. The rest of the ladies went back to talking about the season's fashions, though I aimed a sharp look to my left and into the white, round, smiling face of Maisey Unclest, freshly returned from Paris. Maisey, an only child, was spoiled as milk left in the sun. Pale and puffy as it too. Buried beneath that pretty face was some real ugliness.

"Why, Bertha Mason, you look a mite flush." Maisey kept her tone polite and her voice low. Her smile was unwavering, caught between a sneer and a snicker. "I hope the sun hasn't taken undue toll."

"Not at all." I offered my own smaller grin, adjusting the grip on my cup. "And yourself? You seem to be working that new lace fan for all it's worth. Not another fainting spell, I hope. I'd hate for there to be a repeat of what happened at the Bartletts'."

Maisey's expression tightened. "Oh, no, I'm right as rain."

"I'm glad to hear it." I took a sip of my tea and looked away. "Wouldn't want Gerard to get any ideas." Gerard was the son of a well-to-do merchant, and a prospective suitor Maisey fancied, though he had eyes for Charlotte. Mentioning him often sent Maisey's face spinning through different shades of red.

Maman said girls like Maisey were ignorant as hornets and twice as ill-tempered, especially when they didn't get their way. It was best not to poke at either, but sometimes . . . sometimes things need poking.

At my comment, Maisey made a little noise that sounded like she'd run out of air. She set her cup and saucer down on the nearby side table. A pale blond boy hurried over with a teapot to refill it.

"If I didn't know better, I'd think you were infatuated with one of Charlotte's guests," Maisey said, loud enough to gain the attention of the other girls. "It's impolite to stare, you know."

Four sets of eyes focused on me. I did my best not to flinch, not to let it show that I was caught off guard by the statement. Instead, I simply cleared my throat and shook my head.

"Infatuated? No. I simply think I've seen him somewhere before, and I'm trying to recollect."

Well, that wasn't the wrong thing to say, but neither was it the right one. Instead of letting the subject drop, the girls gathered closer, wanting more information. Who was I speaking of? Where had I seen him? When had I seen him? All the while Maisey remained smugly silent.

"Honestly, there's no need to make a fuss." I waved a hand dismissively. "I'm equally certain I'm mistaken."

"Then there's no harm in saying."

"We promise not to look all at once."

They pressed and chirped for answers but got none, until Charlotte puffed her cheeks and reached to set her gloved hand on my knee. "Oh, come on, Bertie!" The genuine joy on her face settled some of the anxiousness in my belly. "It's my birthday, you *have* to tell me."

"I—I . . ." I felt the heat in my face rise, despite the breeze playing over the grounds, as the girls closed in. "Well, he's . . ." I chanced a glance over my shoulder and, to my relief, Edward was gone. "He's no longer there, I'm afraid."

A chorus of disappointed sighs and groans rose as I sipped from my cup again.

"Was he handsome?" Charlotte asked.

"Oh, quite." I smiled and wrinkled my nose a bit. And he was. It was true then, it's true now. But a handsome face does nothing to make up for a horrid heart.

"Excuse me, ladies," a voice called from nearby, and we all broke apart in order to gaze up at my mother as she gently beat the air near her warm brown face with a lace fan. "I need to speak with my daughter a moment. Bertha?" She extended a hand.

I set my tea on a nearby table and rose, moving to take her arm.

"Oh, Charlotte, dear," Maman cooed at the birthday girl. "Your mother says we'll have cake and strawberries with cream within the hour."

We left the girls chattering amongst one another, no doubt attempting to guess who my mystery man could be, and began to walk, arm in arm. Maman greeted a few people in passing with nods. They lifted hats or dipped their chins in turn. She always was a woman to garner much respect.

After a short ways, I noticed we'd trailed to the edge of the garden, where the crowd had thinned considerably. Maman made a show of looking over the flowers that lined the hedges. I waited patiently for her to say whatever it was she'd brought me out here, and away from prying ears, to hear.

For a moment there was nothing. Then, right when I was beginning to think perhaps she simply wanted my company, she cleared her throat.

"Have you given any thought to the prospect of marriage, my dear?"

The question caught me off guard, not because of the content so much as her choosing there and then to pose the inquiry.

I schooled my expression to be what I hoped was more intrigued than shocked. "As much as you have suggested I give."

"Good, good." Maman patted my hand where it was tucked into the bend of her elbow. "Because I believe I may have found you a suitor."

I was certain my surprise showed this time as my head jerked to look at her.

For her part, she remained completely calm, though the slight curl at her lips betrayed her excitement, and the corners of her eyes crinkled like they did whenever she was pleased about something.

"A suitor," I repeated, to give my thoughts time to catch up to the moment.

Marriage.

As if summoned by the word, memories of Charlotte leapt to the forefront of my mind. They were mostly filled with laughter and conversation, like today. But then there were a few when the two of us were alone, no need for chaperones. I remembered the gentle press of her mouth against mine, the feel of her fingers at my sides or in my hair.

It was never more than that, a kiss or a touch, an exploration of feelings trapped in both of us. We were one another's way out of the snare of society life, a brief reprieve when it all seemed to be too much. And we never wanted it to go anywhere beyond that, so the faint tightness in my chest at my mother's words was more fear than anything else. Fear our connection would be lost, or at least irrevocably changed. I did want to marry. We both did. But I didn't want to lose my friend. Not yet.

"What's wrong, my dear?" Maman inquired. "You seem shaken."

I pushed the fledgling dread aside. "No, I'm fine. I simply . . . never expected you'd want to discuss such a thing here, now."

Maman's eyes creased even further. "I wouldn't, save for the happy chance he is also here. Now. And I would like it very much if you were to meet him."

My previous shock and panic were nothing compared with what I felt in that moment. It was as if I had been turned to stone, unable to move or speak. I'd veritably forgotten what words were entirely.

So I could only repeat her once more. "Meet him?"

"Yes. It seems you caught his eye at a previous engagement, I know not which, but he's been asking after you ever since." Maman took a moment to straighten a bit of lace near my collar, along with my curls and hat. "He's a wealthy gentleman from England here to visit a close family friend, and he's eager to spend a bit of time with you before he has to return to his estate in some weeks' time."

"England? That's so far away." From my family, my friends, my home. All I'd ever known. My heart beat brutishly against my ribs.

Maman nodded, her smile still in place. "And I hear it's absolutely beautiful, my dear. You'll thrive, maybe even meet Queen Amelia the Second, if Rochester runs in the circles he proclaims." Her shoulders lifted in her obvious elation. "And then perhaps I may meet her as well. But first, introductions."

That's when I realized we'd traversed the entirety of the inner wall of the garden to come upon the outer courtyard, where the music was loudest and people milled about in small groups when not dancing across the wide wooden floor. The air was jovial, the conversations peppered with laughter and delight. The wind was gentle upon my face, carrying the bright smell of flowers in bloom. It truly was a gorgeous day, and I was stuck inside myself, unable to enjoy it.

Maman's voice rose around me, and I blinked back into the moment.

"—this is my lovely daughter, Bertha. And Bertha?" She smiled and canted her head slightly, ever the picture of the perfect lady. "This is Mr. Edward Rochester."

I offered my hand automatically as I gazed, shocked, into the familiar face of the handsome stranger I had glimpsed at the theater those months ago, and again today on the veranda. I felt my eyes widen but managed to school the rest of my surprise from my expression as Edward took my lifted fingers.

He bowed partially at the waist with his other arm behind his back and brushed his lips just faintly against the cloth of my glove. "It is a pleasure, Miss Bertha."

Then his eyes met mine, deep and shining. There was a quality to them I couldn't place. It reminded me of the way stars twinkle in the darkness of the night sky.

I dipped my chin, and my body, in the barest curtsy. "The pleasure is mine, Mr. Rochester."

"Please," he said, his demeanor easy as he straightened. "Call me Edward." Then he smiled.

It was the barest lift of his mouth at one corner, and it lent a youthfulness to his already handsome face. Such a countenance promised mischief and fond memories, and perhaps just a hint of danger. The same sort of expression Charlotte wore the first time she pulled me into the drawing room of her family's house and her lips found mine in the dimness of a cloudy afternoon that was brighter from that moment forward. *I'm here to get us both into the best kind of trouble*, that expression had promised then, and had returned to make similar claims now.

And, like that, I was under his spell.

We danced that night, many times. People took notice. There was more than one second glance, pointed look, or hidden whisper that evening, and I for once had no care for any of it. Instead, all my attention was on Edward, because all his attention was on me.

Even when he wasn't spinning me gently across the floor, he was taken in conversation with myself and Maman. She did most of the talking, of course. Asking after his people, his home, his relations. All things she no doubt already knew—it was a mother's way—but she wanted me to hear.

Other gentlemen asked me to dance, and I of course obliged. But after every song spent on the arm of another, Edward would be waiting for me at Maman's side, the two of them caught up in some shared tale that left them both smiling. He was cunning enough to win her over before trying with me. He was also patient, courteous, and—most importantly—kind.

The rest of the evening, Edward remained with us. He listened dutifully as Maman spoke of the magic of the city, telling him of all sorts of places to eat or visit to get a real feel for New Orleans. Once or twice others joined us, some trying to win away Edward's attention, but he remained focused, and I was beyond flattered.

When it came time to depart, he walked us to the grand circle driveway and stood with us while the coach was fetched. Night was falling softly, and as the sun set, the world came alive with new sights and sounds. Fireflies fluttered beneath the swaying trees, painting the air as if with starlight. The fragrance of flowers tickled my nose.

My mother cleared her throat. "I hope you found the evening enjoyable, Mr. Rochester."

"I did indeed." Though he responded to my mother, his eyes were on me, and he smiled that little smile of his. When I could not help but return it, even if only slightly, he finally looked to Maman and said, "I did not expect to be so taken with the city. It is . . . enchanting."

Maman's ever-wise gaze slid over Edward. "New Orleans is beautiful indeed. Perfect for hosting events all throughout each season. I don't know how they might compare to the grand soirées in England, but I hope our quaint celebrations have proven entertaining at least."

"Entertaining is an understatement," Edward began. Then he leaned forward and whispered in perfectly playful conspiration, "And let me just say, the food here is far superior. And I find the company infinitely more delightful." His gaze once more fixed on me briefly, then slid back to Maman. "I may find myself sick with longing for the hidden beauties of New Orleans the instant I leave her shores."

My face heated.

"Well," Maman breathed, her own smile widening. "We'll have to make sure you spend time discovering as many of those beauties as possible. Who knows, perhaps you'll wind up taking a bit of the bayou home with you."

"Perhaps I will," Edward murmured, his voice low.

My breath caught silently.

"Wonderful," Maman said, her expression pleased and more than slightly smug. "Ah, here is the coach. I'm afraid we must bid you good evening, though I do hope we'll see you again. Perhaps you'll come calling; my husband would love to meet such an accomplished young man."

"It would be an honor." Edward bent at the waist. "Mrs. Mason. Miss Bertha."

I managed the softest farewell before Maman swept me toward the open carriage door. "Eyes forward, Little Bird," she murmured. "He's watching, and you must leave him lingering if you wish him to give chase."

My heart raced. "How do you know he's watching?" I wanted to see for myself. I barely managed to keep from turning back.

"A woman knows," Maman said, lifting her chin just a bit. "Especially a mother." She patted my hand and kept her hold firm as we moved along the walkway.

There was a line to bid Charlotte and her mother good night in passing. When it was our turn, she looked at me with wide and eager eyes, her cheeks puffed with barely contained glee. She wanted to know everything about Edward and our evening together, I could tell.

"I'll write you first thing," I promised, my words whispered against her ear as I pressed her to me in a hug.

She squeezed me tight and brushed a kiss to my cheek in the dark of the falling night. "You were beautiful together."

Her words followed me to where the carriage was waiting. The instant I found my seat, I sank into it. Thrilled though I was with the results of the evening, fatigue was starting to win out.

"He was incredible, yes?" Maman asked, as the coach bore us toward home. "And rather charming."

"Mmm." I couldn't manage words just yet.

No matter, for Maman had enough for us both. "The way he described his search for you, like you were a figment of his imagination, a dream he was desperate to remember, if just to experience knowing you once more. This one might be a romantic." She patted her knees with her folded fan. "A romantic with a head for business, what a mix. He's perfect for you. Of course, he'll have to meet your father first, but it'll be a formality at this point. I know a good match when I see one."

"And that's what we are?" I asked, suddenly able to find my voice, though it seemed to have shrunk since I last used it. "A good match?" Smitten as I was, the idea of marriage still made something in my chest twist uncomfortably.

Maman fell silent. Her eyes watched me in the dim light of the moon and the lanterns outside the windows. She swayed with the rocking of the coach, the motion almost hypnotic.

"In truth? I don't know." Maman sighed the admittance. "But I hope. I asked after him as you danced, and he seems to be everything he presents himself as. This is not his first trip to New Orleans; he is known by a few families. And he certainly seems taken with you in a way I've only seen twice."

"Twice?" My curiosity banished my previous anxieties. "With who?"

"Well, your father and myself, of course. Then there were your grandparents. That was love everlasting, the kind I used to read to you about in those books you so enjoyed." She smiled and settled back against the bench. "It's all I ever wanted for you, Little Bird. And I'm going to do everything in my power to ensure you get all you deserve."

She held out her hand and I reached to take it. Her fingers squeezed mine tight, and I could feel the warmth of them through my glove.

Fwump. Fwump. Fwump.

The steady thump of footsteps pulls me from my recollections, and I hurry to put my things away. I manage to get the floorboard back in place and regain my feet in time to brush my hands against my dress and straighten the cloth as much as possible. While I don't care to be presentable for anyone in this house, I don't want them wondering why I look so rumpled. The discovery of my hideaway and the pages within would surely result in the last thing that's mine here being taken from me.

The lock rattles with the shakiness of Marsters, likely drunk, fumbling with the key. I face the door as it opens. My body goes still as death when I notice Grace is holding something. Then a feeling like ice water in my veins flows through me, freezing my very bones as I recognize what it is.

She lays the dress out on my bed, smoothing her hands over the skirt lovingly. It's gorgeous, the deep purple fabric seeming to shine in the low light. Any other time, I'd like to run my hands over the visible bits of lace and folded cloth, but the blossoming dread in my stomach steals all joy I would feel at the sight of such a gown.

"What's this for?" I ask, my voice small. I fear I know the answer.

"For you, of course. We need to get you cleaned up." Grace smiles and presses her hands together in a display of joy that is more repulsive than infectious. "The master would like you to join him for supper."

♪ 14 ♫

FAMILY MATTERS

JANE . . .

"Very good, Adèle!" I smile at her and am delighted when the young girl returns it. "You're coming along quite quickly." Especially considering Emm had told me she struggled with her previous tutor.

"I guess it wasn't as difficult as I thought." Adèle looks down at her work, her smile widening. The expression on her face speaks volumes.

"You've worked hard today, and dinner will likely be ready soon," I say as I look to the clock on the far wall. "Let's put away your things before Emm calls for us."

She hops down from her seat and makes haste in gathering up her supplies. As she does, I inspect the day's pages, flipping through them until my gaze lights upon something in the margins.

It's a sketch of the dollhouse on the other side of the room. Small, with little space for minute detail, but still a very skillfully rendered facsimile. I know my way around a brush and easel, and there is technique here in the way the pencil lines flow into one another. This was taught.

"Adèle?" I turn without taking my eyes off the paper.

"Yes?"

I can hear her placing her books on the shelf. She finishes and hurries over, her small face bright with excitement. I hold up the sheet and point at the sketch.

"Did you do this?" I already know the answer. I'd given her clean sheets to work with.

Her smile wanes and my heart breaks. It shatters even further when her shoulders rise and her gaze moves from the paper to me and then the floor.

"I-I'm sorry," she starts in the small, withdrawn tone of hers.

Before she can get another word out, I lower myself to be level with her, and take one of her hands in my free one. "Don't apologize, not for this. This is brilliant!" I make sure to inject as much of my admiration into my words as I am able. "Where did you learn to draw so beautifully?" And why was she hidden away here in Thornfield instead of learning from some grand master of the skill as prodigies are wont to?

Her hesitation is written all over her face and drawn up in her little body. She doesn't pull her hand away, but she won't meet my eye.

My heart, now in pieces, plummets into my stomach. "Adèle, what—"

"I hope I'm not interrupting."

The sound of my employer's voice startles me, and I almost drop the pages I'd been holding. Simultaneously, Adèle tugs her hand from mine and makes her way over to the dollhouse, where she proceeds to toy with the tiny furnishings in silence.

Mr. Rochester watches her a moment before looking to me as I rise. "I came to let you know dinner is ready."

I steal another glance at the clock as I gather the rest of the pages, making sure to keep the one with the doodle set aside. "I don't believe I've ever known the master of the house to run about gathering staff for meals. Will you be joining us again tonight?"

He chuckles. "I'm afraid there's much I must see to, so I'll be taking my meal in my study. I was on my way back from informing Emm of as much and thought I might look in on the two of you." His gaze roams to the still "playing" Adèle, then returns to me.

"Oh. Well. Thank you for letting us know." I manage what I hope is a smile, my stomach still in knots from my earlier exchange with the girl.

If he notices any lack of sincerity in my expression, he makes no mention or show of it. He merely nods and turns to depart.

"Oh, Mr. Rochester?" I call before he's completely abandoned the door.

He halts and returns, his face an open question. "Edward, please."

"Um . . . Edward." I use the name only at his insistence. It feels far more casual than I would like. The page crumples slightly in my fingers as they curl in response to my discomfort, and I force them still. "I'd like to speak with you a moment, if I may. About a matter of business. And Adèle's studies."

His brows lift in curiosity and he nods. "Very well."

"Thank you," I say before looking to Adèle. "Go on to the kitchen, Adèle. I will join you shortly."

She doesn't look at me, or her father, as she makes for the door, doll in hand.

The sound of little feet against the carpet carries her away.

"Is something the matter?" Mr. Rochester asks.

"No, not at all." I wave away his concern, the page fluttering in my hand. "Only I was wondering, when might I expect my wages?"

His brow furrows. "Your wages?"

"Yes. I am so very grateful for this position, and I take the task of tutoring Adèle very seriously. It's just that . . . it has nearly been a month, and we agreed that I would be salaried twice monthly, minus room and board. I wanted to know when I might expect payment for my first two weeks."

For a moment, Edward stares at me in such bewilderment that I almost begin to doubt my recollection of the passage of time. But I know of what I speak, even if he does not.

"We spoke on the matter, when I first arrived?" I say, hoping to spark some memory of our previous conversation.

He continues to stare at me, his expression unreadable.

I hold his gaze, fighting the urge to shift beneath it. "You asked if I would prefer to receive my wages as a check, or—"

"Oh, merciful heavens!" he exclaims with a bit of laughter, his hand lifting to his forehead. "I remember now. Right. I'm afraid checks are distributed near the beginning of the month. I know you asked for funds directly," he says, preemptively cutting off my protest. "So, when payments are dispersed, I will procure wages for you twice over."

Disappointment, and frustration, twist within me. "Then it will be another week before I am paid?"

The guilt-ridden look that takes his features fits them so perfectly, I can easily believe it's an expression he wears often. "I'm afraid so. And while I am happy to oblige your request after the start of next month, I'm afraid habit has slowed things down for the time being. You see, you are the only one who asks to be paid twice monthly instead of once, and the adjustment affects how my accountants handle Thornfield's finances. Bankers and lawyers are particular about these things."

"I can imagine," I murmur, my irritation steadily rising. It's taking no small amount of my considerable patience to tamp it down.

"I'll have to go into town to do this, of course, so that will tack a few extra days' wait onto the tail end of things, but we'll get you looked after." He smiles, the action reminding me more of a nervous fret than anything.

I take a few seconds to gather myself enough to respond. "Very well" is all I manage at first. Then I hastily add, "There is one more thing. An unrelated matter." Which is fortunate for him, because if I linger on this subject, my irritation will no doubt win out. He's explained himself, and the reasoning is sound if not ideal. I thrust out the bit of paper I've held this entire time. "Do you know what this is?" I ask, then give the paper an insistent flap. So he takes it.

His brows rise toward his hairline as he inspects the sheet. "Basic mathematics?"

I point to the drawing at the edge. "No, this."

He brings the page closer to his face for further inspection, and turns partway into the hall so the light from a nearby window falls over the drawing. After a moment, a breath of laughter leaves him. "Adèle's dollhouse. It's a rather good likeness."

"It's an incredible likeness," I correct him. "Especially for having been drawn by a child."

Mr. Rochester's head whips around so fast it makes my neck ache in the watching. "Adèle did this?" His voice holds the same disbelieving wonder I felt when I first saw the sketch. The paper crinkles as his grip tightens.

"Yes." I rescue the page before it is ruined, angling it further into the light and pointing out the finer details. "Look there, the line work in the shading? She's blended contouring with woven hatching for the roof. That's not something one does intuitively; it has to be learned. Meaning it had to be taught." I look up from tracing the fine work with my nail, and am surprised to find his brow furrowed in distaste.

His mouth twists with the want to say something and the apparent effort to keep from doing so. "What is your point?"

"My point? My *point* is that it can take years for someone to develop such skill!" I wave the page in the air before thrusting it at him again. "And she has done it by the age of ten. With the proper instruction, she could be a master as young as twenty, if not half a decade sooner! That alone would be accomplishment enough to hang her work in installations across the country, the world perhaps!"

I take a moment to breathe, my heart beating quickly in my excitement. Once I've reined in my emotions, I continue, "I asked where she learned to draw so well. My inquiry seemed to wound her, and I was trying—hoping to console her. That's when you walked in. My apologies for upsetting your daughter so."

Mr. Rochester continues to stare at me, eyeing me as if debating whether or not I'm being serious. I am, of course.

After a handful of seconds, he takes a slow, measured breath. He has the look of a man about to say something he's not proud of.

"I should have explained this sooner," he finally says as he scrubs a palm over the angles of his face. "Adèle is . . . not my daughter."

There's a moment when I'm not certain I've heard correctly. I understood the words individually, but being placed in that particular order has made them near indecipherable.

"Pardon?" I say, only because no other words can make it from my mind to my tongue.

"She is not my daughter." He clears his throat, not looking at me. He hasn't since he started talking. "I . . . her mother, Céline, was a good friend. I met her some years past on my travels in France. She was an artist. I sponsored several of her works. Brilliant woman."

There's more to what he's saying, but I've stopped listening. Not on purpose. I'm floundering, lost in the current of information suddenly thrown at me. It's as if someone is holding my head underwater. I grasp at something, anything, to slow the workings in my mind, but I am stuck. I knew Mrs. Rochester had not been Adèle's mother, but to think that neither was Edward her father?

In that moment, every interaction I've witnessed between what polite society would see as a dutiful but distant father and a perhaps incredibly shy daughter morphs. I peer at the memory of these interactions with open eyes, recalling how I once thought Adèle afraid of Edward.

"Miss Eyre?" Mr. Rochester's voice cuts through my muddled thoughts.

I peer up into his face, which is pinched with worry.

"Are you all right?" he asks.

I nod, not quite able to manage words for the few moments it takes me to concentrate on speaking. "Yes," I say, my voice faint even in my own ears. "Yes, I'm fine. Just . . . thinking how I might have upset Adèle."

"Don't fret too much. She knows there was no ill intent behind your inquiry."

"Yes," I repeat, then clear my throat as I come more and more into myself. "You . . . you said she was an artist?" Snatches of what he'd spoken are caught in my mind, thank goodness.

He nods, his expression drawn. "Céline had an extraordinary talent. I'm pleased Adèle seems to have inherited her gift."

Another breath. "What happened to her? Céline. And how did you come to care for a child who is not yours?" I am more curious for the answer to the second question, and I focus on his face.

The look that crosses it is one of carefully composed sadness. Just the exact amount of feeling to be appropriately mournful and not a drop more. It's a paltry comparison to the raw emotion I have seen him display for matters most would consider far less evocative.

"Typhus," he murmurs, his voice low in what is likely supposed to pass as grief. "On my last trip, I learned of her passing. I . . . felt horrible, especially for her little girl. So, I made the arrangements for her to come here, where I could at least provide for her as her mother tried to do."

"I'm so sorry." My words are earnest, but they are not for him. Not entirely. True, he claims to have lost a dear friend, but Adèle lost a mother, her home, and all that went with it. And while most might deem being taken in and provided for by one such as Edward Rochester as the best of any fate, I know such would offer little comfort to the recently orphaned.

"I should be apologizing," Mr. Rochester says, pulling me from my wondering once more.

"Sir?"

"I should have been clearer; your assumption is not undue."

"Yes, well." I straighten my shoulders with a sniff. "Then we can both be sorry, yes? I'll speak to Adèle again, make sure I—"

"That won't be necessary." His voice is hard. "While unknowingly bringing up her mother could easily be forgiven, we shouldn't go pressing on old wounds carelessly, don't you agree?"

I don't. Especially if everyone is simply tiptoeing around the subject, and her, for that matter. Such a terribly isolating experience, and I will not abandon her to it.

While I have made up my mind to do the very opposite of what Mr. Rochester insists, I nod to him all the same. "You present a fair point. Ah, but I've lingered too long, I should join Adèle for dinner. But before I go, may I speak plainly?"

"Could I stop you?" He smiles.

I force one in return. "While I understand that speaking to Adèle about her mother may be too much, she clearly enjoys art. And she's good at it. With your permission, I would like to nurture this talent, as best I can. My own skills are accomplished, and I believe I can impart some knowledge in this as well as other areas of her studies. At least until a master can be found for her. You will consider finding her a master, won't you?"

Mr. Rochester makes a face that says he would like to be done with this and likely would rather it were not brought up to begin with. But it has been, and I will not be moved.

"Very well," he finally says, his tone sharp. It sends a shiver through me, though not the pleasant sort. "You may offer her instruction, insomuch as it does not become a distraction from her other studies."

"Of course not." I dip my head, pleased with this little victory. "I'll provide a list of supplies needed as soon as I am able."

"Yes, yes, give it to Marsters," he mutters before turning and slipping out the door. "Good evening, Miss Eyre."

"And to you, Mr. Rochester." I step into the corridor and watch until he has gone around the far corner. Then, my heart lightened and my step matching, I hurry for the kitchen, eager to share the news with Adèle.

When I find her, she is seated at the dining room table, already eating her meal. She looks to be in better spirits than before. The ache in my chest returns. I feel for her. Poor thing. Her mother dead, her father, well . . . who knows. She has no one.

Had no one. From this day forward, she will have me.

I step into the room and smile when she lifts her head. "Apologies for the delay."

She shrugs as she bites into a roll. "It's all right. I tried to wait for you, but it's so good."

"At least half as good as it smells?"

"Better!" She returns my smile and even gives a little laugh. The ringlets in her hair bounce as she does a little dance in her chair.

I join her at the table, even though I haven't gone to procure my own portion. My rumbling stomach protests, but I ignore it. I've more important matters to tend to.

"Adèle." I wait until she looks at me before continuing. "I like to think of us as friends."

"Me too," she says, her voice still quiet but sure, and it's all I can do to keep from bursting at the seams with joy.

"Good. And . . . as your friend, I want you to know you can tell me anything."

She watches me now, with those dark eyes that seem to know more than the girl ever lets on. As I hold her gaze, I can't help but search for signs of Edward in her face. I find them: her cheekbones, the way her mouth turns down even when she's not upset. There's even a hint of him amid the few angles of her otherwise cherubic face that have emerged in the beginnings of prepubescence. He says she is not his daughter, but I don't think I believe him. I wonder why he would speak false about such a thing, and then immediately what else he might be lying about.

"You mean something in particular," Adèle says, sitting back in her chair just so. "Don't you."

"I do." I offer what I hope she can tell is a sincere smile, hoping to put whatever worries she might have at ease. "I know Mr. Rochester isn't your father. It's all right!" I add hastily when her expression falls, the color fading from her little face. "I wanted you to know that you didn't have to hide it from me."

"I . . . I wasn't hiding . . ." Her eyes lower, her voice barely above a whisper.

"No, I mean . . . I'm sorry. Let me start over." I draw a breath to steady myself. I mustn't let this go poorly. "You didn't do anything wrong. All right? Not a thing."

The way the tension eases from her body helps mine do the same. I lean forward a little, waiting until she glances up so my eyes can catch hers.

"I'm not upset or angry. I'm disappointed in myself for not realizing sooner. And I want you to know you can tell me anything."

Her teeth push and pull at her lower lip, as if she's considering the truth of my words. I find she bites them when she's thinking hard about something.

"Like when something makes you happy or when you have a favorite book or dress. Even secrets." I lean in slightly and crinkle my nose. "I'm here for you, no matter what. Especially if you feel upset, or afraid, or if anyone hurts your feelings. And I'll put ink in their tea. I've done it before."

Adèle giggles and scrunches her face. "Really?"

"Yes. Turns their teeth black and blue for a week!"

This earns a full laugh, the sound so rich and full of joy. It bubbles up out of her so rarely that moments like this are a treasure.

I lay my hand on the table between us and wiggle my fingers in invitation. "Talk to me, all right? I'm here to help, if I can."

She seems to consider a moment before smiling and nodding in return, soon after placing her hand over mine. "Deal."

"Good." I squeeze. She doesn't let go.

Over dinner I reveal that I will also be helping with her art. She is delighted, of course, and when the meal is done she races off to prepare a journal so she may start practicing, at least until we are able to procure the proper instruments. She's rather light on pencils, I've noticed, and she seems to prefer sketching.

"Well," Emm drawls as she stacks mostly empty plates. "Worming your way into multiple hearts, I see."

I look up from helping her clear the table. "How do you mean?"

"You've won over Adèle *and* Mr. Rochester," she says conspiratorially. "I've seen people manage one or the other, but never both. Congratulations."

"Bah!" I say, though I smirk. "There's nothing to congratulate. I came here to do a job and do it well." I follow her toward the kitchen, my own gathered dishes clattering lightly. "Besides, I figured of everyone here you would be the difficult one."

"Oh, would I?" Emm calls over her shoulder. She sets the dishes down on the counter so they can be washed later.

I place my stack beside them. "You weren't exactly the friendliest sort when I first arrived."

"I suppose not. I will admit, though, you've grown on me. Not quite the way you've grown on the mister, though." This time her voice dips suggestively.

"I don't know what you're talking about," I say as I start the process of pumping water into the basin.

"Oh no? Come now, this can't be the first man you've ever found to be smitten with you."

I choke on a scoff. "Smitten?"

"As a buck in springtime. Don't think I haven't noticed the way he talks to you."

I try to see what could have possibly led Emm to this conclusion, and I suppose if I were inclined to find men such as Edward beguiling, perhaps some of his actions could be construed as "smitten." Alas, what I *have* noticed is how his mood is often quick to sour when I question him about anything to do with the state of the house, the lack of any other staff or repairmen—he did claim he was in the process of restoring Thornfield, but I see no evidence of that—and now my wages and the desire to nurture Adèle's talent. A talent she clearly received from her mother, who was likely her first instructor as well.

I work on scraping the leftover bits of food into a bin. "Mmm."

"You go about this smartly and I might be calling you Mrs. Rochester soon enough," Emm teases.

The plate slips from my hand and clatters into the bin. "Oh!"

"Careful," Emm cautions from where she's now elbow-deep in dishwater.

"I've got it." I fish the plate free and set it aside. "And that's enough of your teasing on this matter. There's no chance anything like that would happen."

"Don't sell yourself short, lass. The mister is taken with you, that much is certain."

"Nothing is certain except these dirty dishes. Now start washing." I splash Emm with a bit of water, earning a grumbly laugh. "Besides, whatever interest he may have is not shared. I'm here to do my job and nothing more."

"As you say, lass." Emm chuckles. "As you say."

ى 15 ى

NEVER BETTER, ALWAYS WORSE

BERTHA . . .

Sitting on the bed, I clasp my hands together to keep them from shaking. To keep the rest of me from shaking. I fear I might come apart if I don't press my fingers together so tightly that I no longer feel them.

I want to feel nothing else right now.

But the shaking travels up my arms and fills the whole of me.

I hate to admit that I'm afraid of him, and yet . . .

The bath had been quick, the water more cold than warm. Grace had stood over me like a nursemaid out of some nightmare, humming as she brushed at my hair.

"Oh, come now," she'd said when I first refused to allow her to touch me. "It won't do to have you looking ragged."

"I suppose I'm to present myself as a treasure, then?" I had asked, pressed to the corner of the room and refusing to get into the water just yet. "A polished jewel for him to fawn over?"

Grace had clicked her tongue, chiding. "There are those who don't have such luxuries, my dear. You should count your blessings. Now." She clapped her hands. "Get in and let's have a scrub. Or"—she lifted a finger, cutting off my retort—"I can have Devin come and hold you down while I do it. Unless, of course, you elect to comport yourself as a lady."

My eyes shot to the door. Her threat was real, I knew that much.

The memory of when he'd helped her force me into a dress not long after my imprisonment began, the shame of being seen so, burned through me.

Reluctantly, I obeyed.

Thankfully, the bath was quick, and by the time it was done, the water seemed to have warmed slightly. Possibly thanks to the tears I'd added to the mix.

I hate crying, especially in front of others.

Unlike some, I cry out of anger, not sadness.

It fills me up and, with nowhere to go, bursts forth in great sobs sometimes. I managed to remain mostly silent.

Now, dressed and escorted back to my room, I wait.

But I no longer cry.

Despite my trepidation, he will not have my tears.

Not any longer.

The room grows dark. The sun has set. Nighttime shadows stretch across the gloom.

I light the lamp, now with a touch more oil but never full. It must have been seen to while I was bathing.

The sound of steps floats down the hall and my body goes still. They stop outside my door and, like always, the keys rattle in the lock a moment before the door swings open.

"Come along, dear," Grace calls, all soft kindness.

For a moment, I am tempted to refuse. I am tempted to fight and kick and scream and bite, but it will gain me nothing.

And what would going to him obediently gain you?

"I can carry you, if ma'am wishes," Devin offers, his voice cheerful, as if he would be doing me a favor.

A shudder moves through me. I don't want that man to touch me at all.

And if I refuse, what punishments will Edward enact? Shackles to bind me to my bed? Removing the rest of my furniture?

I rise, my hands still clasped together. With a swiftness in my step, I sweep past the two of them and make my way down the hall. Grace hobbles after me but can't quite match my pace.

There's a rumbling shudder before Devin runs up at my side.

"She can't keep—" He reaches and I yank away from him, a hiss of refusal on my lips. His hand hovers a moment before lowering as he sighs through his nose. "Slow down, is all I was going to say."

Grace catches up to us and takes the lead, setting a slower pace. Devin follows, his presence at my back a looming menace. He is often gentler than Marsters, but that does not mean I am safe with him.

We move in silence through the house and, for a moment, I consider calling out. But before the war in my thoughts can be decided, we've reached our destination.

Grace knocks on the set of double doors.

"Enter," Edward's tenor calls from within.

My shoulders hunch on their own.

Grace pushes open the door and steps through.

Devin bows at the waist and gestures that I follow her.

Inside Edward's study, a fire roars in the hearth despite the lingering warmth from the day. Adding to the glow of the larger flame are lamps set into the walls, lending the space a coziness that conceals something far more sinister.

Edward sits behind his large mahogany desk, ever the handsome monster. His eyes find me, and he smiles. It is a villain's smile, all teeth and self-satisfaction.

He practically purrs, "Good evening, my dear."

Grace shuffles away and I hear the door shut behind me.

I remain there, unmoving, unspeaking.

"The dress is lovely. Brings out your eyes." He pushes himself to standing, and I force myself to remain still.

And quiet.

Watching me a moment, Edward sighs. "Come now, no need for that. Let's have the evening remain agreeable."

"The evening is not what I disagree with," I hiss, my voice low, betraying my anger.

"Indeed not. Come. Sit." He gestures to a large leather chair, one of a pair across from the fire. Between them is a cart carrying two silver domes, a bottle of wine, and a pair of glasses.

I'm certain my confusion shows on my face because, without me asking, Edward offers, "Dinner." He lifts one of the domes and the room is filled with the smell of roast pheasant and truffle risotto.

My mouth waters, yet my stomach roils, and I'm certain I'm shaking again.

"I'm not hungry," I lie.

"Oh, don't be stubborn. I had Emm prepare this specially." He lifts the second dome and another meal is revealed, identical to the first. "Do you remember?"

He knows I do. The sights and sounds of Italy fill my mind, the memories trying to follow, but I cannot get lost. Our honeymoon. Back when I knew him as my husband, before he became the monster.

He sets the domes aside, pours a helping of wine into each glass, then gestures to one of the chairs once more.

"Sit."

There's a hardness to his voice this time, and the sound sends a shudder through me. Again, I want nothing but to remain where I am. To make him come and force me into the seat. But my mind works over the various outcomes of that. Bound, again. Closer scrutiny. Never a moment to myself. Other . . . punishments.

Chin lifted, I cross the room and sink into the chair.

He smiles, pleasant, glowing, then takes his own seat.

For a long while there is no sound save the crackle of the fire and the clatter of silverware on his plate. I am sitting, but I won't eat, no matter how the meal calls to my empty stomach.

I am surprised to find actual silverware has been set out for me, especially after my previous failed attempt to gain my freedom.

"You're not going to eat?" Edward asks, already more than halfway finished with his meal.

"I'm *not* hungry."

"I doubt that. It would be a shame to waste such a fine meal."

I say nothing.

He continues to eat.

Once he is done, he sees to the remainder of his wine before setting it all aside. Then he goes for the cigar box on the small end table between the chairs. Within moments he is puffing away, filling the air with an acrid stink.

When he seems well and truly satiated with this farcical attempt at normalcy between us, he fixes me with those dark eyes. Eyes I once thought were like the heavens and night, now more like a deep pit. They say eyes are the portal to one's soul, but I've long stopped believing Edward has one. He is bereft. Empty. I hate him and his nothing eyes.

"As I'm sure you can imagine, I am disappointed, Bertie." He frowns as he looks at me, smoke curling around his head. "After everything I've given you—"

I laugh. The sound is sharp and sudden, as I am unable to help it. "And what about what you've taken?"

"—and how patient I've been, that you would continue to behave in such a way saddens me." He speaks as if I've said nothing. As if I am nothing.

My fists curl in my lap.

"I had hoped there could be peace between us. Peace, after all, is a sign of a good marriage."

"Perhaps if you had a wife and not a prisoner, you would know peace."

He arches an eyebrow, and I can almost see his mind ticking away behind his nothing eyes, like the gears in a clock. "If I did indeed. Are you sure you won't have anything to eat?"

I purse my lips and hold his stare.

"More's the pity. Especially with what comes next."

The whole of me goes cold. "Next?"

"I don't enjoy having to do these things, but there are rules in this house for a reason. And when you break the rules in such an egregious way, well . . . you leave me no choice." His nothing eyes narrow. While his tone is soft, they are hard. His voice, his posture, his words may be kind, but they will always reveal the truth. "What happens now is your fault."

The door opens and Devin steps in. Something rattles in his hands, metal dancing against metal. Chains. Actual chains. I had perhaps imagined this, but hadn't truly believed. . . .

"No." I push to my feet, knocking the trolley aside. The dishes rattle and clack.

"Please, Bertha, don't make a fuss," Edward says.

Devin advances toward me. I back away, around the cart and farther into the study. Both of them watch me now, Devin with a sort of reservation on his face—the kind you might see when someone regards a wounded animal—and Edward . . . amused. The bastard is amused.

He takes another puff on his cigar.

"Don't make this harder than it has to be, madam," Devin says as he comes at me.

118

Edward's massive desk seems to rise out of the floor behind me, boxing me in. My heart thrashes. The sound fills my ears, pushing my thoughts sideways. My head whips about, searching. There's nothing. No weapon to defend myself. I grab the only thing within reach.

A lantern.

"Stay away from me!" I shout.

Edward's eyes widen. "Bertha, don't—"

Devin comes around the chair.

Edward waves him off, shouting for him to stop.

I hurl the lantern with everything I have. It smashes against the side of the cart. Glass and lantern oil splash along the carpet and the chair I'd sat in moments before. The flame sets them ablaze with a sudden whoosh. The heat is immediate and intense.

Devin shouts something that sounds like a curse.

Edward falls backward over his chair, his cigar flying from his hand. "Water! Get water, you idiot!" he bellows. Devin drops the chains and hurries from the room.

The flames crawl across the floor, stretching between us like the arms of a living thing. Edward finds his feet again, his nothing eyes wide with rage, the firelight flickering in their darkness.

The way his face contorts shakes something loose inside me and I'm able to move where I had been previously frozen in shock. While the blaze has blocked him from reaching me, it prevents my attempt to get to the door. But there's another way out.

I hurry around the large desk to the massive windows on the other side and yank at the curtains. Thornfield's grounds lay before me, washed in the cold light of the moon.

The heat at my back and the possibility of freedom at my fingertips makes me clumsy. I shake so hard I fumble with the latches.

Finally, they come loose. The windows swing wide. The cool night air washes over me. I brace my hands against the sill and throw one leg over.

Something hard strikes me over the head.

The pain is instant and all-consuming.

I feel myself sinking.

Darkness closes around me.

~ 16 ~

WHERE THERE'S SMOKE

JANE . . .

I blow out the lantern nearest Adèle's bed and plunge the room into darkness, save for a sliver of silver light pouring in between the curtains.

The girl is already sound asleep. I barely made it a dozen pages in the book I've started reading with her before she drifted off. Perhaps she was tired after applying herself so diligently to her studies.

Smiling, I take up the nearly empty glass of water and completely empty plate of biscuits we'd shared as a bedtime snack and leave the room.

I close the door carefully behind me, then make my way through the unlit halls of Thornfield.

The house is like a foreign land at night, all long shadows, high walls, and deep darkness at every turn. If it is difficult to navigate by the light of day, then nighttime makes it nigh impassible, but I am simply going to the kitchen to leave the dishes. I know that path well enough.

This is what I tell myself, but it does not keep my shoulders from tensing, or my back from straightening in the wake of an errant chill. The glow from a single candle chases away the thickest shadows, helping me find my way down the long, empty corridors. While I'm certain no literal creatures of the night lurk in the deep corners and hidden crevices of Thornfield, I keep my eyes on the path before me and ignore how the flickering flame makes caverns out of confined spaces, or whispers of movement when there should be stillness.

My mind drifts to tales of boggarts and banshees said to roam the open spaces, and the warnings that often came with them to never look too closely into the dark for fear that something may look back. Clutching my robe closed at my chest, I press forward toward my destination.

Even the kitchen has been reduced to unfamiliar shapes in the dark. I set the dishes for washing in the morning and slip out, aiming to make a hasty return to my own room.

It could be a trick of the light, but I almost swear that the hallways are darker, the shadows deeper on my way back. But then, it isn't what I see, or don't see, that causes my steps to falter.

Crying, loud and clear, echoes through the hall. No, wait . . . laughter?

Perhaps the sounds I thought I'd heard before were indeed the noise of an old house being lived in. But this? This is most certainly not, nor is it a figment of my imagination. It is distinctly human.

I wait, holding my breath.

Then I hear it again, and this time I can tell what direction it's coming from.

"Adèle?" There's no answer.

It couldn't be; the girl was fast asleep when I left her rooms.

But with Grace keeping a room on the second floor, at least according to Emm, and Emm herself staying close to the kitchen, there is no one else.

"Who is there?" I call louder this time, my voice doubling back to me in the dark.

Silence.

Emm's warning from before comes racing back. Mr. Rochester doesn't like it when people go wandering through the house. But this isn't exactly wandering, and I would be honoring his request by remaining on this floor.

Before I even finish the thought, I'm moving in the direction I'm certain I heard the laughter come from.

"Hello?" My voice is a harsh whisper in the night. I'm not certain where Edward's rooms are, but I do not wish to wake him.

I turn a corner and pause. There's no laughter, or crying, no sound save the beating of my heart like a drum, and yet I go still.

I take a deep breath, willing my thoughts to slow. Then another.

My nose crinkles as a sharp and unpleasant scent grips my senses and coats the back of my throat. The sour taste that accompanies the smell helps me name it almost immediately. Smoke, and not the heady, sooty scent of a fire in the hearth but the thick choking smell of cloth and wood and more burning.

Fire. Something's on fire!

I race forward, my candle lifted, nearly tripping in what little light it provides. The smell is strongest this way, and I follow it until I reach a set of double doors. My heart leaps into my throat at the sight of the smoke spilling out along their edges.

"Oh no." I tap one knob and, finding it cool, grip and pull.

The air thickens, making it hard to breathe, even as I press the sleeve of my robe to my face. Through the haze of the heat and the smoke, I see Mr. Rochester—Edward—fighting to stamp out the flames.

Without thinking, I hurry into the room, setting my candle aside. I tear free the curtains hung on one of the nearby windows, then throw the fabric over the fire. Edward jumps as if startled by my presence. He stares for the breadth of a second before going for another set of curtains.

Together, with the heavy material, we beat back the flames.

In the midst, Devin and Marsters arrive with pails of water, dousing the carpet and chair. The smell of burnt fabric and leather coats my throat. My eyes sting and water with it. My chest heaves with both exhaustion and the need for air, robbed of me by my coughing.

Edward looks to be in a similar state. His eyes find mine, and the way he looks at me . . . it's as if he's seeing me for the first time.

"Are you all right?" I ask, the words thick and sticking to the back of my throat.

He nods, swallowing thickly. "I . . . had a little trouble with the fireplace."

"Most unfortunate." I examine the damage. The smoldering bits of carpet and wood. The now ruined curtains used to smother the flame. One of the chairs seated near the hearth appears to have gotten the worst of it, though I see no sign of how the fire made the leap from one to the other. The grate is still in place, unmarred.

Edward is lying, I realize. Again. But why about this?

While he turns to discuss the swift repairs he wishes made with Marsters—repairs the rest of the house has yet to receive—I take in more of the immediate area. A dinner trolley strands to one side, its contents askew. Even still, I can tell it had been originally set for two. The pair of glasses, the silver domes, two sets of cutlery. Did Edward have company for dinner? If so, who, and where had they gone?

Perhaps he simply requested a second portion. Not entirely unheard of, especially if he had planned on working through the night. Still, something about all this seems off.

"Miss Eyre," Edward begins, drawing my attention.

When I turn to face him, he hesitates. His mouth works wordlessly for a few seconds before he presses his lips together. This pinches his features slightly, giving him the appearance of struggle. To do or say what, I can only imagine.

"Master," Devin croaks from nearby. He hoists something metallic from the floor. Chains, from the sound of it.

Edward's expression falls into a scowl. "Yes, what is it?" He barks.

Devin flinches but otherwise doesn't balk in the face of his employer's mercurial mood. "A word, sir, if you will."

Edward's already dour countenance only worsens. "Presently?"

"Yes, sir." Devin steps forward, his foot knocking against something on the floor.

A lantern, I realize. The metal is bent and stained black from burning. Glass litters the floorboards. Is that what started the fire?

"Excuse me, Miss Eyre," Devin murmurs.

I step aside so he and the other men may bow their heads in quiet conversation. About what, I neither know nor care. My focus is on the lantern, then the nearby walls and shelves as I search for where it had fallen from. Not over here; all other lamps appear to still be in place.

My gaze explores the rest of the study, dancing from hook to hook, lamppost to lamppost, until I spot it. There, on the desk, the setting base for a lantern such as this sits empty. The metal is even the same polished pewter. A reading light, or one to work by.

But how did it get over here? It couldn't have simply tumbled or rolled; there would have been oil spilled, more damage from the flames.

It was thrown.

The thought occurs with a suddenness as bracing as a bolt of lightning. Of course it was thrown. Had it been simply carried and dropped, it would not be dented so. But whether it was thrown by Edward or at him I cannot deduce. I simply know that this fire was started purposely, possibly by Edward or someone else.

"Getting rid of the smell will be the hardest bit," Marsters grumbles, drawing me from my reflections. "It'll spread through the rest of the house if it's not handled properly."

As he speaks, my eyes drift still, stopping on the windows behind Edward's desk. One of them is already open. I can feel the faintest hint of a nighttime breeze on my sweat-slicked face.

I'm moving before I can think better of it. "You should open the rest of these to start. That should help with the—"

Edward catches my elbow in passing, halting me. He stares for a moment, a touch longer than some might deem appropriate, but before offense could be taken, he turns.

"On her lead," he bellows, which has Marsters and Devin scrambling to move behind the desk.

Between the two of them, the windows quickly fly open. Cool air rushes in to dull the swelter and ease our breathing. The relief is instant, and I inhale deeply as Edward does the same. Then he steps into my previously intended path.

"You . . . saved me," he murmurs. "The trick with the curtains."

My face is flushed, and I cannot be certain whether it's from my previous efforts, the still lingering heat of the now doused flames, or the crawling unease that has begun its ascent from my stomach. "I've dealt with my fair share of accidents with candles. Heavy cloth is . . . is best. But you are indeed unharmed?"

He continues to stare, his chin dipping in a slow nod. "Not only am I all right, but I am most fortuitous to be sent an angel in the night. It seems I made the right choice in asking you to join us. I owe you my life. I need to find a way to make it up to you."

"That won't be necessary. And besides, Devin and Marsters both—"

"I insist." I feel his hand take mine. His fingers are warm. "But that will have to come later. Devin, Marsters. I've left something important behind my desk." Though he speaks to the two of them, he keeps his eyes on me. "Take care of it, will you? I'm going to take Miss Eyre out for a bit of fresh air."

Marsters grunts, and Devin nods with a quick "Yes, sir." Poor boy still looks out of sorts. I suppose he'd never seen such a blaze up close. I hadn't either, but he seems especially bothered.

Edward, his hand still wrapped around mine, leads me from the study and into the hall, almost pulling me.

With one last look over my shoulder, I am swept away and down the hall. Edward chatters almost nervously about his carelessness in stoking the flames too hard.

Another lie. An unnecessary one at that. Perhaps he had thrown the lamp in anger or frustration. It isn't hard to imagine, given his temperament.

Or, perhaps, there is something else afoot entirely.

17

THERE'S FIRE

BERTHA . . .

Everything hurts. Every inch of me is pain, as if I've been wrung out like laundry to dry.

That's the first thing I notice before I open my eyes.

The next is the feeling of arms wrapped around me, an iron grip tucked beneath my knees and around my shoulders.

I blink, unsure of what is happening.

Everything is dark. I can't see.

Though the ache in my body subsides, there is a pounding in my head that remains ever fervent.

What happened?

Where am I?

The press of arms shifts.

Someone speaks near my ear. The voice is familiar.

I wrack my brain, wanting to remember.

Flashes fill my mind. A window. A fire.

The room was on fire.

"Here we are," a voice says from somewhere nearby.

There's a rattle of keys and then hinges creak.

"Just lay her on the bed."

The arms loosen their hold and I drop. I land on something soft. A bed, I think. I want to sit up. I try. My body refuses to cooperate, but then fingers take my arms, gripping them, pulling.

Something cold and hard curls around each of my wrists. There's a click and the rattle of chains.

Chains.

With that sound, it all comes rushing back.

Edward, in the study. Dinner, then the shackles. The lantern. A fire.

My freedom . . .

I bolt upright in the bed just as Devin fastens the end of a chain to a hook in the center of the floor. The other end splits in order to latch to the manacles now digging into my joints.

"Seems you've gotten yourself in a spot of trouble once again, ma'am," he says with a sigh.

Grace watches from the door, a candle held high to provide light. "More's the pity."

I stare for a moment, dumbstruck as my mind works to piece everything together. I had been so close. So close. And then . . .

My fingers reach to gingerly feel the back of my head. Pain erupts where they touch.

"Would you like a cold compress?" Grace asks.

Devin says nothing else, just yanks on the chains to test them, jerking my arms forward. The metal bites into my wrists, stinging, and he has the audacity to apologize when I hiss with the pain.

He stands, bows, then hastily retreats from the room, as if he cannot stand to be too near his work, as if the truth of it is now somehow newly unbearable. And yet, he waits for Grace in the hallway.

She busies herself with setting out a small metal bowl of water, a rag folded over the edge.

"It's got a bit of mint in it, for your head," she says before joining Devin at the door. "I'll see you in the morning for breakfast, madam."

With that, the door closes. The lock clicks. Their steps drift away. And I am alone.

18

BURNING BRIDGES

JANE . . .

By the time I've dressed and started to make my way down to the kitchen the following morning, my mind is fully abuzz with the possibilities of my discovery in the study. In truth, I didn't get much sleep because of it, and I'm eager to see if my hunch is correct: that someone else was with Edward before, and possibly during, the fire. Emm will be able to tell me if the extra portion was made for Edward himself or a mysterious guest.

Though, while I am eager to know the truth, I'm also not entirely sure what I will do with it. Did this secret second party start the blaze? And why would Edward lie about it? To protect them? To hide something?

Passing by the study, I pause at the sound of voices from inside. I can't tell who's speaking, but they sound angry.

Moments later, who should come storming out but Marsters. He takes one look at me, his face flushed from either anger or drink, before muttering something about troublesome women before stomping off down the hall.

I stand frozen for a moment, watching him go, before taking the last few steps needed to peer into the study.

Edward stands in front of the desk, head bent as he examines something on the surface. Instinct tells me he wants to be left alone, and I try to do just that, but a mutinous floorboard creaks as I make to step past the door. He looks up.

The anger on his face lifts into surprise, then melts easily under a smile that slides into place more from what looks like practice than genuine pleasure, and I recall Emm's teasing from yesterday.

"Miss Eyre." He turns from the desk, setting something on it behind him. "I'm sorry, I didn't hear you."

"I was trying not to be heard." As soon as the words leave my mouth, I want to grasp them and pull them back in. "What I mean is, I was trying not to disturb you."

"You're no disturbance, I assure you. Again, thank you, for last night."

"I'm glad I was able to help." I hesitate before stepping farther through the door. "It's such an unfortunate coincidence, you being in the study when . . . whatever it was caught fire."

Edward tilts his head to the side. "How do you mean?"

"Well, aren't such things by nature unfortunate?"

"So they are indeed."

"But perhaps there is a silver lining, in knowing what caused the fire."

His smile wanes ever so slightly. On the heels of that is a flutter of his lashes. Clearly, I've taken him by surprise. "What?"

"The fire," I say without missing a breath or leaving room for confusion in my questioning. "You were there when it started, yes? Meaning you would know what caused it."

The look that flashes across his face is brief. It is hard. Sharp. And if I had blinked, I would have missed it, but I did not and so I am left open to it. Cut by it. Then it vanishes, and I'd almost believe it a figment if not for the way his grip tightens on his pen. I fight the urge to check for blood I know won't be there, but I feel keenly as if I have been wounded somehow.

I fight to maintain my pleasant expression. I hope it is believable. "And in knowing the cause, you can prevent such in the future, yes? That is what I m—"

"I didn't mind my reach," Edward cuts in. He still holds his smile, but there is an edge to it that wasn't there before. "I went for something on my desk and, not paying attention, knocked over the lantern."

I am immediately taken aback. Two lies in one? The lantern was not simply knocked over; it was clearly thrown across the room. And yesterday, in the immediate aftermath of the chaos itself, Edward claimed he'd had trouble with the fireplace. Now the lantern was the cause?

I could correct him, bring up the excuse provided before. But I'm still uncertain about what's going on. And my new position still remains precarious, especially as I have not been paid just yet. No, I will need to bide my time.

Edward straightens; his smile is all but gone now, and he crosses the room toward me. I back away, nearly tripping in my haste as he steps out of the office and closes the door behind him.

Standing here, this close to him, I can feel his breath as he sighs, almost wearily. He gazes down at me, and there is something menacing in those dark eyes of his. Something that promises ill will even as his smile returns, a pale shadow of what it was before.

"You were heading to the kitchen, yes? To meet Adèle for breakfast?" He offers his arm. "Allow me to accompany you."

This is so much like all the times before, the offered arm and escort. But now my stomach flips. It's fear, I realize, that causes me to hesitate. Out of necessity, I push the emotion aside and take hold.

"How delightful," I manage to say without the shaking in my belly reaching my voice.

I don't miss the somewhat hopeful look he gives me, and I shuffle my stride, hiding the action as I adjust my skirt, in order to put a bit of distance between myself and his suddenly eager expression.

As we walk, I feel the questions practically pressing against the backs of my teeth. Edward's posture has eased somewhat, and I know I risk arousing his ire once more. I debate whether it is a risk I am willing to take.

My mouth makes the decision for me.

"Who joined you for dinner last night?" The words leap free before I've even had the chance to truly consider them. While I don't regret speaking, I do regret letting them fly so easily.

This time the look he gives me is a startled one. "Joined me?"

"The trolley near your desk?" I keep my attention focused in front of us and my air easy, I hope. "There were two plates instead of one."

I don't miss the way his stride falters just so. "Ah. I asked Emm to plate dessert with dinner."

Another lie. The contents of both were clearly full meals, toppled over though they were.

"Mmm." I try to sound thoughtful enough to hide my suspicion. "I had no idea my employer was such a schemer."

"I beg your pardon?" His words are quick and hard, mirroring the line of his jaw. He has to force himself to relax. I can see it in the way he rolls his shoulders backward to loosen them.

"Taking dessert with dinner. You'll ruin your appetite with such a practice."

"Ah." He breathes the word in a faint laugh that's more relief than humor. "As the man of this house, I do believe I'm allowed such liberties."

While few are overly fond of liars, I find they stoke my ire to particularly hot levels. For most of my life people have attempted to conceal the truth in order to manipulate me or my actions. While Edward owes me no explanation for anything he does within his study, nay, his very house, I cannot help the way heat pools in my temples, warming an anger in me.

"Of course" is all I manage in response.

We walk in silence. It's heavy and thick as it presses in around us, cloaking us. A sort of cloud lingering in our wake, and it may be my eyes playing tricks on me in the early morning, but the darkness seems to ripen. Edward's presence is . . . stifling. If this is his usual demeanor, Adèle's reluctance makes more and more sense.

As we walk, I'm mindful of every step I take and how he matches them. Of the way his hand folds over mine where I have his arm, pressing my fingers. Of how he doesn't look at me once as we move along. I want to pull away, to throw up a wall to match his, but before I give in to the urge, we reach the kitchen.

Emm, of course, is busily bustling about, setting out the last of breakfast on the main table. Adèle is already seated, fork in hand, munching happily. When she sees me, sees us, the pleasant expression that had taken her lovely face vanishes in a blink. The fork she'd been holding drops from her hand with a clatter.

I withdraw from Edward just as Emm looks up, then follows Adèle's gaze to us. She seems just as alarmed for a moment before going back to fishing a tray out of the oven. "Breakfast is just about done. Apologies for the delay; the wee one came down hungry, so I fixed her a bit of something."

"No need for apologies, Emm. I appreciate it," Edward says, still smiling just so.

"It smells delicious." I move across the kitchen, partially to get away from Edward but genuinely to take up a plate to begin filling it.

"It does indeed," Edward murmurs behind me. I ignore him, focused on preparing my meal. "Have Grace bring mine to the study when you're done?"

"Of course, sir."

"Thank you. I'll see you for lunch, Adèle."

There's a soft affirmation from the girl and my heart goes out to her.

"You as well, Miss Eyre?" There's a hopefulness and a gentleness in his tone that makes me turn in surprise more than anything.

Gone is the hard expression he wore as we walked together, replaced with an eager vulnerability that part of me doesn't quite believe now that I've seen him lie with such ease. It takes me aback, and I stumble over my answer. "O-of course . . ."

He smiles, looking ever so pleased with that development. "Ladies," he says with a nod.

And with that, Edward takes his leave, and I am left standing there with Emm watching me as she prepares the requested plate, all while looking me up and down with an expression that is far more amused than I'm comfortable with.

"What?" I snap.

"Nothing," Emm sings. "Not a single thing."

I set my plate beside Adèle and, with a promise to return swiftly, I make my way over to Emm, snatching up a random pot lid as I go. "Emm? Could I talk to you a moment?"

The woman eyes me and then her lid, before lifting an eyebrow. "About?"

"This pot. I need it for something, over here." I turn to make my way to the nearby pantry, stepping into it and just out of sight.

Emm doesn't follow immediately, and it takes a bit of hand waving to coax her over. When she finally joins me, looking annoyed, I lift my hands.

"Sorry, I just needed to speak to you away from Adèle," I explain.

"You didn't need the pot for that." Emm takes the lid. "What's all this about?"

"Last night, did you make an extra plate for Edward's dinner?"

Emm frowns. "Grace usually prepares the mister's dinner. Well, plates it. I cook it."

Another lie!

Emm starts slightly when I drive my fist into my palm.

"So, you don't know anything about the extra setting brought to the study last night?" I press. "Whether it was for dessert?"

"I told you, I don't arrange the settings." The crease between Emm's brows deepens. "What are you on about?"

I hesitate a moment. Edward's lie about the extra setting is a sure thing, but I'm once again caught up in wondering whether or not I'm unduly sticking my nose in someone else's business.

Emm watches me, her expression curious but bordering on concern. It's the type of look you give someone when you're not sure what to make of what they're saying, and whether or not you should be worried.

I want her on my side in this . . . whatever it is that's going on with Edward, if there is anything at all, so I throw all my cards on the table, explaining what I saw in the study, from the tray of dual meals to the lantern thrown across the room. I am sure to point out inconsistencies in his account of things, such as how he claimed to bump the lantern when that was not the case. This was after he'd attempted to blame the fire on the hearth. With each word, Emm's face switches back and forth between frowning and wide-eyed surprise. By the time I'm done, she's stroking her fingers against her chin lightly.

"When I asked him about it, he said he asked *you* to plate dessert with dinner for him."

"Well, that's . . . something, all right. Maybe." Emm sets her hands to her hips. "I already told you I don't do the plating."

"Why would he lie about such a thing?" I ask, throwing a glance toward where Adèle is finishing up her meal. We don't have much time.

Emm shrugs. "Why do men lie about anything?" She grins then. "Maybe he's courting someone in secret. Afraid of a little competition, are ye?"

"What? No!" The revulsion that slides through me is followed by a hard shudder. I press back against the shelves to steady myself. "No, I . . . that's not . . ." That thought had not entered my mind at all until now, but it seemed like an awful lot of trouble to go through. And there was no indication that anyone from outside the house was present last night. "No, I mean . . . I think he's hiding something."

Emm sighs softly before plucking an apple from a shelf near my shoulder. She passes it between her hands a few times before clearing her throat. "I came to work for the mister after his first wife passed. Things were . . . stressed, to say the absolute least. And the last woman in your shoes didn't help things." Her eyes find mine again. "This family has been through a lot. It wouldn't surprise me if he was keeping a few things close to the chest."

Emm isn't exactly accusing me of anything outright, but I can tell an allegation when I hear one. "I'm just concerned. I thought maybe someone was trying to hurt him." Among many things. "A lamp was thrown." *At* someone, though I don't say that part aloud. My mind is busy working over what such a show of violence toward Edward could mean. Or perhaps *from* him.

"Maybe." Emm shrugs. "Or maybe it's like he said, he knocked it over. The extra setting could've simply been an additional serving for himself."

Which is exactly one of the possible conclusions I came to as well. But compounded with the other falsehoods he's presented, I cannot help my mistrust. A defeated feeling settles in my chest. I don't know why I wanted Emm to believe me, but it seems I did. Even if I'm not sure what she would have been believing.

"I have to say, that's some imagination you've got on you." Emm snorts.

I manage a smile. "Got me into trouble on more than one occasion."

"I can tell." She reaches to squeeze my shoulder. "Don't let it run away with you." Pot lid in hand, Emm makes her way back to her station.

I follow, rejoining Adèle at the table and tucking into my own breakfast. As I eat, my mind plays over Emm's words. What I saw *could* be nothing. Or it could be any number of things that weren't exactly nefarious. But something about this entire situation will not let me settle. It presses against my thoughts like a thorn in my side, digging deeper with each attempt to dislodge it.

There are secrets in this house, and if they're starting fires, they are dangerous ones.

ꙮ 19 ꙮ

COSTLY CHOICES

BERTHA . . .

"The master would like a word." Grace stands in the doorway. She doesn't need Devin at her back now that I'm tethered to the floor, but he lingers in the corridor all the same. The chains rattle as I shift where I sit in the chair near the table.

I look at her but don't speak.

She holds my gaze, steady, silent, ever patient. Like she's some kindly old grandmother and not my jailer.

"I don't care." The words are more a sigh than anything. I don't have the strength to put any real force behind them.

I haven't eaten in days. The hunger curdles in my gut, twisting, ravenous. One day. Then two. Then three. Over and over, Grace would come in with an empty tray save a wooden pitcher of water and a single whittled cup.

It's been a week since my last meal, and I am robbed of my strength. I drink. I try to write, but my thoughts are harried by hunger pangs and headaches.

This was punishment, I realized swiftly. For what had happened in the study.

"I've been told that, if you go, I am to bring you dinner upon your return," Grace offers. Her voice is light, joyful, as if she comes bearing grand tidings. "There's dessert tonight. Pie."

I almost laugh, the sound more of a cough. "Pie. How tempting." Though the promise of a meal is enticing. I'm almost ashamed to say I'm practically salivating at the very notion of food.

"Come now," Grace says with all the patience and care in her voice that anyone can muster. "It won't do to be rude."

She steps into the room and holds up a key.

I straighten in my chair despite myself. I didn't see where she pulled it from, but it doesn't matter.

"I want your word you'll be on your best behavior," she warns, jutting her chin out.

I nod, and it takes everything in me not to look at the door.

I don't think I have the strength to knock her over and try to get away, but that doesn't mean I don't have the will.

She places the key in the lock at the end of the chain, where it connects to the hook driven into the floor.

My body hums, my muscles tense, waiting for the telltale *click*.

Instead, there's a grunt from the door.

Devin stands there, eyes on me, his brow furrowed. He gives the subtlest shake of his head, like he could read my intentions as if they were written across my brow. Maybe he could.

Clink!

The lock falls free. The chains rattle as Grace takes them up.

I practically deflate into my chair, a sudden swell of despair welling inside me. Metal pulls at my wrist when Grace gives the chain a tug, like I'm some puppy to be led along.

"Come up, then. Give her a hand, she might be a bit weak."

Devin starts across the room, and I muster up the strength to push myself to my feet.

"Don't touch me," I snap at him.

He looks ready to protest, but Grace places the end of my chains into his hands.

"Come on, madam," she says, and reaches to press her hand to my elbow. The touch would be helpful, but I am in no mood to be coddled.

I shake her off and make my way to the door. It's slow going at first, my steps heavy, my feet feeling as if they've been dipped in lead. But I somehow manage to keep putting one in front of the other. Down the stairs, which I would have nearly tumbled down were it not for Grace's help. I accept it begrudgingly. If I were to harm myself, I'd never make it out of here.

"There we go," she coos when we reach the main floor.

Briefly, I debate calling out for help, but decide against it. Edward would not have allowed me to come down here if there were any chance anyone would hear me, and I don't want to end up tied down or thrown in a cellar or something for my trouble.

We make our way along the hall to the study. The space still smells of smoke, though the fire was days ago. My pulse quickens. My mouth dries.

I'd come so close to freedom that night. . . .

Grace knocks on the open door and doesn't wait before leading the way through. When I don't move fast enough, Devin gives the chain a shake. I dig my heels in and refuse to move, if only for a moment, before finally following the old woman into the room.

The stink of smoke is strongest here, of course. My eyes play over the trappings, noting what has been replaced or repaired, poorly, before fixing on Edward where he sits behind his desk. He's reading something, a letter of some sort, or pretending to.

"Sir," Grace finally says into the silence.

I was not going to be the one to speak first. He asked for me, after all.

Edward nods as if just noticing us, as if the rattle of my chains hadn't alerted him to our presence some ways down the hall. He makes a show of folding up the letter, sliding it into a rather delicate-looking envelope—the edges lined in carefully cut latticework—and sets it aside. His hand rests over it a moment and it's then that I realize I'm staring at it.

I quickly bring my eyes back to his face, hoping I didn't betray my interest. The envelope stokes a faint sense of familiarity in me.

Edward smirks. He's seen it. And I curse him for it.

"My dear. When last we spoke, things got out of hand." He sits back in his chair but doesn't remove his fingers from the envelope.

I lift my hands, the chains rattling to punctuate my point. "I wonder why that is."

Edward's smile widens. "You brought this on yourself."

"I don't recall requesting to be chained like an animal."

"As I said, your ungrateful behavior is what landed you in these circumstances. However, I come to you with an olive branch."

More like he had me brought to him, but I bite back on the words.

"I have a gift for you." He drums his fingers against the envelope before lifting it and extending it toward me.

For a moment, I'm not sure what he wants from me. Surely, he can't mean for me to take it, but as this doubt crosses my mind, he gestures with the envelope for me to do just that. Distrust humming through me, and my chains rattling slightly, I step forward and take the envelope. My heart leaps into my throat as I turn it over in my hands, taking in the long, elegant script so similar to my own.

The words jumble together, my mind struggling to make sense of them in my shock.

The envelope is addressed to me.

My fingers shaking, my breath quickening to match the rising beat of my heart, I hastily open it and draw out the paper inside. Unfolding the pages, my eyes race over them so fast my vision doubles. As it was with the envelope, my mind is caught between what it knows and my panic. I blink through it, through the sudden sting behind my eyes, through the wire winding around my heart, and read.

Dearest daughter,

I'm so happy to hear that Edward dotes upon you daily. It has always been my deepest desire to see you so happily married, as I was in my youth.

I blink so rapidly, it's as if my brain has shuttered briefly. I look to Edward, who has his hands folded together, his expression calm. Not eager, not smug, just . . . calm. Swallowing thickly, I look back to the letter.

Tell me, mother to daughter, how are you, my darling girl? Have you met many of Edward's friends? Does he indeed know Her Majesty as he claims? What is it like to traverse the echelons of British society? It must be so different from how things are done here. I imagine there are a number of similarities as well. People and their traditions make for hard breaking.

How are you faring in the English countryside? I hear this time of year makes for beautiful gardens in that part of the world. The willows are in bloom here, and the parks are a paradise. How I miss strolling along those paths with you on days like this. Hopefully, we can do it again soon.

I know I keep bringing up my desire for you to visit home this autumn, sooner rather than later, but I have my reasons besides my selfish want to see you again. It has to do with your father. He is currently faring well, the cooling weather having worked wonders on his cough. But the doctors fear he may not survive the coming winter in his condition.

My sight blurs with tears and there is a fist in my throat. Something is wrong with Papa?

"How long have you known my father is ill?" I demand aloud. My voice shakes. My hands tremble. Beneath my fear, my worry, is a well of rage.

"You should keep reading," Edward says directly.

I want to fly across this desk and pummel him. Beat him bloody with my own hands, choke him with these chains until his eyes bulge and the breath leaves his body. Instead, I refocus on Maman's words.

I've included a pair of tickets for a ship to bring you and Edward to visit. I know it is short notice, but I really must insist.

> *There is a note of joy as well. Your father has been successful in his pursuit to make you the sole executor of the Mason estate. He's gone through all the proper channels so that you will be named his heir. Of course, this is to be folded into your joint holdings as Mrs. Rochester so your children will be able to inherit both, but this is all yours until such a time. Isn't that wonderful? We can celebrate when you arrive! Hopefully, this will give you plenty of time to prepare. Please, my darling, take advantage of this opportunity to spend a moment with your father, in what may regrettably be one of his last. We love you, we miss you.*

Love,
Maman

I flip through the pages in what I know is likely a vain search for the tickets. When I glance up, Edward has them clasped in his fingers. I tremble so viciously the letter flutters in my grasp.

"As I said, I have a gift for you." He draws open a drawer and sets the tickets inside.

I start forward, but the bite of metal on my wrists and the rattle of chains reminds me that I am still bound, Devin on the other end of my leash.

"*If* you do as I ask, I will give it to you." He shuts the drawer, locks it, then makes a show of placing the key in his pocket.

"So, I'm to sit in my room, quiet and obedient, like a good girl?" There is no way I could keep the venom from my voice if I tried. So I don't.

"To start." Edward opens another drawer and withdraws a thin, leatherbound notebook and a pen. He places them both on the desk before opening the first. "This is a statute naming me executor of the Mason estate in your place." He spins the notebook to face me and pushes it across the desk so it's within reach. "Sign, and I'll allow you to return home. Under close supervision, of course."

I close my eyes and force my breathing to slow. I will not allow him to have this moment. I will not let him have my anger.

"And if I do not?" I manage to keep my voice remarkably calm.

Edward makes a show of closing the notebook. "Then you stay here and lose the chance to say goodbye to your ailing father. Your mother will likely follow in her despair, without her daughter there to ease her suffering."

His words are like a dagger to my heart.

"I'd hate to see you choose not to go to his side," Edward continues.

"Choose?" The word is acid on my tongue.

"Yes. Choose." He holds my gaze. "And what a costly choice it would be, for all of us. Though I imagine the financial implications aren't what's most important to you."

I open my mouth, intending to tear into him with all that I am, but a sudden sound startles and distracts me, drawing my attention to the window behind him.

He turns to look over his shoulder just as Adèle races into view from the side of the house. The little one is laughing, the sound of it like music. A joyful, pure thing that almost shatters the ugliness of this moment.

Almost.

She calls to someone, and seconds later a woman who looks to be about my age joins her. The governess. My breath catches in my chest. She wears the sun like a golden shawl draped over her shoulders, same as she did in that dim hallway. I can see her full face this time, round and glowing, glistening brown. She is still stunning.

Now, as she chases Adèle toward the edge of the hedge maze, sharing in her laughter, I regret not having called out to her. Certainly, if she were one of Edward's minions, she would be in here with Grace and Devin instead of out there.

"They do look to be having a grand time," Edward says, pulling me from my thoughts. He pushes himself to standing and moves to place himself between me and the window, his back to me as he watches the pair. "Do you remember the warmth of the sun on your face, Bertha?"

My fingers curl into fists at my sides, crumpling the letter from my mother before I realize and loosen my grip. I think about the boarded window in my room and how he's managed to steal the very seasons from me.

He continues, "Or the feel of the wind in your hair? The smell of the grass, of flowers?"

Adèle and the girl continue to laugh and call to one another, their voices growing softer as they disappear into the tall shrubbery.

"It must be hard, locked away from everything all this time." He actually sounds remorseful, though I'm not fooled for an instant. I know better. I know him. "I hate to see you do this to yourself over and over again." He sighs and turns to face me but doesn't return to his seat.

My shaking has worsened enough that now the chains rattle with it.

Edward looks to them, to the letter clutched in my hand, then back to me. "I can understand this is a lot for you. Seeing as how this ship isn't set to depart for another six weeks, you have some time to . . . think on your options and what would be best for everyone." Now he does take his seat, withdrawing the notebook. "Don't take too long, however. Preparations will need to be made either way. I won't keep you from your dinner. And you may keep the letter, if you wish." He waves a hand, and there's a faint rattle before the chains draw taut and tug at my wrists.

For a moment I don't move. I stand there staring at him, hating him with all of me. I would kill him if I could, I realize. I would kill him, burn this place to the ground, then dance on the ashes.

"Come on," Grace says, her hand at my elbow.

I snatch away from her, eyes on Edward. Tears fall warm against my cheeks. I don't care. Let him think they are from sadness and not anger. Not my rage. Rage that would consume this house and everyone in it.

"Enjoy your dinner," he says to my back.

I follow Grace and Devin through the silence of the house, down the various halls, up the stairs, and to my room, where they lock the chains in place once more. Grace brings me food, and my stomach nearly turns in on itself at the smell of it, but I can't bring myself to eat just yet. She says she will come for the dishes in a bit, then closes and locks the door behind her.

I don't move from where I've sat on the bed, grasping Maman's letter to my chest, tears running down my face. They flow faster, hotter, pouring out from something that's cracking open inside me. My angry silence soon dissolves into sobs. I can't see. I can't hear anything outside of my cries and the beating of my heart.

I want to kick. I want to pound my fists against the floor. I want to scream.

So . . . I do.

~ 20 ~

INVITATIONS AND INDICTMENTS

JANE . . .

I watch Adèle as she concentrates on getting the angle of the bowl just right in her painting. Or, rather, it is a sketch that will become a painting. It will be quite lovely. With Emm's help, I've set out a few dishes and fruit on a table amidst the dry grasses to provide a model. The girl has an adept eye, and took to the easel with, well, ease. This is her third piece in as many weeks!

"Mind the light," I call from where I'm seated in a chair behind her. "You have maybe another hour left before it changes too much to continue."

"All right!" she calls, excitement clear in her voice. She fishes one of the pencils from the little box and darkens a line.

My brow furrows as I watch the way the lead smears just so. Rising, I step closer. As I do, my suspicions are confirmed. The pencil, if it could be called that, is nearly depleted. So small that her little hand brushes the paper while she draws.

"You should use a newer one," I say, reaching into the box to fetch one. My hand brushes wood, but it's the empty bottom. "What? Weren't there more?"

Adèle shrugs, humming softly as she draws. I can't help the faint laugh that bubbles forth as I shake my head. It warms my heart to see her so completely consumed in something she clearly enjoys, especially after how gloomy things have been around the house as of late.

After the fire, Edward became more withdrawn, and when we did see him, he seemed to be harried or in some sort of rush. It's been some time since he last took a meal with us, or even inquired as to Adèle's progress. Something has the entirety of his attention, and I get the distinct feeling that this is not a good thing.

That and more around the house has . . . concerned me. I do not trust what I am being told. Not anymore.

I've taken to writing my thoughts. It's the only way I can work at the knot of my suspicions. Normally, I would talk such things out, but I have no way of doing that here without being overheard, and I do not want to alert others of my mistrust.

It scares me to admit that I've not felt this uncertain since my time at Lowood. The secrets there had been dangerous as well. My mind opens doors to memories I'd rather stay closed, pulling me into the past, where my misery was a constant companion, but not my only one. At least at first.

There was a time when my troubles and fears were soothed by one person. She was a balm against the trepidation that had dogged me all my life. It is because of her that I am here today, and I know I owe more to the memory of her than the hurt that hollows me out whenever she crosses my mind, but I cannot help it.

Again, I wonder what she would make of all this.

"Oi, girl," a gruff but familiar voice calls.

My shoulders slump in irritation. "It's Miss Eyre," I call without looking. I don't have to, to know who it is and that he's speaking to me. I'm the only one he calls *girl*. "And how can I help you?"

Marsters stands in the door, his beady eyes on me. "The master would like a word."

That uncomfortable flipping feeling from before returns. I try not to look at Adèle, who is staring directly at me now.

"In his study," Marsters continues. "Come at once."

There's a series of thuds and rattles as Adèle's bowl of fruit topples over.

Marsters looks at the girl for the first time since coming out here. "Leave that be, miss. I'll come back to bring it in. You can wait for your governess in your room or the kitchen."

Adèle pauses where she had been gathering up her supplies, and instead rises to her feet. She doesn't look at me or Marsters as she passes by and heads for the door, disappearing into the house.

Marsters isn't very talkative as he leads me. I don't expect him to be, in all honesty, and I'm surprised he elected to provide an escort at all. Usually, he just says what he was sent to say and goes about his business. Now he trundles on ahead of me, glancing up and down the halls as if he expects someone to jump out at him.

I almost comment on it when a high wail of a sound echoes along one of the nearby halls. I freeze, my breath catching as I turn. Was . . . that a scream?

"Nnn, dang wind," Marsters mutters, as if reading my mind. He stares down the hall as well, then looks to me, his gaze intense.

"That was the wind?" I ask, not really believing him. It didn't sound like any wind I've ever heard.

Marsters grunts. "Gets bad during springtime, what with the storms."

"Ah." The fact that it is very much autumn seems to have escaped the old drunk. But I don't bring it up. Instead, I glance over my shoulder in the direction of the sound, or at least I think it came from that direction.

Just as I'm about to continue on my way, the thump of footsteps draws my attention. It's Devin, clomping down a nearby staircase, speaking gently to Grace. The two of them pause when they see me. Grace narrows her eyes and Devin smiles, waving. Grace pushes by behind him, jostling him. His smile vanishes, and he looks admonished briefly before hurrying after her as she shuffles off.

"Hnn, maybe it was a scream," Marsters mutters and continues on, gesturing for me to follow. "Old bird likely fell down again."

I hesitate, gazing after Devin and Grace, my eyes flicking briefly to the stairs, but I eventually trail after the old drunk. "I thought the upper levels were off-limits."

"They are."

"Then what were *they* doing up there?"

The old man heaves a sigh, the sort meant to let someone else know your patience is wearing thin. I find I don't care. "The third and fourth floors are off-limits; the three of us keep to the second. You finished your interrogation, or you need to ask a bunch more useless questions?"

"Only a few."

Marsters hisses a low curse. That's when I realize this is the most he has ever spoken to me, at least at once. I wonder if I can take advantage of his oddly conversational mood.

"Why hasn't Mr. Rochester had anyone see to the repairs?"

"None o' my business. And none of yours, truth be told." He spares me a glare over his shoulder. "Just stick to the parts of the house you should, and no harm will come to you. Wouldn't want you falling through nothing."

"No. Wouldn't want that." As we move down the hall, the still-lingering smell of smoke begins to build, and I assume Marsters is leading me to Edward's study.

We finally stop in front of the open doors and Marsters waves me in.

Edward stands near the hearth, a fire roaring inside. He glances up as I enter and smiles. "Thank you, Marsters."

The old man grunts and closes the door behind me before I hear him shamble off. The room smells of brandy, soot, and something else I can't quite pin down.

"Miss Eyre, I have rather pleasant news. A proposal of sorts for you. One I hope you'll accept."

My thoughts immediately conjure my still-overdue wages. It is my naïve hope that, perhaps, they are now to be offered in full. Perhaps with interest. But if that were the case, why would he word it in such a way? I clench that hope and shove it down, praying I've kept my warring emotions from my face as I arch one brow. "A proposal?"

"Yes." Edward huffs a laugh and shakes his head. "Forgive me, I'm out of practice with such matters. A good friend of mine is to be married soon. Incredibly soon. In a week's time, in fact."

"Oh, well, that is soon."

"Yes. I had decided to decline the offer to attend, but I'm reconsidering. Especially if you would do me the honor of accompanying me to the gala."

What could have been either excitement or panic before is definitely panic now. I feel my eyes widen and I cough into a hand when my breath catches. "E-excuse me?"

"I know it's sudden, and I know it's unorthodox, but I've declined a number of social invitations over the past few months and, I . . . I think this would be an enjoyable time. With you, that is." He closes the distance between us, and I surprise myself by not immediately withdrawing. "We would go as little more than confidants, of course. I find your company enjoyable and I think others in my circle might as well."

"I—I . . . well . . . I . . . I'm afraid I have no attire that would b-be proper for a . . . a wedding . . ."

"I took the liberty of having such a dress procured for you. A few, in fact. Among other items." His smile eases. "They all should arrive in time."

"I—I . . . I'm . . ." I reach for the words but can't quite grasp them, save "When did . . . how did . . ."

"Grace took the measurements from one of yours while she was doing laundry. Forgive me, I wanted it to be a surprise, my promised thank-you for saving my life."

For a moment I'm not sure how to respond, even as the words I know I must say knock against the back of my teeth. All I manage is a soft "I . . . appreciate the gesture, sir, but I—"

"No need for thanks. As I said, this is to repay a debt." He takes up my hand then, his warm and large as they envelop my fingers almost as if in prayer. "One I will owe for the rest of my days, but I will gladly spend that long trying to pay it." His smile wanes just slightly, his fingers squeezing mine. "But, if you are determined to thank me, saying yes would certainly do the trick."

We gaze at each other, his expression hopeful, mine likely caught somewhere between surprise and mostly dread. My mouth works uselessly for a few seconds. Then I clear my throat and take a breath. "This is . . . a most gracious offer, Mr. Rochester, to be sure. But I am afraid I must decline, and instead offer my most sincere regrets."

The corners of his smile droop. "Decline?" He sounds confused, as if the very notion that I might even consider turning down his invitation is utterly foreign to him.

"Yes, sir." I take a breath and raise my chin just so.

"Why?" he barks in demand.

"With the greatest respect, sir, I don't believe accepting such an invitation from my employer to be entirely appropriate. I barely know you, and you barely know me. To attend an event so intimate as the wedding of a friend feels . . . fraudulent."

He stares at me, as if he's not quite sure he believes me, but is equally unsure whether he could prove the contrary. "Fraudulent," he scoffs as if amused, though clearly he is not. "And you offer your regrets? They are not remuneration enough for your refusal. In fact, I'm not at all certain you are capable of grasping the true meaning of the word *regret*." His smile has faded completely now. In fact, his lip curls in the slightest sneer before he turns and moves back toward his desk. "But perhaps you will soon."

A chill rides the length of my spine and prickles the flesh along my arms. "Sir?"

He waves a hand dismissively in my direction. "I had not expected to be offended so in my own home, leastwise by you."

"It was not my intention to offend, sir."

"Intended or otherwise, the offense is felt." He lowers himself behind his desk, taking up the pen I have often seen him working with, his expression now carefully blank. Or perhaps it is barely contained contempt I detect upon his countenance. "That will be all, Miss Eyre."

My fingers slowly unfurl from where they had clenched behind my back. "Thank you, sir," I murmur.

"Go, before your presence becomes further irksome."

I am nearly to the door before I'm halted by his voice once more.

"One more thing. In the future, I suggest you weigh *all* your options and the consequences each may bring to bear, both present and potential, before rendering such decisions."

A trembling starts in my middle and quickly spreads through the rest of me. "Of course, sir." I slip from the room as quickly as I dare without all-out running.

PART 3

I would always rather be happy than dignified.

21

SINS OF THE "FATHER"

JANE ...

The next morning, I stand in Adèle's room, slowly tucking pins into her hair to guide the fall of her thick curls. My fingers are slower than I'd like, but what can be expected after such a dreadfully sleepless night, wherein if I did manage a moment of slumber, I dreamt of the shaded halls of Thornfield devouring me whole, my feet sinking into the floor as I walked, the carpet slowly swallowing me like molasses. I drowned, my head held under, choking on shadows as something hidden within sobbed hollowly, begging to be let go.

Now I pay the price for such things, no doubt conjured by my distress at Mr. Rochester's reaction to my declining his invitation. I don't want to go to his friend's wedding, but now I am afraid my position here is in jeopardy. I have no other prospects, nowhere to go except back to Lowood, but I could never return there. For one, I refuse to go back. More importantly, I refuse to snatch away what I feel is the only stable and positive relationship Adèle has had since the passing of her mother. I will not abandon her as I have been abandoned. I will have to find some way to soothe Mr. Rochester's bruised ego, at least for a time. Would that such were not necessary, but I've learned time and again that one's survival hinges on placating the monster when you cannot slay it.

But I must focus on my charge. She is in fine spirits today, likely because she has finished the sketch for her painting and will take to her new oils that have been procured for her. She bounces in her seat, enough that I miss my intended spot twice.

"Hold still," I chide fondly. "Or I'll poke you."

"Sorry!" She then proceeds to try to physically hold herself still by gripping the edges of the seat. This results in her legs swinging, which only makes it worse.

But I smile and work through it. I've just pressed the final pin into place when a rapid knocking sounds at the door. Before I can call for whoever it is to enter, the door swings wide, admitting them.

To my surprise, it's Emm who comes blustering in, her eyes alight, her face bright with excitement.

"What's all this, then?" I ask as she all but slams the door shut, then sweeps across the room to seize me by the arm.

"Is it true?" Her fingers tighten and I wince slightly. "The mister has invited you to accompany him to the Austin wedding?"

I feel my body lock up, and I am unable to move or speak for a few seconds. When I finally shake loose from the spell, I clear my throat. "It's true he extended the invitation, but I have not accepted."

Emm's eyebrows nearly vanish into her hair. "And why on earth not?"

"Because I declined." I don't mean to be short with her, but to be accosted with the memory of Edward's invitation so soon is vexing.

She huffs a breath that manages to sound both chastising and impressed. "Do you know why he made it in the first place?" Her expression takes on a conspiratorial light that I recognize.

I don't care, but, "He says it's because I saved his life during the fire."

"Men say a lot of things to get what they want." Emm gives my arm a squeeze before finally releasing me. "I can't imagine this went over well, the way he's taken a shine to you."

"It didn't. He all but threatened to fire me, I think. Said I should weigh all my options and the consequences each may bring to bear, both present and potential, before rendering such decisions."

There's a *snap* and I peer down to see Adèle has snapped the pencil she'd been toying with clean in two, one half in each of her small hands.

My stomach performs this odd, uncomfortable little flip. I quickly pat Adèle's shoulders to signal she's free to rise.

Immediately she makes for the dollhouse and I begin putting away the box of pins I haven't used, as well as other items left over now that Adèle's preparation for the day is complete.

"And is it that you truly don't wish to go?" Emm arches an eyebrow and sets her hands on her hips, staining her dress white with flour that no doubt had some part in her plans for breakfast this morning.

"I don't feel it would be appropriate. I barely know the man, and he is my *employer*." I stress the last. Surely I cannot be the only one who views things thusly. "And, now that I think about it, no. Perhaps I do not wish to attend. I wouldn't know anyone there, and I'd likely spend the entire evening racked with nerves over it."

Emm looks me up and down in a manner similar to the way Edward did last night. "You look like you'd be able to weather it well enough, all right."

I scowl. "It's not a matter of how I look, it's how I feel. I'll have to ask you to excuse me. I need to finish preparing Adèle for the day." It's a flimsy excuse, but my mood has not recovered from yesterday and present conversation already wears on me.

"As it stands, perhaps you should consider going for yourself?" Emm says, and when I look to her with consternation likely clear on my face, she lifts her hands. "I'm not trying to convince you of a thing you feel you ought not do, but hear me out. Mr. Rochester runs in social circles where someone knowing your name can be the difference between securing sound prospects for employment should the worst ever happen or winding up penniless on the street."

I frown but say nothing. She is not incorrect.

Emm takes advantage of my silence, pressing on. "Having someone or somewhere you might be able to turn, even when grasping the thinnest string of acquaintanceship, would be better than relying on the kindness of strangers. In case you should find you disagree with him on other matters in the future."

There is no fallacy to be found with that part of her argument. That such a fate would befall me is already of concern, like a gnarled oak planted at the heart of my fears. An oak that now bears the look on Edward's face when I rejected his invitation as fruit. The phrase *most displeased* comes to mind, as that is what many of the women in my life called such displays from men. They ranged from understandably upset to frothing rage. For Mr. Rochester, *displeased* is very much an understatement.

"I'll think about it," I say, though my mind is already alight with conspiracy. I wonder if Edward might have told Emm about my refusal directly. Why else would she come to me like this? Did he have some hope that the two of us would exchange such words? That her advice would prod me toward acquiescing? It is mostly conjecture. A great deal. I feel a tad silly, wondering whether or not this was some machination of Edward's to try to sway me. But after yesterday, I wouldn't put it past him.

Emm brushes at the front of her dress with a sniff. "You've got plenty of time to reconsider."

"Is breakfast ready?" I ask, eager for a subject change.

"It is indeed."

I flash Emm a smile, hoping to settle all this for the time. "We'll be along shortly."

She returns it, then slips from the room.

I've barely breathed a sigh of relief when a tiny voice asks from across the room, "Did he yell?"

I look to Adèle, who still plays with the items in her dollhouse, picking them up and placing them in new arrangements. "What?"

"Monsieur. When you didn't do what he wanted, did he yell?" Her voice is soft but steady.

"No, he didn't." Which is the truth, but I have a feeling such a distinction doesn't matter for whatever it is going on in the girl's mind. "But it certainly appeared he wanted to."

Adèle has hold of her doll now, fiddling with the ribbon in its hair. She doesn't speak, but instead glances to her open bedroom door, and then to me.

Understanding dawns immediately, and I cross the room with sure steps to close the door. I even twist the key in the lock, earning a satisfying *click*. That done, I face her, and wait patiently for her to begin.

When she does, her voice is so soft I have to strain to hear it. "He yells sometimes. When he doesn't get what he wants. He's nice at first. Polite. But when that doesn't work . . ." Her eyes aren't wide and fearful as I might have expected but lidded, heavy, with the weight of a knowledge no child should have to bear.

"You can tell me," I remind her. "If you wish. I won't say anything to anyone, especially Mr. Rochester."

She clutches the doll to her chest almost protectively. "You promise?"

I place a hand over my heart and lift the other in the air. "I swear it; I will guard your secret until you release me from this pledge."

Her gaze roams over me, and I can see her contemplating the truth of my words. She has likely trusted others in the past, only to be let down.

Turning away from me, she places the doll in the newly rearranged bedroom, on one of the small chairs. Then she lowers her head, her fingers twisting around each other so tightly her skin is red. She sniffs faintly, surprising me. "He was nice to my mother. At first. We lived in Paris. Maman was . . . an artist." Her fingers continue to twist and pull at each other.

"Like you," I say gently, hoping to ease some of her distress.

It works, even if only a little. Her fingers pause and a smile pulls at her face. "O-oui." She takes a moment to compose herself, and I cross the room to sit on the floor beside her little chair. "Maman told me about him, when I was little. She said my father was a stately man. The type of man who thinks he's the most important person in the room, and is good at fooling you into thinking it too. She said she fell for his charms before she knew better. That's how I happened."

My fingers grip my knees, wanting to curl into my skirts, but I keep them straightened. "You *are* his daughter, then?"

She nods.

"Does he know that you know the truth?"

It's hesitant, but she offers another bob of her head.

Anger coils hot inside me. I knew Edward was a liar, and I had suspected that he was lying about his connection to Adèle, but I had assumed the girl to be ignorant of such things. Children in these positions usually are. But to pose this denial to said child directly, offering all the material bearings of fatherhood while withholding perhaps the most crucial? It's a level of cruelty I cannot abide. Though I will have to wait to vent my anger. Adèle needs me calm now.

"Go on," I urge her gently.

"Maman said she never regretted it, though. Regretted me. And she didn't regret him, at first. When I was little, he would visit her and say nice things. He wanted us to come and live with him. He wanted us to be a family. But he started visiting less and less. And when he did come, he and Maman would argue, loudly."

"What about?" I pry gently when she falls silent.

"De l'argent. Ah, money. He wanted some from her, because she had so much from her paintings. She gave him some, but it was never enough. He would say things like if she loved him, she would help him. Give him more. That she was being so selfish with the father of her child."

The chill that moves through me sets goose bumps along my limbs. So he was willing to accept Adèle when he thought it might earn him something in return? Such cruelties compounded.

"Was it just the money?" I ask. "Did he yell about anything else?"

"He yelled about wanting to marry her. She said she didn't want to. Not because she didn't love him, but because she . . . she didn't want to lose herself." She frowned. "I don't know what that meant."

But I do. I know exactly what it meant, and I feel a sudden pang for Adèle's mother, this woman I've never met but have been connected to through knowing her daughter. No matter a woman's wealth, station, or power, when she is married it becomes her husband's. Everything she is, everything she has, is his.

"He kept asking her to marry him. In the beginning, when he was nice, she would say, 'Ask me again tomorrow.' It . . . it was how they said 'I love you,' she told me. Then, during a bad fight, when they were screaming and throwing things, she said she would never marry him. That he would have nothing of her or hers. He got quiet then, before starting to leave. On the way out, he told her she should . . . should weigh all her options and the consequences each may bring to bear, both present and potential, before rendering such decisions."

Hearing Edward's words come out of Adèle's mouth is like catching a strike to the face. I would reel back if I weren't already on the floor.

"That was the angriest I've ever seen him." Adèle sniffs again, swiping at her nose. "That night, Maman left me in the house while she went to fetch onions for dinner. She couldn't find the ones she'd gotten the day before. She . . . she kissed me and told me to keep a candle in the window. I did. I fell asleep and woke the next day with it burned all the way down. But she never came home."

The ache in my gut spreads through the rest of me. I don't need Adèle to tell me the rest of the story to guess what happened. But I stay quiet, in case she wants to tell it. Because I have the dreadful suspicion that no one has ever let her before now.

Tears spill across Adèle's cheeks. She keeps wiping at them with small, shaking hands. Every time she dashes old ones away, new ones take their place, and another part of my heart breaks off and falls into the empty pit of my stomach.

"M-men came," Adèle murmurs. "They told me they found her floating in the Seine."

I feel my own tears warm against my face, but I don't move. Not to wipe them away or to wrap her in my arms the way I want to. I know that if I do, she'll likely not reach the end of her story, and it is my job right now to bear witness.

"There was a woman with them." Adèle's small shoulders lift. She still doesn't look at me. "She helped me pack my things. Told me I would go stay with my father in England. He would safeguard me and my . . . comment dit-on . . . domaine? Astate?"

Surprise jolts through me. "Your estate?"

"Oui. Left to me by Maman. The woman, she says I am a child and too young. My father will take care of everything until I become a lady. It's what my mother wished. But I . . . I don't think she wished this at all. She would never want this for me. Would she?"

"No. No, she would not." I do wrap her in my arms now, unable to take the cruelty heaped upon her even in her recounting it. I pull her to myself and hold her tight as she shakes and sobs. Her breath catches on each one, her voice cracking under the weight of her emotion. I hold her together, my face pressed to her hair, letting her go for as long as she needs. I don't know how long we sit there, wrapped around one another, but she draws back first, sniffing and wiping at her flushed face.

"I'm so sorry," I murmur.

She says nothing, only sobbing into my chest.

I am sorry about many things. About her mother. About how she has been trapped here. But more importantly, I am angry. So angry my blood is fit to boil. I force my arms to loosen my hold on the girl, lest I hurt her.

My mind is a whirl of thoughts and possibilities and questions. Adèle's mother clearly left her fortune to her daughter. A daughter she shared with Edward Rochester but who he denies. Why? What has he to gain by this? Certainly not the mentioned estate. That would be made easier if there was a familial relation, so what is the reason? And perhaps more importantly, what do I do with this knowledge? My first instinct is to tell someone everything Adèle has told me, but . . . who would believe me? The nearby hamlet is overseen by Edward, and there is nowhere else I would be able to reach for many miles that is not touched by his influence.

Do I quit my job and leave Thornfield altogether? After hearing Adèle repeat the words of Edward's threat, and learning it had been levied against a woman who later turned up dead—a woman who refused to do as Edward Rochester demanded—it's clear I am no longer safe here. Not that I ever have been.

The cries that echo through Thornfield. The mysterious circumstance of the fire. They are unmistakable omens. Danger lurks in these halls. Whether to me, I am not certain. But a fire would have certainly harmed more than Mr. Rochester alone. And while I might be able to flee in the night, I could never leave Adèle to suffer such a fate. Not knowing what I now do. Nor could I make off with her.

While he has denied her as a daughter, he has taken her in as his ward, and removing her from the hall without his permission would be kidnapping. He could have me jailed.

I need to think. I need to string Mr. Rochester along to do so. I need to be patient. Perhaps I will accept his invitation after all, if only to buy myself time. Time to prepare, so I may spirit both Adèle and myself away from here.

"It's going to be all right," I whisper into her hair.

Tremors rack her little body. "I . . . don't want anything to happen to you . . . like it happened to Maman."

"It won't," I promise the air above her head. "I'm going to take care of this. Take care of you." Though I know not how, my determination is no less kindled. I would breathe fire in defense of this girl as much as myself. "And I will find a way to make sure he never does anything like what he did to your mother to anyone else."

I finally draw her away from me, just a short distance. I wipe her eyes and then mine. The two of us sniff and sigh, the only sound in the deep silence around us.

"We should get down to breakfast," I say as I pat my cheeks and take slow breaths. "Emm will wonder what's happened to us."

I manage to find my feet, but am so wrung out by our shared weeping that the effort to stand winds me and I take a moment to steady myself. Then I take Adèle's hand and squeeze her fingers reassuringly. When she looks up at me, her expression still pinched with concern and sorrow, I offer a soft smile. But when I move toward the door, she doesn't follow. Her little feet stay planted, and her hold tightens.

I turn, an inquiry on my lips, but she speaks first.

"He already has."

"He what?"

"Done something like this to someone else." Her eyes hold mine as she sniffs. There's a severity in her gaze I've never seen in her before. "He already has. Or at least . . . I think he's going to?"

I face her, my mind already whirling with the possible horrors of one Edward Rochester. As if conjured by my thoughts, the sound of heavy footfalls along the hall sweeps in around us. The door is closed and the steps are muffled, but I can tell Edward's gait from Grace's shuffle or Marsters's lumber. Devin hardly ever enters the house, and Emm's trod is not nearly so heavy, so it can be no one else.

A shadow passes under the door, pausing in front of it.

Adèle claps a hand over her mouth, her eyes wide.

I swiftly lift a finger to my lips.

The shadow lingers but a moment before continuing on. When the steps fade, I feel my shoulders loosen and hear my relief mirrored in Adèle's sigh.

I'm certain he has gone when I say, "What do you mean, you think he's going to?"

She shakes her head swiftly, and I fear this moment has frightened her out of the telling. But then that determined light shines in her eyes once more. Though Edward has gone, and the coast is likely clear, she whispers, "I can't just tell you about this. I . . . I need to show you. . . ."

‿ 22 ⸙

TWO CAN KEEP A SECRET

BERTHA . . .

I am tired.

I am tired of this place.

I am tired of these people.

I am tired not of fighting, but of *having* to fight.

I am wrung and outstretched, pressed and pulled, twisted and bent, sore and abused.

A lady needs her rest, Maman used to say. Whenever I would find myself unsteady from having spent too much time helping her with the flowers in the garden. Or when I was little and had run myself and the heels of my slippers ragged playing with the dogs in the yard. Other parents might have found such things distasteful in their daughter, especially those belonging to the upper echelons of society. Such parents would have scolded their girls, chided them for having too much energy, too much fight, too much anything.

But not mine.

A lady needs her rest. Maman's fingers would plait my hair against my scalp gently where I rested my head upon her lap. *Just as fire needs air to maintain its flame, a lady needs a moment to herself, to breathe and be, before she can set the world ablaze.*

Oh, I would burn this place to the ground. But while my fury rages bright, my body can only carry so much. And I am tired. And missing my family so very keenly. So I will rest. If but for a moment.

For what feels like the hundredth time I finger the edges of the letter from Maman, thankful that I was able to rescue it from Edward's clutches. Her words call out to me, already etched in my memory. Almost every waking hour, thoughts of her, my papa, and his failing health consume me. They nearly blot out thoughts of escape.

Even though I want nothing more than to be away from here, I cannot manage to think of how I will accomplish this. And I am running out of time in new ways that claw at my heart.

"Maman," I whisper to the quiet. My voice cracks on the burn of tears, my words shriveling up. "Tell me what to do. Help me. . . ." I curl on my side into the bed. My chains rattle, my only constant companions. A reminder of how, every time I believe my torment has reached its peak, Edward manages to outdo himself.

It feels as if my chest is being cracked and hung open. I cry into the crook of my arm, the sound of my sobs echoing in the room, in my mind.

Until another sound joins them.

The sound of wood creaking.

At first, I'm certain it's in my head before— *Crack!*

I sit up, glancing around. The sound is coming from the closet. More creaking. Another snap. Then a solid *POP!*

For a moment I'm not sure what to do. Surely this can't be Grace or any of the others undoing the work of boarding up my escape?

"Hello?" I call out, my voice nearly a whisper in my shock.

I push to stand, the chains rattling as I take a cautious step toward the closet. I can barely see into it. The dim rays of the sun that manage to slither around the boards on my window do little to help.

There's another *snap*, then a soft shuffle of fabric and slippers. Then the invader emerges, and I take her in.

"Adèle," I say like a prayer, my breath tight in my chest, closing off my throat. I smile despite my fear and move forward to wrap my arms around the girl. She returns my hug. I ask, "What are you doing here? What if they catch you! It's one thing to sneak me pencils and paper at night, but another to—"

"Adèle," a voice calls from the closet, echoing me unintentionally, followed by the sound of someone struggling to come through the hole. They grunt and curse softly, then huff an exhausted breath. "Blazes."

The two of us watch as this mystery party emerges. It's the governess, I realize with a start. The one I caught glimpses of during my escape attempt, and then via the windows here and there. She pants lightly as she climbs to her feet, brushing her hands off and adjusting her skirts.

"How did you know about that . . . hole . . ." She trails off as she catches sight of me, jolting to a stop. We gaze at one another, her eyes wide, her mouth dropping open in shock.

Adèle glances back and forth between us more than once before reaching to shake the other woman's arm. This snaps the governess out of her surprise.

She looks to the girl, then back to me. "What in—who—"

"Jane, this is Bertha Mason," Adèle explains. "Or, as she was known briefly, Bertha Rochester."

I flinch as if struck, but I cannot deny the truth. When aghast eyes find me again, I lift my chin in defiance of any judgment or preconceived notions. I don't possess the words to properly convey my feelings on the association, and even if I did, they would surely prove inadequate. Thus, I remain silent, letting the governess take me and then the room in.

I conduct my own simultaneous examination, now that I'm able to get a closer look. She's beautiful, even while covered in a fine layer of dust. One of the ties in her hair has come loose in her exertions. Her chest rises and falls with the blossoming bewilderment that plays across her expression.

"What . . . what are you doing up here?" the governess asks, her voice quiet.

I have to laugh at the absurdity of the inquiry. Is she not a governess, meaning she should possess some measure of intelligence, yes? Adèle approaches now to squeeze me, and I lower my gaze to her face. Her expression is pleading. The governess in contrast appears aggrieved, if only a little.

Perhaps I have been too severe. This girl is not my captor, and while she may be employed by him, she is clearly ignorant of his wrongdoings. And, most importantly, Adèle seems to trust her.

I clear my throat. "Apologies," I say, shifting my stance. As I do, my manacles rattle.

The governess finally takes notice. Her jaw goes slack.

I lift my hands to give them, and the chains, a shake.

"If it isn't obvious," I finally manage to say, "I'm being held here against my will."

The young woman's mouth works as she tries to form words. She looks from me, to Adèle, then back again. "You . . . you knew about this?" she asks, her eyes on me but her question is for the girl.

Adèle nods slowly. "Y-yes."

Recoiling a few steps, the governess lifts her hands to the sides of her head, and her fingers crawl into her hair, pressing to her scalp. It's almost as if she is trying to coax her brain into comprehending.

"How . . . how long have you been up here?" she asks, her breath a whisper of alarm.

I remain calm. "What's the date?" I ask.

"It . . . I . . . ah . . . the twenty-sixth of October." The governess licks her lips.

A weariness settles over me almost in contrast. I close my eyes under the weight of it. "Nearly a year," I murmur, unable to muster the energy for anger.

Her face washes with confusion. Then horror. "A year." The words escape her in a sharp breath. "A *year*. You've been up here for a year . . ." She searches the floor as if it will contain the answers to her unspoken questions.

All the while Adèle watches her, watches me, and watches me watch the governess. There's an unease in the air, though it's not aimed at anyone in particular; it simply is.

The governess presses her hand to her chest, which rises and falls faster now, her breath coming in gasps. She withdraws another step, knocking into my chair before practically falling into it. She looks as if she might faint. Can't have that; someone would surely come to investigate the sound of a body falling.

"And you are?" I ask, throwing her a lifeline, giving her something to focus on.

For a moment it's as if she hasn't heard me, her gaze still lowered. But then she looks up and directly into my eyes. There is understanding in her face, heavy with equal parts sympathy and sorrow, along with a ferocity that catches me by surprise.

"Jane," she says, quiet but clear. "Jane Eyre."

"Well, Jane." I nod in greeting. Imprisoned or not, I've remembered my manners. "I welcome you into my home." I gesture at our surroundings, my words dripping with venom. "Such as it is."

Jane makes a noise that's something between a whine and a laugh, pressing a hand to her face. More giggles follow. She shakes her head, fingers still in place.

"I see you're going to need a moment," I mutter, less than entertained by her amusement.

She snorts. "I'm . . . I'm going to need a few." She murmurs something else, but another sound has caught my ear and panic pricks my heart.

I gesture for quiet, straining to listen. Adèle has gone as still as stone at my side. Jane freezes similarly, both watching me as I pitch my gaze to the floor.

In the silence, I am able to pick out the distinct lumber of Grace's feet. That prick of panic swells. "She's coming!" I whisper, then hurry to pull Jane to her feet in order to push both her and Adèle toward the closet.

"Who?" Jane asks, thankfully aware enough to lower her voice. She shuffles to keep from running over Adèle, who's already disappeared into the dark.

"Grace. If she finds you, she'll tell Edward, and . . ." I'm not sure what would happen, truth be told, but I am absolutely certain the result would prove disastrous, for all of us. "Go!"

"We can't just leave you here," Jane hisses, her hand braced against the doorjamb.

Any other time, I might take a moment to appreciate the sentiment in refusing to abandon me to my circumstances. Presently, I need her to go.

The key jiggles in the first lock.

I shake my arms, hoping the rattle of the chains conceals my whisper. "Then hide!"

For a breath of a second, I fear Jane may refuse. Her eyes flick to the door, and there's something hard in them. A defiance I cannot name but fully recognize.

"Go," I urge. "*Now.*"

Adèle makes a small, frightened noise as she pulls on Jane's arm from the shadows. "Hurry!"

I feel Jane relent as much as I see it happen. She grits her teeth in a silent curse, then takes Adèle by the hand. The two duck into the darkness, drawing the closet door closed.

Almost simultaneously, the bedroom door swings open. Grace shuffles into the room, her arms empty. She's not humming or singing to herself, and instead of her usual subtle sneer, she wears a frown, her expression dubious.

I offer a scowl in return and try to appear not insignificantly put out. It isn't hard. "An extra visit. To what do I owe the pleasure?"

At first, Grace says nothing, simply letting her eyes roam the space. She glances over each piece of furniture, her attention lingering on the boarded window. Then that suspicious gaze slides to me. "I thought I heard voices," she explains as she slowly steps closer.

I hold my ground and explain, "I was praying." It's the first believable excuse that enters my mind. "Is that now an offense worthy of intruding on what little privacy I have left?"

Grace folds her hands together. "If the master deems it so."

I scoff. "Does Edward think himself above the Almighty now?"

She lifts her chin, a play at superiority that I ignore. My attention is instead fixed on the door that remains open and empty. There are no signs of Marsters or Devin. Has she come alone?

Presented with this possibility, the urge to throw myself at the old woman is nearly overwhelming. I could easily overpower her. Tackle her to the ground, beat her. I've imagined it often enough, but it would be for nothing. She doesn't carry the key to my chains on her person. That honor goes to one of the other two. A precaution, I've been told.

And as righteous as it would feel to leave her lying on the floor, she and thus I would undoubtedly be discovered before I could free myself, even with help from Jane and Adèle. So I swallow the impulse. Barely.

"Praying, you say?" Grace repeats, sounding skeptical at best. It seems she's had enough of our tête-à-tête. "For forgiveness after your truly ghastly behavior these months past?"

"For the Lord to strike down my enemies, and free me from the evils of this world." I pour every ounce of animosity I can into the words. It should surprise none of these people how much I loathe them. "Our Heavenly Father hasn't answered just yet. Perhaps He's thinking on it."

For a moment, Grace simply stares at me. She shakes her head and clicks her tongue chidingly. "Such hateful things to ask Him for."

"Hateful prayers for hateful people," I coo. Then my glare takes my face again.

Grace is the first to look away. She smooths her hands over the front of her apron. "You should rest, dear. You sound unwell."

With that, she departs, her concerns seemingly assuaged.

There's the faintest click of the closet knob turning, and the door opens just a crack. I lift a hand, bidding whichever of them is watching—I can't tell—to wait.

"Deliver me from my captors, oh Lord," I say, careful not to project my voice too loudly. "And lay upon their heads the weight of their sins a thousandfold."

As I call down the wrath of heaven, the locks click into place and Grace moves away from where she was no doubt listening at the door. I wait until I no longer hear her steps, then wait several moments more still. Eventually, I release a breath and call a soft "All right."

At first, there's no answer, and I fear they've left. But then the door swings open and they both slowly emerge.

Jane stares hard at the door, then at me. "Bertha Rochester. Edward's wife." Her voice remains a whisper, but her manner is practically screaming.

Bertha Rochester. I've not heard my full married name spoken aloud in some time. The sound of it rounds my shoulders. There is no use in denying the facts, much as I may wish to, so I nod. "Please. Use my maiden name."

Jane licks her lips before speaking again. "They . . . they said you died."

It is not difficult to surmise who she means by "they."

"But you're alive," she continues. "And he's kept you up here this entire time."

I watch Jane work her way through the truth of the matter. She's smart. I can tell, now that shock has loosed its hold on her.

"Surely he couldn't expect to get away with—"

"Claiming I'm dead while secretly imprisoning me in what would be my own house?" When I finally speak, I sound far calmer than I feel.

She frowns deeply. "Why?"

"Money." The answer is simple enough. "My . . . the man I married"—I cannot say *husband*; the very thought of the word sours my tongue—"wants my inheritance. He keeps me here in hopes of somehow gaining it for himself."

A look of disgust crosses Jane's face. "Money. That seems to be a sore spot of his concerning a number of matters. Regardless, we need to devise a way to get you out of here."

There's a small gasp from Adèle. "You're going to help her?"

Jane turns to the girl and all abhorrence in her expression melts under a careful smile. "Of course." Her eyes meet mine over Adèle's head. "However I can."

She means it, I realize. The sincerity in her voice, on her face, catches me off guard. I have to take a moment to recover, and hide this by adjusting my chains so they do not pull as painfully.

Jane's eyes follow the sound. There's that twist of sympathy on her lovely face again. It lingers just a touch longer this time, before vanishing under the same ferocity from earlier. Had she the strength to rip the chains away with her bare hands, she no doubt would. I half expect her to try, all the same.

"Do you know where the keys are?" she asks, her voice hard even in a whisper.

My shrug is halfhearted. "The simplest answer is no."

"And the complicated one?"

"Sometimes Marsters or Devin, depending which one accompanies Grace, and if I'm to leave the room for some reason. Usually Edward's behest." I feel my lip curl. "He enjoys summoning me on occasion, to inflict some new pain or simply to remind me of my current plight."

"And when neither of them has it?"

"Your guess is as good as mine, though my first would be that Edward keeps it. Either on his person or locked away in that damnable desk of his."

Jane sucks her teeth. "We need to find them for any plan to get you out of here to succeed."

"At least we are in agreement on that," I snap before I even realize words are coming out of my mouth. I purse my lips together with a quick breath and aim an apologetic look her way. "My apologies, I'm used to talking with *them*." I fling my hand at the door.

Another smile breaks across Jane's face, wide enough that her cheeks apple with it this time. "No apologies necessary." She falls into contemplative silence. I watch her formulate and dismiss no less than three potential plots, plans, or ideas. None seem to be adequate. When the next similarly fails to satisfy, she stamps a foot. Fortunately, the sound is muffled by the thick, ornate carpet.

This one has a temper on her.

"Damn it," she whispers. "There's no way around the key, so I'll have to riddle out that part."

"Part?" I ask, curious.

"Of my plan. Or what might be my plan. I'm still working on it, I'm afraid."

"Can't Jane just tell someone?" Adèle asks, her small voice laced with desperation. "N-no one would believe me, but maybe . . ."

Jane's shoulders sag, and she moves to wrap her arms around the girl.

"They'd likely not believe her either," I admit. It is a sad truth that the word of a woman would not amount to much, especially against that of her employer. A situation worsened by said employer's station. "And even if they did, Edward would find a way to keep them from searching the house. Or pay for their silence."

"His influence over the nearby authorities would likely aid him in this endeavor," Jane murmurs.

"There has to be someone we could tell," Adèle says. "Someone who doesn't work for him?"

Watching these two discuss the means for my escape, listening to them, do I dare hope enough to plot? To concoct some means to gain my freedom? Part of me balks at the very idea of allowing myself to reach such lofty aspirations once again. The higher one climbs, the farther they stand to fall, and the pain of previous failure is still fresh.

Despite this, another louder, angrier piece of my being rises in rebellion. It asks, nay, demands to know what I have to lose that has not already been taken from me. The risk was worth it before; is it not now? Has he finally made good on his promise to break me?

No. No, I will deny him this and any other victory I am able.

"My family," I say. "They'd believe you. If you wrote them, told them what's happened, that their *Little Bird* needs help, she needs—" A sudden rush of emotion closes off my throat. My words falter, trapped as I am. Contrarily, almost cruelly, I am unable to contain the sob that follows. I press my hand to my mouth, bite down on the flesh of my palm. The sting of the physical does little to dull the ache in my heart, but it is a welcome distraction.

A heavy *thud* sounds from somewhere else in the house. No one moves or says a word, wide eyes exchanging silent questions and cautious assumptions. After at least a minute, maybe two, we dare breathe again in shared sighs of relief.

"We should probably go," Jane says as she eyes the door.

I muster a sound of agreement. "As much as I've enjoyed your company, your discovery will serve none of us well."

Jane's voice is soft. "Likewise. Correspondence to your family will not take long to prepare. Devising a means of locating the key might prove . . . more challenging. And time-consuming." She mutters the last, then immediately throws off any and all blossoming despair. She asks of me, "Will you be all right in the meantime?"

"I'll manage. I have this long."

"Give me a day, maybe two," Jane says. "I'll bring word of whatever I devise."

"How?" I ask. "You can't just pop up here for a visit."

"*I'll* manage," Jane says.

I stare at her, dumbfounded. Or perhaps astounded, I haven't decided. That small smile of hers returns for the briefest moment before it's gone, buried under a thoughtful furrow of her brow.

There's another *thump*, this time closer. And that is definitely the sound of someone approaching, likely sent at Grace's behest.

"You should definitely go," I whisper, though the two of them have already started toward the closet, Jane guiding Adèle ahead of herself.

I abandon the chair in order to throw myself across the bed, hoping the dragging and clatter from my chains is enough to mask their departure.

As the first of the locks is undone, Jane draws the closet door closed, but there's a moment before it shuts, an instant where her gaze finds and holds mine. She sets her jaw and nods. I blink. She's gone. I'm alone once more. Yet, for the first time in a long time, I'm less lonely. I eagerly— and perhaps foolishly, time will tell—allow the faintest spark of hope to flicker to life.

A glimmer. A morsel. But it's there, thanks to this Jane Eyre.

I arm and armor myself with it, then face the bedroom door.

23

FIRSTS

JANE . . .

Once I make it through the hole at the back of Bertha's closet, I reach to help Adèle through. Then, together, we reposition the planks as quickly as we dare to conceal the opening. The patchwork won't survive any scrutiny, but the boards will at least remain upright.

As we finish, I hear the door to Bertha's room open, and she heaves a sigh.

"First Grace, now you. Can I not get a moment's peace?"

Adèle scrambles out of the closet far faster and quieter than I'd expect of anyone. Her uncanny ability to go undetected makes all the more sense. I start to follow when a familiar voice stops me dead.

"She thought she heard something." That's Devin. I recognize the light, almost conversational clip in his tone. Shock ices my body. Even he knew there was a woman trapped up here?

Bertha scoffs. "I'm sure she thinks a lot of nonsense; what does it have to do with me?"

"I'm just double-checking." His voice grows louder, along with the thud of his steps. No, not louder, closer. The realization comes too late for me to run. I hold my breath as Bertha's closet door opens.

A bit of light streams in through the cracks between the planks. The urge to run burns through me, but I hold fast. If I move, he will undoubtedly hear me. There is no excuse I can fathom that would explain my reason for being here.

The light shifts as Bertha steps in behind him, her chains clinking. "Satisfied?" she says, before reaching around him to push the door closed. "Now, can I be left alone? Or do you need to check under the bed for monsters?"

Devin groans faintly, clearly wanting to be anywhere but here. "Good day, madam."

Bertha says something decidedly rude, followed by the sound of the door closing and locking.

I don't breathe again until Devin's steps carry him down the hall and then the stairs after. Then I count to thirty before attempting to climb to my feet. Adèle stands in the middle of the dim room, her eyes wide, her chest rising and falling with rapid but silent breaths. My fear is so clearly written on her face.

Together, on pins and needles, we cross to the door. I listen for any whisper, any hint of another in that corridor. When I am confident the hall is empty, I open the door slowly. There's not a soul to be seen.

I take Adèle's hand in mine, and the two of us sweep from the room—though I make sure to close the door behind me—then move as quickly as we dare toward the stairs. The whole while I strain to listen, to hear any signs of anyone else moving in the house.

As we run, my mind also races. Bertha's presence answers a number of questions. For instance, I now know the source of the wails that echo through Thornfield at night, and there's little doubt in my mind that Bertha is the one who nearly burned Edward out of his own study. I would have done the same, presented with the opportunity.

Other slightly strange but seemingly innocuous occurrences over the past couple of months sharpen with newfound clarity, as well. Grace's unfriendly behavior . Edward insisting no one venture beyond the second floor. The way he avoided talking about his wife as if she had died instead of being locked like some maiden in a tower. The liar.

I'm so distracted by my rising ire that I don't notice Adèle calling my name, until she grabs my wrist with her free hand.

"Jane!" she hisses.

I look to her, my heart hammering in my chest, pounding at my temples. Her little face is red with effort, and her chest heaves. With a start, I realize I've been dragging her along with me, and she's had to work to keep up.

"I'm sorry," I breathe, taking a moment to take in our surroundings. Thankfully, we've reached the first floor undiscovered.

Adèle nods, letting me go and pressing both her hands to her chest. She shuts her eyes and her shoulders slump and . . . I'm struck by what this must mean for her. To learn that her father likely killed her mother, to *know* he's imprisoned another woman in her home, to see him make an example in such a way of any who dare cross him? No wonder she fears him so.

Yet I have no room in my heart for fear concerning Edward Rochester. All I know is anger, and it surprises me how furious I am when I have not borne his transgressions.

But he would do it to me too. Of that I have no doubt.

When it appears as if Adèle has gathered herself, she takes my hand and I lead the rest of the way to my room. It isn't until the door is closed and locked behind us that I allow myself to relax even the slightest bit, though that's short-lived, as I instantly start pacing.

There is a woman trapped upstairs. *Chained.*

"My God," I whisper to the open air as I come to a stop.

"I wanted to tell you," Adèle says softly, her voice tremulous. "But I had to know I could trust you. That . . . that Bertha could trust you." I can feel the girl's eyes on me, watching me, gauging my reaction.

"Trust me for what?" I ask, though I can imagine numerous reasons.

"To help her," Adèle says, her voice lifting in a plea. "I thought Sophie would."

"Sophie?" I asked, my voice strained even in my own ears.

"My last governess. Bertha managed to escape, once. Sophie saw her and, instead of helping, called for Marsters."

I nod as if I understand. I do not. My mind is reeling with the truth of all this. It has been months, and I had no idea. I swallow my shock, force it down painfully, bury it. There is no place for it now, and I don't want to frighten Adèle, or give her any reason to doubt me. But I need to know, "How did you find her?"

The girl shifts, a child's fidgeting hesitation at being caught doing something she should not. She lowers her gaze, and her voice. "I made Monsieur Rochester angry, asking questions about Maman. He is awfully frightening when he yells, so I hid upstairs. I knew it was forbidden to visit the upper floor, but I wanted to go somewhere no one would find me. Hours passed. No one came looking for me, not even Sophie.

"I thought I was alone until I h-heard him shouting. He didn't know I was hiding farther down the hall. He said such . . . horrible things. I saw him and Marsters leave a room and lock the door before going downstairs. At first, I believed he had been shouting at Marsters. Then I heard crying. I wanted to run, but the person sounded so very upset! So, I asked if they were all right. Through the door. That's when Bertha asked my name. I did run, then. But I felt bad about it later, so I went back to talk to her when everyone was asleep."

"And you've visited her since?"

The girl bobbed her head.

"All those times you went missing?" I ask, though I'm certain I already know the answer.

She nods again, glancing up at me. Poor thing looks liable to shake apart.

Instinctively, I wrap my arms around her, drawing her close. I feel hers clutch at me in turn, and squeeze. "When was the first time?" I keep my voice light, soft, even though a maelstrom churns within me.

"This past summer."

So long . . .

When I feel Adèle's trembling cease, or perhaps mine simply rises to match it, I release her in order to pace. She watches me, silent, fidgeting with one of the ribbons that has come loose from her hair.

I should retie it. Later, I tell myself as I walk. And walk. And walk. I should stop, should sit. But if I did, the storm brewing in my chest would surely consume me. If I stopped, I would scream and never stop screaming. So, I force myself to remain in motion. Besides, I think better when I'm moving.

I promised Bertha I would come up with a plan to get her out of here. Perhaps naïvely, and certainly prematurely, but I meant it. Mean it.

"How do we tell Bertha's family what's happened?" Adèle asks from where she's sat herself on the edge of my bed. The ribbon has started to fray.

"I'll write a letter explaining everything," I say as I continue pacing. Though how I will get that letter to where it needs to go is another matter. No one else in the house other than myself can be trusted, which would mean having to make the trip into town myself to post it. Such a request is not without risk. Someone would likely ask why it couldn't be included with the rest of the post. What was so special about this note that it had to go out on its own and with such haste? Normally, I'd believe myself safe from such a breach of decorum by anyone making so personal an inquiry. But after what I've witnessed, I'm acutely aware of the fragility of such supposed securities.

Then there's the matter of what would happen should I manage to send word to Bertha's family. It would likely be months before they would be able to mount a rescue or send aid. Her position is too precarious for such a lengthy delay. Our options are limited, at least for the moment.

There's a knock. Both Adèle and I jerk in surprise. We look at each other, then to the door.

I clear my throat and call, "May I help you?"

The knob rattles. "Why on earth is this locked?" a familiar voice complains.

The relief at the sound of Emm's lilting accent weakens my knees, and I'm at the door before I've thought better of it. I pause, my fingers curled around the key. Does . . . does she know the truth about Bertha? Do I risk asking her?

"Hello?" Emm knocks again.

"S-sorry." It takes a couple of attempts to open the door.

It swings wide to reveal her face pinched in confusion.

"The key sticks sometimes," I say. The lie is an easy one.

"Does it?" She steps into the room and reaches to give it a few testing turns. When the key presents no trouble whatsoever, she arches an eyebrow.

"I said *sometimes*," I stress, hoping to appear just as miffed as she may feel.

"Well, then, you should get Devin to take a look."

At the mention of his name my stomach turns, and my anxiety around asking Emm about Bertha sharpens. Her help would be indispensable, but it's too great a risk. I have to be absolutely sure before I say anything.

Emm shuts the door behind herself and looks from me to Adèle. "Oh, good, you're here as well. I've been looking all over for the pair o' you, you know. You missed breakfast!"

I fight the urge to ring my hands in lieu of pacing and force a smile. "Oh! I'm sorry. We were playing hide-and-seek. She's very good."

Adèle nods agreeably. There is still a flicker of fear in her gaze. I pray Emm does not notice.

"That she is," Emm says in an offhanded way that leads me to think she might not believe me. Or perhaps I am reading into things. "I'd lecture the two of you about missing such an important meal, but lunch is ready. Also, I have a bit of news."

She smiles in that conspiratorial way of hers and won't meet my eye for longer than a few seconds. I'm not in the mood for these games. I want to shake her, to tell her I've had enough "news" to last me a lifetime. But instead, I fold my hands together and wait.

It doesn't take long for said news to get the best of her. "Fine! What's got you staked against fun today? I've just taken lunch to the mister, he chose to dine in the study. I asked if he would like supper brought in as well. He said yes, no surprise there, but went on to request I inform you that he'd like you to join him this evening." Her smile widens, betraying her apparent delight.

At the same time, everything in me goes cold. Had he noticed Adèle and me missing? Was he the one who sent Grace and Devin upstairs? I fight to keep my mounting fears off my face.

Silence stretches as Emm eyes me the way one might eye a frightened animal. "What's this, then? Still bothered about the wedding invitation?"

I frown, confused at first. Then realization dawns. "The wedding invitation," I repeat. In the face of everything that's happened this morning, Edward's "proposal" was the last thing on my mind. But now that I remember . . . a plan begins to form.

Emm clicks her tongue in sympathy for what, I assume, she believes is my display of disappointment rather than distraction. "Don't be too upset. It's been my experience that Mr. Rochester's bark is far worse than his bite." She offers a smile.

That's not what she said earlier, but I don't bring this up.

"Besides," she continues, "one silver lining is that dinner will be delicious tonight."

"Oh, will it?" I feign interest merely to be polite. I don't care a whit about dinner.

"I happen to know the cook." Emm winks, then looks at Adèle. "Hope it's all right I keep you company while Jane dines with the mister this evening? I'm not as good at hide-and-seek, but sweets will be involved."

Adèle nods, her head bobbing once again.

"Then it's decided," I interject, more than ready to speak about something other than dinner plans with that wretched man. "Now, let's see about lunch."

Lunch is uneventful, despite Emm's nonstop chatter. She's excited about dinner, so much so that one might think she was asked to attend instead of I. Adèle and I make quick work of our sandwiches and soup. When Emm asks why the rush, I offer the excuse of our earlier games having eaten into lessons more than I realized.

"And if I am to spend the evening with Mr. Rochester, then we should complete as much as possible so Adèle is not behind tomorrow."

But there are no lessons this afternoon. Despite the small pile of books I've acquired from the library, not a single word is read. The two of us sit in silence, she with her open sketchbook and I with my journal. Neither of us seems capable of concentrating on our respective tasks. The reason is obvious, even if nothing is said.

Bertha fills my mind, and undoubtedly Adèle's. Thrice I pen openings to potential letters to the Mason family, but I don't get much further than a few lines after the salutation. I'm not sure what to say.

No. No, I am well aware of the what; it's the how that worries me. If I don't strike the correct tone, Bertha's parents may believe the letter to be a fraud, an attempt at some cruel ploy. What little time we have could be wasted if they feel they must seek some sort of proof. And if they write to Thornfield proper with questions? Should their correspondence be intercepted, we would be found out. And potentially at Edward's mercy.

You could leave, a small, frightened part of me whispers. *Pack your things, go before any of this comes to a head.* And there is no doubt in my mind that it will.

But I couldn't simply leave. Abandon Adèle? Abandon Bertha? Without at least trying?

Pressure at my knee causes me to look up and into Adèle's round face.

She withdraws her hand almost immediately, but then presses it back. "Est-ce que tout va bien?"

My expression must have been troubled indeed. I manage a smile and let my fingers fall over hers. "Oui. C'est bon. How are your sketches coming along?"

She spares the sketchbook a brief glance where it rests on the nearby table. "I can't concentrate."

"Neither can I," I admit with a sigh. My gaze drifts toward the clock on the nearby mantel. "Dinner should be ready soon."

As if summoned by the mere mention of the meal, Emm appears in the doorway with a smile on her face. "Almost time," she says, clearly still eager about tonight's plans. Perhaps she truly is unaware of everything Edward has done. Is doing. "I've prepared an especially delicious series of courses."

"Showing off, then?" I ask.

Emm's smile widens. "I haven't the slightest notion of what you mean."

"Of course not." I close my journal and push to stand. Best get this over with.

Adèle's hand tightens in mine. "Tu dois être prudente," she near whispers, stealing glances toward the door. "Sois prudente, s'il te plait." The fear on her face is masked, but I know it's there. To think that at such a young age, she has already learned how to conceal parts of herself.

"Ça va aller," I quietly assure her, and myself. It would be a lie to say I have no concerns for this evening. Being alone with Edward is the last thing I want, especially knowing what I do now. But it's that same knowledge that spurs me onward—that, and my half-formed plan to help Bertha and Adèle. "Go on with Emm," I say to the girl. "See if she needs help with dessert."

"I could always use the assistance of such an accomplished pastry chef." Emm holds out her hand and, with one last look at me, Adèle crosses the room to take it.

Emm wrinkles her nose playfully and I'm glad to see Adèle smile in turn. "We'll make sure it's the best cake they've ever had, aye? I'll even show you my secret ingredient for extra sweetness." At the door, Emm pauses to face me. "Feel free to take a moment to freshen up. It will take at least ten minutes to wheel the trolley to the study."

"The quicker the better," I call after them.

Emm's laughter chases her down the hallway toward the kitchen.

As she suggested, I pause to gather myself and my thoughts, which have been chaotic since this morning. Chaotic and consumed by Bertha Mason. It has not escaped me that I am about to share a meal with her captor. Her tormentor. The man who has made her life hell for a year. I will have to smile in his face while he lies to mine, and I will have to be convincing in my ignorance while concealing my contempt for the cur.

For Bertha, I tell myself as I check my reflection in a small mirror hung on the wall. *And for Adele.*

I make my way toward the study. Hopefully, this has given Emm and Grace all the time they need to arrive with dinner. I want this meal over with as quickly as possible. Alas, as I reach my destination, I neither hear nor smell any sign of dinner. This is it, then. Taking a slow breath, I knock.

"Enter," Edward calls from the other side of the door.

I step through, leaving it open behind me. "I was told you requested my company for dinner."

Edward looks up from a smattering of papers across his desk. His hand stills where he was writing something in a ledger that is quickly closed and tucked into a drawer. All with a smile. "I did indeed. Come, sit." He gestures to the set of chairs positioned across from the hearth. I see the damaged one has been replaced with a spare from a drawing room, perhaps. "I'd like an opportunity to catch up. For you to tell me how Adèle is doing, or if you need anything. Besides arts supplies or ingredients for sweets."

I need you to free the woman you're keeping prisoner upstairs, then promptly go to hell! But instead, I force a smile and say, "We do seem to be going through plenty of both." At Edward's instruction, I lower myself into one of the indicated seats, the one farthest from the desk.

He eagerly slides into the other, then adjusts it to better face me. "A sign of a job well done on your part, I'm certain."

I settle back into the chair, my hands in my lap. "Emm said dinner would be delightfully delicious tonight."

"I look forward to it. Would you like a drink?" He gestures to the table between the chairs, a new addition, I notice.

I arch an eyebrow. "Are you offering me brandy?"

"I am. I thought a lady such as you would have a . . . stronger palate."

I offer a light laugh, not really able to help it. "You are correct, sir. Thank you."

He pours, then offers me a bit of amber liquid in a crystal glass. Our fingers touch briefly and my skin crawls. I take a quick sip to mask it. The burn is unpleasant, but I bear it. "Ooh. That will warm you at night." I set the glass on the small table between the chairs, then take a steadying breath. "Mr. Rochester, sir. I wanted to apologize."

He pauses where he'd started to lift a glass to his lips. "For?"

"For my . . . earlier refusal of your generous offer. You see, this is my first ever official position of employ, the first time I'm in control of my life and what happens to it. And the Austin wedding is the first event of its kind that I've ever been invited to as well, and by my employer of all people."

"Seems you're in for many firsts under my roof," he murmurs.

I try to ignore the comment and press on. "Yes, well, as such, I believed accepting your proposal would have been the equivalent to, perhaps, accepting a loan from someone to whom I had no significant personal attachment. Inappropriate. And, I admit, I panicked. But I've had time to further consider your proposal, and the circumstances surrounding it. I've decided . . ."

The way Edward's eyes move over me makes me feel like I'm covered in mud.

"To accept your invitation," I say quickly. "As your friend." This is the last thing I desire, especially after learning of his true nature and that of the secrets he keeps. But Edward is not the only one capable of manipulating people and circumstances. Accepting his invitation means I can guarantee his absence from Thornfield for an extended period of time. Long enough for someone to search his study for irrefutable evidence of his wrongdoing or anything else that might aid us in Bertha's escape. Who will that someone be? I will cross that bridge when I come to it. For now, I will focus on tonight, on dinner, and on trying not to recoil every time my host draws near.

At my words, Edward smiles. It appears easily on his handsome face, and I am reminded that the devil himself was said to have been beautiful.

"Thank you, Jane. I promise you will enjoy yourself." He reaches for my hand, but I snatch it away, covering the motion by grasping and raising my glass.

"Very well. Shall we toast to better understandings?"

He mirrors the action. "And many more firsts. As friends, of course."

As he swigs, I sip. The burn might have been pleasant any other time, but today I cannot help but imagine I've been poisoned. Acid slides down my throat instead of liquor.

As Edward pours himself another—he finished the first after our toast—I let my gaze trail over the still-singed areas on the floor that haven't been covered by the new rug. Well, the rug isn't exactly new. "Is this from the second-floor drawing room?" Perhaps the chair is from there as well.

"Pardon?" he asks, sipping his new drink.

I tap my toe against the rug, and the faintest puff of dust rises into the air. "This is certainly the rug from the second-floor drawing room."

The look Edward gives me is a curious one. "How . . . astute of you to notice."

"Oh, I . . . remember from when I first played hide-and-seek with Adèle. That day you found me on the third floor?" I watch closely for a reaction that doesn't come. Edward continues to gaze at me evenly. "I tripped on the edge, so I'd recognize it anywhere." I make a show of looking around the room again. "I suppose the curtains from there wouldn't really match." I force a bit of amusement into my tone to disguise my inquiry and gesture to where one of the windows now sits naked.

I want him to think I'm genuinely curious, not that I have any ulterior motives for asking. It's a dangerous line of questioning, knowing what I know, but one I would have pursued even if I were unaware of Bertha. That is why I ask it. I don't want him to think I'm acting unlike myself.

He chuckles faintly, though there doesn't seem to be any real mirth behind it. "No, but the color and cloth combination I requested has to be specially made. They'll deliver them by the end of the week."

"Lovely." I lift the glass in cheers of this "good news." "Wouldn't want people to be able to see everything you're hiding."

That does earn a reaction. He coughs faintly into his glass, patting his chest as he does so. "What I'm hiding?"

"Through the window," I say, and smile. "Wouldn't want anyone to just be able to glimpse the secrets of the mysterious Edward Rochester."

"Ah! Ah." He gives another forced laugh. "I suppose not."

There's a knock at the door, and I say a silent prayer of thanks as Edward moves to open it. Emm steps through, pushing a cart similar to the one that had been in here the night of the fire. She places it in front of the chairs and removes the two trays. The smell of beef, stewed vegetables, and grains fills the air and, despite my unpleasant company, my mouth waters. I realize I haven't eaten very much today. Too . . . distracted.

She pours us each a glass of wine and then departs.

"Thank you," I call after her.

"Indeed." Edward settles into his chair, taking a deep sip of his brandy.

The two of us eat in amicable silence. The clinking of silver against china fills the quiet. I eat some and drink a bit of the wine—my preference to the now unfinished brandy—though I am careful not to take too much. I need my wits about me.

"So," Edward begins, taking up his now empty brandy glass and moving to get a bit more. "About the Austin wedding."

My grip tightens on my cutlery. I do not wish to speak more of this cursed wedding. But I know I must.

Drink in hand, he retakes his seat. He sips, waits a beat, then sets the glass down, his eyes lifting to mine. His expression is open, lending his face a vulnerability that I might have fallen for had I not learned the truth today. And such truths. "Jane, I wanted to—"

"Do you think you'll remarry?" I blurt. I need a moment. To think, to be sure of my next actions or words.

His mouth snaps shut, and he gazes at me with what I believe to be genuine shock. It only breathes but a moment before he shutters it away behind that carefully constructed mask of his.

I take a bite of my meal while I wait for him to answer. It's a fair question, one that isn't technically about his wife. At least not yet.

"Why do you wish to know?" he finally asks, his voice measured.

Because you imprisoned your wife and likely murdered your lover. But I don't say this. Instead, I simply shrug. "I've known a widow or two in my time. One felt her husband could never be replaced and was content to live the rest of her life alone. The other quickly remarried, felt she did not have a choice. I've always found the various responses to such circumstances, while unfortunate and of course grievous, to be somewhat sweet. A testament to the *love* between husband and wife."

Edward wipes at his mouth with his napkin before flinging it onto the table. His eyes flicker dangerously when he looks at me. "I may. I may not, and it's not a topic I wish to discuss."

And I know when not to press my luck, as it were. "Very well." I nod and refocus on my meal.

Edward, however, continues to stare at me. His hands press to the arm of his chair, fingertips tapping erratically. "What of you, Jane? Do you intend to marry at all? Have a family?"

Now it is my turn to sputter faintly. "I beg your pardon?"

"Do you want children, Jane?"

Even though I hear it again, I am still surprised by it. That is a question I did not expect. "I . . . imagine I might. Someday. I've never really had a family. I mean, I have extended family, yes, but I'm not particularly fond of them."

"Oh?"

"Does that surprise you? You aren't the only one with an uncomfortable past. Perhaps we can exchange stories, someday."

"Perhaps not." His tone is tight. His words clipped.

"Hiding from the truth is not helpful, Edward."

His eyes narrow. "What do you mean?"

"I mean . . . I understand the past is hurtful. What happened to your wife."

"I said—"

"I know. But sometimes what we want isn't what's best for us."

"If you know what's best for *you*, you'll silence yourself."

I blink in surprise. "Excuse me?"

"I already told you, I don't wish to speak on it. Don't test my ire on this matter, or you will regret it sorely." There's a weightiness to his threat, an undercurrent of malice I've glimpsed in him here and there, more and more as of late. Of what makes him capable of what he's done to other women in his life.

I draw in a slow breath, my mind working over the words available to me. I must choose my next ones carefully. "You agreed that we are friends."

"I did," he says in a low and even tone that betrays none of the danger beneath. Like the still surface of water concealing monsters from myths.

"As your friend, you should know I would risk your anger if I thought it would help."

"And who said you need to be so damn helpful, hmm? God almighty, can't you mind your business?"

"I'm simply asking because I fear . . . I think Adèle might oftentimes feel she is to blame for your poor demeanor. Children concoct more elaborate fantasies from less."

He snorts. "So, my demeanor is poor now."

"It could stand to be improved," I press without missing a beat. "My point is, your desire to escape your past could be affecting her in ways you hadn't considered. I doubt you've spoken to her about it all, explained everything?"

"Of course not. She's a child, how could she possibly understand?"

"I bet she could, if you give her a chance." And I'm struck with another idea. One that might not work, but is worth a try. "And I bet, once you explained everything, not only would it strengthen your relationship with her, it would open other avenues for her. For instance, did you know she has no friends? I've asked."

"She has you."

"But I'm not her age. Having someone you can relate to in that regard is essential for a young lady. Knowing your place among your peers and all."

"What does this have to do with my past?" He swallows what remains of his brandy in one go, and my throat burns just watching. "Which you continue to bring up despite my many requests you don't?"

"If your late wife had family, perhaps Adèle has cousins she could write to or visit. Or . . . something like grandparents could be a balm. Just so she doesn't feel alone all the time. I know she isn't your blood relation, but the bonds could be genuine despite this." I hope my ruse works and feel it might when Edward falls silent in what I believe is genuine contemplation.

"So you're curious about my wife's family." The hard edge to his words is back. "In case Adèle has cousins?"

"Well . . . yes. Your late wife's family is your family, after all, and thus, in some part, Adèle's. She is not your blood relation, so I'm fairly certain neither you nor anyone else has considered this possible connection for her, and she does need to form connections. You don't even have to be involved!" I add on. "If it's too painful for you, I'll take care of everything. I just need more parchment, envelopes, and an address or two to send the letters."

The silence that spills between us is deafening. That contemplative look remains on his face, and for a moment I pray that my ruse might bear fruit.

"Have you mentioned this little idea of yours to Adèle?" he asks.

"No, I thought to get your permission before—"

"Good. Don't. And don't speak of my wife or her family again, to me or Adèle, am I clear?"

My mouth works briefly, disappointment making my face hot. I purse my lips together and nod. So much for that.

"Dinner is over," he mutters, and stands before stalking over to his desk. "As is the conversation. I wish to be alone." He lowers himself into his chair, glaring at me the entire time. "Get out."

✑ 24 ✑

HER SPELL

JANE . . .

With dinner being rather eventful, I'm more than glad to take my leave of the study and Edward. I make my way to the kitchen, where Adèle and Emm chat over dinner, the smell of biscuits lifting into the air.

Adèle looks up as I enter. Emm does as well.

"That was quick," she says.

"He wanted to be left to his work after we finished," I say, my jaw and words tight.

"I take it things went well?" Emm looks at me in that way that people sometimes get when they seem to be reading more of you than you'd hoped to reveal. "The mister behaved himself?"

"Well enough," I say in answer to both questions, though the sigh in my words possibly gives more away than I'd wanted.

Adèle straightens in her chair. "You're all right?" she asks, her voice small but firm.

"She looks all right to me," Emm says.

"I'm fine." I look to the oven. "It smells like the biscuits are nearly done."

"A second batch." Emm pushes to standing and moves to peer in at them. "There will be plenty for all."

"Set mine aside, please. I'm full. Dinner was delicious, by the way."

"I told you it would be." Emm winks.

And I smile. She seems to be magical like that.

I look at Adèle. "Why don't you spend the rest of the evening helping Emm with her biscuits. I've a few letters I must write, and I need a bit of time to go over your lesson plan we discussed earlier." I hope she can understand what I'm not saying as well.

The girl nods, her lips tight in determination.

Emm fusses with her apron. "I'd better go make sure someone nabbed the cart from the study. Won't take long, then you can be on your way."

"Thank you, Emm," I call as she disappears into the hall.

The instant Adèle and I are left alone, I step around the table in order to wrap an arm about her shoulders. "Finish with the biscuits, then come find me. Be sure to sneak a couple for me, hm?"

She gazes up at me, her lips pursed, the light in her eyes an uncertain one. I wrap my other arm around her and squeeze. "I'm all right," I whisper into her hair. "It will all be all right. Especially with biscuits," I say, louder this time.

She squeezes me before finally withdrawing. "Do you have a plan? To help Bertha?" Her voice is quiet, but I still glance around, toward the closed door that leads to the back of the house, then the doorway where Emm disappeared just moments before.

"Maybe. At least the bare beginnings of one, but this is not the place for such conversation."

She nods and squeezes her arms around by waist.

I kiss the top of her head. "Go on and finish eating. And I meant what I said about sneaking me a few biscuits."

The smile that pulls on her face soothes my sore heart.

On the way back to my room, my mind turns over the impossible task before me once more. Free Bertha, or somehow get word to her family. I didn't think to have her write the address down for me when we were with her before, and I'm not sure when I'll be able to get it from her, even if Adèle feels able to try the method I've been devising for carrying notes between us.

In truth, I'm not completely comfortable with her taking such a risk, and I don't believe I ever will be. At least, not when I haven't risked the same myself. And if the letters are discovered on her, our ruse will fall apart. No, I need to leave her out of it, as best I can.

By the time I've reached my room, I've an idea of sorts. Not the best idea, but it's there. I spend my evening writing a letter to Bertha's parents.

Dear Mr. and Mrs. Mason,

My name is Jane Eyre. You don't know me, but I know your daughter, Bertha. I am an employee of her husband, Edward Rochester, who has been keeping her locked away in Thornfield Hall since bringing her to England. I wish I had time to completely explain the circumstances under which I've come to know your daughter, but they are unpleasant, and I would rather spare you those details.

Bertha is physically well, but a prisoner here. I am trying to devise a way to free her, but with Mr. Rochester's sphere of influence, I've little opportunity to do so without risking provoking him. I've reason to believe that he has killed in the past to maintain this charade he's built around himself, and the last thing I would want is for either your daughter or myself to end up his next victim.

Please, if this letter finds you, send help as soon as you can. If we manage to find freedom beforehand, I will write to tell you. Bertha loves and misses you terribly, and she wanted me to tell you that your Little Bird needs help, so you would believe my words are true.

In the meantime, I will do all that I can to protect your daughter.

In service,
Jane Eyre

It took me hours just to write those few lines. The ink is splotched here and there where my pen rested for too long as I tried to think of what to say and how to say it. I wanted to convey the urgency of the situation but didn't want them to fear the worst.

I'm rereading the page and my script for what feels like the tenth time when a faint knock sounds at my door, and I in turn knock my knees against the bottom of my desk when I jump.

"One moment," I call as I massage away the sting with one hand, and carefully place the letter in a drawer.

I open the door to find Adèle and Emm standing there, a plate of biscuits in Adèle's hands.

"Special delivery!" Emm sings, smiling brightly as I step back to allow the two of them into the room. "I'm afraid I tinkered a bit with your recipe, but I'll let the results speak for themselves."

"Oh, did you?" I bite into an offered biscuit, and the swell of sweetness and cinnamon on my tongue does wonders for my worried mind. "Oh, they're delectable," I say around a mouthful of soft deliciousness.

"Extra butter and sugar always does the trick." She winks. "Among other things. Now then! Biscuits are delivered; think you'll be all right with going off to bed now?" she asks of Adèle.

Shocked, I glance toward the window to see the sun has set and the sky is barely burning with what's left of its radiance. I was so caught up in writing the letter, I hadn't noticed! And the fire in my hearth had provided enough light I couldn't tell the change.

"Oh goodness, I'm so sorry. I didn't realize the time."

Emm waves off my concern. "Think nothing of it. I was happy to keep an eye on the wee one. We even planned tomorrow's dinner together."

"Thank you," I say to Emm. "Really." And I wonder again if we shouldn't tell her about Bertha and Edward, but I want to check with Bertha herself first. "I'll get her to bed."

Emm nods. "Very well. I'll see the both of you for breakfast, then."

"Good night," I call, closing the door behind her and facing Adèle, another apology on my lips. "I'm so sorry, I didn't realize . . . I was writing a letter to Bertha's parents. Though I've no idea where or how to send it."

"I could slip her a note asking for an address," Adèle offers.

"You could, though I'm not completely resolved to having you take such large risks." Yet I'm certain almost any plan I come up with would call for just that.

"I want to." She lifts her chin, jutting it out a bit. "I want to help. I couldn't help Maman; I want to help Bertha."

The slight waver in her voice pulls at my heart, and I feel my resolve coming undone. I heave a sigh, taking another bite from the biscuit I've been holding. "Let me sleep on it."

Adèle nods, not looking at all disappointed. I didn't say yes, but I also didn't say no.

"Come on, then. Let's get you to bed."

I lead Adèle back to her room and get her changed and into bed quick enough. She's asleep only a handful of pages into the book, and I find I'm grateful. I'm not certain I had the usual one to two chapters in me tonight.

After tucking the blankets around her, I make my way back to my own room and prepare for bed myself. I climb beneath the covers and lie there, staring into the dark, waiting for the fatigue that has been crawling through me since leaving Bertha's closet to finally claim me. Only it doesn't.

I'm not sure how much time passes before I finally throw the blanket aside and sit up. I can't sleep. Because I can't quiet my mind. It's still trying to figure out a way through all this, and I need . . . I need Helen. She was always there to talk me through my plots and ploys at Lowood, offering advice or suggestions. Sometimes fruitful, but usually just to aid me in slogging through the mess inside my own head. I need to talk this out with someone, and there's only one person I can do so with.

So, before I think better of the foolish endeavor I'm about to undertake, I press a few pillows beneath my blanket to create what I hope is a convincing ruse of me lying in bed. There's no reason to think anyone would come checking to make sure I was still here, but old habits die hard, and such a ploy was necessary whenever Helen and I would sneak off for a moment alone together, then eventually I would go to be by myself.

Pushing the thoughts aside and breathing through the sudden tightness in my throat, I head for the door, though I pause when I catch sight of something in the faint dimness of the moonlight. The plate of biscuits still sits on the table where Adèle placed it. I pick it up, and then, with a deep breath, I slip out of the room.

The house is silent and still, like a giant beast fast asleep, as I move through its bowels. I walk along slowly, allowing my eyes to adjust to the darkness brightened here and there in beams or patches of nighttime glow that manages to peek through windows or skylights. I move as fast as I dare, which is still fairly slow, keeping both eyes and ears out for anyone who may similarly be walking the halls to clear their mind after troubling dreams and to grab a late-night snack. At least, that is the story I'm prepared to tell.

Eventually, I make my way up three flights of stairs, to the forbidden wing of the house and the hallway I'm mostly certain leads to Bertha's room. I'm not entirely sure—Thornfield looks so different at night—but when I approach a door and notice the plethora of locks upon it, I know I've made it to the right place.

Hurrying, or as close to it as I can manage, I enter the adjacent room and close and lock the door behind myself, just in case. I'm careful to hold the knob so I can slowly release the tumbler in silence, and do the same with the latch. Then I listen for signs of anyone else stirring, coming to check. But there is nothing but silence and shadow, and I breathe a sigh of relief.

Crossing to the closet, I'm still careful to be quiet as I lower the boards we placed earlier. I'm halfway through the hole, my nightgown catching on the splintered wood, when a voice rises from farther in the room.

"Who is there?" Bertha whispers in the shadows.

"It's me. Jane." I hurry to my knees, my eyes narrowed in the darkness. I blink rapidly, surprised at my sudden difficulty seeing when I had been able to navigate the house just moments ago.

A hand presses to my elbow, startling me.

"Sorry," Bertha says when I jump. "I'm here." Her fingers are warm and soft, and I press mine over them to squeeze.

"Why are *you* here?" she asks, her words ghosting along my cheek where she has leaned in to keep her voice down. "What have you found?"

"Nothing, yet." I feel my own disappointment threatening to pull me under; I can only imagine how she feels. "But I have a plan, or the beginnings of one. And I wrote a letter to your parents."

She's so close I hear her breath catch.

"I need to know where to send it. Could you write down the address for me?"

"O-of course." Bertha moves away from me, and there's the faintest hint of jasmine left in her wake. Her chain rattles ever so slightly and I hurry forward to take hold of it, lifting it from the ground.

She pauses, and though I can't see her, I hear the shift of her feet against the floor. She's no doubt looking at me, wondering what I'm doing.

"So they don't make so much noise," I whisper in answer to a question she didn't ask.

She doesn't say anything, but instead moves for the window again, the chain tugging lightly in my grasp. It's heavy, but not so much that I can't hold it comfortably, letting the cold, hard links run over my fingers instead of noisily along the floorboards.

There's the strike of a match, the faintest thump, and then the light of the lantern explodes across the darkness. Bertha stands there blowing out the match as gold illumination folds in around her, draping over her head and shoulders like an enchanted cloak, falling against her light brown skin, setting it aglow.

This time my breath catches as I take her in. She's just standing there, but in the blue nightgown folding around her body, dipping to follow each curve thanks to how she's turned, she looks like the sun herself come to stand before me.

And, like that, I am under her spell.

25

SPEAK

BERTHA . . .

I've never been a self-conscious girl. What with people telling me how pretty I am since I was in swaddling clothes, I learned early on how to manipulate a room and those in it for what I wanted. When other girls would gasp after I said or did something too bold, and their mothers would titter disapprovingly behind their fans about my "lordly" bearing, Maman would always find some way to make sure my confidence was seen as an asset, something to be desired.

Fortunate is a man who wins a wife who knows how to run her house.

If I were looking for a partner in life, I'd want someone who knows how to live it.

Never too soon to learn the value of being able to keep one's head in all situations.

I have received all manner of glances and stares in my life. But when I turn from pulling the board free from my window and find that Jane Eyre is staring at me . . .

I forget myself completely.

The way her eyes hold me in place steals just enough of my strength that I have to lean back against the wall.

"W-what?" I ask, my voice flaking away under a tide of insecurity the likes of which I've never known.

"What?" Jane asks in turn as she tilts her head, like she's unaware of the way the air between us has thinned the slightest bit, leaving me somewhat breathless and feeling all the more foolish.

Perhaps I had imagined her widening eyes and the rise of her chest, when it was my own breath that caught. Especially when I noticed the chains in her hands, her fingers curled, as if ready to pull me toward her.

"Nothing," I mumble, far too low for her to hear. "You were just . . ." I wave one hand, giving my mouth time to catch up with the words bouncing around in my mind. "Standing there, staring." That's it. I've imagined the entire thing. "I thought something was wrong."

"No! No, nothing's wrong," Jane says as I silently scold myself for imagining things. "Besides you being trapped here, of course. I was simply imagining how he might like being trapped in here. Locked away."

I shake my head as I step past her and toward the bed. "I've wondered the same myself so many times. Would that I could see his face when the locks latch."

"If all goes according to plan, you may get the chance."

I want to believe her. Desperately. And I am determined to have my freedom one way or another. "Let me get something to write with."

It doesn't occur to me that I'm revealing one of my greatest secrets until I'm pulling the paper and pencils free, but I don't stop. I can trust Jane, something inside me says. Something reassuringly certain. I settle onto the bed, and Jane does so as well. That's when I notice she's brought something, the shapes distinct even in the low light.

"Biscuits?" How absurd. And sweet. I feel the giggle threaten to bubble up. Heavens, when was it I last laughed? I don't remember.

"Yes. Adèle made them. I thought . . . well, they won't make things better, but they can't make them worse. Unless you don't like sweets. I'm sorry if you don't, I didn't think to ask, not that I would've had a chance to ask before now, I just . . . assumed . . ."

She brought them for me. This fact stuns me briefly, enough so I'm not sure what to say in response. It's been so long since anyone has shown me kindness unpartnered from some cruelty, that I'm not exactly sure how I should respond. Then I remember what one does with biscuits, and that I likely seem ungrateful sitting here like this. So I take one up and bite into it.

The crumbly blend of spice and sweetness melts against my tongue, and I'm half-certain this is the best biscuit I've ever eaten. I can't help but sigh my delight as I barely resist shoving the rest of it into my mouth. "They're delicious." An understatement.

Jane smiles, her gaze softens, and she lifts her chin just a bit. "I'll tell Adèle. Glad you like them."

I finish the biscuit off before turning my attention to scrawling out the information she came for, offering the slip of paper over even as I nab another from the plate. "That's where you can send the letter. What did you say? In the letter," I ask before biting into the treat. This one tastes better than the first, though I don't let the deliciousness distract me.

Jane's brow furrows, and for a moment I wonder if she's having trouble recalling.

"I . . . I told them the truth. That you're being held prisoner in your own home—"

Anger strikes through me hot as lightning. "Thornfield will *never* be my home." I'm not sure how I managed to keep from shouting, though I have learned fury burns cold as well. Sometimes it blazes bright and hot enough I feel I may burst just holding it inside me, and sometimes . . . sometimes it seeps through me, blistering my being until there is nothing left but numbing bitterness. There is ice in my heart, even though my words are fire on my tongue. I will burn. Or I will freeze.

But then there's the faintest touch against my hand where it rests in my lap. Jane's fingers squeeze mine.

"I said they shouldn't believe whatever they've been told by Mr. Rochester or anyone else." She scoots toward me, the bed shifting under her weight. Her eyes find mine in the dark, and I can see her worry for me in her gaze. Her genuine concern, so different from when Grace tuts about how I need to do this or that for my own good. "That they need to come or send help as soon as possible," Jane continues. "I was certain to assure them that you're unharmed, physically. You are, aren't you?"

I hold her gaze, because I can do nothing else in that moment. I can say nothing else. There is nowhere for the fire or the frost to go. I'm . . . trapped. And yet, Jane is here to rescue me. The truth of that is suddenly clear. Even though she declared this her goal hours ago, some part of me hadn't been able to fully believe until now, sitting in the dark, the moon as the only witness to this girl's genuine concern for me. I believe.

The flames die down, and the frost thaws the barest bit.

I pull away, not wanting to let them go just yet. The anger keeps me going. "As I can be, I suppose," I finally manage, my gaze falling.

"I told them their Little Bird needs help," she continues, "as you said. Little Bird; is that a pet name?"

"Mmm." I'm glad for the change in subject. "Yes. From when I was a child, though my mother used it clear up to when I left her standing on the New Orleans port. It's because Bertie, which I am called by friends, sounds like birdy."

"That's incredibly sweet. And New Orleans." She sits back, though her eyes don't leave me. In fact, they move over me, appraising, and her lips curl slightly. "That explains the accent."

"I have an accent?" Again, laughter escapes me, just the barest bit, but it's there, and I wonder if Jane isn't some secret sorceress casting a spell to bring me joy. "I couldn't tell."

"Oh yes, quite distinct. Beautiful, really. That's where you're from, then?"

"Born and raised."

Somewhere in the house, there's a thud. We both go quiet as the air seems to thicken, the silence becoming a scream to fill the nothing around us. I listen, straining to try to hear something, anything, any sign of approaching steps. But they don't come.

Eventually we relax, and I all but melt against my pillows in relief. I've not felt the fear of discovery so keenly in so long, and it's only because I've allowed myself to hope.

Jane has given me hope.

"You . . . should probably go," I whisper, trying to breathe through the quaking that's moving through my middle. "I don't want you to get caught."

"I won't. Get caught, that is. This isn't my first time sneaking around in the dark." And then she lifts a biscuit and chomps into it like we haven't spent the last few moments too afraid to breathe too loudly.

I can't help it, I'm laughing again. This time, I have to lift my hand to help muffle it. I've lost all sense this night, it seems. And yet, for some reason, I don't care.

"I'll go eventually, but first? First, I'd like to hear more about your home. Your family, your life before all this. If you don't mind."

When I shake my head, it's so subtle, I don't know if she'd notice, so I answer aloud. "No, no. I don't mind, I just . . . thinking about home, about being away from here, hurts. So, I don't do it much. Plus, no one listens."

"I'd like to listen."

I've lost count of the number of times I've been struck silent since Jane crawled out of my closet with her plate of biscuits. It's the oddest thing. I'm not one to get tongue-tied around others, and here this girl has managed to steal whole sentences from me. Or, rather, in an unusual turn of events, has managed to get me to hand them over. I can't remember when I last eagerly carried on conversation with another soul. Even though we have to do it in the dark, whispers shared in a breath of space between us, I'm glad for it.

I've missed being with someone.

"I miss the willow trees," I murmur. It's a silly thought, but one that doesn't hurt so much. So I start with that. "They won't be in bloom for months, but it's always a spectacle." I close my eyes and sink even farther into my pillows. "I remember how they looked standing watch across the lawns as the wind snatched at their leaves and plucked at some of the freshly formed blossoms. They litter the air like diamonds. Beautiful, like something out of a dream. Can you picture it?"

"Yes," Jane whispers, her voice awed. "I can."

I paint a picture of my home from the memory of my heart, and speak of my beloved New Orleans. I speak of my friends and family, what they would likely be doing right now, who would be hosting what parties and why everyone who's anyone would be in attendance. I speak of my life before Edward Rochester, a life that feels worlds and eons away from now. Back before I knew how easily dreams could turn to nightmares.

When she asks how I came to be here at Thornfield, and assures me I don't have to say if it hurts me, I affirm there is little pain in the telling, save wishing I had been less naïve. For the night Edward took my hand, kissed it, then danced with me, was to me like something out of a fairy tale. I tell her how that same enchantment carried through the following weeks, casting a spell over everything. The fact that a handsome lord of vast lands and wealth had taken an interest in me seemed to set the bar for the other gentlemen of New Orleans. At least a dozen more suitors sent their letters over the next few days, all of them adorning gifts of flowers, fine dresses, and a number of items that would make any young lady swoon. The memory is still fantastical.

I remember how Maman was beside herself with excitement, though not for the suitors themselves. It was the ritual of the thing, and what lay at the end.

"This one promises to come calling before the week is out," she had said one pale blue morning as she leafed through the letters while we broke fast in the parlor. "And this one says he will arrive by this afternoon. Clearly you are a priority."

"You speak as if you don't already have the house in order to receive the whole of the parish." Papa flipped through his newspaper, held up as a barrier between himself and the "circus," as he called it, but I knew better. He was just as eager and attentive about all of this as Maman.

Maman huffed a breath through her nose. "That is simply because your wife is always prepared to take advantage of any and all circumstance for the betterment of this family."

"A blessing we all reap the rewards of." Papa took a loud sip of his coffee.

Maman set the letters aside. "Hopefully this will spur Rochester into acting quickly. Prepared as I am, a swift proposal will no doubt save a lot of time and effort."

"And money," Papa murmured.

Maman ignored him, instead looking to me. "Are you finished, dear? I want you to try on all three dresses I have arranged so we can decide which looks best."

"Nearly." I'd honestly picked over my meal more than partaken of it, my stomach was so tied in knots. I wanted to see him again, I realized. Wanted to hear his voice, wanted to watch the dimples in his cheeks appear when he smiled ever so faintly.

Nauseating. That must be what people mean when they say someone is love-sick, but I didn't know better at the time.

"Good." Maman sat back in her large, cushioned chair and plucked a few grapes from the tray on the table. "I remember my days of being courted. I received just as many letters as this." She pats the pile. "Though not all at once, mind you. However, there was one note in particular that stuck out amongst them from the very beginning." Her eyes trailed across the table. "I could tell whoever wrote it was . . . different."

Papa flipped through his paper, clearing his throat faintly.

"It was six pages long, describing my beauty, the way the sun itself seemed dim in my presence, how my voice could put a choir of angels to shame. Compliment after compliment." Maman waved her hand with a flourish as she described the details of the letter. "That was simply the first two pages. Then came the promises to take care of me, assurances that I would want for nothing. That my children, should I desire to have them, would want for nothing. That I deserved the world and everything in it. I must admit, I was smitten by page four."

I smiled as Papa flipped another page, though he'd gone backward. I doubted he noticed, being so distracted by pretending he wasn't absolutely engrossed in Maman's tale.

She sighed and sipped her tea. "But then I had to settle for your father."

That's when Papa unwittingly gave up the game, sputtering as he lowered the paper, his light brown cheeks puffed. "Settle?! Now see here!"

Maman and I burst into laughter, which only grew louder when we noticed his confused expression. Though he caught on quick enough.

"I swear, Faye, you can be the devil's own sometimes." He snapped his paper open.

Maman rose from her seat, wiping tears from her eyes. "Now, now, Ernest, no pouting." Coming around behind his chair, she leaned in and folded her arms around his neck from behind. "After all, according to your essay, my sense of humor is one of the numerous reasons you asked me to marry you."

Papa grunted but said nothing, though I noticed the way he tilted into her.

They sat there like that for what felt like eternity in an instant, basking in one another, her cheek pressed to the top of his head. One of his hands came to hold her wrists where they crossed over his chest.

Eventually Maman kissed the top of his head, right in the center of his bald spot—it was slightly rouged from the many times she'd already done so today—and withdrew. "I need to get Bertha ready."

I took that as my cue, and both of us departed the parlor, Maman talking about which dress she thought she'd like most and me lost in the memory of the moment my parents just shared. So in love, even after all that time. It warmed my heart, and filled it with a desire I hadn't known until then.

I wanted what my parents had. What was shared between them. What they gave to one another and created anew together. I wanted the magic only love seemed capable of casting. And I'd believed, hoped, I'd possibly found it in Edward.

I tell Jane of these desires in me that have turned to regret. I share with her stories that had been shared with me, of Maman and Papa's courtship. She smiles and the apples of her cheeks rise with her soft laughter. I revel in the sound of it, in her. I don't want this night to end. I don't want her to go.

So I continue to speak. And speak, and speak, and speak, unable to stop the words even if I tried. They flow out of me in place of the tears I can feel rise to burn the backs of my eyes but never fall free. I am like a cup running over with water, full to bursting. And though I feel my breath quicken, and my lungs burn as if I am drowning, I *am* drowning, yet I keep pouring, because—for the first time in so very long—there is someone who will drink. Someone who will listen. Someone who will hear me. And I finally acknowledge that small part of myself buried deep in the darkness of my icy heart that had feared I would die here without anyone outside these wretched walls having ever known I lived.

That I live.

✺ 26 ✺

PROMISES

JANE . . .

I can't sleep.

According to the clock on the mantelpiece, it has been two hours since I returned to my room, and I *can't* sleep. My mind is filled with Bertha. Her face, her smile, her faint laughter, the way she looked standing in the moonlight.

When I close my eyes, I can easily picture her, but I won't trap her in that room in my thoughts. Instead, my mind conjures the willow trees she described when she told me of her home. She stands beneath one, draped in a powder-blue dress, all lace and frills, with a parasol resting against her shoulder. She's waiting. For what, I don't know.

I hope it's me.

The suddenness of that thought shakes me from my imaginings and I sit up, shoving aside the suffocating blankets and kicking my feet to the floor. A groan bubbles up inside me and I swallow it down while digging the heels of my palms into my tired eyes. I want to sleep. I should sleep.

But still I cannot.

Because I cannot rest while knowing the truth, her truth. The injustice of what's happened will not allow me to lie still.

"Be patient," I can hear my Helen say, as she had a dozen times before, whenever I grew anxious about anything.

The last time she said such words to me was on a night similar to this one, all silver light and sleepy shadows draped across the world. We'd snuck out of bed and, after nicking an apple to share from the kitchen, slipped out of one of the third-floor windows near the headmaster's office. The danger of getting caught was great, but this window in particular was the only place where the pipe for rain runoff had come loose from the side of the building; the two of us could use it and one another's help to climb to the roof.

The pipe wasn't fully broken, so Brocklehurst had yet to pay for its repair, but there was no telling when that could change. Still, the risk for a bit of uninterrupted privacy was well worth it. And, of course, there was the view. On clear nights, like this one, I could see all the way to the horizon as a thousand dancing lights floated across the heavens. They sparkled and shone and, though they seemed distant and cold, filled me with a warmth that seemed otherworldly. Though that could very well have been the result of Helen's hands up my skirts on many an occasion.

But not that night.

That night, my anger warmed me, though Helen did everything she could to cool it.

"Be patient," she had said.

"There's a difference between impatient and angry," I shot back at her. She set a hand on my shoulder, though I didn't move. My ire was still raw and fresh, and I didn't want it soothed. I stayed there with my knees lifted, my arms wrapped around them and my chin resting on top. I must have looked like a petulant child, but I didn't care.

"You misunderstand." Helen scooted closer, wrapped an arm around my back and rested her head on my shoulder. "You should be rightfully upset you were passed over for the teaching position, but I speak of the future." She toyed with my hair while she talked, pausing here and there when she was distracted by a loose strand or curl.

"What of the future?" I asked when it seemed she'd forgotten her train of thought again.

She blinked those big brown eyes at me and smiled. "Our future. Together. Leaving this place."

I sighed, some of my roiling emotions tempering. "You love teaching." She'd been doing it for nearly a year by then, and I had hoped to join her. "I don't want you to give it up."

"That's the beauty of me doing what *I* want." She winked, a hint of her laugh on the cool air. "You'll see. I'll save enough for both of us to go anywhere. You'll have your pick of teaching positions then." Her fingers coaxed mine free from where I gripped at my elbows. "We'll get a house together with room for a garden. I'll grow tomatoes and sprouts; you'll tend to the rosebushes."

"Rosebushes?" I asked around my own laughter.

"Oh yes, and mums. We'll have a little dog, a cat or two, and one day other little things, perhaps? It'll be perfect. So, be patient."

It sounded perfect. Enough so that I was able to let go of my anger in order to latch on to that dream. I'd never wanted something more in all my sixteen years than I wanted to reach that future Helen described. I tilted my head to rest against hers, then snaked my arm around her waist, holding her close. She felt thinner under the layers of her dress.

"Perfect," I repeated. "You promise?" I lifted my pinky from where our fingers were woven together.

She chuckled and curled her finger around mine, like we used to do when we were little girls. "I promise that and more." Then she pulled me close and we held one another until the sky threatened to pinken with the coming day.

That was the last night I sat on the roof beneath the stars with my Helen. The memory of it is burned into me, and I can see it as clearly as I can see the furniture in my room here at Thornfield, many miles away from Lowood.

I was robbed of her and all the promises we made to each other not six months later. Remembering is a bittersweetness that I almost cannot stomach, and yet that memory is what urges me from my rapidly cooling bed and to the chair at my desk. I light the lantern there and set out my pen and paper. Then I begin to write.

When the words have run dry and I've nothing else, I scrawl out a valediction and sign my name.

The rapping at my door sends my heart knocking just as hard, and I startle so badly I bump my knees against the leg of my desk. Again. Pain dances through my lower body and I hiss softly.

"Y-yes?" I call, hurriedly folding the letter and pressing it into an envelope. Then I slip the entire thing into a drawer, turning the small key in the lock that I've never had occasion to use until now.

"Oh, so you're awake," Emm's voice calls jovially. "And here I feared you'd died in the night, or been spirited away by some thief, to be so late."

"Late?" Alarm shoots through me. I look to the window to see more than the usual faint outline of light from when I normally wake. The sun is well into rising.

"Aye. When you and the wee one hadn't made your way to the kitchen by the time I finished breakfast, I feared the worst," Emm explains as I hurry around to get myself together for the day. "Well, perhaps not the worst, but I thought there might be reason."

"Y-yes!" I've flung my nightgown aside and have snatched articles from the drawers, more than I'll likely need but I don't care, leaving a bit of a mess in my haste. "Sorry! I didn't sleep well."

"Ah, it happens. Don't hurt yourself!" Emm calls when I bump into a chair while rushing, stubbing my toe and cursing faintly, though not faintly enough, it seems. "Take your time, I'll get the girl up and dressed and meet you in the kitchen."

"You don't have to do that!"

"Think nothing of it, lass. See you soon." Emm's steps fade before I can get a word in.

I'm left standing there, my thoughts spinning, Bertha's words bouncing between my ears. Despite Emm's insistence, I rush to get dressed, and am put together enough within moments. On my way to the door, I pause at the desk. I hesitate before unlocking it and withdrawing the letter, slipping it into the pocket on my skirts. If an opportunity presents itself, I'll find a way to get it to Bertha.

Carrying such a thing is a risk, but there is no reason to believe anyone suspects me, so this is fine. For now.

I will be fine, I attempt to reassure myself, and I repeat the thought again and again until I reach Adèle's room just in time to see her and Emm step out the door.

The girl's face lights up when she sees me and she moves in for a swift hug. I *oof* lightly as a bit of wind is knocked out of me before folding my arms around her.

"She was concerned." Emm watches, a smile on her face. "I told you Jane was fine, just slept in a bit is all. Happens to everyone."

"I'm sorry I made you worry," I say into Adèle's hair, rubbing her back gently.

She squeezes my waist.

"I had a dream you were locked up." Her voice is muffled, though I can still hear the tremble in her words.

My mind instantly goes to Bertha, and an odd flutter moves through me, along with a sharp pang of understanding for Adèle.

"Oh . . . oh, Adèle." I pull back so I can get her to look up at me. My fingers brush away a couple of stray tears from red cheeks. "It was just a bad dream. And you know what's best the morning after nightmares? A bit of dessert with breakfast." I look to Emm to confirm.

"Oh, I'm certain I'll be able to scrounge something up," Emm says, her smile widening.

I match it with my own and tap Adèle's chin lightly. "Right, then. Let's go."

We continue down the hall and are nearly to the kitchen when Grace shuffles into view from the adjacent corridor. Normally I ignore the old woman, as there is no love lost between us, and I intended to do the same this morning, though she's carrying something that snatches at my attention.

Panic sweeps through me, swift and debilitating, and I stumble to a stop before I can help myself.

Clutched in the old bird's bony fingers is the empty plate of biscuits I'd taken up to Bertha.

27

FOOLISH

BERTHA . . .

I practically fall out of the bed when the door suddenly swings wide, jarring me awake. I just manage to fetch my dressing robe in time.

"Breakfast, madam." Grace shuffles in and pauses, surprise written on her face as she takes in my appearance. "Sill in bed at this hour?" She tsks and moves to set the tray on the table.

In the hallway, Devin's gaze meets mine before he averts his eyes and turns aside.

At least one of them has some manners.

"And just what were *you* up doing in the wee hours of the night?" she asks as she sets out breakfast, and my entire body goes cold.

"Pardon?" I ask, hoping my voice doesn't betray my unease.

"Oh, nothing." Grace waves a hand dismissively. "I was just making a bit of fun. The governess was also late to rise this morning. Emmaline had to be sent in to wake her up."

"Ah," I say, to cover my sigh of relief. "I didn't sleep well," I offer by way of explanation.

"No? I'm sorry to hear that."

"No, you're not." The suddenness of my words surprises both of us, though when Grace looks at me, I hold her gaze, unwavering. I meant what I said, even if I didn't mean to say it out loud.

She goes to setting everything out, though as she works there's no attempt at small talk or conversation. Seems my words have robbed her of her own.

Good. I'm not in the mood to listen to her talk.

"I'll return to retrieve your dishes in an hour." Her task complete, she moves toward the door, though she pauses, her eyes on the bed. "What's that there?" she asks as my gaze drops to the blankets, and everything in me turns to stone.

The plate of biscuits, now empty, rests partially tucked beneath the corner of the blanket. A hasty, ill-thought attempt at concealing it, but there was nothing else to be done. And I know, mere inches away, rests the pages of my makeshift journal. I had been too slow in gathering them together after sharing them with Jane last night, and now they are but a flick of the wrist from being exposed.

Grace reaches.

My heart lodges itself in my throat.

She lifts the plate to inspect it, her brow furrowed.

I waver slightly, caught between the relief that she didn't lift the blanket and the dread that she's still discovered this much.

She looks at me. "What's this?"

My throat closes and I have to draw a quick breath through my nose to keep from gasping. "Dessert." My voice doesn't shake, despite the fact that the rest of me does. I clasp my hands together in front of me to hide their trembling. "It was left from last night."

Grace eyes the plate a moment, then looks to me again. Out in the hall, Devin has turned his attention toward the room again. He's even taken a few steps forward, abandoning his usual post of tilting against the opposite wall.

"It's not made of wood, so it can't be from last night." Grace turns and moves forward into the room, glancing around as she goes.

Devin fills the doorway with his presence.

I loose a shuddering breath and swallow thickly. "Fine," I say, letting some of my quivering into the word. "It's from last month. I kept my dessert to eat later and hid the plate in my drawer." I also let my shoulders sag in resignation. "I've been waiting for a chance to sneak it back onto another tray, but it's been wooden dishes ever since; I never had a chance." It's a flimsy lie, but I can't have them deducing the truth.

Devin snorts. "Broken china can cut as deep as any knife. You sure that wasn't your plan, ma'am?"

"If that was my plan, it would make more sense to break it, don't you agree?" I don't have to fake my glare. "I simply didn't want to get into trouble." My stomach turns as I lower my voice, happy and yet hating that I manage to sound chided. "Besides." I shake my leg to rattle the chain. "Broken plate or not, I wouldn't get far."

"Too true." Grace shakes the plate in the same way she's often wagged a finger. "You shouldn't conceal things like this. But it's good you told the truth. The master will be pleased at your improved disposition."

Another churn in my middle at the mention of Edward.

"Go on and have your breakfast before it cools."

The two of them depart, the locks clicking into place behind them. I don't go to the table, the unease moving through me having stolen my appetite. Instead, I lower myself onto the bed.

I wait until their steps fade and I'm certain I've been left alone before drawing back the blanket to gather the loose pages and quickly dropping to the floor to hide them away. It takes three tries to slide the floorboard into place because of how badly my hands shake. I tuck them between my thighs and squeeze, breathing deep, attempting to force calm that I know is unlikely to come.

It seems that Grace has accepted my lie, which is fortunate. Though I can hardly believe I allowed such a thing to happen. I should've sent the plate with Jane last night, but I didn't think . . . it never occurred to me. I was so wrapped up in being able to speak to another person, someone who wasn't a danger to me, that I let my guard down.

Jane Eyre got me to let my guard down.

That alone should be reason enough for me to mistrust her, to mistrust all this all over again, and yet the thought of her offers comfort to my still-rattled nerves. I shut my eyes and latch on to the fleeting feeling of warmth the memory of last night conjures. I can picture her face in the dark, the moonlight shining against her profile. She smiles at me, the expression gentle, as I speak of home. Of Maman and Papa and the willow trees behind the house.

I spoke of much last night, more than I've spoken to anyone for the better part of a year. In truth, I'd almost thought I'd forgotten how to have a civilized conversation.

For a moment, I wonder if I'm being foolish. This could be some elaborate ruse by Edward, to what end I'm not sure. Dangle hope and a chance at freedom in front of me, only to snatch it away with another betrayal. The cruelty alone would be adequate cause for him, I imagine.

But no, I won't think of him, not now. Not when my thoughts had been so pleasant just a moment before. And so, I let them return to last night and the serenity those few stolen moments with Jane provided.

I'd like more, I realize. Another chance to talk, to feel human again.

For now, I settle for the memory, and breakfast, which is cold by the time I start eating. No matter; I've little enough appetite as it is, considering I ate a plate of biscuits not that long ago. That thought invokes another smile. I'll have to thank Jane for them. The sweets and the smiles.

And I'm still smiling when a faint tap at the door takes me by surprise. At least, I think there was a tap at the door. I didn't hear anyone approach, and I don't hear anything else for another moment or two, before it happens again.

Tap. Tap tap tap.

That's when I realize that it's not coming from the door but from the closet. Before I have a chance to rise to investigate, the door swings open and Jane Eyre emerges, brushing at her skirts as she does.

"Jane," I murmur, keeping my voice low despite the way my heart leaps in surprise at seeing her here. "What are you doing here? Grace could be back at any moment!"

"I had to check on you." Jane crosses the room, her eyes roaming over me as she approaches, her brow furrowed in concern. "And Adèle is keeping her busy by asking the proper way of making a cup of tea. She'll likely give a demonstration, so I've time enough."

"And you won't be missed yourself?"

She waves a hand, as if my concerns are little more than dust to be swatted aside. "Yes, yes, I'm fetching something from my room. Enough about me; are *you* all right?" Her hands hover in the air, just shy of falling to my shoulders.

For a moment, I'm not sure what to say. My mouth works, but my mind hasn't caught up to provide words to speak. Eventually I stammer out, "I-I'm fine, why would—"

"I saw the plate," Jane whispers as her entire body sags with relief. "From the biscuits. Grace had it and . . . I'm so sorry, I should have thought to take it with me."

"Ah," I say as realization settles over my previously tumultuous mind. "Don't worry, I managed to explain it away. You're not the only one with a clever tongue." I smirk, hoping to dispel her concerns.

It seems to have worked because she lowers herself onto the bed beside me, despite my earlier warning about Grace's return. Adèle offering a distraction or not, it's too dangerous for her to be here. I start to say as much, but her hand falls to my knee, and my words are trapped in my throat.

"Good. I'll be more careful in the future. I promise." She squeezes and I swear I can feel the warmth of her touch through my gown.

I look up from where I had been studying her fingers. "Like now?" My brow arches high. I imagine I look like Maman often did when she scolded me or Papa.

Jane's gaze drops briefly before lifting to find mine through the veil of her lashes. "I was worried," she admits, her voice nearly too low for me to make out the words. "I had to know you were well."

Something . . . happens in my chest that I can't quite describe. It's a fluttery sensation that fills me up, but at the same time I feel like I've been emptied out, my insides replaced with clouds or mist. "Fine as I can be, at any rate." I breathe the words more than say them. Then I shut my eyes to gather myself. What in the world is wrong with me?

The touch at my shoulder causes me to jump.

Jane withdraws her hand quickly, her expression once more concerned, but now there's something else there in those brown eyes. "You're certain you're all right?"

"Yes," I sigh. "I'm just tired. We were up rather late last night."

The smile that pulls at her face is bright and beautiful, and her eyes play over me once more, this look very different from the worried one before. "Late morning? Me too. Sort of." She pushes herself to her feet, most likely intending to go.

And she should. I've already expressed how foolish it is for her to have come in the first place. And yet, I'm grateful she did.

"Here." There's a rustle of cloth as Jane fishes something from her skirts. An envelope. She holds it out to me.

"Oh." I reach to take it from her. "Thank you?"

"Read it when you like." Jane nods, her smile widening. "I'll try to come back tonight. If I don't, just leave a response in the closet." With that, she returns to the closet, lowering herself in order to climb through the wall.

I trail after her, my fingers playing over the paper of her letter, still folded and tucked against my palm. "Be careful," I whisper into the dark.

There's a rustle of fabric, and then silence descends. I don't hear the retreat of Jane's steps, nor the approach of others, so I assume she has slipped away without being noticed.

Again, my attention falls to the envelope, so I draw out the letter, unfold it, and read.

Bertha,

I know you have little reason to look for the good in anyone who works in this house, but I'm grateful you've extended such grace on my behalf. Grace that I in all rights do not deserve but will do everything in my power to honor.

As I said, I will send my letter to your parents as soon as I am able to deliver it to post myself, and whilst I wait for such an opportunity, I will look within Thornfield's walls for means to end your imprisonment too.

I'm grateful to you for sharing your story with me. Not just what's happened since meeting Edward, but what you've described of your home and life in New Orleans. It sounds lovely, and I imagine I'd like to visit someday. Your family sounds wonderful as well. I swear to you, I'm going to do all that I can to make sure you're able to see them again.

Sincerely,
Jane

My chest is a whirlwind while reading. It happens and again and again, and when I reach the end of the letter for the fourth time, I'm once more near to bursting with a swell of emotion I cannot quite place. I've grown rather adept at being able to find the sour in such sweet words, but I see none of that here. This girl is genuine. And foolish.

Very well, Jane Eyre. If you are foolish enough to make such a gamble, then perhaps I will be foolish enough to believe in you.

28

REGARDS

Jane,

Your last letter states that, despite my warning, you still intend to go through with the plan you described the other night? I must insist again that you take heed when matching wits with Edward. I would die before paying that coward any sort of compliment, but it would be foolhardy to underestimate him. He is a shrewd and cruel man whose machinations have thus far gone undetected by the wider world. His web, while relatively small, is strong. Keep a clear mind and watchful eye, lest you be ensnared.

Truth be told, I don't know if I believe you when you say that we can do this. That escape could come so easily. Even now, I fear this is some cruel trick by Edward, using you, using this, to buoy my hopes, only to sink them into deeper, darker waters. But Adèle trusts you, and that girl has more sense than most. I want to trust you. I do trust you. Forgive me for speaking my broken heart.

Regards,
Bertha

29

SINCERELY

Bertha,

I want to assure you one last time that you don't need to worry about the wedding. I am well aware of the danger Edward Rochester poses. I am also aware that men such as this do not often think twice when the world gives them what they want. By leaning into his attempts to enthrall me, I will be able to lead him from the end of the leash he's convinced he's placed around me. If anyone is in danger of being taken in, it is not I.

In addition, I maintain confidence that accepting the invitation ensures both Edward and Marsters are out of the house for an extended period. If you are able to hold Grace's and Devin's attention for any amount of time, it will leave only Emm to discover Adèle, and she rarely leaves the kitchen. It is a lot to trust a child with, but that girl is far more intelligent than many I have met, as you have mentioned yourself.

Though I must confess no small amount of worry concerning you. While I am away enjoying a night of feigned frivolity, you will still be a prisoner. And though I am aware how hard we work to put an end to this evil, it persists in this moment, and I cannot bear the thought. Yet I must, for you, bear the reality. Though I will go with him, know that my mind and heart are with you. And Adèle.

As always, please tell me if you desire anything from the kitchen or the garden, or even the town proper. I can add your requests to my own, and no one would be the wiser. I want to help you in every way I am able, and as always my focus is on your freedom. Take heart. We can do this.

Sincerely,
Jane

PS Apologies for the cold biscuits, but they are fresh. Made just this morning. I thought the kerchief, while less tidy than a plate, would be easier to hide when you're finished.

30

FURIOUSLY

Jane,

I worry. Despite your assurances. I worry very much. This is not a reflection on you or any lack of faith in your capability, merely my knowledge and understanding of that horrid man. I worry what he may do to you if he discovers anything that has transpired between us. If he were to feel you have outlived whatever usefulness he sees in you. That you should share a fate similar to mine or worse fills me with such dread and trepidation.

Perhaps my thoughts are selfish in part, as well. My worry is for you first and foremost, but I would be lying if I did not admit to some concern also for myself. I know not what I would do if one more good thing in this world were taken from me, and you are one such good and wonderful thing, Jane. The thought that he would harm you in any manner fills me with such a rage that I feel I am no longer myself in those moments. I am anger. I become fire. I would burn them all for harming you.

Please take care. Please be cautious. Please be careful.

Furiously,
Bertha

31

WONDERFULLY

Bertha,

I am at a loss for words in the face of your wrath. Knowing I am not the focus of your ire allows me the distance and safety to stand in awe of it and of you. I cannot remember a time anyone else was ever stirred to such severity, such ferocity on my behalf. My Helen was not quick to anger. She would defend me, vehemently in fact, in her own way. But her patience and peace are what often calmed the storm of my heart whenever it was stirred by anger.

It is strange, I must admit, that I feel a similar quiet come over me when I read your letters. When I glimpse your fire and feel its warmth even in cold paper and ink. I've no doubt your blaze would consume any and all dangers in our path were you given a chance to loose it. I pray you have such an opportunity, in the end. I pray your freedom, when hard-won, presents so perfect a prospect for recompence that your righteous anger would turn the night to day. For I know the pain of holding a sun's worth of rage inside.

You are a wonder, Bertha Mason. A marvel and a glory. In you I feel I have found my own furious maelstrom's match.

Wonderfully,
Jane

32

CORDIALLY

Jane,

It seems you are to repay me in kind for stealing your words, for now you've stolen mine. I've never heard nor read such passionate promises, though I imagine you are sincere in what you say.

You strike me as sincere about much. I've spent most of my time here braced for the next lie, the next cutting barb or cruel taunt, but it never comes. Not from you, or your letters. I look forward to them and the peace they bring. The peace you bring.

Much as I am loath to admit it, I find myself hopeful as of late. It is as fragile as a flower, but I guard it closely. Thank you for being the seed.

And please, be careful.

Cordially,
Bertha

PS The biscuits were delicious.

33

FONDLY

Bertha,

I'm happy you enjoyed the biscuits. It's my Helen's recipe, though I made a few adjustments. She always enjoyed things a little sweeter than I did, my Helen. You remind me of her in many ways. Just as strong, just as determined. Even your way with words. . . .

Have you ever tried your hand at writing? I don't wish to make light of all that has happened, but whenever you talk about your life before, I find myself transported to the places you describe. I can hear the people at the theater or the birthday party, the rise and fall of their conversation, their roll of laughter. I can picture your parents as they sweetly tease one another over breakfast concerning the prospect of your courting. I swear I can even smell the fruit and flowers on the table in your mother's parlor.

Even when you speak of this house and the people here, your words vibrate with the force of emotion, and I cannot help but be moved. It's as if I've given myself over to the tides to be swept out to sea, into the arms of the goddess Calypso hidden in the waves. I face her majesty, her might, and her rage, all with no fear of drowning. I don't know where these waters might carry me, but I am eager to find out. To say you inspire me is to understate the matter.

Fondly,
Jane

34

AFFECTIONATELY

Jane,

To answer your question, I've not given any thought to writing or any other pastimes. Perhaps I will give it more consideration in the future. A future away from here. A future I had begun to fear I would never see, but you are starting to change that.

Alas, I am no goddess, for surely no goddess would suffer such a flush at your words, which are equally powerful. Your words are as magic, and you have bewitched me. I like to think, had we met earlier in life, we might have been fast friends. An impossibility, as we were born with an ocean between us, but that is what dreams are for. And who is Helen? Tell me more about her, please?

Affectionately,
Bertie

ご 35 ご

DU BUREAU DU PRÉFET DE LA SEINE

JANE . . .

The house is as quiet as a church the day after Easter. In my many weeks here, I never noticed just how oppressive the silence is. Certainly, I took note of the emptiness, the shadows hiding in every corner, and I had noticed how . . . barren everything was, but the way the quiet filled the space, pushed everything else out, takes on new meaning now.

Perhaps it's because I'm so aware of every noise I make as I pretend to play hide-and-seek with Adèle. It's a story we've concocted so we can bide our time mapping the fastest and best-concealed routes from Bertha's room to the stables out back. Once she is free and we have proof of Edward's misdeeds in hand, we must make haste, the three of us. There will be little time to spare.

As I wander the halls, all these unoccupied rooms, these locked doors, look back at me with curious, questioning eyes . . .

What are you doing here?

What are you looking for?

Do you want to know what's inside?

Do you?

The sound of my breathing and the beating of my heart is like a roar in my own ears, so loud I'm afraid it'll bring Grace running from wherever she vanishes to during the day. I see her less and less often now.

As Bertha's warden, her absence on the first floor concerns me. Has she noticed anything? Is she watching her charge more carefully? Bertha says Grace doesn't visit more often than usual, but her room is on the same floor. Perhaps she is listening, watching, for signs of trouble.

Or perhaps my nerves are getting the better of me as the days wear on. Soon we will put my plan into motion.

I pause at a window, movement outside drawing my attention. Marsters has drawn the coach around in preparation for a trip into town. After breakfast, Edward declared a few last-minute things to attend to before the wedding tomorrow. He explained to Emm that she need not prepare anything for his lunch, but he will be back in time for dinner. This will be the first time he's left the house for any great length of time since my arrival, and it's too good an opportunity to waste.

I've decided to sneak into Edward's study while he is away. A risk, I know, but no more than the one Adèle would have taken tomorrow night. And, if I do this right, then she'll never have to make the attempt herself.

Abandoning my current path, I make for the front of the house as fast as I dare. I've a plan to buy us a bit more time.

When I reach the door, it's wide open and Edward is already stepping out.

Anger and revulsion flood me at the sight of him, but I swallow it. It nearly makes me sick.

"Wait," I call, coming down the stairs.

"Come to wish me off, then?" He turns and smiles, then lifts his hands. "I remember, your wages. Don't worry, I'll retrieve them."

I shake my head, forcing my own smile in turn. "No, no. Well, yes, I suppose. But I wanted to ask a favor of you."

He says, "Name it," as he faces me fully.

I fidget, as if unsure about asking the question, and I am, but not for the reasons one might suspect. "I want to make something. Another dessert, like those biscuits you so enjoyed," I add when he arches an eyebrow. "And I need particular ingredients."

"That's something Emm would be better suited to assist with, wouldn't you say?"

"Normally, yes. But the idea struck me this morning, and her next visit to the grocer isn't for another week yet. I don't want to wait."

His smile returns. "Impatient."

"A familial curse, I'm afraid."

He nods to himself. "What are you making?"

"It's a surprise."

"Won't my fetching the items ruin it?"

"Only if you know my grandmother's recipe." I step forward then and set a hand on his arm. "Adèle's done so well in her studies. I want to reward her."

Edward lifts his gaze from where my fingers squeeze. "Very well. What shall I bring back?"

My smile brightens and I search through my skirts for a bit of paper and hand it over. "It's not much, less than half a dozen items." But it will take him to at least three shops and, hopefully, add a couple more hours to his journey.

Without opening the note, he passes it to Marsters, who grunts but says nothing else.

"Anything else I can do for you?" He sounds so sincere. "You've everything you need to prepare for the wedding?"

I fight back the grimace that threatens to overtake my expression and shake my head. "That is all. I had better get back to the game. Adèle will wonder if I've abandoned her. Safe travels to you both." I dip my head and turn toward the kitchen, eager to get away.

The door closes behind me and I only make it a few steps before spinning on my heel and retracing my path to the front hall. I peer through the curtains, watching as Edward climbs into the coach and Marsters shuts the door. Soon enough, the horses kick forward and draw the coach down the path. I wait, my breathing loud in my ears again, as the team grows smaller and smaller, farther and farther away from the house.

When I can no longer tell if the speck at the end of the road is the coach or my eyes playing tricks, I move away from the window and toward my actual destination.

The door to the study is closed, but not locked. Inside, the smell of smoke is still thick. There are fresh flowers and potpourri to try to mask it, but I fear there may be little more to be done to remove it other than to wait it out.

Closing the door behind me, I hurry over to the desk. The lamp has been replaced. There are papers stacked here and there, letters and other missives, though nothing telling as I flip through them. I try the drawers, searching for flashes of either Adèle's or Bertha's names, anything about them or the tickets Bertha mentioned.

Inside the first drawer rests extra supplies for writing letters. Paper, pot, pen, nothing outside the ordinary for a study. But there are also wads of paper that have been tossed here instead of out with the rubbish. Something that angered him but was too important to throw away, perhaps.

Plucking a few of them free, I pull them open and press them flat as best I can against the desk to read.

To one Edward Fairfax Rochester of Thornfield Hall,

This correspondence concerns the matter of a debt owed to Schroders Bank and Lender in the amount totaling some 25,000 pounds sterling.

My eyes practically vibrate over the number, and I have to blink rapidly to clear my vision. *Twenty-five thousand* . . . The rest of the letter instructs Edward to contact the bank to make arrangements to begin repayment before the end of the season, or he could face consequences up to and including legal charges and a stint in debtors' prison.

I press open the next letter, scanning it.

Edward Rochester,

This correspondence concerns a personal matter pertaining to the repayment to one Reed Ingram in the amount of 34,000 pounds sterling for a personal loan. The terms of the loan, agreed upon by both parties mentioned, was that payment would be remitted monthly in the amount of 2,500 pounds, beginning in April of this year and continuing until the total was reached, with the final payment being 500 pounds.

As of the issuance of this letter, four consecutive payments have either been missed or were far less than the agreed-upon sum. As legal counsel for Mr. Ingram, I have been instructed to inform you that failure to make the next scheduled payment in the full amount will result in filings with the local magistrate.

There is more, but I move to the next letter. Another debt. And another. There are a few notes where some debts have been paid, large sums, then more letters asking for loans, all of it going back weeks, months, years. Amidst them are less pleasant letters, written in a quick, sharp hand, the paper poor and stained. They bear the names of gambling houses, pubs, street dens.

Rochester,

Time's up. This ain't no bank or gentlemen's bargain. The next letter from you better be a time and place I can collect what's owed, or you'll lose more than a pretty pocket watch. Go to the

peelers about this again, and I might have to retract the rather
generous offer I made last I was in town. See you next month.

Carlisle

Edward Rochester looks to have bet the very land upon which his home stands a time or two. There are even liens on the house, though they appear to have been resolved. He gambles, borrows money to pay back the parlors or what he's previously borrowed, shifting it all around, never letting it settle. It's a web, a sticky, tangled knot, and it's impossible to find the center.

No wonder the man hasn't given me my wages or paid for the upkeep needed to prevent Thornfield's fall into disrepair. Edward Rochester is a liar and a charlatan, one who has managed to coast on his name and status and the notion that he is wealthy.

Hastily, I crumple the papers and return them to their proper place before moving on to the next drawer. There look to be even more letters, but I only have so much time. This drawer holds a cigar box and a cutting set. I shut it and move on to the next.

I find nothing of import in the third and fourth drawers, but in the fifth rest envelopes both long and short, still bearing slowly crumbling seals. They are numerous and rather official-looking. I don't know where to start until I spot a scrawl of French across the corner of one.

Relatif au domaine et aux exploitations de Varens.

It occurs to me in that moment that I do not know Adèle's full name, having assumed it to be Rochester for so long, but what else could correspondence in French be pertaining to?

Inside the envelope is a series of pages, the first of which bears the seal of the bureau du préfet de la Seine. They comprise a letter in duplicate, one in French and the other looking to be an English translation. I read and quickly discover this is an official missive declaring Edward Fairfax Rochester the guardian and steward of Adèle Varens.

It outlines substantial evidence presented during an investigation that proves his closeness to the Varens family, as well as his ability to give the now orphaned girl a home. Witness testimony from Céline's neighbors—Céline is named as Adèle's mother—paints Mr. Rochester as an angel sent from heaven to watch over the child. "It's what she clearly would have wanted," one woman declares.

My stomach turns and I am overcome with the urge to rip the letter into pieces. Mr. Rochester's depravity is on display plainly here, bolstered by the hand of governmental authority. No wonder he feels as if he is beyond reproach.

There's another missive describing what is to become of the holdings and estate of one Céline Varens. The fortune is to be passed in its entirety to her daughter, Adèle, once she comes of age. Until that time, both child and fortune, now in a trust, will be remitted unto the chosen guardian. Save for a monthly stipend meant to see to Adèle's needs, the trust itself will be untouchable until she is able to claim it. The stipend itself is not without restrictions.

Proof of spending will be required at the end of each month before the following month's payment is to be released. There's even a clause that stipulates a seizure of the account should anything untoward befall the girl before she is old enough to take on the trust herself. If such a tragic event were to occur, the fortune would go to various orphanages throughout Paris.

Adèle's inheritance is relatively safe, and more importantly, so is she. If harm comes to her, he will lose the money. Good.

I flip ahead through a few pages of a ledger for the estate. While Edward's personal finances appear to be in shambles, the state of this account is impeccable. No doubt the pressures of external auditing and the threat of losing what he has worked so hard to steal are to thank for that.

Turning back to the letters, I read for more details concerning the trust. Perhaps there's a means to unshackle Adèle's future from Edward.

My eyes flit over paragraph after paragraph, taking in what I can. It's not until I reach a section titled Familial Clause that I pause. I read slower here. As I take in each word, there's suddenly too little air in the room.

The unexpected *click-click* of tumblers at the door sends my thoughts scattering, save one. Edward has returned, and I am going to be discovered here with the truth he's worked so hard to hide.

I have but seconds before the door opens, and still so much of the letter to read. In a split second, I drop the entire thing into the drawer. It lands with a thunk I hope went unheard, and as I shove the drawer shut, the door swings open. Someone steps inside. There's a distinct shuffle in their steps and, when they start to hum, my suspicions are confirmed.

Grace has come in, singing faintly to herself. I pray silently that she doesn't stray too far into the room. I have little reason to be crouching behind Edward's desk, game of hide-and-seek or not. This area is off-limits for such things.

Her steps bring her closer.

I press a hand over my mouth, certain she can hear my faint gasp.

Something atop the desk shifts before a few items rustle.

It's the moment I know I'm finished. I'm caught.

But then . . . I'm not. With more shuffling steps and the sound of her voice fading, Grace slips from the office, closing the door behind herself.

Even after she's gone, I wait for minutes more before finally standing, though my legs have turned to pudding and can barely hold me up. I need to leave before I'm caught. I've already done too much. I've located what I can and unfortunately will still have to rely on Adèle for the rest. I take one last moment to check the desk and make sure everything is where it should be.

I briefly make note of what I've found and where. That way, when Adèle returns tomorrow night, she will spend less time searching and more time on her work. Then I hurry for the door, closing it behind me.

"What do you think you're doing?"

My heart leaps and I spin to find Grace standing in the hall, watching me. She must have doubled back.

With my fear a hardened lump in my throat, I curse myself for not listening before exiting.

"Oh goodness, you startled me," I say, stalling as I wrack my brain for reasons, and to try to keep the fear clawing at my thoughts at bay. "Adèle has gone through all of her pencils again. I was hoping to find a spare."

Grace eyes me like she's not sure if she believes me.

"Do you need help?" I point at the rather large vase she's carrying. It's the one from Edward's desk, only now it's full of fresh flowers instead of nearly dead ones. That must have been what she was doing earlier.

"No," she says quickly. "No, I'll manage. And I'll let the mister know you're needing more supplies. Now, off with you."

I nod and move toward the kitchen. It's not until I'm farther down the hall that I hear her enter and close the door behind herself. My heart kicks beneath my ribs and I can only pray I left no trace of my presence.

ᦒ 36 ᦒ

RENEWED VOW

BERTHA . . .

> *Helen was such a friend to me. She was more than a friend. She was . . . everything. I loved her, for my part. As completely as I think I am capable of such. And now I sit here, staring at the words I've not spoken aloud since losing her. I loved her.*
>
> *I think you would have liked her. She certainly would have liked you. Oh yes, Helen would have liked you very much, for I like you very much. Which is why I will ask the impossible of you.*
>
> *Please do not worry for me tonight, keep . . .*

I stop reading, lower the letter, and squeeze my eyes shut against the ache of tears. My heart is in my throat and my stomach has fallen around my feet. My breath catches continually. Something roils in my chest. I feel a rush of nausea and unease wrapped around one another. I am afraid.

But it is not for myself that I fear.

I lower myself to the mattress and try not to think of the danger Jane has put herself in. Despite my warnings, she will go with him tonight. And despite all her reassurances, I remain terrified.

The trembling in my hands has moved through my entire body. I quake with it, uncontrollably. It sends me to my knees, my stomach

247

heaving with it. I fear I may be sick, but I swallow everything. I swallow it and bottle it up somewhere inside me. Some unfathomable place able to contain the storm brewing.

I finish reading Jane's letter. She continues to assure me everything will be fine. She insists so much I sense that perhaps she, too, is afraid, and in trying to comfort me offers scant comfort to herself. I can see her so clearly in what is not said. These scribbles on paper provide a window into her, into me. And I realize now that it is not only fear I hold, but guilt. Guilt that she might wind up harmed for helping me.

Lying here, I make a promise. A renewed vow in place of the one Edward made and broke. And for the first time since being locked in this room, I do not think of escape. Instead, I imagine all the hell I will rain down on this place if he lays a finger on a single hair on Jane's head. Resolve slides through me, cold and calming. My mind turns from freedom to vengeance.

If I could not gain one, I would take the other.

∽ **37** ∾

YOU MAY NOW TAKE A BRIDE

JANE . . .

With the dress properly laced and my hair pulled into place, I look queenly. The dresses Edward claimed to have commissioned are beautiful things but were obviously once Bertha's. The initials *B. M.* were casted on the ornately molded metal of the trunks they were delivered in. While I silently seethe at the audacity, a part of me is comforted at the thought of having something of Bertha's with me. I will need it tonight.

I gaze at my reflection, amazed at the image of the girl who stares back at me. There's a faint dusting of deep bronze on my cheeks, and my lips have been painted red. My hair is pulled atop my head and allowed to fall in ringlets thanks to a handful of hours with Emm, some careful instruction from me, and a hot comb. She's long since gone off to prepare dinner, so I sit at the vanity that came with the room and work in a few more pins to hold it in place. So far, all I'm managing to do is make my scalp ache and itch something fierce.

There's a knock on my door.

"Could you get that for me?" I ask Adèle, who had been assisting with pins in the back of my head.

The girl hurries over to open the door. Grace stands there. She smiles at Adèle, then looks at me. I see the reflection of her eyes run over me, taking me in. Her lips twist faintly.

"Well. Aren't you fetching." She says it like an admission, a confession she is loath to make. Whether she is irritated at the truth or because she could not believably lie is up for debate.

"Aren't I?" Indeed, I am, though I don't believe she meant the compliment.

"The mister would like for you to be in the atrium at the top of the hour and prepared to depart." With that, she shuffles off without another word.

Adèle and I watch her go. I look back to my reflection. With a spritz of perfume, and a few moments waving my hand in my face and coughing at the overpowering smell, I find I'm ready.

Ready as I'll ever be, at least.

I turn to Adèle and take her hands in mine. Her small face is set in determination, her lips pursed. She has a look I've seen on many girls in my time, a look that almost seems out of place on her. She's ready for tonight, far more than I am. I know this. Yet I remain hesitant. No one will hurt her, I tell myself. Even if she is discovered. Edward needs her in one piece for his plan to work. She will be fine.

She will be fine.

"One more time," I whisper.

She takes a slow breath. Her voice is quiet when she says, "After you and Monsieur depart, I am to wait in the kitchen with Emm and my sketchbook. When Grace comes to the kitchen, I excuse myself to go play."

I nod encouragingly. Bertie is to send Grace to fetch something from the kitchen. Then she will do her best to keep the old woman and Devin—who will likely accompany her, with Marsters out—occupied while Adèle acts.

"Go on," I encourage.

Adèle swallows. "I go to the study and find the letters you describe." She pats lightly at her pocket where my list is tucked. "When I'm done making copies, I leave those and keep the originals. While I am at his desk, I am to search for any sign of the tickets."

"Good. And if anyone catches you?" I ask, trying not to let my worry seep into my voice.

She says, "I cry and tell them I was alone and afraid; please take me to my room." Then she leans forward and smiles faintly around a whisper. "But I won't get caught."

A surprised bit of laughter leaves me before I can help it, and I clap a hand over my mouth, my eyes wide. "Well," I say when I've regained myself. "They don't stand a chance." I smile and she returns it before wrapping her arms around my waist.

"Be careful," she says into my dress.

"Escort me to the front?"

"Of course." She offers me her arm, which I take, then leads me down the hall and toward the atrium.

I can hear Edward and Marsters conversing quietly as we approach, though they stop when I step into the room.

Edward has gone still beside Marsters, blinking rapidly as he takes me in. "Miss Eyre," he says before swallowing. "You . . . you look lovely . . ."

"Thank you," I say. "Adèle helped me prepare tonight."

Edward clears his throat and looks to Adèle, who scooches behind me just slightly once more. "Well done, my dear."

I lift my chin, adjusting the scarf about my arms. It's black, to match my shoes and the ribbon around my throat.

I give Adèle's hand a quick squeeze.

She backs away as I step through the door.

The coach is waiting for us. I can hardly believe the sight of Marsters, dressed in a suit and a bit more polished than any other time I've ever laid eyes on the old grump. I nod in passing where he holds the door open. I climb in first and settle onto the bench, directly in the center, leaving no room to be joined.

Thankfully, Edward claims the seat across from me.

Marsters shuts the door. The coach rocks as he climbs into place, and soon we're off.

The ride is rather uneventful. Edward remains quiet, smiling on occasion. I don't miss how his eyes trail to me more often than not, and how his gaze lingers.

I'm doing this for Bertha, I tell myself. *For Adèle.*

And in no small part for myself. While he hasn't imprisoned me, I've no doubt he would. And he has stolen from me. Far less than what he's taken from others, but he is a crook. And I will see him pay. That gives me comfort and makes the ride bearable, even when he attempts to speak to me about my day in preparing for the evening.

I answer him quick and easy, though never let the conversation carry on.

This goes on for the better part of an hour or two, until, finally, we begin to slow. I chance a look out the window. We're drawing along a lengthy path, similar to the one that leads to Thornfield. It is lined with trees that provide an avenue of shade. A number of coaches lead the way and follow after us.

Eventually, we break into a wide circle around a large fountain that spills crystal-like water into the air. Across from it sits a massive house, much larger than Thornfield estate. It's like something out of a fairy tale, polished white and stone.

Our coach stops and, shortly after, the door opens. Edward steps out and I allow him to help me down. Give him what he wants. He offers his arm, and I take it with a murmured thank-you. Around us, other ladies and gentlemen do the same, and soon we're making our way toward the grand entrance.

Edwards greets a few fellows by name in passing, introducing me in kind. I smile and nod and recite, "It's a pleasure" more times than I can count, and we haven't even reached the doors.

When we do, I marvel briefly at just how large they are. Everything here is so much bigger than Thornfield. These people, this friend of Edward's, must be incredibly important. I wonder who it is as we stop long enough for Edward to produce his invitation and hand it to one of three butlers stationed just outside the entrance. The man takes the embroidered stationary, looks over it, then looks down his somewhat lengthy nose at the two of us.

He smiles and hands the envelope back to Edward.

"Welcome, Mr. and Mrs. Rochester," he says.

"Thank you," Edward says, without correcting him.

My face heats. "Ah, I'm n—"

Before I can get the words out, Edward ushers me forward.

"We can't block the entrance," he says as we sweep into the main atrium.

I can hear music spilling out from somewhere, I'm not sure. The sound mingles with the full thrum of voices as people speak to one another politely, greeting each other and catching up in pockets of conversation here and there.

Edward guides me through most of it, clearly having been here before, toward another set of doors also flanked by servants. Stepping through, we enter a world of bright light, sparking crystal, music, laughter, the smell of wine, roses, and sweets, of savory broths and meats. It is a veritable explosion of sight and sound, so much to try to take in at once.

I stand stunned for a moment before a faint tug at my arm brings me back to myself, and I trail after Edward. All around, ladies dressed in finery and gentlemen in the same speak with one another, either standing or seated at large round tables draped in white and covered in silver, china, and crystal. Beautiful faces swim in and out of my vision, some with tawny and umber-brown skin glittering in the crystal light, others porcelain pale and shining. Servants move in and out of the crowd carrying trays topped with flutes of golden, bubbly liquids. Everywhere, there is laughter and smiles.

My stomach twists. I feel so out of place here. Of course, I know my manners, as society dictates I must, but that knowledge does little to easy my anxieties. All it would take is a misstep here, a spilled drink there, a dropped fork or out of turn word, and the facade of this gorgeous gown and pretty paint would fade away.

My Jane is queenly indeed. I hear Helen's words as clear as if she were at my shoulder.

"Here we are," Edward murmurs into my ear, close enough that I feel his breath on my skin. I shift to the side and away from him as he draws back my chair.

Thanking him, I settle into it. My eyes continue to roam the room, from the high windows along the far wall and the glimpses of blossoming trees and hedges beyond, to the small group of musicians near a massive table at the front of the room, where it looks as if the bride and groom are already seated.

"Would you like a drink?" Edward asks.

"Yes, please," I say.

Edward lifts a hand, and sure enough, a tan young man in a waist-coat appears practically at his call, lowering a tray for both of us to take a flute.

The first sip sends bubbles dancing along my tongue. They tickle my nose, and my face scrunches slightly. I don't much like the taste, though.

As I try a second sip, there is a faint chime of a bell, and the crowds begin to disperse, heading for the various tables. Several couples join us, Edward rising as the ladies seat themselves, the gentlemen all shaking one another's hands.

Edward greets the women in kind—it seems they all know one another in some way—before he looks to me.

My spine straightens immediately, and I almost feel as if I am back at the school, being judged for my improper posture.

"I was certain we wouldn't see you this evening, Rochester," says one of the men, a round, elderly dark-skinned fellow with whitening hair and a beard to match. He sits nearest Edward.

A woman not as young as me but not as old as him settles at his side. Her tawny complexion practically glows against the ginger of her gown, and I cannot help but be entranced. "Let alone with your wife," she says, flashing me a smile.

I blink, taken aback yet again in so little time. His wife?

A rebuttal dances on my tongue, my lips parting to free it. But Edward leans forward. "I almost didn't come," he admits, smirking faintly. "But when your companion is as lovely as mine is, you manage." There's a chorus of agreement followed by laughter. My opportunity to correct the assumption has passed.

As if summoned by my thoughts of him, he looks to me and smiles. I don't return it, instead taking another sip of what I'm sure is champagne.

A Chinese gentleman, younger than the first, joins the discussion as it turns to an event from earlier this month, an engagement party Edward had missed. As they speak, the women have started their own conversations, talking about the new dresses they've seen other ladies wearing, and some of the old ones. Too old, in fact.

"I believe I've seen her wear that particular frock thrice now," says a pale red-haired woman—German given her accent—as she flutters a pearl fan in her face.

There's no need; we're not outside, and the temperature isn't all that warm, but I say nothing of it.

The red-haired woman looks at me, her blue eyes taking me in from head to toe.

"Now that's a lovely color on you. While it is an appropriate fall palette, it gives you a springtime glow."

I smile and dip my head slightly. "My ward helped me select it."

The looks that cross the ladies' faces are impossible to miss, a mix between surprise and something near to distress.

"Your ward?" asks an older white woman.

"Why, yes. I'm—"

"Far too modest sometimes, my dear." Edward drops a hand to take one of mine, lifting it and patting it, smiling at me reassuringly as he does.

He addresses the table. "Technically, Adèle is my ward, but my Jane has already developed such devotion to and affection for her. She taken charge of Adèle's education, shown her how to manage a kitchen, has even encouraged a love of art in the girl. I've never met a finer caretaker."

The compliment catches me off guard and leaves me staring for a moment. He speaks the truth, but the way he's phrased the entire thing does not settle well with me.

"Good on you," one of the gentlemen says.

"How lovely," a woman adds.

"Lucky girl," says another man.

"A girl needs a mother," a second woman agrees.

Mother?! I slip my hand out of Edward's. "Well, no, I—"

"And I did not come out to talk of life back home." He bursts into laughter, the other gentlemen following. "Where did that waiter—ah." He lifts a hand, the man from before returning with another tray of glasses.

Another round of excited and accepting chatter. I smile, despite the discomfort coiling in my stomach. It tightens when I think I hear the words *perfect for him* and *it's been so long* among them.

Before I can think more on it, there's a ringing of a bell toward the front of the hall. A gentleman standing before the table where the bride and groom sit shakes a small silver bell to gather the attention of the now seated crowd. He then sets it on a tray, which is whisked off by another servant.

The man looks to be somewhat younger than Edward, handsome as well, his dark hair curling around his pale face. He lifts one of the flutes into the air just so. "Many of you have known my brother as long as I have. Some longer. So, you're likely more surprised by this turn of events than I am."

There is a chorus of well-mannered laughter.

"To imagine he, who once grew faint at the very thought of marriage, would be sitting here today." He turns to hold the glass out to the couple.

A gentleman who resembles him though looks older, and a woman around Emm's age or so, smile at him from where they sit at the table, he dressed in finery and she looking like an angel encased in cloudy gossamer.

"I've no doubt this is due to you, the new Mrs. Austin. You've brought out a side of him I never thought I'd get to see, but that I'm happy to have been introduced to. You make him a better man, which I thought was impossible. And your future together looks brighter than anything I could have ever imagined for him." The man's voice grows quiet, just briefly, before he swallows.

There are several soft murmurs and sniffs here and there, a few at our table. I would be lying if I denied the tightness in my own throat.

"Here's to you, brother, and now you, sister. To Mr. and Mrs. Austin." He lifts the glass higher, and there's a chorus of echoed sentiments as other glasses are raised.

I raise my own, giving a boisterous "Hear, hear!" along with everyone else.

The best man, I assume, faces forward again. "My brother and his lovely bride bid you all welcome to our family home. Please, avail yourselves of dinner, drink, dance, and merriment!"

With that, the music picks up and servants sweep in, trays on their hands. Steaming plates are soon set out and dinner begins. There is polite conversation all around, the low murmur filling the hall. Even at our table, the gentlemen speak of business matters, of hunting and ventures across the seas. The women talk of the last event or wedding they attended, of fashions and festivities.

Finally, one of the women fixes me with a look. "It's nice to be a guest and not the bride, isn't it? So many eyes on you, judging you, taking you apart piece by piece."

I can't help but notice how Edward shifts beside me, taking a sip from his brandy glass that he requested be brought out as he attempts to hide that he's listening to what I'm about to say.

"I haven't attended many weddings." I manage a smile. "I mostly looked to my studies or other means of bettering myself. Marriage was not one of those things."

The woman chortles, though I'm not sure if she's amused by what I've said or that I've said it. "I suppose with a face as fetching as yours, prospects were aplenty. Edward must have had a fight on his hands."

"In more ways than one," he says with a smile.

More laughter, more smiles.

The realization of what they mean dawns on me, and a shock of horror moves through me. "I didn't—"

"Do any of you know if the happy couple will move in here or if they'll take the southern house?" Edward asks, brows lifting as he looked to the group.

Like that, the conversation shifts away from possible weddings and plans for them, though I don't know what they talk about next. A buzzing fills my head, pushing out all other sound save for the rapid beating of my heart.

Welcome, Mr. And Mrs. Rochester.

My vision doubles.

Let alone with your wife.

A feeling like fire fills every part of me.

A girl needs a mother.

My gloved hands clench into fists atop my thighs.

This was his plan. From the moment he asked me to attend the wedding with him. To pass me off as his wife. I am a pawn, and now I finally know my place on his board.

The anger burning inside me threatens to spill outward.

I refuse.

And I want to scream my refusal in his face.

But I don't want to ruin someone else's celebration. Today is an otherwise happy occasion, and I can deal with Edward Rochester and his half-truths later. And as much as I might like to strangle him in this moment, a dead man cannot pay for his crimes.

I don't touch the rest of my meal, and I don't pay attention to the conversations as they continue through dessert. While I've no taste for the pastries being set before us, I've had more than two flutes of champagne and am eager to get started on a third.

Soon couples begin to rise from the tables and make their way toward the massive empty floor at the center of the room as a waltz picks up. Even the bride and groom look to be making their way toward the floor to dance.

Two of the couples seated at our table rise as well.

I watch them, trying my best not to give away that I'm also watching Edward. He finishes his drink—I'm not sure what the count is for him—and sets the glass down.

I stand. "Pardon me, I must find the powder room. I'd like to freshen up."

"That sounds like a marvelous idea," says one of the younger women. "If you'll excuse us, gentlemen."

The other ladies rise from their chairs, the gentlemen as well. In an attempt to not trigger any alarm, I set a hand lightly to Edward's arm where he stands beside me. "Back shortly."

With that, we make our way to the edge of the room and to the door, where my tablemate asks for directions to the powder room.

As she receives instruction, I peer up and down the wide corridor, where pockets of guests are gathered to speak once again. There are so many people present, it's almost obscene, and all for a wedding! I wonder just what sort of influence the bride and groom have when I notice my companion has already ventured off in some direction, and I no longer have sight of her.

I wait before drawing myself to the side. A quick glance around tells me that I'm relatively alone, given how everyone else appears to be drawn up in their own conversations.

I just . . . needed a moment. I needed a chance to gather myself, my thoughts, for what I was certain was happening.

People are making assumptions about my relationship with Edward, and he is stoking them. I don't know why such a thing surprises me, and yet it both does and does not. This escapes all reason I can muster. Why would he do such a thing? Surely there is no benefit save fooling a room of what I assume are his friends.

So many questions fly through my mind, but the one that I settle on is, what am I going to do about this? I've already decided against causing a scene, but speaking the truth does not require fanfare. I will simply correct any further assumptions made, interrupt whoever is speaking to ensure I am heard, rudeness be damned.

Resolute, I walk back toward the main hall.

Upon entering, I search the crowd for signs of Edward. He is no longer seated at the table, and there is a large number of people dancing across the floor. Eventually, I spot him near the head table, where he converses with the groom and his brother.

He glances up, catching my eye, then shakes the groom's hand before making his way across the floor toward us. With each step that brings him nearer, I feel my heart kick against my ribs. He smiles, ever pleasant, as he comes to a stop in front of me.

"I trust all is well," he says.

"Quite," I say between clenched teeth. "I hope I didn't interrupt."

"Not at all. In fact, you rescued me, in a way. The excuse to dance with my lovely companion is as good as any to break away from conversation." He lifts one hand, holding it out expectantly. "Join me?"

"O-oh, I . . . I'm not much of a dancer," I say, despite my earlier promise. "I'm afraid I'll make a fool of myself in front of your friends."

Edward chuckles. "It's a simple dance, and you're a bright young woman. I'm certain you'll pick it up quick enough. And don't worry about them." He sweeps his gaze over the gathered crowd. "There are things much more worthy of gossip."

He takes my hand and moves as if to lead me out onto the floor, but I remain firmly planted in place. "I'm sorry, but I'd rather not."

I don't miss the look that flashes across his face, tight and surprised, before it's buried under that quick smile.

"Just one dance, it won't hurt."

"I'd prefer to watch, thank you."

I look around, noticing what Edward has not. Those nearest us, while not fully ending their conversations, have stopped to look.

"We've come all this way," he continues.

I smile. "And I'm a bit tired."

"You're my guest."

"Please, this isn't—"

"Show off that lovely dress of yours." He tugs insistently this time, almost enough to pull me forward.

I plant my feet and snatch my hand from his. "Edward, I said no."

I don't mean to raise my voice. As a matter of fact, I'm certain the exchange went mostly ignored, given how the lively music undercut by the dull roar of the party never lets up. But we've certainly gained the attention of those nearest us, at least a dozen or more heads turning toward us.

Edward stiffens, his fingers closing where his hand had held mine. He chuckles, the sound forced as he glances around and takes in our surroundings for the first time.

"O-of course," he says, his voice soft but low.

His entire body is tense, the lines in his face pronounced as he forces a smile. "You're tired. Such excitement can be a lot for a new wife."

My ire burns stronger. "I am not—"

"We'll go at once," he says, raising his voice, his eyes flashing with the silent promise of . . . I'm not sure, but it sends a chill through me. "Allow me to make my goodbyes, at least. We're not all so rude."

With that, he spins on his heel and marches toward the front of the room again. As he goes, the line in his shoulder eases, and he melts back into that boisterous air, so different from the tight, angry thing he was a moment ago. I watch the transformation with no small amount of shock. I should have seen this coming. I did see this coming. But knowing you are about to be hit by a train does not diminish its force.

I stand there, shaking just so, very aware of the eyes on me now, of the whispers passing between lips and ears, of the judgment being cast. Half of me doesn't care; let them judge. The second half envies the resolution and strength of the first.

I leave the dining hall, marching down the corridor and through the front door, out onto the main walk. Along the way, I grab a champagne flute from a tray carried by a startled servant.

The crowd thins as I go, with fewer people scattered about. Eventually, there's little more than a couple looking for a moment alone here or there, and then I am alone.

Drink in hand, I set myself down on a nearby stone bench and upend the glass, draining the whole of its contents. When I am finished, I remain unsure of what to do with myself. The answer won't come. There is only fear. And fury.

I turn at the sound of approaching steps.

On his way toward me, Edward looks stoic. His faced wiped of all expression. He steps past me without a sideways glance and continues toward the edge of the pathway.

Upon spotting him, one of the runners goes for the coach. It hopefully will not be long, as we are the only ones out here taking such an early leave. He paces as he waits. I approach, keeping a healthy distance.

Neither of us says anything.

Eventually, blessedly, the coach begins to make its approach, the runner hanging from the side. When the coach comes to a stop, he opens the door and Edward climbs inside.

After I am seated across from him, the coach lurches forward into the slow pull toward home.

For a lengthy period of time, there is nothing but the creaking of wheels and the stomp of hooves on the dirt. Edward watches the scenery go by outside the window and I watch him.

We are nearly home when, finally, he clears his throat. "I am . . . disappointed, Jane," he says.

I remain silent, letting him continue.

He looks to me, his expression pinched, pained. It's brief, before he returns his attention to the window again. "After everything, I did not expect to be disrespected in such a way."

"Disrespected?"

"All I requested was a dance. At my friend's wedding. I asked; you agreed to come. I got this dress. I've provided every opportunity for you, just like—" He cuts himself off, his jaw tight and his teeth bared before he takes a slow breath. "I did not know you were so ungrateful."

"I—I . . . I'm not ungrateful. I'm anything but ungrateful!"

He slams a fist into the cushion beside him.

I jump, my heart leaping as well.

"Don't . . . interrupt me." Now he looks at me directly.

The sun has set, and the moonlight cuts against the angles of his face. Bathed in silver light and harsh fire from the glow of the lanterns, he is a study in opposites. There is the calm of his voice weighed against the fury in his expression, and there is such fury.

His nostrils flare with it. His fingers are clenched with it. The muscles in his jaw work with it. He is unpredictable when angry, and I am certain Edward Rochester means to do me harm.

"I've given you everything you ask," he says, his words even, his voice low and tight. "And you spit in my face. That will not happen again. I will not be embarrassed like this, do you hear?"

I stare, my mouth working uselessly. I can't think of anything to say, my attention on where his fists rest against his knees, just an arm's length from my face.

"Do you hear?!" he snaps, his mouth twisting.

I recoil with a jolt, my back pressing into the bench.

The coach rocks as we come to a stop. Edward reaches to grip the handle, holding the door closed, his eyes never leaving me. "If you value your position here, and don't want to find yourself on the street or back at that school, I suggest you think long and hard about how you treat those who've been kind to you." He pushes the door open and slips out into the night.

PART 4

When we are struck at without a reason,
we should strike back again very hard;
I am sure we should—so hard as to teach the
person who struck us never to do it again.

⤳ 38 ⤳

A TOKEN

JANE . . .

I wake to sunlight streaming through my window and across my face. I shield my eyes with one hand as my mind struggles to catch up with itself, similarly to how I struggle to sit up. Why does my body feel so tight? Tilting up on my elbows, I realize what the issue is.

I'm still in my dress from yesterday.

The memory of the wedding, the ride home, and Edward's words comes crashing back into me. The house had been quiet when I entered last night, all gone to bed, none but Marsters awake to witness the fury aimed at me. Were it a weapon, I dare say I could have been struck dead on the spot. Instead, Edward simply harassed me the entire way to my room, and when I closed the door continued to shout through it for the better part of an hour. I did not dare venture out then.

The fact that there has been no further shouting, no additional rousing, leads me to believe that Adèle was successful in her venture without detection. I told her to go to her room and wait for my return, that I would find her the following morning. This morning. I plan to do just that, but first I need to get out of this damned dress.

With a grunt, I struggle to my feet. I'm tired and sore and stiff in various places. I happen to catch a glimpse of myself in the mirror as I move toward the trunk where I've shoved all my things, a preemptive

267

packing of sorts. My hair askew, the bit of color on my face smeared against my skin, I look like death prepared for a ball.

Without anyone to help me, it takes a while to remove the dress, and a bit of soap and water here and there, especially my face, makes me feel less like I slept in a barn. I shove the dress into the wardrobe and check my reflection properly this time.

When I open my door with the intent to make my way to the kitchen, I'm stopped by the presence of a vase on the floor. It's full to bursting with a smattering of flowers, the colors brilliant, their perfume already wafting over me. There's a letter tilted against it, and I bend to pluck it up. Edward's seal rests over the fold.

Sighing, and knowing I should put the letter away unopened, I let my fingers pull the wax loose and unfold it. There are only two words written.

Forgive me.

—*E.R.*

I take the letter and the vase to a nearby table in my room, set them down, and walk out. The house is surprisingly bright as I make my way to the kitchen, and it's then that I notice a number of the curtains have been drawn open. Sunlight pours in through the somewhat dirtied panes, but it's still more light than the entire time I've been here.

Adèle's door lies open and her room empty. For a moment, panic's icy fingers claw at my throat, and I cannot breathe. But then I tell myself that if she had been discovered and carted away, her things would not be here, and certainly not neatly pressed into place. Emm must have taken her to breakfast, as she often does if I am unable to for one reason or another. So I set my step toward the kitchen.

As I approach, I hear Emm going on about a new type of spice she'd like to try if we could get some in.

Another familiar voice answers her, and stops me cold.

"It sounds delicious; I look forward to tasting it."

I recoil a step, with the desire to turn and go back to my room, lock myself away until he . . . I don't know, until I won't have to face him! But I can't do that.

I *won't* do that. I will not run. I never have, and I don't plan to start now.

Rolling my shoulders back, I lift my chin in defiance of my earlier fear. Then, before I can think better of it, I stride into the room.

Silence greets me, as do three sets of eyes.

Emm peers at me from where she stands near the stove. Adèle watches me from where she sits at the table, as usual, and beside her . . .

Edward glances up from a book open on the table between himself and Adèle. He smiles.

I fight the urge to shudder.

"Good morning. Or is it afternoon?" he asks Emm, though his tone is more amused than admonishing.

I let my gaze linger on him briefly. He would dare? Pretend nothing transpired between us last night, that his words were not flung at me like stones, that his wounded pride was not wielded in attempt to bludgeon my own?

In an instant all my earlier resolve to not let this get the better of me crumbles. All sense that I shouldn't provoke him deserts me until I look to Adèle.

I smile for her, easily. And it's genuine. She seems so afraid, her shoulders hunched, her eyes shifting back and forth between Edward and me.

"Morning," I say softly, hoping to reassure her. I greet Emm as I move to take up a plate. "What did you make?"

"Jane," Edward starts.

I ignore him. "It smells delicious. I caught scent of it the instant I opened my eyes."

"Jane," Edward tries again, a little louder but not necessarily forceful.

Emm looks from me toward the table and then back again a few times.

"I hope it hasn't gone cold." I thrust the plate in her direction. "I know I'm a little late this morning. Last night did not agree with me."

There's a heavy sigh and the sound of a chair scraping the floor.

Edward approaches, though stops far enough away that I can't reach him. Even with the frying pan temptingly close.

"Jane," he says, and then heaves a sigh through his nose. He meets my gaze briefly, then lets his drop. "Last night was . . . not like me."

"Then who was it like?"

The noise Emm makes would have been comical any other time.

His brow furrows. "I admit I was delighted when you changed your mind and accepted my invitation to the wedding and had hoped . . . well, that's irrelevant. I let my feelings on what could have been get the better of me, on more than one front." His frown deepens, and he purses his lips.

I say nothing, letting my silence speak for me. My jaw aches, it's clenched so tightly.

A handful of seconds pass before he manages to gather himself enough to continue.

"It was . . . supposed to be an event I attended with . . ." His voice falters, and he clears his throat, all while steadfastly avoiding my gaze, I notice. "She was supposed to go with me."

It takes me a moment to realize he's speaking of Bertha. The very woman he has locked upstairs like a caged animal. Such remorse on his face, in his words. How did I ever fall for this? The deception rankles.

"While I understand," I begin, grateful my voice remains steady, "that is no excuse for your behavior."

Edward nods, looking dutifully admonished. "I know. And I'm not trying to make excuses, I simply wanted to explain myself. Grief . . . makes us different people."

"You are not the only one to know grief," I shoot back at him. "Nor are you the only one to know anger at not getting what you want. Your explanations sound a lot like excuses."

His shoulders tighten, but he wears his apology on his face openly, his expression twisted with remorse. The man has clearly had practice. Years of it. A proficient liar.

"I will not suffer such indecencies," I continue. My indignation and ire are true, but I keep them cooled at the edge. I want to appear close to my end, but not there. Not quite yet. "I *will* leave, before I allow this." It is a partial truth, because I would never leave without Adèle, and now, without Bertha. But just as Edward weaves his webs, I now weave mine. My gaze slowly travels the room, first to Adèle, who watches both Edward and me. There is fear written across her small face. Fear for me. Emm has politely returned to her task of preparing lunch, and is looking at no one, but I can see the line of tension drawing up her shoulders.

Finally, my eyes find their way back to Edward.

He still has not lifted his gaze, and while anyone else might see his tight shoulders and white knuckles and think he's a man chagrined and trying to contain his numerous apologies, I know it is most likely he is fighting the urge to strike me, either physically or verbally. I have gambled against the violent nature of him.

When he speaks, his voice is deceptively soft. "I hope you can come to forgive me for my rude and completely unnecessary outburst, and how I treated you. I hope I can win back your trust, and I pray I have not too badly damaged our friendship."

"You can start by giving me what is mine."

The confusion on his face both irritates and pleases me. Irritated because he has already forgotten what we've discussed yet again. Pleased because, if he wishes me to stay, he can only surmise he has no choice but to do as I ask.

"My wages," I clarify when it seems he's still lost. Realization flickers like a spark across his face, and he opens his mouth. To agree, I assume, given the way his expression lights up. "Doubled," I add before he gets the words out. "To account for the delay."

He jolts, mentally stumbling over what he was about to say, my demand clearly catching him off guard. He gazes at me, his eyes less open now, less friendly. The barely concealed contempt with which he regards me is familiar. For a moment, I think he might refuse. Finally show just how unsound and dangerous he is.

And I would meet his fury with my own now that it can no longer ambush me. What happened at the wedding, what happened in the coach, is not merely a caricature of the man. The mask has been removed, and yet he wishes to carry on the charade.

I have known men like Edward Rochester. I know what they are capable of. I know that they will weave pretty lies and promises to cover ugly truths.

And I know how to use such against them.

I clear my throat and settle my shoulders back, lifting my chin. "Doubled," I repeat quietly. "And we can put this whole messiness behind us."

A lie for a lie.

He releases a breath that sounds and looks like it's one he's been holding his entire life. His body sags with it. The brief, calculating glint in his eye is gone, but not forgotten.

"Thank you," he breathes. "Thank you. For your . . . unwavering kindness. You are the epitome of a lady, Jane." He reaches for my hand, then seems to think better of it, which is good because I would have pulled away, and likely slapped him.

Instead, he turns his over and waits for me to offer mine. "While it will take until I next go into town to pay you, allow me to make this gesture. A down payment, if you will."

I look him over before lifting my hand and resting my fingertips against his. His touch sets an unpleasant shiver through me.

Instead of taking my hand fully, he adjusts his grip in order to turn my hand over. Then he presses something into it and curls my fingers around the object before I can see what it is.

"A small token," he explains. "I had planned to give it to you regardless, and I know it can't make up for what happened on its own, but I'd like for it to be a start." He releases my hand and makes his way around to rejoin Adèle at the table. "And don't worry about lessons for the day. Take a moment to yourself. Whatever you'd like to do. It can be a day of painting for her." He smiles before taking up the book and closing it. "Let's go into the library, Adèle, and leave Jane to her day."

Adèle watches me, her expression unreadable, before rising to her feet to follow Edward out of the room. She spares me a brief glance over her shoulder, mouths the words *thank you*, and then slips out of sight.

"Are you all right?" Emm asks softly. "It seems something happened during the wedding."

"I'm fine," I say, wishing to avoid the unpleasant memories. "It was only a misunderstanding."

"Well then, lunch will be ready within the hour," Emm says. "Though I imagine you're hungry for having missed breakfast."

"A little," I say, finally opening my hand to see what's been placed there. It's a bit of silk cloth, white in color, wrapped around something hard.

While Emm busies herself with pulling together leftovers from the meal that morning, a bit of bacon, porridge, and eggs from the look and smell of things, I finally unwrap the gift.

As a chain of dazzling silver spills over the side of my hand like water, my heart kicks against my lungs. Bright red flashes in the light, ringed by sparkling white, the stones each winking at me.

"Oh," I breathe.

"What?" Emm asks, coming around to get a look at what's in my hand. "Oh my word . . ."

I finally manage to lift my free hand and, carefully, catch the chain between my fingertips. Dangling from the end is a band of silver folded in on itself. Diamonds trace the outside of the twist, and seated at its center is a ruby the size of a thimble.

Hanging from the chain, the setting and the stones are further exposed to the light, and now send a twinkling of dots scattered around the room, and at the center, a deep and bloodied haze colors everything. This . . . this has to be worth at least a year of my wages, if not more.

I glance after Edward, though he is long gone. I know he meant for this to dazzle me, to bring me swooning back into his good graces, and he into mine. But instead, a cold twist of discomfort moves through me. Of mistrust.

"That's . . . that's quite a gift," Emm says before setting my plate on the table. "There you go."

"Thank you," I say. "And it is." I sit the necklace, still wrapped in the kerchief, on the table as I take a seat. I turn the pendant over to find an inscription on the back.

B.M.

~~5 **39** &~~

RIGHTEOUS FURY

BERTHA . . .

I stare at the necklace where it flickers and shines in Jane's hand. She was correct in assuming it belonged to me. Given to me by my grandmother mere weeks before she passed, it was supposed to be an early wedding gift.

A ruby bordered by diamonds signifies true love. May this gift bear such love to you. Her thin, frail fingers had gripped my hands as she looked at me with all the sun in her smile. Then she pressed the necklace into my palm, the same way Jane does now.

I continue to stare as I did before. My fingers trace the jewels, the settings, the chain and clasp.

Before I can think better of it, I've flung myself into her. Her arms wrap around me with her little "Oh" of surprise. She squeezes and I lose myself for just a moment.

"Thank you," I whisper, feeling the heat of tears fill my face.

Her hold tightens, and one of her hands cups the back of my neck. "You're welcome."

I break away before the flush crawling up my neck reaches its destination and turn to find somewhere to hide my recovered trinket. Perhaps under the bed with my journal?

As I contemplate the matter, Jane lowers herself onto my mattress.

She's got a look on her face that says she's in a mood. "He gave it to me to apologize for his behavior last night."

The elation conjured by the appearance of my necklace sours at this. Jane wrote to me about what happened night before last, both during the wedding and after. Then all day yesterday I secretly wanted Edward to make one of his rare appearances so that I might claw his eyes and snatch his throat, that he might never look upon her or speak to her again. Alas, as is too often the case, my rage remains impotent.

"Giving me your things, introducing me as his wife. I believe he's . . . trying to pretend I am you," she said, her agitation clear. "Or at least trying to convince the world."

Even after everything, after all Edward has done, Jane's words take me by surprise. "To what end?" I lower myself to crawl beneath the bed, carefully wrapping the necklace back in the kerchief Jane provided and tucking it beneath the loose floorboard.

She still hasn't answered by the time I stand. I find her staring at a piece of crumpled paper. Her grip is tight, her jaw set. "This is from Edward's desk," Jane says, her voice deceptively soft. "It's part of a contract or official decree. Adèle was successful at secreting away the pages."

I settle beside her to read and am surprised to find its in French, though not deterred by it.

Jane points to a section titled Familial Clause: which stipulates that the only means to circumvent the hold placed on the child's trust is if the guardian were to marry and the two adopted the child outright.

"This is concerning Adèle?" I ask.

"Yes," Jane says. She more breathes the word, as if the truth behind it has been some great burden to bear and she is happy to share the load. "He's penniless. Destitute. We found debt notes and calls for collections from banks and other holdings. *Threats* from gambling houses. It's why the house is in shambles, why he hasn't paid my wages, and I'm certain he never will. He's doing everything he can to stave off anyone looking for their pound of flesh. And now he's concocted a way to make himself flush with Adèle's inheritance."

Between the letters and visits, Jane has revealed the depths of Edward's evil concerning Adèle's mother. That poor girl, drawn into all this at that age.

"Why did he not fence the necklace?" I wonder aloud. "It would have paid off at least a portion of those debts, I'm certain."

"True," Jane murmurs. "But fencing jewelry belonging to the wife no one has seen in over a year? Likely to lead to uncomfortable questions. You and your inheritance are worth far, far more." She taps lightly at her chin in thought. "Or he is biding his time. If he has to run from his debtors, the necklace is something he can carry on his person if he is unable to pack anything else."

Jane has begun to pace again. Her steps are quiet, but I steal a glance toward the door, trying to listen for signs of Grace or any of the others.

"He's been in debt for years," Jane mutters. "You were supposed to be a solution. Or, rather, your fortune was. A woman of means and title from the Americas, unaware of his dealings and unknown here. According to the letters, your dowry was only enough to convince his debtors to give him more time, during which he was to wrangle you out of your fortune. But the five-year probationary period on your trust meant he wouldn't have the money soon enough. There are letters stating as much that date back to just before your arriving at Thornfield."

My hands shake as I read and listen, the words sometimes confusing in my sight or hearing, but it is more than enough for me to understand. "That's why he cannot simply kill me. If I am not alive to claim the trust, he cannot touch it. Not while my parents live."

Jane thrusts a finger my direction. "Exactly! He needed more money, fast money. So, he went to Céline, who turned him down." Jane falls silent at this. The furrowed expression tells me all I need to know.

I've been aware for some time that Adèle's mother was dead and that's why she was here. The girl told me herself, one night. What I did not know but should have suspected was Edward's possible hand in the woman's untimely demise.

"The bastard." My words are barely a breath in the air.

"He killed her," Jane says just as quietly. "He killed her and then stole her daughter in hopes that being Adèle's caretaker would open the way to her mother's fortune. But he can't touch her money either, not until she's grown, *unless* . . ." Jane taps the letter in my hand.

She doesn't have to say the rest. I am able to piece it together myself. "He and his wife adopt her."

"Right. A wife he's imprisoned in his house, who will certainly not help him in any regard. And he cannot simply marry another woman unless you are declared dead, but if that happens your fortune is forfeit as well." At this Jane stills entirely. She wraps her arms around herself and slowly comes to join me on the bed.

For a long while neither of us says anything. I stare at the page, then at Jane. Back and forth my gaze travels, until the press of a warm hand in mine draws my full attention.

"He knows after locking you away up here, you would never help him. So, he finds someone who will. Who he believes he can manipulate into doing so." She huffs a faint laugh that is more incredulous than amused. "Take your place, at least long enough to finalize the adoption."

Jane falls silent, watching me. Her free hand fists in the blanket, her shoulders lift. What little sunlight manages to pour into the space wreaths her in flames to match the fury I can feel from here.

"He thought I would fall for him so easily," she nearly growls. Her anger is . . . in a word, breathtaking. "Gave me gifts, expensive things. Items that any girl would be delighted to receive, especially from a potential suitor."

There's a faint twinge of shame that I have to push down in order to speak. "Don't be too hard on yourself. I fell for his schemes. Enough so I married him, willingly even." I still remember how Edward treated me with fabricated kindness, even love. He was so convincing. I thought I was the luckiest woman alive.

"He even let others at the wedding think we meant something to one another. The bastard!"

"Jane, your voice."

"He won't get away with it," she says quietly. And then again, louder, she promises, "He *won't* get away with it." She takes up both my hands now, squeezing them.

I gaze into the face of an avenging angel.

"I'm going to get you out of here," she continues. "We will all be free. You, Adèle, and me. I'm going to get *us* out of here."

The ferocity in her gaze is enough to burn away my fears. What's left behind is a sort of determination bolstered by her bravery. I press her hands in return. "I believe you." And I do. God help me, against all odds, I do.

Jane nods, a smile pulling at her lips but a moment before she purses them. And then, without warning or preamble, she leans toward me.

I gasp, rooted in place as her face dips near mine. But then, at the last second, she turns, and her lips touch the corner of my mouth.

Then she is drawing away. "I'll write to you," she whispers over her shoulder. "Soon, to tell you about my idea once I've laid the foundation. We have our evidence; now we need to find a way out. In the meantime, are there any other belongings you want me to keep an eye out for?"

I shake my head slowly, my hand against my cheek, near where I can still feel the heat of her mouth on my skin. Then I remember. "A pearl necklace. Grace was to have it repaired for me. It's been months."

"I will watch for it. If anything changes, I'll write sooner."

I nod. I don't know if she sees it, for she's disappeared into the closet. There's a rustle of fabric, a soft farewell, and then she's gone.

⁓ 40 ⌇

DEBTS LAID BARE

JANE . . .

After tea, Adèle elects to spend the evening with me in my room under the guise of using the light from my window for her latest study in art. Her idea. The girl is brilliant and has a mind for what Helen used to call circumstantial deception. Such is true of most children, but Adèle wields the ability like a master swordsman cutting through the assumptions of her opponents with deft swiftness. She allows them to blind themselves to the truth, thus allowing the lie to take root on its own.

She sits on the floor amidst a sea of paint pots and brushes, a canvas carefully laid out to try to discern the best angle for the setting sun. Though instead of sketching out the subject of her proposed portrait, she is re-creating a map of the house from memory. I meant it when I said she was likely the one who knew this place best, and that knowledge will certainly help with the plan to free Bertha.

A plan that I hope soon comes to fruition. Helen was the thinker, of the two of us. And I was the doer. Not that either of us was incapable of the opposite, but . . . well . . . we had our strengths and found strength in each other. But now, it's just me.

Or so I think, because a faint sound draws my attention to Adèle once more. She leans in over the canvas a bit further, her dress tucked beneath her knees, her tongue caught between her teeth in concentration, as she finesses something on the map. Even though the lines are faint, I can make out some of the intricacy from this distance. She is thorough. Whatever plan we manage to concoct will no doubt be made stronger for her efforts. I cannot help but smile. While I have been robbed of my Helen's genius, I have met the seed of its equal in Adèle.

I look back to my own work, pages and pages of practiced scribblings where I've attempted to disguise my handwriting a number of ways, or mimic someone else's. I've penned copy after copy of what is essentially the same message, saying it different ways, changing various words to affect the tone of the message. This current rendition is the closest I've gotten to anything I'd consider myself proud of, or that might work. Setting the pen aside, I inspect my handiwork.

Rochester,

It's your lucky day. I know you've been holding out on me. I know about the girl. I know about her mother, the artist. And I know what you did and what you have. But I've decided to forgive you, for double. That's fair, I think. I'll send one more letter with a time and place. Be there. Say nothing to no one. No questions. No correspondence. Do and say nothing until you hear from me, or people will be very interested to hear what I've got to say.

Carlisle

The letters are still a little curved here and there, not as jagged. I write the letter again, farther down the page. Then I turn it to write sideways. Twice more on the back. I practice at least a dozen times until the handwriting resembles what I can remember, then I write it anew on one of the clean sheets. Hopefully the ink smudges conceal any telling flaws.

My work done, I rise and toss the practice sheets into the nearby fire, watching as the paper catches light, then curls inward, burning away.

Now I need only wait until the opportunity presents itself to slip this in with the post, and then we'll see if the seed of my plan takes root. It's a risk, to be sure. Edward might see through the ruse, or reach out to this Carlisle and discover the truth. But I'm betting if he's coward enough to do all he's done to those he deems weaker than him, he's too cowardly to move against someone he views as a threat.

Let's see just how Edward Rochester fares in this great gamble of his when he's no longer the player and is merely the pawn.

Setting that letter aside, I pull out paper and begin another one, only for this, I need disguise nothing.

Bertie,

First, I want to apologize that I've been be unable to visit you. For at least a week I've been "afflicted" with dreadful headaches that no amount of rest, tea, or fresh air seem to relieve. Likely due to the fact that these pains are a fiction. I requested laudanum, and was finally given a bottle. Lo, I've made a miraculous recovery! Just in time to accept Edward's invitation to dinner this weekend. He's been asking for days now, and is thrilled I'm finally well enough to join him, especially since he will soon find himself needing to go into town on business the following morning if my forging attempts are successful. This presents the perfect opportunity, as close to perfect as I believe we may get.

During dinner, I'll slip some of the tonic into Edward's drink, just enough to settle him into a deep sleep. He always sees to it that we are not disturbed, save when the courses are served. Adèle will delay Emm, providing me with a chance to search his study once more. We were unable to find the tickets from your parents in our last attempt, but this time I will turn every drawer inside out if I must.

Then I will call for aid. Upon finding their master, and my similarly inebriated self, we will both be put to bed straight away. I've measured the dose in the hopes that, by the time he wakes the following morning, it will be too late in the day for him to do much aside from make himself presentable before departing. And, while he is away with Marsters, I'll drug Devin and Grace similarly. Then we can make our escape with Adèle.

I hate to deceive Emm, she's been nothing but a friend to me, and I have been in sore need of meaningful companionship. I've written her a letter, one I'll leave explaining all of this. She deserves to know the truth about the man who has employed her, to protect herself from his wrath when all is said and done. And soon it will be done. It's going to happen, Bertie. It's finally going to happen.

Plant your seed of hope, that we may grow it together.

Faithfully,
Jane

41

YOURS

Jane,

Now I am the one left without words, having reread your last letter so many times that I'm fairly certain the paper will crumble away to ash if handled but once more. In truth, a part of me had feared this moment would never come. That I would remain locked away for the rest of my life. At least I will have Jane and her letters, I thought. Imagine, I'd condemned you to being stuck here in this house with me. I hadn't figured how or why that would be the case, just that I was unable to imagine enduring that possible future without you. You and Adèle are the only friends I have here.

In truth, it feels at times as if you are the only friends I have in the entire world. I know my family still cares for me, and I left friends home in New Orleans, but that seems like a lifetime ago. A different life entirely, in fact.

I think of the Bertha who lived that life. How naïve and foolish she was. I hate her for being tricked so easily. I hate myself for being hard on her. What happened wasn't her fault any more than being stuck here now is mine. And yet, my anger still burns. Isn't that strange? To be furious in one's understanding.

I know Edward is to blame, and while I am overflowing in my rage for him, there is still just enough space for rage at myself, irrational as that may be. So very strange. It's as if there is a storm trapped inside me, threatening to burst forth. I cannot control it; I cannot guide it; I can only unleash it. Watch it lay waste to everything around me. I often wished it would. Or that lightning would strike and set it all ablaze. Such imaginings often consumed my thoughts.

The storm is calmer now. I have you to thank for that, I think. Your seed of hope has sprouted into a great willow. Now, when the maelstrom in my heart threatens to engulf my very being, I think of you. I think of you, and I am able to hide myself away within the willow's branches and wait for the storm to pass. There is room for more than the anger. There is room for the idea of joy again, for laughter. My heart is lighter. I feel more like the girl I once was. Thank you for that, Jane.

Yours,
Bertie

PS Edward drinks both bourbon and whiskey. He picked up a taste for the former while in New Orleans. Whiskey will hide the taste of laudanum best. So I've heard.

42

ALWAYS

Bertie,

Why, Bertha Mason, however did you come by knowledge of what best hides the taste of laudanum? You are a shrewd one, another thing you have in common with my Helen. So many things. While I wish with all I am that she were still with us, and that you had never come to this wretched place, please don't think me cruel in the saying, but I am glad to have met you. I am glad to know you.

It is funny, in a way, how I used to imagine my future with Helen, a little house we would share together, with a small garden. Maybe a chicken or two, perhaps other animals. She, and I, and all that was to come spread before us. Any other outcome seemed impossible. And then the impossible happened in losing her.

I didn't think I would recover. In truth, a part of me never will. And I certainly never thought I would find the strength of heart to give mine to another in her stead. Another impossibility. But I feel that all things are possible with you.

I think of you as well. Often. I think of your smile, and all I would do to have you smile at me, because of me. I think of what it would be like to take you far away from here. I think of going to the theater, or attending a party. I think of a little house with a big kitchen and an even bigger garden, full of flowers. I think of making you cakes and biscuits and other sweet things, of taking tea with your family. I think of dancing beneath willow trees, all with you.

My confession likely comes as a surprise. Or perhaps it does not, and you've already decided to ignore what you have seen coming, but I had to speak the truth of my heart. You planted that seed, and this is what has grown from it. Forgive my forwardness, and my foolishness, but you are worth being foolish over.

Always,
Jane

43

ETERNALLY

Bertie,

I find myself at a crossroads of sorts. I would never wish you ill but would name myself a liar if I said I did not hope there was a reason you haven't answered my last few letters. I had feared the worst, that you had been carried away in the dead of night, and I had not stirred whilst my heart was stolen away unto darkness. I am relieved to find that is not the case, but now a new concern arises. You have received my letter and have elected not to respond.

Perhaps I said too much? Perhaps I've done too much? Please, know that I am sorry, and I meant no imposition. In fact, I would sooner cut off my right hand than slight you in such a way.

I miss hearing from you. I miss what our letters have become. I miss the laughter I could hear in your words, the way your voice would fill my head as I read them. I miss my friend. I miss you.

If it would suit you best, you can burn my confession. Throw it into the fire with the others, and let the ash fill this void between us. While I have professed my love, I would not do so if it meant losing my friend. And you are so dear to me.

Can we go back to before I ruined it all? We can pretend that letter never happened. Please. Our plans to escape this place still hold true.

Eternally,
Jane

44

RESPECTFULLY

Bertha,

Another day without word from you.

    This will be my last letter. Tomorrow night, I take dinner with Edward. He has announced that he'll be away on business the following day just as we had hoped.

    Everything is in place. Adèle and I are prepared. Please, provide some sign that you are as well. I cannot imagine you would not be, but I don't wish to assume more than I have.

    Soon, this will be over.

Respectfully,
Jane

PS I am with you. However you would have me.

45

LOVE

Jane,

~~I didn't know what to sa~~
~~Your confession took me by sur~~
~~I'm sorry~~

My silence these past days must speak volumes, and I realize the message sent is far from what is in my heart. Your words, your declaration, have shaken me to my core. At first, I thought the letter some cruel jest. That you did not intend what you had written, that somehow I had read it wrong, had strung the words together to find meaning that wasn't there, even if it was what I desired.

I read and reread and reread again, over and over, to the point that I'm certain I could recite the words by memory. And they never changed. Not a single syllable. They remained unmoving, solid, and sure. As I read, my heart began to pound, and I thought of when last someone had confessed such.

In truth, I loved Edward. And I believed him when he said he loved me in turn. Here I sit, because of love, so I thought. So convinced of this I was that fear took hold of me. Terror, in truth. Terror so sharp and wild, it stirred a hurricane in me. A terrible, clamorous thing that robbed me of all sense and thought. I was afraid of what had happened, that it might happen again.

*But then I closed my eyes and thought of you. I imagined you
waiting for me beneath a willow tree, the same one that grew
from your seed of hope. I imagined joining you there, both of us
safe from the maelstrom. I was still afraid, but I was not alone. I
was with you. I am with you. I want to be with you. If you would
have me. Please say you'll have me.*

Love,
B

I stare at the words until my vision starts to swim with them. My hand shakes. My chest heaves with the swell of my panicked breaths. I don't know how long I've sat here, hunched protectively over the now useless sheets of paper where I've started this letter at least half a dozen times. Twice as many additional attempts are scattered in wads of crumpled parchment across my bed. Sunlight spills into my room in slits, meaning it's likely well into the afternoon and approaching evening. Or maybe it's a particularly sunny day.

It shouldn't be so difficult to sign my name . . .

Creeeeeeeaaaaak.

The groan of wood snatches at my attention, and before I take my next breath I am out of my bed and across the room, yanking the door open. The chains clatter noisily behind me.

"Jane?" The flutter of my heart shakes my voice, wringing my eagerness free.

Adèle gazes up at me with those wide brown eyes caught in the bands of sunlight. Her mouth forms a silent O of surprise, her hand frozen where she's placing another letter on the floor of my closet.

"Bertha!" Adèle scrambles the rest of the way through, climbs to her feet, and flings her arms around my waist. Her hug is tight, her face pressed to my middle.

After taking a few seconds to swallow my disappointment, I fold her into my hold, returning her squeeze. "Quiet now, Grace might hear," I murmur, despite my earlier call.

"You haven't been leaving responses to the letters," Adèle says into my dress.

"I—I know." My throat is tight, the words catching. I swallow to smooth the way. "I'm sorry. Is . . . is that from Jane?"

"Yes!" The girl finally withdraws and offers the folded bit of paper I spied in her hand. "I know she delivered one just last night, but she said it was important."

I take the folded slip of paper with trembling hands and murmur my thanks.

Adèle nods, watching me with those eyes. There's something about her gaze, some understanding that seems ancient, especially when the rest of her is clearly so young. I look away, crossing to the nearby chair and table—where more of my failed attempts to write a response are scattered—and lower myself to sit.

This letter looks like all the others, only I know it won't be. Something has changed. It's my fault, of course, but I'm afraid all the same. I don't open it right away. Instead, I stare at it, and try not to get lost in the storm once again brewing inside my chest.

"You should read it," Adèle says, her voice so soft, so small, I almost don't hear her. But her tone is gentle yet firm.

I swallow thickly and slide my fingers along the length of it to stretch it out. There aren't very many lines.

Bertha,

Tonight it begins. If all goes according to plan, by this time tomorrow you will be a free woman, on your way home to your family. I'm happy to be part of that, and to have come to know

*you, Bertha Mason. Burn my letters. I've burned yours, and the
journal. We must be cautious from this point forward.*

Be well,
Jane

So very few lines. She had so very little to say, when before we wrote volumes to one another. And her tone . . .

I fold the letter up and set it on the table. "How soon until dinner?"

"She's preparing for it now," Adèle answers without moving from where I sense her still near the open closet door. "Won't be much longer. She asked me to bring that to you, to make sure you knew what was happening."

Swiping the tears from my face, I rise and set my shoulders. "I've something for you to take to her." I snatch the paper I've folded, unfolded, refolded, and unfolded again so many times it is likely to come apart at the creases.

The start of my signature sits there, branded against the faded white. My earlier fears, the frantic doubts that had plagued me since Jane's confession, seem to fall away. Why was it so difficult to sign my name?

Because I was doing more than that. I was making a declaration. One I had made before. One that was used against me. I was afraid of what had happened in the past, and I let that fear shackle me to the present, possibly denying me a future of happiness with Jane.

No, I've decided. I won't let fear stop me.

Edward Rochester has robbed me of enough. He cannot have her too. He cannot have what we share.

I won't allow it.

I sign my name, and hastily scribble a short message.

Love,
Bertie

PS I can't wait to run away with you. We can be foolish together.

Folding the letter, I extend it to Adèle, then pull her into another hug. "Thank you, sweet child. For being so brave. For all you've done."

Adèle squeezes me again. "It'll all be over soon," she murmurs.

"Yes," I say, my voice cracking beneath the weight of emotion settling in my chest. It's overwhelming to think about. "Yes, it will. See you on the other side?"

Adèle nods before turning to hurry into the closet. There's a rustle of cloth and a faint scrape of wood as she puts the planks back into place.

Then she's gone. I can't even hear her departing steps. She's like a ghost, haunting these halls as much as I. Together our spirits shall be set free.

I wonder if Jane knew that her coming to Thornfield would have such an effect.

Or if she's truly aware of what she risks by going up against Edward.

Fear takes me. True fear, the kind that hollows you out by turning your insides to foam.

Oh, Jane, my Jane. Please. Be careful. . . .

46

LOSS

JANE . . .

Sitting at my vanity, I stare at my reflection while Emm presses one last pin out of at least a dozen into my hair. A girl I only partially recognize stares back. She has the same brown skin and angular features I do, the same dark eyes, but there is no joy in them. It's as if the light has left her soul.

I know that look. I know that feeling. Both hounded me in the months following my Helen's passing. Only there is no death to mourn here.

But there is still loss, a part of my mind whispers, gentle and low. It's the same part of my mind that told me there was nothing to read into Bertie—Bertha's silence. That I was simply being impatient. That I was imagining things to be worse than they truly were. That all would be well. A part of my mind that was, unfortunately, outmatched by a much louder, crueler voice that scolded me for what I'd done. I'd gone and ruined a good thing by expecting more.

Both voices have been present for as long as I can remember, and while I had learned to silence the second, rowdier one some time ago, today it seemed to sense the chink in my armor. The weak link in the chain holding up my constitution.

"Now what's this long face for?" Emm asks as she presses another pin into my hair from the side.

I wince as it slides across my scalp.

She touches my cheek gently in apology. "Surely you can't be too fussed about dinner, seeing as how you accepted when you could have declined."

"It's not that," I answer truthfully, though I don't offer much else.

"Oh, good. I didn't think it would be. You don't seem the type to do what you don't want." Emm rests her hands on my shoulders, now finished with my hair. "But ye look like someone's had a go at ye. Come on, then, tell me all about it."

For a moment, I consider. Telling her about Bertha and the plan would lift some of the weight I feel, if only briefly. The reprieve would be welcome, and I know Emm would likely not only sympathize but offer aid. But Bertha has trusted me, and I cannot betray her.

And that isn't the only reason I say nothing. Part of me, that obstinate, chiding part that's decided to rear its ugly head, is protective of this particular pain. The one that once surrounded every thought of Helen, and now has turned its attentions toward Bertha. My hurt is a secret wound, one I've barely been allowed to nurse on my own. Perhaps that part of me is afraid of speaking the truth of the matter. The longer I can remain silent, the longer I can pretend it never happened.

"I'm not feeling well, is all." I lie as I have lied for the better part of a week. Today, right now, I can taste the bitterness of it. I offer a smile and let my hand fall over Emm's. "I'll be fine once I get some food in me, I think."

Emm's expression brightens and her fingers squeeze. "You bet your bonnet you will, especially with what I've prepared tonight. Something nice and heavy to settle upset stomachs and nerves. Seems the mister is a mite anxious as well."

"Oh?"

"Mmm." Emm hums as she adjusts the collar of my dress. It's one of Bertha's, from the chest he's given me. Again, I am both appalled and

297

comforted by this. While I abhor having to feign ignorance of what it is Edward is trying to do by dressing me like a doll in her things, I continue to take comfort in the fact that he unwittingly binds Bertha to me. That he ensures her presence fills my thoughts instead of him.

"I think it's to do with his trip into town tomorrow," Emm continues. She lifts a perfume bottle, another gift from Edward—another of Bertha's belongings, considering it's half-empty—and sprays me.

The scent of lavender and the faintest hint of mint fills my nose, and the desire to find Bertha, pull her into my arms, and claim her lips in a kiss fills my heart.

I push it down deep and try to focus on breathing.

"Is something amiss?" I ask, as if I don't know exactly what's happened.

"Oh, I wouldn't know the whys and what-fors. Honestly, I wouldn't want to. Men tend to complicate things unnecessarily, and I prefer to steer clear of it all. Though I must say I'm still surprised you agreed to this and all." She pins me with a knowing look via the mirror that I'm unable to hold.

I turn away. "In truth, I had thought to refuse him again. But he will be gone for a handful of days, and I'd like him to think favorably on me when next he visits the market."

Emm's smile takes a sly twist. "The better to shower you with more gifts and trinkets."

I shift in my chair to conceal my wince. "All the better. Men like to believe women have their purpose, so let them serve theirs. He desires my attention; let him purchase it like he does everything else he sees as valuable. I will not be cowed or bullied, but I may allow myself to be earned. Besides, a man like Edward Rochester is no stranger to working for what he wants. If he wishes to endear himself to me, it will be on my terms."

"You are a shrewd one, Jane Eyre. Brilliant really. I wish I had a mind like yours when I was so young."

My laughter and smile are genuine this time. "You say that as if you're some spinster. You're barely five years my senior."

"Half a decade is a lifetime, depending on your circumstances." Emm's reflection winks at me.

The knock at the door is sudden and takes the both of us by surprise. Emm taps my shoulder and crosses the room. As she does, I quickly check the lining I stitched both to the inside of my skirt, near the hem, and the much smaller one tucked just inside my collar. It will conceal the small bottle of laudanum I've prepared, while the other acts as a pocket for me to tuck away the documents we've taken from Edward's desk with room for any more I may find tonight.

The stitching on both is solid; I do good work. I finger the bottle, warmed by being pressed to my skin.

"Jane!" Adèle's voice bursts into the space, startling me.

Emm steps back to let the girl into the room.

I rise to stand. "I thought you were going to work on your latest painting this evening." It was a portrait of a quaint little street in Paris, the view from a balcony framed with flower boxes. Rather lovely.

"I was, but . . ." Adèle's fingers go to her waist, and my heart flutters.

That's where she tucks letters between deliveries, just in case she runs into anyone in the halls.

Heat rushes through me, though it is swiftly tempered by a fear that settles in my stomach. I swallow the want to be ill.

"I needed to ask you something." The girl's voice softens in secret meaning.

She has a letter from Bertha. What might it say? Did she rebuff my affections? Or, perhaps, more frightening a possibility . . . did she return them? I'm eager to know, I *must* know, and before I can think about it, I'm moving toward Adèle with purpose.

"Of course, I can—"

"Ahem."

The clearing of a throat stops me dead in my tracks, and has all three of us turning to the door, where Grace's stooped form partially fills the frame.

She watches us with that mistrustful, disapproving glint in her eye. The open disdain on her face when she looks at me manages to shake me from the brief spell of possibility cast by the words left unsaid between Bertha and me.

I manage to rein in my enthusiasm and regain my composure, my mind swimming with the knowledge that I nearly gave up the game. Heavens, am I really so far gone? Already so fully engulfed in Bertha that the mere possibility of correspondence with her sends all common sense fluttering from my mind like startled birds?

Yes, that gentler, quieter part of me insists. *Yes, you are.*

"The master awaits," Grace says, the grit in her tone grinding my thoughts to a halt.

I bite back a curse and hope my disappointment doesn't show on my face. To be certain it doesn't, I force a smile and pull Adèle in under the guise of a hug while Emm and Grace speak briefly about tonight's meal.

"I'll read it later," I whisper into the girl's hair.

Adèle nods and squeezes me in turn. "Be careful."

"Always."

We part, and I make to slip from the room. Grace and Emm already wait in the hall, the former turning to shuffle in the direction of the study without a word.

"Best not keep him waiting, then," Emm murmurs. "I'll go make sure everything is ready to be brought in."

She disappears down the hall. Behind me, there's another impatient "*Ahem.*"

I sigh and smooth my hands over the front of my dress. Bertha's dress.

"You know, if you're having a bit of trouble with your throat, a sip of laudanum might work wonders." I spin to face Grace but don't make to follow her just yet. "I've some left in the bottle Edward procured for me, I could fetch it for you before we go." It's a risk mentioning the laudanum at all, but hopefully calling attention to the fact that I've left it in my room will further insulate me from suspicion.

Grace peers down her long, thin nose at me, and narrows her yellowing eyes. "That won't be necessary. Come along."

I make a compliant yet dismissive sound at the back of my throat before following her. We walk in silence, our steps an uneven rhythm that fills the hall in lieu of the conversation that would rise were it Emm escorting me. Too quickly we are at the open door, and Grace gestures for me to enter.

As I do, she wraps her knuckles against the frame. "Jane Eyre for you, sir."

Disgust ripples through me. I am not *for* him and never will be, but I meet his gaze when it lifts from whatever he is reading on his desk.

"Edward," I say, dipping my chin slightly.

"Jane." The smile that takes his face is equal parts stunning and cutting, the latter because I know the ugly truth behind that pretty facade.

He rises and comes around his desk. I even offer my hand when he reaches for it.

"Thank you for agreeing to dinner tonight," he murmurs, his lips brushing the back of my knuckles with his words.

It takes everything in me not to snatch away as a feeling like worms digging beneath my skin crawls up the length of my arm.

"I almost didn't," I offer in quick reply, then arch an eyebrow when he frowns slightly. "I still feel under the weather. And you, Mr. Rochester, have yet to do right by me."

"Truly?" He straightens, his earlier enthusiasm slightly dimmed. A wave of his hand dismisses Grace, and I hear the study door close behind me.

"Indeed. I am owed two months' wages. Doubled, yes? And now, nearly three." I tap my fingers against my chin as if in thought, ignoring the dark look that takes his expression. "Well, I suppose we can forget such matters for tonight, given the value of that necklace."

"Right . . . the necklace," he murmurs, his gaze trailing to my collar. The area where the concealed bottle digs lightly into my skin prickles as if burning, a beacon to draw his attention, though I know the fabric is smoothed over. After a moment, his eyes find mine again and he says, "You aren't wearing it."

"Well, I can't wear it with everything, now can I? That wouldn't be fashionable at all." I step past him and over to the pair of plush chairs, lowering myself to the one farthest from the desk. "It clashes with the jeweled clasps on this dress."

Edward scoffs but moves to follow, lowering himself to the cushions, his attention still rapt on me. "But this isn't some social affair, it's simply dinner with . . . a friend."

"Mm." I lift my chin with the sound. "Perhaps. Bad habits have a knack of developing when one is lax in such things. Besides, I wanted to put on airs a little. I've had so few opportunities to do so in the past. I'd like to imagine there might be more in the future, but for now, dinner with you will more than suffice."

It's a mixture of sorts, both insult and compliment swirled together like a fine cocktail; bitter but enjoyable nonetheless. At least, that's what I hope. For a moment I'm afraid the tone I've striven for has missed the mark, but then another, softer smile splits Edward's face.

"You are a rather unusual woman," he says.

"So I've been told, usually by those who intend I be affronted." My other brow lifts, and I eye him expectantly.

"That is certainly not the case in my regard," he says quietly. "I simply meant, and I know I've said something to this effect in the past, that I've never met anyone quite like you."

Liar, I silently seethe, knowing Bertha sits, waiting, just two floors above us. But, once more, I smile, mostly to conceal the sneer I feel pulling at my face. "And you never will again, so I suggest we both take advantage of such a momentous occasion."

"And how might you propose we do that?" There's no mistaking the suggestive tone his voice has taken, though I ignore it entirely.

"I propose a toast! When Grace returns with the first course, have her fetch champagne. Surely you keep a bottle or two in the house, in case the need arises."

Edward's lips thin. No doubt champagne is an expenditure he can ill afford to make, but he would never say so out loud.

"I've a better idea," he says, climbing to his feet and crossing the room to where he keeps his liquor. I noticed the lack of a fire in the hearth, despite the chill that seems to cling to the air this time of year. "Lady's choice."

"Whiskey," I say after a few seconds of "deliberation."

"A woman after my own heart."

The clink of glass and slosh of liquid prelude his return to my side, a glass in each hand. I take the one he offers with thanks and pretend to sip. The bit of amber that does manage to slip past my lips still burns, so my wince is genuine.

"Yes, a good whiskey is worth just about any price." He takes a hearty sip from his own glass, his lips curling above his teeth briefly.

"I wouldn't know, I hardly ever buy it for myself, but I do enjoy it when I can." I keep the glass in my hand, my fingers wrapped around the lower half to hide the fact that, no matter how many sips I take this evening, the liquid will not lessen.

"You should have a drink with me more often, in that case."

"Is that entirely proper?"

"You don't strike me as a woman who cares about impropriety."

"I don't, but only to a degree that I can afford it."

"How do you mean?"

"Well, while I am apt to speak my mind on any and all things, and do as I please, with little regard for how others might perceive me as a result, there are still certain topics of conversation or actions I find personally distasteful."

"Such as?" He sips slow from his glass this time as he eyes me over the rim.

I let my attention move toward the cold, dark fireplace. "Such as attempting to inquire about such things. At least while still on the first drink of the evening."

The frown that had begun to pull at Edward's brow eases, and he settles back into his chair with a chuckle. "Very well, then. You wanted to make a toast?"

"Oh! Yes." I clear my throat and sit forward in my chair, portraying perfect eagerness as I lift my glass. "To . . . unusual women. May we remain unchained in all ways except the ones that matter to us most."

Edward falters briefly before mirroring my pretend sip with a deep one of his own. So deep, in fact, he rises in order to refill his newly empty glass. And I take that opportunity to dump half of mine into the pot of a nearby plant.

There's a knock on the door before it swings inward. Grace has arrived with the first course—though I know Emm has planned six— which includes a bottle of wine. I smile as Grace pours both of us a glass.

Taking up the one nearest me, I lift it in cheers, then drink. Edward does the same as bowls of soup are unveiled beneath silver domes.

Three courses, and perhaps two bottles of wine and as many glasses of whiskey later, I watch as Grace wheels out the cart piled with the dishes from the meal so far. She struggles with it at the door for a moment and, were she anyone else, I might've helped her. Instead, I pretend to sip at another whiskey as Edward recounts some daring tale from his boyhood that I cannot be bothered to truly listen to. If he later wishes to discuss details I cannot recollect, I'll blame it on the drink.

And in terms of drink, it looks like he's well into feeling the effects of his. I should hope so, with as much as he's had. He hasn't matched Marsters just yet, but one might get the distinct feeling that he's making an attempt, what with the slightly glassy quality to his eyes and the tinge of pink flushing his cheeks. My, how I wish that delicate flush was due to my smacking him both ways across the face.

"And *that* is why I am still the best at cricket in the entire region," he finishes with a prideful smile.

"Fascinating." I rub at my arms as if warding off the cold. I've been doing so for at least ten minutes, hoping he takes the rather obvious hint. But he's been so busy talking about himself the entire time.

He pauses in lifting his whiskey glass to his lips, eyeing me up and down. "Cold, my dear?" His words aren't slurred and he's still very alert, though unobservant.

"Mmm, a little."

"It would be my pleasure to warm you up."

I don't miss the wink and simply smile in return. "Perhaps warm food might do the trick."

"Perhaps. But there are other ways."

"In truth. Though it looks like you're almost out."

He blinks, confusion taking over the suggestive look in his eye. "Out?"

"Of firewood?" I gesture with the hand holding my nearly empty wineglass before sipping.

"Oh, well, so it seems."

"Two logs should provide ample enough warmth for the rest of the night."

I dangle the bait ever so slightly, and the look that transforms Edward's face tells me he's found it. The rest of the night indeed. He's no doubt imagining what I might mean by that, and what he'd want me to mean. He can imagine all he likes.

Setting his glass on the nearby tray with our as yet untouched course, he rises to his feet. "This won't take but a moment."

I turn my focus to the food, lifting the silver domes to reveal the small dishes with little bowls of some sort of paste. Across the way, Edward takes up one of the last logs, swaying with a huff of frustration as he does. His state has turned this simple task into a bit more than he bargained for, which is what I had hoped.

He fusses with the flint, attempting to birth the beginnings of a flame as I pluck the bottle from the pocket hidden in my collar. With shaking fingers, I empty the contents into his glass, my heart beating around my ears. The liquid burns darker, noticeably so. My panicked pulse tries to deafen me as I quickly tip a portion of my whiskey into the glass. Some of it splashes onto the table and I swallow a curse.

The deep brown color lightens, some of the amber returning to the liquid, but only barely. I pray he doesn't notice.

There's a crackle and a bark of victory as he finally coaxes the flames out of hiding. It startles me, and I fumble in trying to twist the top back onto the bottle, dropping both into the folds of my skirts on my lap.

Edward stands, adding the second log. My entire body is given to trembles as I hurriedly snatch up the bottle and slip it back into the pocket near my collar. I'm settling into my chair when he finally returns to his.

"There's your fire, my dear. It's not exactly roaring, but—"

I wave a hand dismissively. "It will no doubt do the job. Now then, where were we?"

"Something about keeping warm the rest of the night?" He leans forward, his elbows braced against his knees. His drink goes untouched.

I try not to let my eyes drift toward it and instead hold his gaze. "Actually, you were telling me about your various sportsman titles."

"And you were looking practically bored to tears the entire time."

My faint chuckle is genuine. "Only when it came to cricket." I sip my wine, slow, hoping he'll mirror me again.

"Ah, you wound me." He doesn't take up his drink.

My hold tightens on my glass, and I pray my frustration doesn't show on my face. "I've lost my taste for this vintage." I set my glass down and puff out my lips in the barest pout.

"I could have Grace bring in another," Edward offers.

"Or you could pour me just the tiniest taste more of . . ." My whiskey glass glints as I shake it slightly.

Amusement lights his eyes, his face framed by firelight. The devil himself must have a face like that.

"A third? Don't you think that might be a tad much for one night?" Despite his words, he takes my glass.

"You keep count of your drinks, Edward Rochester, and I will tally mine."

His chuckle is warm and low, pitched so by the liquor no doubt catching up to him. "Very well, though I'm afraid that might be it for both of us." He lifts the now empty decanter.

"Oh, pity." My pout deepens. "Just fetch more on your trip tomorrow."

"Yes, yes." He offers the drink, making sure to brush my fingers with his. Instead of the fluttering flush I'm no doubt supposed to feel in his mind, my stomach twists in revulsion and I have to hold myself fast to keep from yanking away.

He retakes his seat and, damn it all, ignores his glass once more. He opens his mouth to speak and I lean forward to swat at his arm where it drapes over his knee. Confusion takes his face.

"No more stories, not before our toast." I raise my glass.

Edward arches an eyebrow slowly. "We toasted earlier. Twice, in fact."

"Well, yes, but we've finished the bottle. It's bad luck not to acknowledge it."

"What sort of wives' tale is this?"

"The kind I take very seriously." I gesture for him to join me. "Come on, now."

There's a moment when I fear he won't, but then he heaves a breath and lifts his glass. I raise mine higher before drinking.

The entire thing. There isn't near as much as there has been in the other pours—I'm certain I've killed that poor plant—but it's enough to feel it. The burn starts on my tongue and scrapes along the back of my throat, roaring all the way down. It coats the sides and roof of my mouth. I can even feel the sting in my teeth.

Edward makes an appreciative sound as he too drains his glass, not to be outdone by a woman. His face twists far more than I've seen it do, and he lifts his now empty glass as if inspecting it will somehow answer whatever questions he's asking himself. It's likely the bitterness from the laudanum he's hung up on.

"Oh my." I touch my lips and flutter my lashes as tears prick the corners of my eyes. "Make sure to get this exact brand." My now empty glass clacks against the table.

"Mmm." Edward smacks his lips silently, still puzzling out the odd taste.

"I suppose we've enough wine left to finish the next course. Two courses? How many have we had?"

"I lost count." His eyes trail to the empty decanter across the way.

"Is something the matter?" My voice cracks toward the end of my question, and I clear my throat. "Oh, little stronger than I anticipated. Pardon me."

"I'm . . . not sure . . ." He frowns, though it's not at anything in particular, from what I can tell. "How was your drink?" he asks.

"Strong." I pat my chest lightly for emphasis. "Is it true they say the bottom of the bottle is the strongest? I feel that might be true."

Edward looks at me, and his expression eases. "Another . . . another wives' tale?" Now he *is* slurring his words. He presses a hand to his face.

"One of many, though this one may be true. My goodness, I feel a little light-headed." There's a breathy quality to my voice.

He digs the heels of his hands into his eyes. "That's not . . . there shouldn't . . ." With a sudden burst of energy, he surges to his feet, jostling the cart and the dishes atop it, startling me as well.

"Edward?" I ask, the fear creeping into my words genuine. "What's wrong?"

"I . . . I don't know, I . . . mmphng . . . Rrrnn." Those last few sounds aren't even words. He takes a stuttering step forward, then rocks backward, landing in the chair with a *whump!* and scooting it across the floor several inches. His body goes limp, his legs splayed, one arm draped over the side.

At first, I don't move. I barely dare to breathe. I stare at him, my heart pounding so loud I'm sure it can be heard throughout the house. I strain to listen, trying to catch wind of anyone approaching to investigate. But nothing happens. No one comes.

I shake loose of my shock and push to my feet. Edward's chest rises and falls so slow I'm half convinced I'm imagining it and he's actually dead. Killed by my hand. I cross the space between us in inches and reach to set my fingers just beneath his nose. The instant warm air brushes my skin, I snatch my hand away. He's alive, the bastard, but asleep. It worked.

I swallow the celebration bubbling inside me and hurry across the study, sweeping in behind the desk to begin tugging open drawers. Papers flutter; journals and ledgers thunk against the wood. There's so many, so much, but I must start somewhere. I'm careful to go through one drawer at a time, my eyes sweeping over written or printed pages, searching for words and names to identify what I've found.

Letters to one lender. From another bank. To different houses in the area. The correspondence I planted from one Mr. Carlisle. I smirk as a small swell of satisfaction rises in my gut but don't have time to revel and instead continue searching. More letters from a few of the names I recognize from the wedding. Edward snorts and I freeze. I peer at him over the top of the desk. The back of his head is visible lain against the spine of the chair, his arms draped over the sides. He doesn't move.

I press a hand to my chest. It feels as if my heart is going to burst clean out of it. I had feigned my light-headed flush before, but now my vision wanes slightly in the beginnings of a swoon. My nerves and the whiskey no doubt. I try to shake it off and continue.

I've finished with two of the four large drawers and have only opened the third when there's a knock.

My entire body goes still as stone.

My stomach bottoms out.

My heart lodges itself in my throat.

And my eyes find the door just as it swings open.

∽ 47 ∾

BETRAYAL

JANE . . .

I'm caught. There is nowhere for me to go, nowhere for me to hide, as the door to Edward's study swings inward.

Emm sweeps forward, a tray in hand. "I hope you're ready for p—" Her words dry up as her eyes take in the scene, sweeping back and forth and growing wider each time.

Her gaze finally locks with mine.

"Jane?" she whispers, shock clear on her face and in her voice.

"Shut the door!" I gesture wildly. I am relieved to see it's her and no one else, truly, but my panic is still fluttering in my ears and a healthy dose of fear is right behind it.

Emm fumbles briefly as she twists to kick the door shut before moving to set the tray on the trolley. Her eyes move to Edward and she gasps, drawing back.

"I—I . . . did you . . ." Her voice is quiet, thready, and quaking.

"No," I hiss as I return to my task. "He's just drunk is all."

"Oh." Her relief is palpable. "Because that . . . that would have been unfortunate to deal with." She crosses the room, her steps quiet and hedged. I think she's still staring at him.

Eventually she joins me at the desk, knocks against the top of it to draw my attention. Her brow is furrowed, her concerned gaze still dancing between me and Edward. "The man passes out drunk, and you decide to rifle through his things? I did not think you capable of such betrayal, Jane Eyre."

I huff an annoyed breath. "It's more complicated than that. He . . . he hasn't paid me since I arrived. I'm looking for my missing wages."

Emm seems to reconsider her stance at that, or reconsider reconsidering. "Is that all? While I understand your exasperation with the matter, do you really think this is the best recourse? You're stealing! The man opened his home to you, and you've betrayed him."

"Have I? Well, he's done *far* worse." I take a breath and focus on lowering my voice where it had begun to crest with my irritation.

Emm snorts in that way of hers that so oft amused me, but now only serves to fan the flames of my ripening ire. "Withholding wages isn't *much* worse than steal—"

"He's imprisoned a woman!" I bark. The words are out of my mouth, and I want to grab them and force them back inside before they have a chance to register.

But it's too late. Even if she wasn't looking at me as if I'd grown a second head, it would still be too late.

I had hoped for a different reaction. Something other than the skepticism in her eyes. Even though I understand the dubiety of the situation and the reasoning I have given, part of me wanted her to believe me simply because she is my friend. But that makes no sense. I know that, and pause in what I'm doing to meet Emm's gaze. "Her name is Bertie—Bertha Mason. She's locked upstairs right now."

Emm continues staring at me, her gaze flicking to Edward's slumped form every few seconds. She swallows thickly. "W-what?"

"Edward married Bertha for her money, then imprisoned her. Long before you arrived." I speak as I continue to search, pushing this drawer closed and opening another. "He's been doling out her possessions, cutting away pieces of her, biding his time. And he may have killed another woman in France. I can't prove that part, but Bertha is upstairs, right now, and I'm going to free her."

Something catches the light where it rests at the bottom of the drawer.

I reach in and my fingers brush against something solid. When I lift my hand, a string of iridescent pearls dangles in the air, twinkling in the low firelight. I peer deeper into the drawer and spy a pair of keys. My breath catches; a silent prayer that these are *the* keys is interrupted when I spy a thick envelope. My heart kicks when I see MASON scrawled across the top. Inside is a ledger.

Closing the drawer, I flip open the ledger. *Everything* is here. Letters from Bertha's parents, documents regarding their marriage, and most chilling of all, a contract for the official adoption of Adèle Varens, by Mr. and Mrs. Rochester. My assumption had been right.

There're also inquiries concerning inheritance law from America and methods of folding it into law here, and a mess of other things surrounding Bertha. And tucked between it all are the two tickets Bertha spoke of for the ship next week.

Pressing everything back into place, I hug the ledger to my chest and release a slow breath. I could cry. Instead, I swallow the tears and quickly tuck it and the pearls into the pocket I've sewn into my skirt.

I hurry to my feet, ready to tell Emm the good news, but she's no longer standing near the desk. A quick glance reveals she's stepped over to peer down at Edward where he's slumped even further in his chair.

"Are you sure he's all right?" Emm asks, leaning in over him just so.

She is the one near him, but it's my skin that crawls. "Far better off than he deserves."

Her eyes trail to the nearby table, where the whiskey glasses still sit. "So you said. And what is it you plan to do now? Surely, he will have questions when he wakes. Suspicions."

"He may," I say. "But when we are discovered in such a state and taken to bed having had our fill of drink, he will wake in the morning with witness accounts of what happened. Whatever suspicions arise, I will not be at their center." I make my way quickly across the room to my chair, settling into it. "I was lucky you came instead of Grace, otherwise this would've never worked. After he leaves tomorrow morning, with your help, I can get Bertie to safety. And Edward can pay for what he's done."

I can't keep the heat from my words, or my gaze as I look at him. What will happen after tonight is not in my hands; any ramifications Edward is forced to endure will likely be quelled by his connections and status. But Edward Rochester will not terrorize Bertha or Adèle any longer.

"Bertie?" Emm asks, lifting Edward's glass and sniffing it.

"Bertha Mason. Bertie is . . . a pet name."

"Laudanum," Emm murmurs, impressed. "There were no headaches, then?"

"What does that matter?" I smooth my hands over my dress before crumpling it up again strategically. "All right. Emm, please, I need your help. Find Grace to tell her you discovered us in such a condition as this."

"Clearly this ruse was long in the making. You are quite clever indeed, Jane Eyre. Cleverer than most, by far."

I pause, watching her as she sets the glass down, tracing the lip of it with her fingertip. "Ah . . . my thanks. But please, time is of the essence, I don't know how long he will—"

"But not as clever as you think."

Something sharpens in her tone enough to cut through me, leaving my words dangling in empty air. "What?" I barely have breath enough to form the single syllable.

"It really is a pity." She pats Edward's cheek. Hard.

He winces and shifts with a grunt.

And my heart is in my ears. "Don't!"

"I like you. Truly." She pats him again. Harder.

His eyes roll beneath his lids.

"But I can't allow this to continue." She lifts her hand.

"Stop!" I'm across the room and gripping her raised wrist in an instant. "What are you doing?!"

The calm on Emm's face, in her eyes, is such a startling contrast to the storm wailing inside me that I'm struck speechless. She regards me with open contempt.

I don't understand.

She snatches free of my grasp, moving toward the desk. "'Dear Miss Eyre, I hope my correspondence finds you well. I am pleased with your decision to accept my offer of employment as governess in Thornfield Hall.'"

Where my heart thrashed in my ears a moment before, it now drops into my stomach with enough force that it threatens to pull me to the floor. My mouth gapes uselessly.

Emm makes her way around the desk, her steps slow, measured, her eyes on me. Her fingers trace the edge of the wood. "'As such, I will send for you at the earliest possible convenience. A coach will arrive at Lowood the morning of Saturday of next week. That is the sixteenth. I trust this will provide plenty of time for you to make the necessary preparations. Room and board will be provided as part of your wages. Please bring anything else you feel you will need.'"

As I continue to stare, my body unable to move, my limbs turn to lead, the air in my chest all but water for how well I am able to breathe. The trembling starts in my gut and moves through the rest of me. I feel I am coming undone, bit by bit, pulled apart like so much clay.

"'Regards.'" Emm lowers herself into Edward's chair and settles back, making herself comfortable. "'E.'"

I stare. I can do nothing but stare. Stare and gasp for breath that refuses to come. My vision waxes and wanes in time with my pulse.

When I finally find my voice, it flakes as badly as the rest of me. "E-E . . . Edward's letter . . ."

"Not Edward's. Mine." She waves a hand as if unveiling some grand exhibit. "Well, he agreed to the entire thing, but it was my idea. Fishing through advertisements for governesses, looking into ones he could potentially woo. Women of specific status, with no other prospects, who would gladly welcome the attentions of such a man if they were offered. The first one, well . . . you know what happened to her."

Adèle's previous governess. Yes, I know what happened to her, but my words have abandoned me again. I swallow thickly, trying to regain them. The room continues to swim. Though the fire has dwindled, the temperature is stifling. I can't breathe.

"And then came Jane Eyre." Emm smiles wide, a hint of her friendliness returning. "An answer to our prayers."

"O-our?"

"Mmm. Edward owes my family a great deal of money. And when he married that Yank upstairs"—Emm points toward the ceiling—"it was thought he would have it. But it has been slow going. Slower than suits our needs. So I came. To help him find a replacement for her. Someone to stand at his side as Bertha Mason, long enough for the ink to dry on the checks."

She knew about Bertha. The realization rises beneath me like steady ground, providing me a foundation on which to put myself back together.

First comes the anger.

Emm knew about Bertha and did nothing. In fact, she helped keep her here.

"Seems we'll have to start over again," Emm continues, unaware of the rage rising inside me, righting my thoughts. "All that time and effort, wasted. And poor Adèle. She's grown quite attached to you. But it can't be helped. Oh, come now, don't look at me like that. It's not personal, it's business. And, as I said, I really do like you." She folds her hands upon her lap, looking most pleased with herself.

"Who are you?" I demand, though there's little force behind my words as I'm gradually coming back to myself.

"I'm exactly who I claimed to be. A cook. Though I suppose I neglected to mention my former employer holds one of Rochester's largest debts. I was sent to keep an eye on the man, lest he steal away into the night. I assume in the asking, you want a name." She dips her head, as if in a bow. "Blanche Emmaline Ingram. But I prefer to be called Emm, as you know."

Ingram. The name is familiar. I recall it from one of the letters I discovered.

"You . . . did all this . . ." I'm shaking. So is my voice. I sound afraid. I am furious. "Helped him imprison Bertha. Lie to her ailing parents. Plotted to steal everything from her. Did you have him kill Adèle's mother, too?"

Emm's brows lift in what appears to be genuine surprise. "No idea about any of that. Edward's not exactly a choirboy. You don't get in deep with my lot by being a moral man."

Edward groans, shifting in his chair. My heart seizes in my chest once more. If he wakes, I'm done for. And Bertha . . .

"This has been fun, but it's time to put an end to the game." Emm rises from the chair, moving toward the cord that will summon Grace, or Devin, or Marsters.

Before I can think, I'm racing across the room. Emm barely has time to bark a startled shout before I slam into her. There is pain from our collision, and again when we hit the bookshelf behind her with a crash. The tomes topple down around us like stones in an avalanche.

Emm snarls and tangles her fingers in my hair, yanking at the braids and curls she'd so precariously pinned in place earlier. We shriek in one another's faces, fingers pulling, nails scratching. Something digs into my wrist and rakes across my face. Pain, white hot, drags along my nerves. We're a tangle of limbs and fabric.

Her palm strikes me across the face, and I see stars.

She shouts for me to get off her, screaming for help.

I say nothing. I save my words, my breath, my strength for beating her senseless.

With a shout, Emm's knee drives into my stomach, forcing the air from me. I lie there, stunned, my lungs twisting to try to take in air. Emm scrambles to her feet. I struggle to follow, snatching at her skirts. She kicks out at me, and I get a hand around her ankle, tripping her. She crashes to the floor in front of the hearth, and I crawl in over her.

She thrashes and howls like some wild thing dying in the woods.

The fire poker is in my hand.

I bring it down across the back of her head.

Emm goes still beneath me.

I raise it again but hesitate. She doesn't move. I can't tell if she's breathing, and panic stabs through me. Emm is . . . was . . . my friend, at least for a time. The thought that I've brought her harm strikes *me*; though I know it shouldn't, I cannot help it.

"E-Emm," I whisper.

She doesn't respond.

"Emm!" I shake her shoulder.

Edward groans, shifting in his chair.

My fear and worry vanish. I have to move.

Clambering to my feet, I stumble across the study and throw open the large door. The hall is blessedly empty, and I break into a run, poker in hand.

I have to get to Bertha. I have to find Adèle. There's no time.

Doors and windows rush by me as I run. My lungs burn. My head throbs from where Emm slammed it into the floor.

The house is silent. Far more silent than it should be for what has happened. The sun has set, and the looming shadows menace me from the corners.

Still, I run, through the house, up the stairs.

I encounter nothing and no one, reaching the room beside Bertha's. I don't care about being silent as I fling open the closet door and scramble through the hole in the wall, emerging on the other side and stumbling into Bertha's dimly lit room.

And there she is, seated on the bed, stunning and beautiful as the night I first laid eyes on her.

"Jane!" She jumps to her feet, her chains rattling, her eyes wide in surprise, and growing wider as she takes in the sight of me. "What—"

"We have to go!" I tug the keys from my pocket.

Without a word, Bertha pulls the bindings taut.

The chains come loose with a clink.

"What's happened?" Bertha asks as she shakes free.

"We have to find Adèle. We have to get out of here, it—"

Bang!

The door rattles on its hinges as someone shakes it by the knob from the other side.

"Open it," snarls Marsters, his words slightly slurred. "NOW! Make sure they can't get through the other side!"

Steps thud into the adjacent room, blocking our only other exit. We're trapped.

"Get behind me," I whisper.

The locks on the door click as they're undone.

My wild breathing steadies.

Behind me, Bertha whispers my name. Her hand slips into mine.

My wailing pulse begins to calm.

Whatever happens, Bertie will be free. I'll deal with what comes after.

The knob turns.

I squeeze her fingers, then let go, lifting the poker to brandish it with both hands.

The door swings open.

༄ 48 ༄

RUNNING

BERTHA . . .

"Jane!" I whisper. There's so much I want to tell her, so much I need to say.

She squeezes my hand. My heart beats wildly in my chest, like a trapped bird trying to escape its cage.

The door swings open.

Marsters and Devin push into the room.

Jane swings wildly, screaming as she does. She nearly takes off Marsters's head. He barely manages to dodge, dropping to the floor, unable to halt his momentum.

Devin comes at me, reaching. Jane swings again and the end of the poker catches him across the face. He cries out, but before he's finished feeling the pain of her first attack, she swings again, catching him across the middle. He drops to his knees, but now he has hold of the poker.

She yanks at it, kicking him. I do as well, aiming for his face, but my movement is halted when a hand grabs my ankle and hauls me off my feet. The instant I hit the floor, Marsters is on top of me, his breath hot and rank in my face, his eyes wide and wild, yellow and feverish in his efforts. His hands close around my throat and begin to squeeze.

The pain is unlike anything I've ever felt. It rolls through me in great waves, bubbling in my chest as my lungs struggle and fail to take in air.

Darkness crowds my vision, pushing it sideways.

I can't, I . . .

"No!" Jane screams.

Marsters shouts, and the weight of him lifts off me. I can breathe again. The relief of it is so sudden I'm left light-headed, coughs wracking my body, threatening to shake me apart. My throat is on fire.

The room tilts on its axis as I push myself up.

Jane thrashes on the floor where Marsters has hold of her, or rather she has hold of Marsters. To the side, Devin is regaining his senses, pushing himself to his knees.

"Run!" Jane shouts.

Her nails rake across Marsters's cheek, leaving lines of red. He howls in pain while I struggle to rise as well, my legs folding under me like wet grass.

"Get away from here!" Jane commands, her voice cracking. "GO!"

And just leave her here? How could I? *I can't!*

But then my eyes find hers, wide and fearful and . . .

Go . . .

Tears well, the sting sharp as knives. I push myself upright. My head pounds in protest. My legs have locked, but I force them to move. I will do this one thing she has asked of me.

I run. Stumbling into the hall, catching myself against the wall.

My heart in my throat, and my eyes burning to blinding, I run.

Down the hall and around a corner.

My legs nearly give out twice on the back stairs. The voices above me continue to shout, Marsters sending Devin after me.

I don't stop. I can't stop. If I do . . .

I reach the main floor.

CRACK!

Fire erupts in my left thigh, sending me crashing to the floor. It feels as if my leg is being ripped from my body. I stare at the red blossoming along the tear in my dress where I clutch at my thigh, then at the figure standing near the stairs.

Grace fumbles with a pistol, her thin lips drawn in a sneer. "She's here!"

I grit my teeth against the pain and haul myself upright again. The door is just ahead. My leg screams with each hobbling step, and I nearly fall twice more before reaching it and throwing it open.

Darkness greets me, and I fling myself into it.

More voices join Grace's. Devin's.

Edward's . . .

I don't know what he's saying. I don't care.

I keep running.

The night air is hot against my face. So are my tears.

I keep running.

The moon and the stars are bright above me.

I keep running. . . .

୬ 49 ୧

WHERE THEY MAY

JANE . . .

Pain in my arms and my face drags me from the darkness of sleep and I blink my eyes open. My head throbs, and it takes a moment for my thoughts to crystallize, but when they do, I sit up. The world spins and the agony that had pulled me from my sleep spreads to encompass all of me.

"Wouldn't move around much if I were you," a voice says.

A man sits across from me where I lie in a bed. The light of the lantern dances over his red hair and thin face.

Devin.

He lounges in a chair beside my bed. No, not mine. Bertha's.

For a brief moment of panic, I search for signs of her, but there are none.

"She got away," Devin murmurs, settling back in his seat. He winces, pressing a hand over his stomach. The area around his eye is beginning to puff and purple.

Good. I'm glad it hurts. I hope he's pained the rest of his miserable life.

I glare at him as I sit up, slower now, carefully.

He looks on me with sympathy, almost. "You really shouldn't put up such a fight when people are trying to help you," he says.

"Help? Is that what you think you're doing?" I snap back.

He opens his mouth as if to reply, but the sound of approaching steps stills his tongue, and my heart plummets. I push myself to the edge of the bed as the door flies open and Edward enters.

His face is a storm, his fists tight at his sides. He grips something in his left hand. Papers, I think.

"Where is she?" His voice is calm despite his obvious fury.

I lift my chin and hold his gaze. I will weather him. I am not afraid.

"Tell me!" he roars, eyes wide and wild where they hold mine.

For a moment, I do and say nothing, save watch him. He shifts under my scrutiny, looking to Devin, then back to me.

"She's gone," I say, my own calmness startling me.

Edward's expression twists with rage. "I gave you everything. Luxuries. Fine clothes. Jewelry. Run of my home. I offered you more, and here you . . . ungrateful. You're all ungrateful."

"Like Bertie was ungrateful when you locked her away, planning to steal her family fortune?" My accusation rings clear in the thick stillness of the room. "Or how about Adèle's mother, when she refused you? Then you threw her into a river."

Edward's face goes bright red, and he takes a step toward me. Fear kicks in my heart, but something stronger holds me steady. I will not be moved.

"Where is she?" He repeats the question as his eyes slide to Devin.

"Gone, sir." Devin lowers his gaze before gesturing to me with the hand not wrapped around his delicate middle. "This one let her get away. Threw herself at Marsters so she could get by."

"She . . . sacrificed herself?" The way he asks the question sends a cold feeling through me.

"That she did, sir."

"Well. Emm's assumptions were right." Edward lifts papers that had been crumpled in his hand, holding them out for me to inspect.

My insides froth up at the mention of Emm. The twist of the knife at her betrayal is still fresh, still painful.

Edward snorts. "She's alive. Concussed, but well enough to tell me what you had planned. Smart. But not smart enough." He waves his hand to draw my attention to the paper in his fingers.

It's a letter, I realize. I recognize Bertha's elegant script. For a moment, I'm confused. I burned her letters, and the journal.

"You seem surprised," Edward mutters. "We found this in Adèle's room."

A gasp escapes me before I can catch it.

The letter Adèle brought me before dinner. . . .

"It seems my dear wife has developed a fondness for you. Do you share her affection?"

I say nothing. I can't. My tongue is stuck to the roof of my mouth and my lips no longer function.

"Oh, yes," Edward says as he looks me over. "Of course you do."

He turns away from me and begins to pace. "We need to prepare for my wife's arrival."

"You think she's coming back?" Devin asks, his confusion clear as mine.

"I know she's coming back. We have something she wants." Edward looks to me once more, and the truth of his words pricks my heart. Bertie will come for me, no matter how much I don't wish her to. Because I would come for her.

And now we will both be doomed.

50

MRS. ROCHESTER

BERTHA . . .

When I'm certain I'm not being pursued, I double back. I haven't managed to make it far, the wound in my leg hampering all progress. I've bound it with fabric from my dress. It's not as bad as it could be, little more than a graze, but the pain feels so much larger, so much deeper. It slows me, and I already have so little time to spare. I get as close as I dare, sticking to what shadows there are. I circle the house, listening carefully for signs of anyone who might be stirring.

My mind works over the possible ways I can enter when I hear a sound that draws me up short. Sniffling, crying, quiet as a whisper. I follow the sound to find Adèle, tucked behind a bush. I call to her softly, then dare to be a little louder.

She pokes her small head out of the brush and gasps.

I hold a finger to my lips to quiet her and beckon her with a quick wave of my hand.

She hurries over to me, whispering breathlessly, "They have Jane! She's locked in your room, I couldn't stop them, I'm sorry."

Holding the girl to me, I nod slowly. My room. Of course.

"We can get her out," I whisper. "Can you take me to her? Without us being seen?"

Adèle sniffs and wipes her eyes. "I can try."

327

I manage a smile for her. "We can do this." I whisper the words Jane wrote to me many times. "We will do this."

She nods again and turns to lead the way into the house, through a side door that was likely used by staff at some point. Slowly, carefully, we move through the otherwise quiet though brightly lit house.

There's no sight or sound of anyone else, and I can only imagine where they all are and what they're doing. Up the stairs and down halls, our going is slow, and my wound howls with the effort to stay upright, but I grit my teeth and bear it.

Soon we reach the hall that I am oh so familiar with and slip into the room beside the one that had been my prison for so long. At the closet, I hesitate. I don't want to go back. Something tells me if I do, I'll never leave again. But . . . Jane's in there. I pull the wood free and crawl through. For a moment, silence presses in around me save for the beating of my heart.

"Jane?" I whisper into the darkness.

Then, with a strike of a match, light filters in. A lantern is lit and turned up. Two lanterns, filling the room with light.

Marsters holds one, Edward holds the other, and Jane is nowhere to be seen.

"Welcome home," Edward says. "Mrs. Rochester."

⤳ 51 ⤶

FORGIVEN

JANE . . .

I pace the floor of Grace's room, which has been locked from the outside. Grace watches me with a scowl in place of her usually judgmental expression whenever she glances up from a needlepoint she's working on. She's cross with me for poisoning her employer.

"It wasn't poison," I'd told her. "But perhaps it should have been."

She called me rude.

I laughed.

And so, she's been here, my quiet companion. Silent and glowering. I want to take that needle and jam it into one of her eyes, but that won't solve my current problem.

Though it might make me feel better for a while.

I still when the sound of the lock draws our attention. The door swings open, and Marsters steps through.

"Come with me." It's not a suggestion, and I'd refuse if not for the grip he has on my arm. He drags me the short distance to Bertie's room, but I don't make it easy for him, fighting the entire way.

At least until we reach the open door, and the fight leaves me entirely.

Inside, Edward stands looking completely calm. To his right, Bertie has placed herself in front of a terrified Adèle.

"No," I whisper as something breaks inside me.

329

"What did I tell you?" Edward announces as if he's made the most delightful discovery.

Marsters pushes me into the room and follows, closing the door behind us.

My eyes stay on Bertie. "Why did you come?"

"We all know the answer to that." Edward waves the pages of Bertie's letter in the air before tossing them onto the bed. "Now then, since I have everyone's attention." He looks to me and his expression softens. He places a hand on his chest, and for a moment, I could almost believe he's the gentleman he's played at being these past months.

"I didn't want things to be this way, Jane, but you're forcing my hand. All of you are forcing my hand. Because you don't know better, so you can't do better. Ungrateful, like I said. But! We can put this messy business behind us." He aims a finger at Bertie. "You *will* sign your executorship over to me. Or I'll be forced to do away with poor Jane."

"Don't listen to him!" I shout, and barely blink before Edward steps between us and his hand strikes me clear across my face. I hit the floor.

Adèle screams.

"Leave her be!" Bertie shouts.

My head rings as I pick myself up. "I-I'm all right," I stammer out.

"For now," Edward says softly. He gestures and Marsters takes hold of my arms. "But that can change fairly quickly." He lifts a finger. "Don't interrupt me when I'm talking. It's rude. Now, Bertha. If you don't want Jane to come to further harm, you'll sign over your holdings. And Jane, if you don't want harm to come to Bertha, you'll behave yourself while you're a guest here in my home. Perhaps I'll give you a nice room up here; that way the two of you can be close. But not too close. Can't have you planning little coups again."

I look to Bertha. That defiant light in her eyes, that fire I've come to adore, I see it flickering, lessening. Dampening.

I shake my head, but even as I do, even as her eyes hold mine, I know what she plans to do. I can't let her, I can't . . .

"As you wish," she whispers.

"Good. And I'm truly sorry you won't get to see your father again, but that's your own fault for going along with this"—his waves a hand—"folly. Perhaps you'll learn a woman's place. Both of you. You set a bad example for the child."

My eyes move to Adèle. Or at least where she was, but she's no longer behind Bertie. Movement to my left draws my attention, as well as everyone else's.

Adèle grips a lantern, raising it above her head. Edward starts to say something but, with a shriek, she lets it fly.

The glass shatters. Oil splashes across the carpet. Flame follows.

Edward bellows to put it out and Marsters lets me go, grabbing for blankets on the bed. That's when I spot the other lantern on the nearby table. I go for it.

Edward howls my name as my fingers grip the metal, the heat searing my hand, but I don't care. I lift it and slam it to the ground, sending another plume of flame across the rug. It eats at the cloth and the carpet; the blankets are soon consumed, and in a flash, the entire room is alight.

"Come on!" I shout above the roar, waving Bertie and Adèle toward me.

They push past the men trying to fight the flames.

Edward snatches at Bertie's skirt. She spins and slams her fist into his face with a roar and he lets go.

The fire is spreading. Adèle reaches me first, her arms around me and mine around her. Bertie is behind her and I throw open the door, pulling the two of them from the room. The fire follows, as if it intends to give chase as well.

"Run!" I shout.

Adèle races down the hall, with me and Bertie coming after her, but Bertie is having trouble. Her leg, the blood loss, it's catching up to her, I realize.

"Here, lean on me," I whisper as I get up under her arm and the two of us hobble along together.

Adèle reaches the top of the stairs and turns to us.

"Look out!"

Something batters us from behind. Pain radiates through my body. I lose hold of Bertie as I go tumbling the last few feet to the rail, slamming into it. The wood breaks under my body, and I feel gravity pull at me. I scramble, trying to latch on to anything as I fall, my fingers catching on the edge of the floor.

I'm left dangling over the grand stairway as fire crawls along the walls, the ceiling. My arms strain. My eyes water. I cough against the acrid scratch of smoke in my nose, my mouth. My hands, branded by gripping the lantern, feel as if someone is driving needles into my flesh as I hold tight.

Other hands grip mine and Bertie's beautiful face comes into view. She pulls, shouting my name, but then lets go when something hits her side. She rolls away, groaning in pain. I can barely see through the thick black. I scream for her, for Adèle, but neither answers.

Instead, Edward kneels above me, his face contorted in fury where I hang, helpless, as fire consumes the house. His eyes are wide and wild, the flames reflected in them. He lifts something overhead, poised to strike me down.

I close my eyes.

52

FORGOTTEN

BERTHA . . .

The fire is everywhere. The heat of it presses in around me, around us, as I struggle to lift Jane back onto the landing, where she dangles from what's left of the banister.

Adèle is somewhere beside me, I think. I'm not sure. I can't be sure, not in the blaze and the smoke.

I grip Jane's arms and pull, despite my failing strength.

Something hits my side and sends me sprawling. My hands lose hers and I cry out in pain and fear. She drops, but her fingers still grip the edge.

Edward looms over me. He kicks me, forcing the air from my lungs. I'm dizzy with the pain.

Another blow lands. This time on my wounded leg. I scream. The hurt burns hotter than the flames that threaten to take us all.

Edward calls out to Jane.

"You're right, you know. About what I've done. Who I've hurt. Bertha. Céline. Not that it matters." He sneers as he regards us, a monster of a man toying with his prey, moving slowly, deliberately, as if everything isn't burning around us, threatening to cave in and kill us all. "What's one more dead woman." He draws back to strike a final blow against Jane. My Jane. And struggle as I might, I can't save her.

I can't go to her. I can barely cry out for her. He's going to kill her. And then he will kill me. I know this to be fact. And I can do nothing about it.

There is a shriek but not mine. And not Jane's.

Adèle races forward, throwing herself bodily against her father's back.

For a moment everything stops. Time slows. I see Adèle, her face drawn up in fury. Her small body practically vibrating with it.

I see Edward. He turns, grasping at the wood, but his fingers can't quite catch hold. He looks at Adèle. The surprise on his face when he goes over what's left of the rail will forever be etched into my memory.

And then he's gone.

For a moment nothing happens. It's all stillness and fire. But then there's a loud crack and a beam drops from the ceiling into the hall behind us, jolting me from my shock.

I push myself up, my side and my leg alight with agony, and crawl to where Jane still dangles from the banister. With Adèle's help, we pull her up. She climbs onto the landing, throwing her arms around me and the girl, holding us close, but not for long.

"We have to go!" I croak out.

Jane takes my hand, hers slick with blood. She takes Adèle's. The three of us press to the wall and make our way down the stairs.

Edward, still alive, howls in pain, clutching at his legs where they are bent at odd angles—white sticking up through red, clearly broken—and he tries to draw himself away from the encroaching inferno, but it is no use. Thornfield is devoured. We skirt around him as far as the fires will allow and as near as we dare, his fingers snatching at our feet in passing. Jane lands a sound kick to the side of his head, turning him over.

He thunders at us, obscenities and threats, pleas to help him, consequences if we don't.

Jane turns Adèle away from the sight and into her arms, hurrying for the door. The two of them make it through.

I stop in the doorway and face him as he tries to pull himself toward it.

As I gaze at him, the house behind him aflame, my prison burning and crashing in, I don't feel the anger I thought I might have. I don't feel fear in the face of such danger. A sense of calm has taken me, despite the roar of the fire, the cries from Adèle and Jane behind me, the threat from Edward before me, and the pain in my own body.

I am relieved in a way I've never felt before.

There is no need to do it, but I find myself compelled to step forward. I take hold of the massive knob on the front door, and pull it closed behind me.

~53~

HOME

JANE . . .

The Thornfield fire burns so brightly it's as if the sun has risen early to linger on the horizon. The orange of the blaze is almost beautiful from a distance. I watch it over my shoulder as we pull farther and farther away, the clomp of the horses' hooves beating a steady rhythm in the dirt.

Beside me, Bertie stares ahead, not once looking back as I have done many times. In truth, I'm afraid that someone may come riding out of the dark, accusing us for what has happened, but we are alone on this road, the three of us.

We sit on the bench of the coach, Bertha between myself and Adèle, with the girl's small head cradled on Bertie's lap while she threads her fingers through her hair. I guide the horses along, my thoughts loud in the silence.

Edward is . . . really gone. He has to be; there's no way he could have escaped.

But what of Grace, Devin, and Marsters? What . . . what of Emm . . .

The sting of her betrayal still burns fresh in my heart and brings tears to my eyes even now.

"What are you thinking about?" Bertie asks, her voice quiet in the night.

I look at her, then back to the road. "Nothing. Just . . . taking it all in. Wondering what to do next."

Adèle straightens then, looking at me. "Where are we going to go?"

"I have something of an idea." With some difficulty, and a twinge of hurt, I gather up my skirts in order to get at the pocket within.

Bertha laughs as I lift the ledger. "Don't tell me."

"The tickets. A few bonds. All the paperwork and evidence we could need. And." I hold out the string of pearls.

Bertha's breath catches. "Maman's pearls," she whispers, taking them gingerly in her fingers. Her eyes glisten in the starlight. "Thank you."

I say nothing, because nothing needs to be said. Instead, I take the reins in one hand so I can wrap my arm around her. I pull her close, her body solid and soft against mine, the scent of her filling my senses. Her eyes find mine in the night. Our lips meet. It's slow and careful, soft and sweet. And my entire body is abuzz with it.

When we break free of each other and I draw back to gaze at her face, I set my fingers to her cheek as she did to mine.

"What was that for?" she asks, her voice barely a whisper.

"You know what it was for." And then I'm kissing her again, and all I can think about is how she feels. How she tastes. How I want nothing more than for this moment to continue forever.

A giggle from Adèle finally causes us to break apart, but I don't let go. I've decided I'm never going to let go of her again.

"You still didn't answer me," the girl says, smiling at us. "Where are we going to go?"

"Home," Bertha murmurs, dropping her brow to mine.

I squeeze Adèle again, then trail my fingers along Bertie's arm.

She finds them and weaves hers with mine.

I am, indeed, home.

ACKNOWLEDGMENTS

As always, I begin by thanking my heavenly Father for all He has blessed me with. For the way He has made so many things possible, the doors He has opened, the opportunities He has provided. I am grateful each and every day for what I have been allowed to do at this point of my life, and I pray I get to continue doing the work I love. To my Agent, Victoria, here's to another one, and many, many more. Carolina, my editor, thank you for weathering the storm with me on this one. It was not easy, but we got it done. To my beloved family, I love you, and I hope I continue to do you proud. Book after book, story after story. And to the Black girls brave enough to live and love for themselves, however that might look, you are queenly, indeed.

ACKNOWLEDGMENTS